THE DROWNED FOREST

Never gets to the story
Good writing. Bad story
development

ALSO BY ANGELA BARRY

Endangered Species and Other Stories
Gorée: Point of Departure

ANGELA BARRY

THE DROWNED FOREST

PEEPAL TREE

First published in Great Britain in 2022
Peepal Tree Press Ltd
17 King's Avenue
Leeds LS6 1QS
England

ISBN13: 9781845235376

Printed in the United Kingdom
by Severn, Gloucester,
on responsibly sourced paper

ACKNOWLEDGEMENTS

Before and during the writing of this novel, I have drawn on the expertise of many people. I owe a debt of gratitude to the following who were so generous with their time and whose knowledge was an invaluable resource: Madalena Almeida, Alexander Barry, Ibou Barry, Dr. Jolene Bean, Father Julio Blazejewski, Ian Cameron, Sheelagh Cooper, Patricia Dangor, Arthur DeSilva, Jane Downing, Dr. Mark Guishard, Catherine Hay, Grisell Almagro Lightbourne, Peter Miller, Denis Owen, Bob Richards, Sandra Taylor Rouja, Jean Foggo Simon and Wendy Tucker. I wish to acknowledge the irreplaceable contribution of the late Teddy Tucker.

Many thanks also to Ruth Thomas and Dr. Kim Dismont Robinson for assistance with this book as well as for their pivotal role in developing Bermuda's culture.

I would like to recognise the support and input of Dr. Graham Mort, who guided me through the early stages of this journey.

Lastly, my grateful thanks to Jeremy Poynting who wielded his editor's pen with rigour and insight and to Jacob Ross whose skill and encouragement helped me to bring this book to completion.

In loving memory of Michael Gilkes who made a huge contribution to the writing of this book, and whose poem about the process of its composition is included, as a tribute to him, at the end of the book.

Dedication

For
My sister, Pat and my brother, Bob
With love

The season has come and the water is warming. A new storm spins round a still centre, a furious disc of wind and cloud dark with rain, feeding on the heat of the ocean.

It swings northwards, grows stronger, churning above the tormented waves. On the horizon is a lonely atoll, an island in the belly of the ocean.

The people of the island are hurricane people. They've learned the lessons of sea birds, of surf and doom-laden air. They batten down and take to their beds.

The night slips through their windows and troubles their sleep. For some, the images they see are of the ocean covering sea-mountains, engulfing the sacred forests, rising ever upwards, and faster than before, leaving the people marooned on this hook-shaped rock. Even asleep, they cling to it.

For others, the vision they see is of the wind that makes the ocean heave and fashion hills out of water. The winds howl, the trees writhe and the sleepers lie low as the breath of God roars over them. The last thing they see in the agony of their dreams is a great wave, rising, curling, cresting, suspended like destiny above them.

Written there by wind and water are the stories and the histories of the people. The wave breaks with a terrible power. But their stories do not drown.

HISTORIES

The past is never dead. It's not even past.

William Faulkner

CHAPTER 1: STARTING OUT

Nina

Nina hesitated on the doorstep of Sweet Airs and watched as Tess, in full hostess mode, looked Genesis up and down and then pulled her inside.

Setting foot on the estate for the first time, Nina had expected to feel what she always felt when confronted by conspicuous wealth – a pleasant sense of superiority over those burdened with privilege. History was not on their side. But all the sharp comments she'd managed not to make to Tess during the past few weeks and the flashes of irritation she hoped had not been visible on her face had all receded and been supplanted by concern for all things Genesis.

Nina could see it, feel it. That day in Family Court.

The magistrate, a woman with a severe grey bun at the nape of her neck, made her pronouncement.

'You…' She cast steely eyes on Genesis, 'are at a crossroads and you…' glancing at the three women, 'have stepped forward to try to guide her onto the right…' The girl's head was down. Was she listening? 'Miss Smith, stand up!'

Genesis stood, tugging at the hem of her school sweater. Finally, she looked up.

'Miss Smith… Your assault on a fellow student involved a degree of violence that merits severe punishment.' The girl's hands stopped fidgeting but her face was blank.

The magistrate leaned forward. 'I could lock you up.' She paused. 'I *should* lock you up!'

The girl's body swayed and Nina could see her hand trembling as she grasped her sweater. The thought *Not so tough* sounded in her mind.

The magistrate sat back in her chair. 'But I'm not going to.' She leaned forward again, forcing the girl to meet her eyes. 'But let's get this straight. Mrs. Nina Fox has agreed to act as your legal guardian until you are eighteen and Mrs Alexander and Ms Pereira have committed to play an active role in your life until then. They are giving you the chance to be different. To be better. Without them, it's jail time at the Youth Facility and after that... They are the ones giving you the chance, not me!'

They had all known Genesis at different times and in different ways. Lizzie was first, when she had become the troubled eleven-year-old girl's 'Big Sister'. As a young woman making her way in the island's business community, Lizzie's participation in the Big Brothers and Sisters of Bermuda was the sort of thing that looked good on a resume, Nina thought. She had been next, meeting fourteen-year old Genesis when she'd shown up at the clinic wanting to avoid getting 'knocked up'. Finally, Tess had only recently become involved but brought with her the full weight of her women's organisation.

In the time since the court hearing, Nina had struggled to find common ground with the other two. It was all so difficult without Dee. Even when they argued, when he got on her last nerve, what had kept them together had never been something imposed from above. It had been a feeling coming from deep in the earth, through the soles of their feet right out through the ends of their hair. Dee. Nina forced her thoughts away from him. Last week's meeting with the probation officer had reminded her of how different all other relationships were. Genesis's only hope was for the three of you to work together, the probation officer had said. It would be an act of will. As Nina stood there, hesitating, she felt nothing but uncertainty about this gathering which was supposed to seal their commitment.

To make things worse, Rosie was now in the mix.

'Got someone with me in the car,' Nina said when Tess ushered her in. 'She won't come in. Rosie. Mrs. Rosie Fox.' With people Nina knew, the name would have been enough, but not here. 'My mother-in-law.' Lizzie and Tess exchanged puzzled glances. 'My husband's... my late husband's mother.' Nina could feel things start to slide until she focused again on the girl and the three days she had been with her. Rules, regulations, lessons, sermons – she had thrown the book at Genesis, who'd responded with compliant phrases and expressionless looks. It had been a disturbing performance.

First, she had to deal with Rosie.

'She appeared at the door when we were leaving home... threatened to turn around and walk back to St. David's.' Tess and Lizzie made exclamations of astonishment. 'So I brought her along. She seemed fine on the way but as soon as we got here, she announced she wasn't going anywhere she wasn't invited.'

Tess opened the door further, craning her neck to see where Nina's car was parked. 'How old is she?'

'Ninety-two.'

'Is she all there?'

'Of course! As all there as she's ever been.'

'Just hard-headed then.' Tess slipped on her sandals. 'Like mother, like son?'

That was Tess. Assuming she'd known Dee. Nina's resolve wavered. 'Oh no, thank God. Chalk and cheese, mother and son... Their eyes. That's all Dee and Rosie had in common.'

'If it's an invite she wants, that's what she'll get. Go in and sit down. Too hot for the terrace. Be back in a...' Tess disappeared around the corner.

Nina and Genesis joined Lizzie in the front room. Beyond the wall of glass and the mosaic-tiled terrace lay the Great Sound, ablaze in burnished gold, celebrating high summer as July slipped into August.

'Million-dollar scenery.' Nina surveyed the enormous front room. 'Inside and out.'

'She calls this place the gallery,' whispered Lizzie, as though not to disturb the family portraits, the paintings and sculptures.

Nina watched Lizzie give a nervous little toss of her head and then stretch back on one of the soft leather sofas. Trying to look like she's used to this. Lizzie was so transparent. From the corner of her eye, Nina glanced at Genesis who was sitting beside her, her back like a rod and her profile like carved black onyx.

Lizzie broke the silence. 'So what you doing for Cup Match. Going to the game?'

'We always go to Horseshoe Bay for First Day,' said Nina, 'About fifty of us. Sisters, grandchildren... you know... Cup Match!'

'We barbecue First Day,' Lizzie said, 'and then...'

'Here we are!' Tess was flushed and smiling as she came in with Rosie Fox in tow. Rosie, once she'd freed herself from Tess's hand, made her way over to Nina and planted herself in front of her.

'You never told me we was going up Old Man Darrell's house! If I'd of known, I'd of been the first one out! But, of course...' Rosie addressed Tess. 'How could I recognise the place with all the messing around you done to it. Knocked down this and put up that.' She paused, fixing her eyes on a cluster of portraits of whiskered patriarchs. 'I remember them, though!' She sat down and faced her audience.

'I used to come up here. Years ago. To bring Old Lady...'

'My grandmother...' Tess said.

'To bring Old Lady Darrell enough fever grass to last a month. Going through the change, she was. Yes sir. For sure, if I hadn't of, she'd of gone upside somebody's head with a cleaver.' Rosie gave a satisfied humph and started rummaging around in her large canvas bag. When she looked up, everybody was looking at her. 'What I do?'

'Nothing, ' Nina said. 'We're glad you came in.'

'Sure got a funny way of showing it. Staring...'

Nina tried to see Rosie with the eyes of the others. An old woman with Attitude in shapeless, washed-out clothing, her flattened breasts sitting on an accommodating waist. A St. David's Island face, where Africa, Europe and the Americas met in an arresting combination of colours and textures – copper-brown skin, full lips, straight black plaits down her back, two white wings kinking at her temples. And those unblinking green eyes.

'No manners!' Rosie grumbled. She bent over her bag again, withdrew some knitting, placed the end of the needles under her arms and started working the thick wool. She stopped when she caught sight of the girl.

'So, child... Who are you?'

Genesis looked at Nina in panic.

As a veteran of innumerable encounters with her mother-in-law, Nina knew when to intervene. 'Come on now, Rosie, I introduced you in the car… This is Genesis.' Nina touched the girl lightly. 'She'll be staying at the house for a while.'

'Genesis, you say?' said Rosie. 'What kinda name is that, girlie?'

'It's a book in the Bible.' Her voice quivered.

'So's Deuteronomy and Numbers,' said Rosie, resuming her knitting.

'Well, actually, as names go, it could be a lot worse,' said Nina. 'Much worse! Bermudian names… Lukeisha, Markeysha…' Lizzie and Tess started to smile. 'Shawnika, Shay-ronne, Shah-nayd…'

'And what about the French ones?' Tess said, laughing. 'Or should I say, the French wines?'

'You mean like Champain…' said Lizzie. 'P-A-I-N. And Bo-Jah-Lay?'

'Then… then…' Tess said, 'There's El Dash Ay.' She stood up. 'The letter L, then a dash, you know, the punctuation mark…' Tess's finger cut the air with a horizontal line. 'Then – the letter A.'

'L – A!' Nina and Lizzie screamed in unison.

'I know him!' Genesis shouted over the hooting. 'He was in my class! Don't people have the right to…' she mumbled sinking back into the sofa.

'Relax, G,' Nina said gently. 'We're not mocking anybody. It's just that a name should mean something.'

'Like yours?' Rosie didn't look up from her knitting. 'Bernina.' There was a pause. 'After your Mama's sewing machine.'

Genesis started laughing so hard that tears sprang from her eyes, eventually collapsing across Nina's lap. Nina laid a gentle hand on the convulsing back and felt tears seep through her skirt. Without raising her head, she knew Rosie was watching her, with those eyes so eerily like Dee's.

'Oh, excuse me,' a young male voice came from the open glass door. 'Mrs. Alexander?'

'Hugh!' Tess gushed. 'Come! Come!'

As he stepped out of the shadows, Nina passed a cool eye over him and wondered why his mama had never shown him how to use an iron. She noted, too, that both Genesis and Lizzie were sitting at attention. Then only Lizzie continued to study him.

Tess introduced her new tenant. 'Recently arrived from England...'

'Wales, actually...'

'Been with me a week.' Tess pointed vaguely beyond the terrace to a small cottage near the water. 'Working down at AIOS. Big brain!' She made a big brain gesture with her hands. Hugh blushed and sat down.

'So, what brings you up here?' Tess asked. 'Thought you'd be out with your mates. The holiday starts tonight, you know.'

'I wondered if I could borrow an adapter for my laptop. I'd like to do some work over the...'

'Work?' Lizzie voice went up several notches. Smoothing down the front of her white trousers with red-tipped fingers and leaning forward to offer a view of her cleavage, she said, 'Work! Don't you know it's Cup Match?' She turned a broad scarlet smile on Hugh. 'August first and second! I can't believe Tess didn't tell you. Cup Match is about play!'

'I don't know too much about it. A cricket match, I think...' he mumbled.

Lizzie pranced over to Hugh's side. 'Cup Match is a four-day party! Just an excuse for a good time...'

'It's more than that.' Nina had had enough of Lizzie's hair-tossing antics. 'More than a good time. It celebrates the ending of slavery.'

'Yeah!' said Lizzie, with a wave of her hand. 'That too.'

'What do you mean "That too"?'

'Oh God, Nina...' Lizzie groaned.

Feeling a flame radiating up from her chest, Nina pursed her lips and managed to say nothing.

'Yes, it is about Emancipation.' Tess wore a smile of sorts. 'But it's also about our beginnings. Sir George Somers. Shipwreck. *Sea Venture*...' When her eyes met Nina's, the smile had vanished. 'You know,' Tess persisted, 'the first day is Emancipation Day and the second... Somers Day.' She paused. 'Fair is fair.'

'Well, that's true. Technically. But everybody knows that Cup Match was started by black people to celebrate being free. Free from Sir George and all his descendants! This Somers Day business was just tacked on.'

'Well at least you all have a day. What about us? After all the time we Portuguese have been here, what do we have to show for it?'

'Well, all the supermarkets and construction companies for a start...'

'See what I mean? No respect! Still second class. Not black and not quite white. Still just onion diggers...'

'Hey, you lot...'

'Isn't all that money recognition enough, Lizzie? And, Tess, I don't know how you people can put Somers Day in the same category as Emancipation Day. Sir George Somers was blown onto this island by a hurricane. Pure accident! Anything black people have achieved has been after a long, hard...'

'You lot!' Rosie managed to be heard above the raised voices. 'When you're finished quarrelling about who did what to who, I got one question.' The sight of Rosie wavering on unsteady legs startled the combatants into silence.

'Where de food?'

Shamefaced, Nina apologised to everyone and Lizzie and Tess did the same. Tess resumed her role as hostess. On the terrace perched high over the darkening water, they were soon being served canapes and recovering a jokey yet disengaged level of conversation. Hugh hovered on the fringes. Genesis silently observed. Then they toasted Cup Match – both days, Portuguese egg bread and, in deference to Rosie, St. David's mussel pie. They toasted Genesis and wished her all kinds of good things in the future – finishing high school, going to Harvard, getting a job, marrying a millionaire, learning to knit.

When they were leaving, Rosie stopped in front of the portrait of one of Tess's forefathers. She peered intently at the austere, bearded face, then stepped away.

'Didn't say a thing,' she said. 'Least I couldn't make out what he was saying.'

Everybody except Nina looked confused. She glared at the old woman for a moment, then took her arm. Instead of moving, Rosie put her bag down.

'It's time to go, Rosie,' Nina said.

'Not yet.' Rosie faced them all – Tess, Lizzie, Genesis, Hugh and Nina. 'Next time you want to fuss and fight, listen to what they have to say.' She aimed an arthritic finger at the portraits on the wall. 'Them! And all them others that made you!' She calmly picked up her bag. 'Listen. Even if you don't like what you hear.'

The party broke up. Nina dropped Genesis off at Salt Cay and began the long drive to St. David's. The place where her beloved Dee was born and now slept overlooking a placid bay… Not a word was spoken until they reached Rosie's house.

'Rosie, you need to stop your foolishness! About dead people talking. I told you about that! And to do it tonight! In front of those people… In front of the girl! They probably all think I'm as crazy as you now… I could never understand why Dee never stopped you from talking like this. The one thing I never understood…'

She helped Rosie out of the car and walked her to her door. It was a clear moonlit night and every blade of grass stood vivid and bright in the darkness. Beyond the yard, there was the gurgle of water over rocks. But it all seemed sour and threatening to Nina.

Before going inside, Rosie turned to Nina and said, 'I just know what I know.'

Hugh

Hugh had not spoken to a single soul for over thirty-six hours, not since the gathering at his landlady's house. Although he didn't mind his own company and had no desire to join his new colleagues on the island's great let-it-all-hang-out holiday, the enforced solitude had begun to weigh on him.

Until now.

He couldn't make up his mind about what was the worst thing about this island. The list was long. It was too small. It was too complacent. Too full of itself. Utterly unaware of its sheer insignificance. But underneath the veneer of sameness – the red post boxes, the Marks and Spencer's, the plumed Governor – he recognised that the island was unfamiliar to him; it didn't have the British class system for one thing.

After a month of island life, he divided the people he'd met into two groups – his colleagues at the Atlantic Institute for Oceanographic Studies and all the rest. 'All the rest' had been ably represented by Tess, her guests and their unfathomable wrangling. He would keep well away from them. But his colleagues were also a disappointment. Professional – yes. Clever – yes. But most of them had been born on a yacht that sailed them straight to the world's best universities. He'd had to swim up rapids to get where he wanted to be. And where was their passion for the ocean that was supposed to unite them all? Four days ago, he'd seen a newspaper article describing how a local diver had brought up an ancient tree root from a reef thirty feet beneath sea level. Proof of a living forest of cedars from some distant past, drowned by the rising sea. He had gone running out of his office to share his excitement. Nobody cared. They had all caught Cup Match fever. He was as out of place with these scientists as he'd been with the bickering women at Sweet Airs.

But all changed when he opened a large brown envelope that a colleague had casually given him as they'd left work to start the holiday. On it was written: 'Everything you need to know about Buddy Darrell. Knock yourself out!'

The envelope contained a newspaper article and a glossy book about the exploits of Buddy Darrell, a legendary old salt whose life's work was carried out beneath the waves. There was also a DVD which, for the next hour, he watched on his laptop, and then watched again, uncut silent footage of Buddy Darrell's retrieval of the ancient root. The man himself was old with a thatch of white hair, but as he entered the water and swam down to the reef, his body had an obvious energy. Buddy had uncovered a strange object looking like a giant spider clinging to a rock. He'd attached the root by a steel cable and gave the signal to his boat, separated from him by thirty feet of ocean. As the cable went taut, the water became opaque as sand and coral and long dead life forms whirled around. At last the 'spider' began its journey towards the rocking hull above.

On the deck of Buddy's boat, three men stared at their find as the seawater drained away from it. Buddy sliced a thin triangle from the mummified body and brought it to his nostrils. Then his face broke into a broad smile.

'It still smells of cedar!' Hugh said out loud.

There was a knock at the door. Tess. She spent the first five minutes berating her husband for being a no show, again. He'd called from New York to say that he wouldn't be home until Saturday at the earliest.

'Yesterday I sulked,' she said, 'but today I said to myself, Hell! It's the second day of Cup Match and I need to get on the water, Richard or no Richard. And I want you to come too. Simmons has already brought the boat around.'

Hugh took a deep breath and looked up at the ceiling, angry at this interruption.

'Got something better to do?'

Such a bully! No wonder the husband's never here... Then a thought occurred.

'Do you know Buddy Darrell?'

'Sure. He's my cousin. Third or fourth or fifth...'

He gave her a crooked smile. 'Here's the thing. You tell me all you know about Buddy...'

'And in exchange?'

'You get the pleasure of my company.'

'Deal!' They spent what was left of the morning filling coolers with food and drink and loading them onto *Miranda*. Tess told Hugh about Buddy and the nebulous way families were related who'd lived on the island for generations. She rambled on about the nineteenth-century father who had married off his nine daughters to the sons of all the important white families, making them, in one fell swoop, a single clan. Like Queen Victoria and the crowned heads of Europe, she said.

Hugh told her about the potential significance of Buddy Darrell's find. The archaeology of the sea, he said, his eyes shining. The submerged landscape of the ocean... She threw him an ice-cold Heineken and called him a poet.

The phone rang and Hugh saw a cloud scuttle across Tess's face. 'Genesis is coming,' she said. 'You know, from the other night.'

Hugh remembered the woman with the white trousers, the red nails and the tossing hair. 'Erm... Which one was she?'

Tess laughed. 'The girl. Some long story. Nina's at the hospital with her uncle, and Genesis needs looking after.'

'She's a bit old for that, isn't she? She must be...'

'Seventeen. Nina says she'd sooner leave an infant by itself than leave this girl to her own devices at Cup Match.' Tess sighed. 'Probably right.' She closed the lid of the final cooler. 'Don't worry. Genesis won't give any trouble. She's too smart for that.'

Half an hour later, Genesis was giving trouble. No amount of cajoling could persuade her to step down and cross the small gap between the dock and *Miranda*'s spotless deck.

'Well, I give up!' Tess flopped down.

'May I?' asked Hugh.

'Be my guest!'

Hugh leaned towards the girl, trying to establish eye contact. 'Do you know how to swim?' His tone was firm.

Genesis looked off to the distance. Her lips twitched and then belligerent eyes swung back and collided with his. 'No.'

'Well, then,' he said, 'I have something for you.' He went into the cabin, came back with a bright orange life jacket and handed it to her. 'Put this on. It will keep you safe for the whole trip.'

For what seemed like several minutes, she hesitated with the jacket in her hands, fingering its straps, pressing and prodding its rounded contours, examining the life-saving potential of its fabric. Finally, she threaded her arms through and secured the belt around her body.

Still, she stood rooted to the dock.

'Would you like to come on board now?' Hugh extended his hand and smiled encouragement.

Grabbing the proffered hand, Genesis came aboard.

Tess grinned, jammed on a faded pink straw hat, mounted the eight steel steps that led to the upper station and took the boat's controls and began barking orders at Hugh. 'Get that grappling hook. Port side. Pull in those lines. Watch the buffers!'

He knew his way around a boat. The dock cleared and all the lines safely stowed, he went aloft, breathed the sea-scented air and felt the heat of noonday beat down on him. He glanced at Tess, her hands loose on the wheel, the brim of her hat blown back, a contented smile on her lips. He noticed a mark on Tess's left arm, and she caught him staring at it.

'Impressive, isn't it?' She extended her arm. 'Sometimes it

looks like a spider, sometimes an ink blot.' It was raised, dark against her tanned skin and nestled near the crook of her elbow. 'We all have it... since forever...' She laughed and put her arm back on the wheel. 'It's the family brand!'

The boat cut a clean line across the Sound until they reached the bridge that joined the mainland to the islet.

'Hugh! Lower the outriggers now!'

He released one of the towering outriggers from its clasp and then, squeezing behind Tess, released the other. Slowly, the tall arms descended from their vertical position and reached out to the side. Cutting both engines, Tess lined the boat up to pass beneath the bridge. With power reduced, the churning wake disappeared and the boat, now sitting low in the water, rose and sank with the rhythm of the waves.

Hugh could see Genesis huddled on the padded seat at the stern. 'Come up!' he called out. 'We're going under the bridge!'

He watched as, all arms and legs, she leapt to her feet and flew up the steel steps to the upper deck. The bridge placed itself between them and the sky for a few moments; by the time they were on the other side, Genesis was smiling.

'Where we going?' she asked.

'East. As far as we can go,' said Tess. 'A nice trip for a newcomer to the island.'

The island was on their starboard side. It was a perfect day and the colour blue defied anyone to find names for all its varieties. There were lots of boaters out, all waving and calling hello. The jetskiers chose bravado over gentility. They wove in and out between boats, between rocks, sending up arcs of spray, to impress the girls hanging onto their waists. Hugh drank in the watercolour houses with their white roofs, the rusty remains of a pontoon bridge, the alternation between rocky shoreline and sandy beach, people bobbing like dots in the water, bright-coloured tarpaulins sheltering picnickers from the sun.

Tess began to talk about boats.

'It's in the blood,' she said. 'In my family, even if there was no house, there was always a boat. Daddy used to say that I could swim before I could walk. Grandpa taught me to sail... And cabin cruisers like this, I've been crewing since I was a teenager.'

'Why *Miranda*?'

'Oh! After *The Tempest,* of course. That and Sweet Airs too.'

'Very… literary of you.'

'My grandmother. She made my grandfather call it Sweet Airs. Before that, the house name kept changing, thanks to…'

'Those men in the portraits.'

'Exactly. But then Grandma Lottie stepped in. She was… how to put it… a miserable old bag. But she loved Shakespeare. It reminded her of the England she'd had to give up to marry Grandpa Nate. For her, one of the few good things about Bermuda was its connection with *The Tempest.* Forced all her grandchildren to read that damn play at least once a year and…'

'Oh, look! A turtle!' shouted Hugh. 'No, two!'

'I see them!' Tess cried, clapping her hands in excitement. 'Look!' She took Genesis by the shoulders and held her in position. The girl caught sight of them just in time with their heads up like green periscopes swivelling around, before they dived. Standing next to her, Hugh felt her soft exhalation of breath and a sound like 'Wow' passing through her lips.

From then on, there was nothing but delight over what was in the water and what was on the land. There were sightings of fish, birds and the strange displays of those humans on the shore who had not gone to the game. Tess was a font of knowledge of island lore which Hugh received with amused scepticism. Even Genesis joined in once or twice.

'That's where they landed,' Tess said. 'That scrap of beach over there.' She pointed with her chin towards a small rough strip of sand. 'Sir George Somers.'

'Well,' said Hugh, saluting. 'Here's to you, Sir George. It's your day!'

At last, *Miranda* turned away from the open ocean and entered a lagoon with sandy coves surrounding it. They dropped anchor and within minutes Tess and Hugh were in the water, leaving Genesis on deck in her life jacket.

Hugh set off with a vigorous stroke, heading for one of the little islets until he slowed down and looked about him. The water was aquamarine, translucent. The light was hard for his eyes to adjust to: almost unbearable in the sky, brilliant on the land, bent and mysterious in the water. He closed his eyes and saw the red mist of his lids. When he opened them again, first there was just the glare, then the harbour and the islands gaining definition. He looked over at Tess, floating on her back as though asleep.

Hugh felt at peace. The sea always chased away the clumsiness he felt on land with people. It cleared his mind. His lids fluttered shut. He heard an unfamiliar sound and opened them again. Two white birds were directly overhead. They had long curling tails and a fine black stripe along the wing. They hovered for a moment, beating the air, calling. As they flew off over the smooth water, their breasts absorbed its tender blue.

'Longtails,' Tess said.

Hugh felt too languid to reply.

'Doesn't talk much, does she?' Hugh said at last. 'The girl.'

'Oh, she can talk plenty. She's had it tough, poor kid. Trying to give her a break. The three of us. It's early days yet. Could go either way.'

'She any good at school?'

'Depends who you talk to. Mostly, they'll be glad to see the back of her. Got a short fuse... But, for what it's worth, I think there's something there. A brain...'

They glanced in her direction. Genesis was where they had left her, her body huddled like a tight orange knot, Tess's pink straw hat on her head. When they heaved themselves back onto the boat, Genesis looked relieved. They lazed, they ate and they listened to the cricket score on the radio. Somerset was batting but, as usual, Tess said, it looked like the game was heading for a draw. She pointed out Nonsuch Island Reserve and Hugh reeled off all the information that he had recently acquired about it.

'See the longtails?' Tess asked Genesis when there was a pause.

'You mean them big white birds? Yeah, I saw 'em. They were... kinda... kinda...'

'Beautiful.' Hugh smiled.

'I guess.'

'Genesis.' This was the first time he had called her name, the first time he had really looked at her. 'You like Nature?'

Not waiting for a reply, he moved his chair closer. 'I want to tell you about something great that has happened...'

Genesis started to play with the bottom of her t-shirt.

'She might not be interested,' Tess warned.

'Last weekend, some divers went thirty feet down and retrieved an ancient cedar root from a reef...'

Tess gestured to a place beyond the entrance to the harbour but said nothing.

'And apparently the root is in good condition. They don't know how old it is yet but they're going to find out. The point is... that we have evidence that the coral reef used to be land that sustained trees. Forests! And the island used to be much, much bigger. Until the sea came in and covered it up.' He knew his words couldn't convey the thrill he felt.

Genesis eventually looked up. 'I'm supposed to care?'

Tess rolled her eyes, scraped back her chair and started to collect plates and cups with the maximum of noise. Hugh stood up and said, 'This is your world. You have to find out about its past. That way you can protect its future.'

'I'm supposed to do these things? Me?' Her eyes were furious and she struck her chest when she said 'Me'.

'Yes. You. And me. All of us!'

'Back off,' Tess whispered in Hugh's ear.

'Look, man. Gimme a break!' Genesis leapt up. 'How long you been here? In my country? And telling me what to do? I don't give a shit about your goddamn reef! Or root. Or whatever the hell it is.'

'Time to go!' Tess said.

'Think you know so much!' The girl's anger mixed oddly with the colours of the life jacket and straw hat. 'Both of you! I heard you talking. Shakespeare and all that crap. Now this. Always want to make us look bad!'

'Genesis, I think you should stop now.' Tess's voice was quiet, professional.

'Tess! Stop babying her!' Hugh turned to face the girl. 'You accuse me of knowing things as though it's the worst thing in the world. Well, young lady, you're wrong.'

'Don't give me that "young lady" bullshit! You don't know me!'

His face was aflame. 'You're at school. Learn something, for God's sake!' He strode to the bow and yanked up the anchor.

Genesis followed him, repeating, 'You don't know me!'

Tess engaged the engines and they were off, out of the lagoon, around the exposed headland, back along the coast, all sunlight drained from the day.

When they were nearly home, Genesis climbed to the top deck and tapped Hugh on the shoulder. He flinched.

'Sorry,' she said.

He gave her a nod of acknowledgement.

'You're just in time to do some work,' Tess said. 'Lower the outriggers.' Tess paused. 'The fishing poles. Let them down.' Genesis scrambled from one side of the boat to the other, unclipping the poles and seeing them fall to the side, as they sailed beneath the now gloomy span of the bridge.

Simmons was waiting for them at the dock to drive the boat back to its moorings. Back in his apartment, Hugh logged onto his laptop and replayed the raw footage of Buddy's descent into the ocean, his harvesting of the root and the triumphant moment when he found that the essence of that long-dead tree was still alive.

Only after he had played it again did the knots in his stomach begin to loosen.

Genesis

Man! Some Cup Match! No matter where I been livin, I always got away for it. Four days runnin wild. Last year. Sixteen. With the shortest shorts on record. Me and my girls rollin from party to party. Just had to smile and those guys playin Crown and Anchor parted with some of their winnings. They won. We won. Got our share of dollars. Somebody hit a six and everybody scored.

This year. No shorts. No dollars. In this big empty house with Nina comin soon. Genesis you screwed up. She won't say it but she'll mean it, whatever she says. She and those two other bitches. Got me locked up on their planet. Planet Hot Flush, Planet Lockdown, Planet Tight Ass. And today. Tried not to talk. But that expat guy made me. I'd of been okay if he hadn't of crowded me. Talked crap, put his chair right in my face and *demanded* that I say somethin. I mean…

It's like when I gave it to Kalrita. There's a mouth flappin in front of me and I have to make it stop. I'm warnin you, Kalrita, stop laughin at my shoes my clothes my hair. Stop asking me how many homes I've lived in. Askin how come I ain't got no mama no daddy… Stop. I pull my arm back, don't care what trouble I get into. I give her one. Then another. Don't care about the blood pouring from her nose. And another. Until they have to drag me off her… It felt just like that with whatever his goddamn name is. Pinning me in a corner and talking *down* to me.

Feels like a century since those bitches got me on their planet. Not even a week yet. Full-time in Nina's house of rules. Do this do that don't put that there don't say that this is my brother sister nephew aunt uncle great-niece this is where my parents are buried brush your teeth wash that off your face turn that off this is where Dee's buried… Part-time with Tess and the Mansion. I always been cool with Tess. She posted bail and it was never do this do that with her. But it didn't feel good at that dinner. Nina's old auntie with them spooky eyes. Nina and Tess and bimbo Lizzie acting like they wanted to fight. Didn't mind that. But can't stand the way they treat me like I'm their pet project.

Yesterday Cup Match was supposed to start, but it was the First Day from hell. Five hundred of Nina's close relatives on the beach all eatin chicken and starin at me. I swear some of them nephews are Babylon – checkin me out, like they seen me before in some line-up. Worst of all was the way everybody wanted me to go overboard. I tell them no. They look at me funny and then go back flingin themselves under the waves. Now who's crazy?

Couldn't sleep last night wondering about Second Day. But I was saved. Kind of. Early this morning, there's noise comin from the bedroom next door where the uncle with no teeth is sleepin. Soon the three of us are at Emergency waitin with the other people who drank too much rum, ate bad coleslaw or broke something partyin. The uncle's breathin loud, sittin there, out of it. He turns round and smiles at me and I see yards of gums. That's some smile! He looks at me… like he knows me. The doctor gives him some pills and tells Nina to take him home. Nina calls Tess and I'm shipped up to The Mansion like a Fedex package.

Thought my troubles were over. Then I saw the boat. No way. No friggin way. Don't know how I get on board even with that stupid life jacket. They leave me alone and all I can see is what's goin on behind the boat. Bubbles from the engine and these two, like, hills of water. Identical. In the middle of the hills there's this dark line with no bubbles and no matter how fast the boat's goin those hills of water never change. And the dark line between them either. Can't stop lookin down at it and thinkin about things that have happened to me, but it's like I can't remember what the things are only that they happened. Then the boat stops and the hills and the trench disappear. Now the water rises up and looks like it's gonna pour into the boat. I take off up those steps to where the others are.

Everything's okay until the expat guy starts in on me. He should of stopped pushin. Less than a week with them and I've messed up. Nina's lecture will go on for hours. Don't matter.

Nina'll be here soon. She told me that you can train your mind to be positive. Think good thoughts... What happened good, today? The sun felt good. Another good thought? Those big white birds were nice. Scary but nice. Anything else? Somethin not messed up. With that expat boy, I just mouthed off. I could easily have cracked him one and I know he wouldn't of hit me back. So I *chose* not to beat his ass! That's positive, ain't it?

And... and... I said sorry!

CHAPTER 2: WORKING IT

Tess

'The address is here. Come through.' She beckoned Hugh through the gallery into the library. The morning sun poured in through the large window, across the wall of rare books, the ranks of paperbacks, the photographs, the awards, the family treasures, the lustre of cedar shelves.

'This room... I just love it,' she murmured.

'Impressive,' Hugh said, taking in the quiet beauty of the space.

Tess copied down Buddy Darrell's contact information and handed it to Hugh. Surveying his rumpled appearance, she added, 'He's gonna love you! You have his dress sense.'

'I don't know about that.' Hugh ran his hand through his hair. 'So many famous scientists must come seeking his advice. All I have is a piece of paper...'

'Well, Dr. Hugh, in this island, you have to use what you've got to get noticed. No experience? Use that PhD! Tell Buddy what's special about what you studied. Make it up if you have to. But be confident! Own it! Work it! That way you'll stand out from the pack.'

'That's not really my style, Tess. But...'

'It works. Believe me.'

Hugh continued walking around the room, peering at the titles, occasionally touching the spines. When he reached the photos, he stopped.

'These are your ancestors?' He looked along a row of photographs in plain silver frames.

'Yes. But not distant ones. I knew almost everyone in those pictures. Nothing further back than my grandfather's generation.

Before that, nothing but paintings.' She pointed to a photograph of a man in a straw hat surrounded by a bunch of tow-haired children. 'That's him. My grandfather. Can you find me?'

Hugh examined the row of freckled faces until he stopped at the one right next to the tall man. She was the only one looking up at him.

'Well done, you! Yes. Grandpa Nate was the one who made this room into a library.' Tess looked around her. 'Used to be a dumping ground for tools, fishing tackle, animal feed...'

'Looks like he was a very busy man!' Hugh peered at a series of pictures featuring the same upright, smiling man at different stages of his life.

'Yep! That's Nate! At the Yacht Club. Reading the lesson at St. Anne's. In the boardroom at the Bank. Sailing. In the House of Assembly. On the golf course... Yes. He did it all. He made it all happen.'

'I don't follow you.'

'Made it happen. He and a few others. Turned this...' Tess flung her arm out, encompassing the island. 'This pile of rocks that people shunned, into, well, a playground for the rich and famous!'

'How did that happen?'

'After World War One, they changed the Isle of Devils into Paradise. It's all here in these.' She pointed to a row of sleek, sealskin diaries, each bearing the year and the name Nathaniel Darrell. 'In one fell swoop, they created tourism, the thing that's put food on every table. They hired a queen.' Tess lightly touched a model of cruise ship crowned with three red and black funnels and traced the words *Queen of Bermuda* on it with her fingernail. 'Not exactly this Queen but her predecessors. The cruise line that established the first regular service between New York and Bermuda.

'When Grandpa Nate and his cronies saw the island going down the drain after World War One, they knew they had to act fast. I don't know whose idea it was, but in a few short years they put together three pieces of a solution. Piece one – attract America's super-rich with lots of leisure time. Piece two – make it a beautiful place for them to play and hang out with people like themselves. Piece three – establish a way to get them to that place.

'Et voilà! By the end of the 1920s, the wealthy travelled here in cruise ships, played golf and built houses in one of the most beautiful corners of the island – tidied up to make room for them.'

'Tidied up?'

'Yes. Just like Nate created this library from a room good only for dumping stuff, he and his buddies did the same thing for the country. Because of them the tourist industry was born.'

'And all of that was done with… no pain for the island. I mean, for the ordinary people who lived here.'

Tess gave him a quizzical look.

'I wouldn't say that. Did they do things we would find politically incorrect now? Sure they did! But if they hadn't, you certainly wouldn't be sitting here today. You can thank my grandfather for your being here.'

'I'm sorry, Tess, but I can't agree. Don't want to be rude but there's no connection between me and your grandfather. My grandfather was a miner who died of black lung disease when he was forty. Your grandfather and mine – they don't share anything!'

Tess said, 'You're not in Britain now. Here we had slavery for over two hundred years, so for the average black Bermudian, my grandfather, your grandfather, you and I, we're all the same.'

Hugh was silent, then said, 'Thank you for Buddy's address, Tess. Be seeing you.'

Tess rose to stop him. 'Look, things are changing here. I see it every day in my job. When I'm with clients, I wait for the moment when I can see their eyes change. From seeing only my white skin to seeing me as a person who can help them change their lives. And more and more, that moment comes.'

Hugh nodded. As he was leaving, Simmons appeared at the door.

'Morning, ma'am. Just wanted you to know that I'm taking *Miranda* to the boatyard for servicing. You won't be able to use it for…'

'It's all right, Simmons.' And she waved him away and hurried towards her car.

During her drive to work, she wondered about the version of her grandfather's life that she had given Hugh. And the version of her own. She hoped that at least was true.

Hugh

Hugh looked over the letter, was about to sign it but put his pen down. When was the last time he had written a letter rather than an email or text? And in longhand... It seemed like something from the past. He glanced at Buddy's photo. Yes. The handwritten letter was appropriate.

Dear Mr. Darrell,

My landlady, Tess Alexander, suggested that I write to you. I have not been on the island long, having come out from the UK at the end of July to take up a two-year appointment at the Atlantic Institute of Ocean Science as a researcher.

Let me introduce myself.

So far, so good. But Hugh had a sinking feeling when he read through the rest of the paragraph.

I'll begin by telling you how privileged I feel to be working at such a world-class institution as AIOS. Following my doctoral studies, for which I received the BERA Award, and three years working in Australia, this is my first experience of the Atlantic world. My brief is as part of the Coral Reef Management team, looking in particular at the recruitment and population of Siderastrea Radians.

Oh God! Hugh groaned. A self-satisfied arse...

I have been made to understand that you are something of a scientist yourself, although the print and broadcast media emphasise your treasure-hunting skills!

Patronising and verbose...

So, as one scientist to another, I must express the depth of my excitement at your discovery and extraction of the ancient cedar root from the reef at Gurnet Rock... I would like to put myself at your disposal.

Pushy...

And although I have not been on the island long, I feel I know the waters well already and must confess, they do not seem to be a treacherous as many have tried to make me believe.

Know-all! Condescending! And this, the result of hours of labour?

More than anything, I would like to meet and talk to you. I understand that the root will soon be on display. I cannot wait to see this ancient survivor of a time when much more of the Bermuda Seamount was above water.

Please let me know if and when I may call on you.

This was the only part of the letter that sounded genuine. Hugh read the whole thing again. It would only work if Buddy Darrell was impressed by degrees and high-sounding words. But if Buddy wasn't, he would see that he was some green Johnny-come-lately trying to catch hold of his coat-tails. Hugh rewrote the letter and put it in the mail.

A few days later, his own letter was returned to him.

Sweet Airs Cottage
September 28, 2002.

Dear Mr. Darrell,

I'm a scientist working here and would love to meet and talk to you about your discovery at Gurnet Rock. I understand that the root will soon be on display. I cannot wait to see this ancient survivor of a time when much more of the Bermuda Seamount was above water. Please let me know if and when I may call on you.

Sincerely,
Hugh Denham

Underneath in bold black script were the words:

We're unveiling her next Saturday, October 12 at 6 o'clock. Bring a friend. I'm going out to Gurnet Rock the week after. Come on along, if you like.

Buddy

Lizzie

'Hello.'

'Hello, Lizzie. It's me.'

'You're going to have to give me a clue.'

'It's me! Hugh!'

'Hugh?'

'Hugh Denham! You know. Tess... Tess Alexander's tenant.'

'Oh, that Hugh. Didn't recognise you. Hello, Hugh.'

Silence, then Lizzie heard an intake of breath.

'Well... how have you been?'

'Fine.'

More silence.

'I know it's been a while since I last called... I've been very busy. At work, you know.'

'Really.'

'I know I was supposed to call and we were supposed to go out a couple of weekends ago...'

She heard his words sliding towards apology. 'Were we? You were supposed to call?'

'Yes! You remember... Don't you? We were supposed to go to the cinema.' Lizzie wished she could see him. There was a new kind of phone that let you see the person you were talking to. She needed to get one!

'But I got so busy at work... I just didn't get around to it. I guess you're angry with me...?'

'Me? Me, angry at you? What would make you think that?'

'Well, the way you're talking now. You sound angry.'

Lizzie noted the change in Hugh's tone. He was pushing back. She would have to ease up or she might lose him altogether.

'You've got it all wrong, Hugh. I'm not mad. I live a busy life. Like you.' She heard a sound she could not identify. Was he shifting from one foot to the other? Moving pens around the desk in front of him? 'I just assumed that your timetable didn't include me. And that's cool.'

'You see...' Hugh's uncertainty had the ring of the confessional. So easy for a Catholic to recognise! 'I'm not very good at keeping on top of phoning and going out and things like that...'

Lizzie shook her head. This was what too many hours in libraries and laboratories did to otherwise normal heterosexual males. She almost felt sorry for him.

'Lizzie? Are you still there?'

'Yes.'

'I'm sorry about the other day.'

'Week.'

'The other week. About not phoning the other week. But I would like to see you again. This would be a nice occasion. Something you'd like.'

'I'm listening.'

'Well… er… they're having a big unveiling of an ancient cedar root at the Maritime Museum next Saturday. The twelfth. You know. It's been in all the papers… Lizzie? Are you still there?'

An ancient cedar root. She struggled to stifle a yawn. 'Uh huh.'

'It's going to be, well, a big do. Local dignitaries. Some people, scientists, from overseas. I'll even make an effort to dress properly… I'd like you to come with me.'

All right. But he would have to work to get her there. He'd made her wait too long, and an ancient root?

'I can't,' she said.

'Can't or won't?' There it was again, the edge in his voice. He was not the pushover she thought he was.

'Can't. I'm having Genesis that night.'

'You mean the girl that you and Tess fuss over?'

'Yes.'

'Can't she stay home? By herself? She's practically a woman!'

'No. She's staying with me that night. Nina's busy. The only solution is if I bring her.'

'Please don't!'

'Why not?'

'I find her somewhat… abrasive.' Lizzie's ears pricked up, but she didn't interrupt. 'And anyway, I thought that afterwards, we might be able to go and have a drink. Maybe a meal. Try to catch up a bit.'

'Either I come with her or not at all.'

'Wouldn't it be nice to spend the evening together? Just the two of us?'

'Hugh, next Saturday, it'll be a threesome or nothing at all. After that, we'll see about a next time.'

Lizzie suppressed a smile. With the men she was used to playing games with, the mere mention of the word 'threesome' would provoke some suggestive response. But not from Boy Scout Hugh from the Welsh Valleys!

'All right then… I mean, great!'

'What's the dress code?'

'Oh! Buddy told me to wear to tie.'

'High end of Smart Casual. What time?'

'Six o'clock.'

'We'll meet you there.'

'Bye, Lizzie!'

'Bye.'

Lizzie smiled at the phone for a second.

Genesis

She's gone. Tending her flock.

Late Saturday afternoon and evening. On duty. Like clockwork.

Not her day job, though she takes that beat-up nurse's bag with her, like she's on some TV show. No! This job she gave herself! Makin the rounds. *Makin interventions* in the lives of all her loser brothers and sisters, nieces and nephews and all their husbands and wives, girlfriends and boyfriends. Keepin them on the straight and narrow.

And now I'm on that straight and narrow street, too. In Nina's house with the stupid name. Salt C-A-Y. Pronounced KEY. When I asked her how come a key was made of salt, she cracked up. Right there in my face. Then comes some long-assed story about how her mama's family came from some crappy island… Ticks? Tucks? Turks? Like I care.

Why do I have to go out with Lizzie tonight? I wouldn mind stayin home and cranking up my sounds. Like *Work It.* MISSY MISDEMEANOUR ELLIOTT! Coulda been doin Missy's dance moves, right here in Nina's kitchen.

Is it worth it, let me work it

I put my thing down, flip it and reverse it

But I'm not workin it. I'm waitin for Lizzie to take me to some damn museum. Just sittin here at the mercy of them bitches. They're the ones that's workin me! The three of them think they got me covered. Especially Nina. Gave me a room to myself. Good. First time I don't have to share with some snot-nosed bed-wetter. Doesn't feel like mine, though. OK, she let me paint it yellow and choose the curtains. But none of that can make up for what she made me do with my things. Get rid of my clothes. First week! Straight after Cup Match. My clothes! She said they made me look like a ho. *Too provocative*. Then she buys me all this other stuff. Expensive. In colours that match. Just like hers! With the same job to do. Keep everything under wraps. Boobs, belly, ass. Everything. Seventeen and looking like a friggin nun.

Nina scares me. It's not just that she wants me to get through this year without getting into trouble. So does Tess. Another Public Service award for her. Airhead Lizzie, too – for her resume. They all want it more than me. I just don't want to be locked up. Learned two things bouncin in and out of people's houses when real little girls were bakin brownies or goin Vacation Bible School. Don't get knocked up. Don't get locked up. I check out the girls I know. Knocked up. Locked up. Or both. Those three crazy bitches gave me a break when I needed one bad, but they're making me pay. Big time. Makes me want to rip their heads off.

But Nina wants something more. Wants me to... dunno... Yeah. When she's not pissin me off, she's creepin me out. And she's so sneaky. You think she's sayin one thing and then, when it's too late, you find she's sayin somethin else. Somethin that's got some lesson, some *moral* to it. That's how she rolls. Nothin is ever what it seems!

Like the other night. She took me over Black Horse to get lobster. My first time – though I didn't tell her that. And it tasted well! I thought we were goin to have it there in the restaurant but, no. Takeaway. We drive somewhere, then we walk through a whole lot of scratchy bushes. All of a sudden, we're standin on the shore. No people. Just trees behind us, and the sun setting over the water in front. I'm sittin fightin with the lobster; she's askin me if I see some island over there. Which one? There's lots of them. Nonsuch, she says. I carry on eatin but she's all hyped up about it being a nature reserve and bringin back some bird from the brink. But that's just background music. Her voice changes. *It used to be a reform school.* She says this not lookin at me. And there it is. The moral. There's always been places for people like you, Genesis. So keep your little tail quiet. She never says the words. She doesn't have to.

But the lesson isn't over! See that little point of land, that peninsula? My mouth is full of garlic butter and peas and rice so I grunt yes. Called Tucker's Town. Then starts another long story. How her daddy's family and other families were cleared out of that place in the 1920s to let rich Americans play golf and build big houses there. Then without taking a breath, she's like, I read this week's report from school. Your teacher – Mrs Powell? – says you haven't chosen the topic for your social studies research project. Maybe you should find out what happened back in the 20s…

That's Nina! Always workin her corner with some hook. She gives you lobster, sunset, stories. But what she's really dishin out is reform school and stick-woman Powell. All part of her plan to make me into what I'm not.

Same thing again before she went out. Worse this time.

We're at the sink. She's washin, I'm dryin. I want to bitch about havin to go to the museum with Lizzie. But bitchin about anything is out of the question. Not with Nina. So I sulk. Ask in a miserable voice why I have to go and look at some stupid root… when I could be reading good books, or thinkin about the Lord. She gives me the look. I shut up. Then she says I have to broaden my horizons. I been here three months. I must of heard that a thousand times.

Out of nowhere it comes. My horizon is pretty broad, Nina. Broader than yours will ever be. As I'm sayin it, there's a flood of faces and feelings that I half remember. I turn my back on Nina and scream in my head for those tears to keep the hell away.

It goes quiet. The only noise is Nina movin around, wringin out the sponge, wipin off the countertop and finally scraping a chair to sit down. Then a big sigh.

G, see that jar on the window sill?

Something's been there a couple of weeks. I'm only now seein that it's a jar.

Just add some water, she says. Not too little. Not too much.

I hate this kind of instruction and after I've added a few drops, I hold it up for her to see.

A tiny bit more.

I squeeze a few more drops from the faucet.

Now bring it over here.

We sit at the table lookin at this old peanut butter jar with toothpicks holdin a dried-up seed on the rim.

It's the beginning of an avocado tree, she says. I always wanted one.

From the bottom of the seed, there's something like threads curlin down through the water. Coilin like a bunch of snakes. Where the snakes start, there's something else going up, straight through the seed, up and out, breakin through. A tiny shoot with a couple of bright green leaves on the top.

A few weeks from now, she says, Uncle Jack will plant it in a pot and later in the yard.

How long will it take for you to get avocados?

Years. Many years of fertilising, rain, shine and crossed fingers. I hope I'm around to taste the first one.

The root looks nasty, I tell her.

Not nasty, G. Alive. That's what life looks like. The root is the beginning of everything.

No it's not. It's the seed.

What! You want to be a lawyer? She laughs. I never like that laugh. Like she's laughing at me. G, she says, the seed on its own can't do anything. It's the seed and the water together that make the root. And the root triggers new life.

I look again at those thin snakes winding around each other.

Put it back on the sill, G. Let it get the evening sun.

When I cross the kitchen holding the jar, I know for a fact that this was one of Nina's lessons. Not quite sure what it meant – but it was there.

CHAPTER 3: CEDARS

Lizzie

'Oh, there you are! Been looking all over for you!'

All Lizzie could see was the girl's back forming a dark silhouette against the glass case.

'Sorry. Just checking it out.' Genesis glanced over her shoulder at Lizzie then turned back towards the box. Her outfit was sober and Nina-sanctioned, making her look out of place among the white wine and finger food and all the Smart Casual ensembles.

Lizzie shook her head and stepped closer to the exhibit. For the first time in an evening full of obscure discourse from scientists, impassioned accounts from deep sea divers and approving noises from a well-heeled but clueless public, she looked at the thing that was generating all this talk.

'Ugly!'

Worried that she'd been heard, especially when she compared her reaction to the fixed concentration of the girl, Lizzie looked again at the object.

It was a root. Lizzie had seen plenty of trees blown down by gales, their roots exposed and obscene in the open air. She had never before seen a root cut off from the rest of the tree – as if an inept photographer had shot a random pair of feet instead of the whole body. It was bigger than she'd expected, a monstrous spider, with some of its legs amputated, perhaps two feet across and half as high, with its top worn to the texture of an elephant's hide and its splayed limbs clutching vainly for soil and solid rock. It looked as though the upper section had been incinerated, leaving the lower tentacles pale in comparison. Lizzie gave an involuntary shudder. The display board above the root was certainly more inviting than this cadaver and she turned to look at an image of the island, as it now was, floating on an ocean in graduated shades of blue. There was also an outline of what the island would have been, when this root had been part of a living forest of cedars.

The text read:

> *In the lifetime of this cedar root, retrieved from the reef at Gurnet Rock on July 26, 2002, Bermuda was approximately 25 times larger than its present size. During the intervening millennia, the sea slowly covered its original forested landmass, leaving the twenty-one square miles that we inhabit. What happened to Mount Bermuda also happened to the other two volcanic seamounts to our south-west, known to us as the Argus and Challenger Banks. Because of global warming sea levels continue to rise. The discovery of this root gives us an insight into the past of both our island and the sea that surrounds it. Knowledge provided by the Gurnet Rock root will shed further light on the nature of sea-level rise worldwide and what it will mean for communities such as ours which are completely defined by the ocean.*

More doom and gloom! That was not what she wanted from this evening.

'Wait here,' she told the girl, 'I'll get Hugh.'

She slid through the crowd, dispensing indiscriminate smiles and hi's. He was huddled in a corner with Buddy Darrell, bending slightly, his tousled brown hair almost touching Buddy's straight white thatch. One slim, the other stocky, one still flushed pink, the other with skin permanently mottled by a lifetime's overexposure to salt and sun. Both were squirming in their correct clothing. Both were smiling and talking at the same time. Kindred spirits... Hm, an obstacle. Hugh was a challenge. Educated, with plenty of employment possibilities, presentable looking even in his natural rumpled state, he had potential. She even agreed with her mother on this point! But so far, he had not responded to the tactics which had left a whole string of corporate attorneys, insurance operatives and actuaries gasping. The challenge was the only thing preventing her from deleting his number from her phone.

She moved towards them.

'Hello, Hugh. Are we ready? Oh, are you Mr. Darrell? So happy to meet you at last. I've heard so much about you. And, this evening! What a triumph!'

Ten minutes later, Hugh, Lizzie and Genesis were out in the car park, arranging to meet at *La Siciliana* for dinner.

In the low buzz of the restaurant, punctuated by the rattle of plates and the clink of glasses, Lizzie looked at Hugh and saw something more than a resume and a bank account. It was an acquaintance. That was the correct word; it was neither a friendship nor a relationship. They had been out for a drink with other people twice, had met at Tess's a few times, had talked on the phone. And that was it. Not much there. While they ordered and were served drinks, she remembered the day they'd met. Coming on to him hard and feeling him back away. She sank back in her seat, overcome with embarrassment. What made her act like this? Time for a new start. She'd have to camouflage her hard edges.

They were in a booth that seated four, she and Genesis against the wall, Hugh sitting facing her.

'I love that Buddy Darrell!' she began. 'Such a wonderful human being! This island doesn't know what a treasure we have in him. The whole evening was so exciting!'

Hugh looked up, his eyebrows raised. 'I'm really pleased you enjoyed it, Lizzie.' He smiled. 'I wasn't sure you would.'

'Who wouldn't?' she made an expansive gesture which included Genesis who was demolishing a large pizza. 'And Buddy...' she continued, giving up the attempt to articulate the scale of his magnificence.

'I've never met anyone like him.' Hugh put down his fork and looked into Lizzie's eyes. 'Someone who knows the sea. From the inside.' He lowered his gaze and started twirling spaghetti around his fork. 'You know, he's taking me out to Gurnet Rock next week. I can't tell you what a thrill that's going to be...'

The waiter came to ask for dessert orders and Hugh had still not succeeded in telling them what it felt like. Dessert did not interrupt the flow of words. Taking a breather from her large slice of strawberry cheesecake, Genesis sat gazing around the room. Lizzie hovered over her fresh fruit salad, holding on to the moment when he had looked at her, for the first time without trepidation or awkwardness.

At last, he took a breath to blow on his coffee and Lizzie leapt in. 'So, Gen, how's everything going at school?'

'Everything's safe.'

'She means OK,' Lizzie explained. 'I used to try to answer my mother like that and she'd give me a whack.'

'No, really. Everything's safe,' Genesis said. 'Well… let's see… I haven't been bad,' she continued with a mocking smile. 'Haven't sworn at any teachers. Haven't taken a swing at anybody. No trace of Attitude. No mark under C, mostly Bs. And one A. How's that?'

'What did you get the C in?' Hugh's question wiped the smile from her face.

'Maths.'

'Hmmmm.'

Feeling a quiver in the air, Lizzie stepped in. 'What was the A for?'

'Social Studies.'

'Go on!' Lizzie's face and body shouted encouragement.

'Well... I had to write the outline of my research paper. The teacher thought my topic was good. I'm researching the way they kicked black people out of Tucker's Town in the 1920s. So they could build a golf course.'

The smile on Lizzie's face remained but started losing its gloss. 'Wow. That's… that's… well. Not a lot of people know about it.'

Genesis leaned closer to Lizzie. 'Did you know that Nina's people were one of the families that were forced out? She's the one told me about it. I get to interview some of her old aunties and stuff.'

'When you say they were forced to go, what do you mean?' Hugh asked.

'Forced mean forced.' Genesis threw Hugh an acid look. 'The government and the money people – same difference – they got them out. Chucked a few dollars at them and told them go live someplace else.'

'Sounds like the Highland Clearances,' Hugh said.

Lizzie winced.

'How come everything that happens here must have happened someplace else? Someplace you know about?'

'Because it probably has. It was bad when they did it in the Scottish Highlands in the 19th century. It was no doubt bad when it was done here.'

Genesis sucked her teeth.

'Anyway. That's what's happening in school. And Nina's helping me.' Genesis returned to her dessert. 'And Tess.'

'I can help you too,' Lizzie said.

'How?'

'My grandfather – my Vovo – died years ago when I was a little girl, I hardly even remember him… Had a scratchy moustache that… And well, he built that golf course and the club. He and a bunch of other men from the Azores. They were brought over to do that job. Most of them had to go back as soon as it was finished. But my Vovo met my Avó and he stayed.'

Lizzie found herself inadvertently adding a fourth spoonful of sugar into her coffee. 'I can find out details for you,' she said. 'My grandmother would love to talk about it.' She cocked her head to the side and added, 'But only for you, Gen. I don't like digging up the past. What's done is done. Not a thing we can do about it.'

Hugh was signing off on the bill when, as though it were a sudden thought, he asked Genesis what she'd thought of the root. Her expression showed that she had not expected another direct question from him.

'It was… safe.'

Hugh looked straight at her.

'I thought… It was good the way it showed that we were so much bigger than we are now. Twenty-five times bigger! You get sick of being small. It's even better than being an iceberg. An iceberg goes down deep into the water. There's so much more than you can see. But it doesn't go to the bottom of the sea. We're a mountain! I didn't understand a whole lot of what you all were saying. But what I saw was that we're a mountain. I'm a mountain!'

'Goodness!' Hugh said. 'You did like it.'

'And the root itself… well, it looked… alive.'

'And, in its way, rather beautiful.'

'I guess…'

‘Time to move,’ said Lizzie, fiddling with her phone. ‘Just excuse me a minute.’

Genesis

I hate this bullshit place and this bullshit room and these bullshit yellow walls and the bullshit trees that make so much friggin noise when the wind blows and all those bullshit vegetables she makes me eat – *You want to clear up those pimples, don't you?* – and all her bullshit rules. I hate the way I can't even *think* the word fuck without her being in my brain telling me not to… And I hate that other bullshit house, with its bullshit swimming pool and bullshit boats and bullshit maids – not even black. FILIPINOS! I hate the way that blonde one always wants to be my bullshit friend. At least Nina doesn't try that! I just hate her bullshit ponytail with so much Clairol in it you could drown a bullshit army. But most of all, I hate the bullshit bitch that calls me Gen!

What I do her? What I do her skinny ass? I didn't do nothing! Nothing! I went there – for Chrissake, I didn't want to go no bullshit museum. But I went because I'm playing their game. I went… dressed like a nun, as always. There's something to look at. I look at it. I keep quiet. Those people didn't want to talk to me and I sure as hell didn't want to talk to them. Then dinner. At least I could have a grease without Bernina talking to me about fats and carbohydrates and what they do to my skin… I switch off as expat boy goes on and on about who knows what… Skinny-Ass is making a move on expat boy but doesn't want him to know. I'm the decoy. She wants to make him hot for her and then make him wait till she's ready. Ha! She's ready! I understand all this bullshit and don't give a crap. I'm there for the pizza and the cheesecake and I'm thinking about those poor bastards at the Home and their chicken nuggets and Chef Boyardee. But things aren't going to plan for Skinny-Ass. I don't want to be in the mix but she pulls me in. That's when we start talking about my project and she tells me about her grandpa and then expat boy jumps in with his crap about England or wherever. And that pisses her off too. But like she's scared to say anything to him. I'm not. I tell him. How come you think you own everything, even what happened here in 1920? He's not scared either. What he thinks, he says. So before we left, he asks me what I think about the root. I tell him. That's where I went wrong. Should of kept my big trap shut. Should of said it was safe. Before I know what I'm doin, I'm tellin him I'm a mountain... A mountain. What kind of bullshit person am I?

Before we leave, Skinny-Ass goes to the bathroom and puts in the call. Tells Nina I embarrassed her. That I wouldn't talk to the people at the museum. I wouldn't say a word. And how rude that was. And when I did talk, I was rude to expat boy and eventually I was acting *inappropriately* towards him... Nina was waiting for me when I got home.

So I told Nina I didn't do nothing. Didn't act any kinda way with expat boy. Appropriate or inappropriate. Answered his question. That's it. I told her Lizzie's the one with the problem. Remember the way she acted when she first met him? She's the one with the problem. She's the one...

Nina didn't say much. Only that she's disappointed that the evening didn't go well. She says goodnight and went to bed.

I been in this room ever since. All night. Can't sleep. Can't stop my mind from screaming. Even when I don't do nothing, I get the blame. I can hear those birds out there making their noise and now there's light coming through the window. Guess it's not a big deal. I'm not being thrown out of the house. But I feel like storming into Nina's room and asking her why she didn't stand up for me. I know why. She don't trust me – like I don't trust her. That's why I feel bad. Because when she feels bad, she can go to a hundred close relatives and talk. And so can Tess and even HER. They all have somebody. Not me. Not here at least. Ever since that teenager pushed me into the world and didn't have the sense to stay alive long enough so I could remember her. Joy. Stupid name. I hate that name. Hate that bullshit name.

This is so fucked up! Got to get out of here before I suffocate!

Wow. Outside. So cool...

Oh, no. Over there under the trees... Crazy Uncle Jack. Too late. He's seen me. All I need.

He comes over. Smiles and shows a yard of gums. I always get a kick when he does that. Not one tooth. But he don't care. Smiles anyway. I say morning to him and he nods and goes back to messing around with the trees. He stoops down and swirls his hands around the base of every tree. Gets all the fallen leaves and anything else that's there, even the soil and loosens it up and swirls it around. He does it with all twelve of the orange trees and all ten of the grapefruit. How I know how many? Anything I know about this yard comes from Nina. It always sticks, even though I don't want it to. Twelve orange. Ten grapefruit. Used to be more back in de day.

Crazy Jack goes about his business on his knees swirling that dirt around. Got to give it to these old people. They don't mind getting dirty. Me! Just as I'm growing my nails back – after Nina made me get rid of the acrylics. No friggin way I'd put my hands right in the dirt!

But standing here is safe. Can't see the sun yet but the sky's light. Everything's quiet. Nobody on the roads. The only sound you can hear is those friggin chickens makin off the way they do this time of day. I close my eyes. Something makes me open them and there's Crazy Jack, standing right in front of me, holding out something for me to take. I look down and it's a ratty old bag. I don't want to touch it but the way he's holding it, I can't say no. It's like that with old people. They tell you do something and there's no way you can say no. I take the bag and though it makes me squirm, I throw it over my shoulder the way he does.

As we're leaving the yard, he stops and puts his hand on the trunk of the big cedar tree at the gate. He runs his hand over the trunk. His hand must be hard because I can see from here how rough that trunk is.

'Tree!' he says and smiles his gummy smile.

I say yes and we carry on walking. I know where we're going. When Jack comes to spend every second weekend at the house, he wakes up early Sunday morning and goes down the beach for seaweed to put under the citrus trees. And when he says 'tree', he don't mean no orange or grapefruit or cherry or banana or any other kinda damn tree. He means cedar. Like there used to be all over the place when he was young. Nina told me.

Can't believe how fast he walks! Holding his cane with one hand and the end of the crocus bag with the other. We go up the hill on a path running along Sister Rita's house. It's pretty steep but he's going like a bullet. He's seventy years older than me so I try not to pant as we make it to the top.

We stop. Catch a glimpse of the water. Can't really see it because we're going down into a tunnel of trees. But we can hear it! The waves breaking on the shore getting closer and closer. He stops again. With his cane, he points to the trees crowding around us. Dark inside this tunnel but I can see his face. Serious. No gums. He raises his cane and strikes the nearest tree. I feel scared. Looks like he's about to go off. He strikes it again and says, 'No. Tree. No. Tree.' Says it over and over, each time looking at me. Finally – because it's like he's giving me an order – I look closely at the tree he's hitting and all the others that are surrounding us. Not special enough. Not cedars. I say it out loud. They're not cedars! He nods. I don't know what else to say and start feeling scared again. Then Jack throws his arms wide and looks up and all around him, turning his body this way and that. In a whisper he says, tree, tree, tree. He stops, looks at me again.

I stare into his face, black without a wrinkle, with one of the broadest noses I ever seen in a human. I understand. 'There used to be cedars here. Lots and lots of them. A long time ago. But they're gone.'

He smiles and we start walking again.

We're the first people on the beach. Everything clean. Sand, water, air, sky. When the sun finally comes up out of the sea, I feel like clapping. There's loads and loads of seaweed. It's fresh and stinks of fish and Jack and I almost fill our bags. When we're finished, he goes into the surf like he's part of it. He don't care that he's wearing his shoes and clothes. Every time the surf runs up to meet me, I take off, don't want it to touch me. He shakes his head. Swings his bag up over his shoulder. Time to go. When we reach home, he puts his hand on the cedar, the one at the gate. It looks to me like a soldier standing guard over the house. Take my bag out to the back and empty it onto the pile. Jack's already arrangin the seaweed into one level patch. When it's dry, he'll put it around the trees. Twelve orange and ten grapefruit. Nina said.

Noises are coming from the kitchen. Nina making Sunday breakfast. Smells good. I start to hurry but make a detour first. I go to Jack's soldier tree and put my hand on it. It's rough against my palm. But it's not just the tree trunk I'm staring at. My hands. Covered in sand and soil, bits of tar and seaweed, my nails gritty and chipped. I'm still holding them out in front of me when I get inside. Nina takes a look at them. I know she's gonna make off about bringing that dirt into her house. But she doesn't. Just smiles and turns back to the stove.

Nina

For anyone with a drop of Bermudian blood, codfish and potatoes garnished with parsley and anointed in olive oil. Hard-boiled eggs, quartered. Tomato sauce laced with onion, garlic and hot pepper. White sauce for the fainthearted. Lime wedges. Sliced avocado. Johnny bread and loquat jam. Sweet fig bananas. Orange juice. Tea. For any Jamaican friend who might stop by, ackee and saltfish. For any Trinidadian, buljol. Sunday breakfast, an open-house ritual that had been going in this house for as long as anyone could remember.

Despite all the running around she did on a Saturday, Nina always managed to get most of the Sunday breakfast preparation done that day – the peeling, the chopping, the sautéing. The salt cod had to be soaked in readiness for its eventual transformation into three distinct guises. Then, early on Sunday morning, when all was quiet, she would finish the fish dishes and cook the Johnny bread in the heavy iron skillet. She'd put a white cloth on the table, arrange the platters, have a shower, sit down with tea in a china cup and saucer – she hated mugs! – and think of Dee. Always Dee. Soon the first of her family would arrive – usually her sister Rita, as she lived closest. Or maybe one or two of the girls from work, some nieces or nephews... They would come and go, on their way to or from church, or, for the younger ones, whatever they did on a Sunday – running on the beach, going to the gym, doing their grocery shopping, taking a child to its babydaddy for the day. From the morning into the early afternoon, they would come. She could rely on her sister Janet to bring homemade rolls or gingerbread but, as the eldest of her parents' eight children, she had made this weekly event her own, though really it was the property of the whole family. She provided the venue and the food. All the rest –

the arguing, the diaper-changing, the hand wringing over the latest teenage transgression, the reminiscing – she let them get on with it. With one proviso – that when she returned from church around two o'clock, her kitchen would be clean and all the food gone.

Backing out of the driveway, she waved at Rita, making her way down the hill. Rita would make sure none of the young ones harassed Uncle Jack. Then she thought of the look on Genesis's face when she'd come into the kitchen with the old man, both of them smelling of the sea. Uncle Jack would be safe! She swung onto the South Shore Road, sank back into the seat and let the car bear her away.

She was going to church. That was all she ever told her people, so they'd stopped asking. Recently, she'd only sporadically attended the church into which they had all been born and Born Again. Nobody could understand it. One of her sisters said it was because she was going through the change. Another thought she had a secret lover but that was a nonstarter because everybody knew she wouldn't do that to Dee's memory. The waters were further muddied by Nina-sightings at other people's churches – Pentecostal, Methodist, Brethren, Unity, Presbyterian, Salvation Army, Baptist, Church of God, Church of Christ, Church of God in Christ, Lutheran, even Anglican and Roman Catholic. Somebody was prepared to swear that she'd been seen at the Ethiopian Orthodox church... This trail had gone cold.

Nina smiled as she thought of their thwarted detective work, but her church-hopping was no joke. She had lost her faith. Utterly. What she was left with was a void, not a gaping hole but an empty space – in the shape of a building with a steeple and tombstones out in the yard. She wanted to renounce God and all of His works – the God who had taken away the man she loved. But no matter how hard she tried, she could not outrun Him. He existed all right, but He couldn't care less. Everywhere she looked, she found proof of this – in some of the disasters in her own family; in the people she met at the family planning clinic, lost young girls about to become mothers, and somewhere in the shadows, young boys equally lost and unable to be fathers beyond the moment of sowing their seed. There was her island, a triumph of Mammon, if ever there was one and what did you see on the news? Always the victory of the strong and corrupt over the weak, the poor, the starving... Whatever happened to *Blessed be the meek for they shall inherit the earth*?

No, girl, you hate Him because of what He took from you.

She turned off the main road into a narrow lane with a fallow field beside it. There she saw the brilliance of the morning as the sun's light poured through every cleft, every fissure of air visible between the crowding green arms of the trees. They jostled for room, these two ancient inhabitants of the island – the olivewood's demure oval shape contrasting with the flamboyant gloss of its leaves, and the cedar, taller, tougher, with the broad span of its arms, covered in tufted foliage of the darkest green. Unseen birds made claim to their territory in lovely song. The pounding in her head was easing, and with the fresh breeze of October in her face, she walked the rest of the way.

According to the pamphlet, the chapel had once been a labourer's cottage, but when Nina saw it first a few months ago, she felt sure that labourer had been a slave. Nothing else could account for its presence on what had been one of the largest estates on the island. This morning, it was not its history but its beauty that stunned her. At the edge of the sunlit wood, it gazed over the Sound, spread out below like a silken sheet. The cottage was no bigger than her living room and it had a large water tank attached, a throwback to the times before tanks were sunk underground. Strange angles and buttressing gave further evidence of its age, as did the blinds at the windows, pushed and held wide open by poles. Its walls were covered in a limewash so white that it hurt Nina's eyes. Outside the chapel, overlooking the water, were two grey cedar boughs, hammered together in the shape of a cross.

Nina stepped into the chapel and through the gloom took in the six bare pews, the plain crucifix and the small tapestry of the magi. She stumbled to sit, clasped her hands and closed her eyes. But she did not pray. She could not. All she could do was shut out the world and try to find... *a balm in Gilead to heal the sin-sick soul*. She sighed. Whatever she thought, whatever she felt, always came out in these, the words of the bible. She could not even grieve in her own language.

Dee had been dead for just over nine years. She'd had to force herself to stop thinking in terms of months, weeks and days. It had become pathological. She'd had to break that habit and get back into life. Her loved ones were relieved to see her the way she used to be – immersed in her work, her church and her community, a ministering figure in their world. Doing the Sunday breakfast. Being Nina.

How wrong they were! Her grief at losing Dee got worse as time went by. She saw him in her dreams, she heard his laugh, she felt his presence, especially when she was home by herself. There was no comfort to be found in these encounters because although she could see those green eyes lit up with laughter and hear the raspiness – no, the rascality – of his laugh, he was still separate from her, behind a veil, *across the bar*. In the eyes of the world, he had not been a great man, or a brilliant man but a decent man, who worked hard, who made people laugh, who loved his family. Who loved his wife. *No longer twain but one. Till Death do us part.* Another lie! She was still married – to a dead man. How could she praise a Lord who gave her such a love, then take away its earthly form and leave her soul with an ache that nothing could assuage.

Oh, Love that wilt not let me go…

She opened her eyes and looked around the chapel. Such an unlikely sanctuary, this former slave cottage made into a church by the Christian foundation that now owned the estate. Twice a day, two nuns sang mass in plainsong. That was it. No preacher, no congregation, no sermon. Just the ancient chant twice a day. She'd been there once when they had done it and even though she'd been quite taken by the ethereal sound, she preferred the chapel silent of everything. But then, in that silence, came the second pain. She and Dee had not been able to have children. Wrong! *She* had not been able to have children. Infertile, or, to use that great word from the Bible, barren. As barren as a stone, with a womb colonised by ever-increasing clusters of fibroids. Then the miracle. A tiny life began. At last, against all the odds! Even now, her body tingled at the remembered joy and hope of those few weeks when she'd walked on air. It ended as suddenly as it began. Only Dee's tender care had prevented her from entering the circling darkness that threatened to swamp her mind. *It's a curse.* They were the first words she'd said to him – that she, a nurse and midwife, was unable to grow a baby that would have been theirs, and hence the most loved child on this earth. Because he was there to bear her up, she had been able to endure it... *I rest my weary soul in thee*. They had talked about fostering, maybe adopting. In his practical way, he had reminded her of all the children who had lived with them over the years, the children of siblings, the children of friends, children waiting to be fostered, all who needed care in an emergency. Their lives were full. They had each other. She had argued that it wasn't the same as a child they could call their own. Back and forth they went... the pros and cons and every aspect of parenthood. Then the cancer came. The talking stopped.

One thing she was prepared to tell this God – if He were ever interested enough to ask – was that she had already had her fair allotment of suffering. There must be no more. She would not allow it. She shook her head so hard that a decorative pin in her hair flew out. Genesis, she thought, stooping to pick it up. Why did I do it? Why did I let her in? It began the day three years ago, when she'd walked into the clinic and asked for the pill so she wouldn't get 'knocked up'; the period that followed when she became a regular at the clinic, still wild and alone, still not wanting to get pregnant; and the day when Tess Alexander called, representing her organisation for vulnerable children, wanting her to be a support and advocate for Genesis. Now this troubled, troubling girl, whose understanding of the difference between right and wrong was fluid to say the least, was living in her home. When Lizzie had complained about her, Genesis kept on saying that she hadn't done anything wrong, over and over, almost as though she needed to convince herself.

Nina brought her hand down hard on the pew in front of her. She had to remain detached! Her nursing training would help her not to get too involved, because, if she did and it all went wrong, she didn't think she would survive. She could not do this to herself. What would Dee have made of it all? Would he have counselled her to keep her distance or give the girl what she'd never had? Was she destined to become a mother at fifty-seven? Like Elizabeth, the cousin of Mary, who gave birth to John the Baptist when she was already of a great age? If that was written for her, would she have the strength to face it?

With body clenched and head bowed, Nina remained motionless until she heard the slamming of a car door and the murmuring of voices. She walked towards the tiny altar and saw that the word 'Joy' was embroidered on the tapestry. Nina sighed, burdened by those three letters.

Joy. A sad name. A short life. Joy. The mother of Genesis. Joy, who had left her child to face the world alone... The girl says she has not a single memory of her. Can that be?

Before she pushed the screen door to go outside, she turned for one last look. There was no plastered ceiling, just rough-hewn boughs of cedar, exposed bones keeping the building together. Could she be strong enough to be a mother to Genesis? If she were to try, it would be on her own terms. Without Him.

She nodded a greeting to the family who had come to see the church and as she made her way to her car, the trees sighed and gave her a whole verse of the hymn that had been stalking her.

Oh Joy, that seekest me through pain
I cannot close my heart to thee
I trace the rainbow through the rain
And feel the promise is not vain
That morn shall tearless be.

CHAPTER 4: THE PENINSULA

Lizzie

For most of the drive, the passing scenery escaped Lizzie. Her head was too full – deadlines to be met, clothes to be sourced online, dates to be made or cancelled. Then suddenly, the sea was there, its broad blue arc on her right, silencing the chatter.

The work was terrible, breaking hard stone in the hot sun.

She could see the sentence written on lined paper and could hear the words read in halting, accented English.

She had been given that paper over a week ago. She'd been at home, hesitating outside her grandmother's door…

'Avó!' She'd knocked and slowly counted back from five. 'Avó! It's…'

'Elisabete.'

The old woman's eyes were wary. Despite her diminutive size, she barred the doorway.

'Can I come in? I hope I'm not disturbing you…'

Avó looked at Lizzie without blinking, then turned inside. Following her dowager's hump made her look less forbidding. Lizzie did not try to pretend that this visit was normal. There was silence as Avó picked up her rosary and seated herself again. Lizzie perched herself on the carved wooden chair that her father sat in every evening after supper. She didn't know how to start.

'You wish to speak to me about your grandfather. Your Vovo.'

'Yes. That is true.' Lizzie's tongue felt large in her mouth and the Portuguese came out in awkward bursts. It had been so long since she'd been alone with Avó, so long since she'd really thought about her, even though they lived under the same roof. Long ago, under the subtle tutelage of their mother, she and her brothers had left Avó behind. They went to Sunday Mass together, they ate Sunday lunch together and, on special occasions, Avó was wheeled out for public viewing. Only for her youngest son, Lizzie's father, João, did Avó continue to live. He had acted as intermediary for this encounter.

The walls of the room pressed in on Lizzie – the crucifixes, La Biblia looking ominous on the table, the crochet work frothing everywhere and the old woman in mourning black, decades after her husband's death.

'There is something that you want to know?'

'Yes, Avó. I have this person... She's doing some...' She couldn't remember the Portuguese for 'research'. 'She is looking for some...'

'Informações.'

'Thank you, Avó. This girl I know. This friend. She's doing "research" – she said the word in English – on the history of Tucker's Town. I know that my grandfather came here to work in Tucker's Town and...' Lizzie started to fumble for words again. 'I wondered if you could tell me any details of when he came and what he did.'

Lizzie wasn't sure she remembered him. She was four when he died. For a moment, there was a complete blank – no name, no face. Nothing.

Avó retrieved a white envelope from the table, and took a sheet of paper and a photograph from the envelope. She cleared her throat. 'When your father told me what you wanted, I wrote this.' As she unfolded the lined paper and handed over of the photograph, they still avoided each other's eyes.

'Manuel Da Silva Pereira was born in Sao Miguel, Açores in 1902, on 16 May. His family had a farm that did well until the war. Then there was nothing but ruin and hungry mouths. Manuel heard that they were looking for men to work in Bermudas. He was only eighteen years old but he left his family and came. He and the others, mainly from Sao Miguel, but from the other islands too, built the golf course. Then they built the clubhouse.' She paused. 'Mid Atlantic Club.' Avó enunciated the words with care. 'The work was terrible, breaking the hard stone in the hot sun. Our men worked until they dropped. The big men wanted to send them all back when the club was opened. But by then, something had happened. My father had met Manuel and found out that he was the son of someone he knew back in Açores. One day, he brought Manuel home to meet me. I was fourteen years old. We got married and had five children. The only one living is your father, João. Manuel died in 1972, on 27 February. He was a good man.'

Lizzie remembered staring at her grandmother's signature.

Maria Madalena Da Freitas Pereira.

It was only then that she'd realised that Avó could read and write English!

She swerved, narrowly avoiding a moped overtaking on the other side of the road. Flustered, she pulled over. 5 - 4 -3... Her breathing eased. The photograph was not like the one she knew well – so faded that all you could see was one figure in white, one in black, both blurred beyond recognition. This one had weathered the years in defined shades of sepia. A very young man – an adolescent – leaning on a spade, his eyes dark brown, his skin dark olive. His smile hopeful. 3 - 2... Going back in time was her least favourite thing. Even recent time. But this stirred something in her, something painful – to think of her ancient grandmother as a girl bride walking down the aisle towards her boy groom.

She looked around. Without realising it, she had already driven into Tucker's Town. There was nothing urban about this town. Green dominated. Not a building in sight, but the green of the hedge-lined lanes branching out from the main road, winding towards the hidden mansions of the rich and super rich. Old Money. New Money. Didn't matter as long as it was green.

Greenest of all was the golf course as it undulated away from both sides of the road, sometimes looking like green velvet, sometimes like rolls of green baize. Sometimes, rarely, it almost looked like grass. Even the trees had the sheen of a manicurist's finishing coat.

This was Tiago's kingdom. Tiago, her favourite cousin, her defender when she was a child, was now Director of Course Maintenance at the Mid Atlantic Club. He had promised to show her what their mutual grandfather had created. He was there in the clubhouse parking lot, waiting for her with a smile and a bear hug.

'Hey, girl! Let's go find Manuel.'

Lizzie struck a pose. 'Will I do?' Her hand swept down from head to toe. 'That dress code sheet you sent me cost me a lot of money. Had to buy every damn old-lady thing that you see.' She stepped into the cart, laughing. 'No ripped jeans, no sneakers, no tube tops...'

'Eisenhower and Churchill played golf here and between holes, decided how to get world peace.' Before switching on the ignition, he turned to her. 'It's called class, baby!'

They shot off onto the course, Lizzie smiling, relaxed, her hair whipping around like a dark flag. Tiago had had this effect on her when they were children and now, here he was, with wife, kids and mortgage, still making her feel... normal. Only for him would she sit acquiescent while he gave her the tour. Tee box, fairway, green, rough... The terminology washed over her but she couldn't help but be pulled into what she was seeing. She was silent as Tiago spoke of open spaces carved into woodland; greens, pristine as though newly born; gentle hills and sharp inclines; sand traps cut into the green like the paw prints of some giant bird. The Mangrove Lake, graveyard of overconfident golfers. Even without his enthusiasm, Lizzie could see the engineered beauty of the course, though she wondered about the value of the colossal task of creating and maintaining this perfection.

Finally, they reached the eighteenth hole, where the tree-lined cliff dropped sheer into the Atlantic. Tiago pulled over and turned to her. 'So, *prima*, why are you here?'

'Why am I here? I told you on the phone. I'm helping this kid. She's got this Tucker's Town thing. Said I'd help her... I told you!'

'Yes.' Tiago got out of the cart, gave his back a good stretch and patted the beginning of a pot belly. 'See this? Never had this when I was working outside all day.' He looked towards the ocean. 'I don't buy it, Lizzie. Okay. You want to help the kid. Fine. You make an appointment to see Avó. Now already that's huge. In your house! In your mother's house! Then you call me – all crazy, all *luoca*. Need to talk to me. Need to see the place where our Vovo landed aeons ago. Need to, need to...'

He turned a stern face towards Lizzie. 'What's going on?'

Lizzie raised her foot to stamp but looked down at the grass just in time. But Tiago had seen and started to laugh.

'All right. Genesis does have this project. That's true. But... It's just that... for me there's now...' Her hands snapped out in front of her around an invisible box called 'Now'. 'And there's Back Then.' The box disappeared behind her. 'And you know me. I live in Now. Why would I want to live in back then? But when the whole project thing came up... I had to step up. Couldn't have those two old babes get one over on me. I had to defend my turf! Had to produce a Tucker's Town ancestor. And there he was. Vovo!'

Tiago threw up his hands. 'What are you? In a gang?'

'No. I have to get them to respect me.' She sighed. 'That's when it all fell apart. I had to see Avó. I had to go in her room. Hear her voice. Hear her read. See a picture of Vovo when he was just a kid. At work right here... When it was hard stone in the hot sun.'

'So?'

'Don't you see?' Her eyes pleaded with him. 'Back then became now. I couldn't escape it. And I can't escape them.'

'Why do you want to? They're your grandparents. They broke their backs for you.' Lizzie recognised the tone. He'd used it when he, at thirteen, would try to explain something to her, then four. But now she was the one who needed him to understand.

'I am educated, Ti. With a plum job in re-insurance. Great prospects. Good looking.' She took a little bow. Tiago responded with a shake of his head. 'I am of Portuguese descent. That's it! I'm not a Por-dee-gee... or a Gee! I have nothing in common with what people associate with Vovo. Poor. Immigrant. Agricultural worker. Manual labour... His name was Manuel for God's sake!'

Tiago grabbed her by the shoulders and shook her. 'Without them there'd be no me. No you. They made us!'

Lizzie pulled away from him and went to sit in the cart with her arms folded.

Tiago joined her. 'I'm sorry I shook you, Lizzie.'

'And I'm sorry you didn't understand.' She didn't care that he'd shaken her. What had hurt was the appalled expression on his face. 'Guess it's back to square one with my family. Nobody gets me. Not even you.'

As they headed back, Lizzie spotted a graceful clump of cedars on the cliff edge, bending away from the Atlantic breeze. Several yards away stood a lone tree, with sparse, gnarled branches, bent double against the wind.

'Why's that tree on its own?'

'It's old. We're trying to save it.'

Back at the car park, they stopped for a moment to look across the inlet that separated them from St. David's Island. Its landmark lighthouse shone scarlet and white in the afternoon sun. Before she left, Tiago leaned into her open window and touched her shoulder. She looked straight ahead. 'You should get rid of that old tree. If something doesn't fit, you need to get rid of it.'

Tiago kept his hand on the roof of the car as she began to reverse. She stopped and looked into his puzzled face.

'I had to do that once. And it made me into the success you see now.'

'Lizzie!' Tiago put both hands up to his head. 'Come round for dinner! The kids haven't seen you for...'

She didn't hear the rest as she slammed the stick into drive and put her foot hard on the gas.

Nina

'You've spoken to the others?' Nina asked.

'Yes. Lizzie's finding out about her grandpa and Tess says she thinks there could be something in her library I could use.' The sound of sucked teeth filled the car.

'What?'

'People having their own libraries...' the girl muttered. 'Crazy!'

'Yes... I guess.' Nina slowed down as she approached the junction and swung right onto the coast road. A grey and sullen sea stretched beyond it. 'Looks cold, doesn't it? Isn't it amazing that all three of us are personally connected to the Tucker's Town story. Not to mention Rosie!'

Snatching a sideways glimpse, Nina caught sight of the corner of the girl's mouth hardening, then relax again.

'That's it!' The thought was so definite that Nina wondered whether it had actually slipped out of her mouth. She turned away from Genesis and allowed herself a self-satisfied smile. She had long thought the girl used her face as a blank canvas on which she posted a series of images, according to what she wanted others to think. She suspected a tough brain behind the images, always in control. Recently she was beginning to read little signs of things less willed – tiny but real – in their fleeting dash across the girl's face.

'Are you worried about talking to Rosie?' Nina chose her words with care. 'She can be a bit…'

'Weird… No disrespect. I know she's your people.' Genesis turned towards Nina. 'Why did we have to bring Rosie into this? Everything was cool. My project was cookin! Tess could give me an ancestor. Lizzie too. As for you, you even had family who were thrown out of Tucker's Town. I had all I needed! Then in comes Miss Rosie…'

'Don't ever call her that to her face!'

'In comes Rosie, then.' Her voice dropped to a whisper. 'To confuse me with them spooky green eyes…'

'G, you have to hear what Rosie has to say. What I can tell you is just what I found out years later. She's the only one who was there when it happened. The only one of us who actually witnessed it.'

'You think stick-woman Powell could care less whether my project is real or not? She'll just be looking for the right number of words and how wide the margins are and how many pictures there are. And *appen-di-ces*!' Genesis was mangling her sweater again. 'When I told her what it was going to be about, she gave me a funny look.'

'You're imagining it,' Nina said with a laugh.

'She thinks I'm an F kind of person and whatever I do, she'll find a way not to give me an A.'

'It's showing again.' Nina reached over and touched the girl's shoulder. Genesis flinched.

'What?'

'You know… The chip.'

Nina heard her take the kind of breath required for a tirade, but what came was a slow expulsion of air, ending in something like a laugh.

'You don't get it, Nina. You'll never get it.'

'Maybe... But look! The entrance to Tucker's Town! Coming up on the right!' Moments later, they had passed the fork in the road that was so heavily obscured by foliage that it seemed to lead nowhere. Genesis spun round to look.

'Did I ever tell you about the one time I went to Tucker's Town?'

'Of course! You went with your friend and when your daddy found out, he wouldn't let you go again. If it had been me, no daddy could of kept me from that place. I'd of grown up and come steppin into that place, with all my bling blazin. I'd of show'd them!'

Nina shook her head. 'Well, it wasn't you, thank God!' There was silence except for the rhythm of the windshield wipers keeping the fine rain at bay. 'Anyway, let me tell you about the time I went there.'

Genesis sank back into her seat and closed her eyes.

'I had a friend. She and her family used to go there once every summer because they knew the caretaker of one of those big houses. All very hush-hush. One year, they invited me. Must've been seven, eight. I was so excited because I'd heard that the place was supposed to be... magical.

'They picked me up early because it was so far. A beautiful day! All of us talking in the car. Then everything went quiet. Tucker's Town. With a guard in a sentry box and a heavy chain across the road.'

'Did you need a passport?'

'No.' Nina laughed. 'But it was like another country. First it seemed like nothing but the golf course. Then came the houses... Massive... you could only catch a glimpse of them through the trees. The house we were going to was not what I expected. Big but dark, with all the furniture covered over. The owners hadn't been for years. There was a real swimming pool... Nobody had them those days... Had green slime all over it.'

'Yuk!'

'But, girl, outside... Wow! On one side, this perfect beach with big, thundering Atlantic waves. And on the other, the loveliest, calmest stretch of water and the pinkest sand I'd ever seen. We went wild that day, my friend, her brothers and I – in and out of the water – running wild, screaming… We were just playing fools. But later that day, everything changed.'

Genesis opened her eyes.

'It was late afternoon and we went looking for conchs. All of us, the caretaker, my friend's parents and we children. We were on the beach – the calm one – when we see this outboard motorboat coming closer and closer to the shore. Two people in it. We could see them. They could see us. They called out. "What are you people doing here? This is private property! Not for you! No coloureds here!" That was the man.'

'What you all do?'

'We children huddled around the grownups. We could feel something terrible going on with them. Especially the men. But my friend's mama started mumbling something we couldn't understand because she seemed to be grinding her teeth at the same time.

'After a long time, they started up the engine again. As the boat started to move, the woman on it shouted out, "Go home! Niggers!"'

'You see! I don't understand you old people! If that was me, I'da gone out there and kicked some ass!'

Nina looked at her.

'What you do then?'

'Nothing. We were all scared. All except my friend's mother. She was mad as hell. Her face and neck had gone completely red. Of all of us, she was the only light-skinned one, the one with the straight hair. "I *am* home!" she finally screamed. "My people were from around here!" But the boat was already gone.

'We wanted to leave. Our day was wrecked. But the caretaker said we should still go and see the conchs. To get the nasty taste out of our mouths.

'We walked over the rocks to a cave scooped right out of the shoreline. The cave had a deep pool and we stood there looking right down to the bottom. The water was so clear.

'Then, my friend's mother dives in and goes all the way down. We could see her on the bottom grabbing hold of something on the wall of the cave. We could see her hair waving around and those pale legs and arms of hers wrestling with something. I'm holding my friend's hand. She's turned to stone watching her mama. Not coming up. Her hair waving at us. Nobody says a word. Just watching. Her feet touch bottom. All this sand starts spinning around and we can't see her anymore. Just clouds of sand where she used to be.'

Genesis twitched and broke into a coughing fit, hard, dry coughs that stopped as suddenly as they began.

'A few bubbles break open on the surface of the water. My chest is hurting. I can feel my friend shaking. Then she's calling *Mama!* Repeated over and over.

'My friend's father can't swim so the caretaker's throwing off his shoes to jump in when the sand settles and we can see again. There she is. Pulling at something with all her might. Suddenly, she shoots away from the cave wall and up she comes. Like a fish. Like a mermaid, like in a fairy tale. Her hair, her eyes, her mouth – and we can see her, gulping and spluttering. Both of her hands come up over her head. They're holding something… this huge dark shell shaped like a horn. Covered in barnacles and God knows what and streaming with green sea grass and pink underneath. When she finished gasping for breath, she gave us a smile… the kind of smile that everyone who saw it would never forget.'

Genesis's brow was furrowed in a frown. 'Seems a lot to do for a stupid conch.'

'I never set foot in Tucker's Town again,' Nina said. 'I've had many chances since then but could never bring myself to.' She paused. 'Too many mixed-up feelings. The thrill of being on forbidden soil. The water and the sand. The fun. The fun suddenly ending with that word ringing in our ears. And my father's fury afterwards…'

'Did you think that your friend's mama was going to drown?' Genesis asked in a small voice.

'Yes. We all did, even though she was a strong swimmer. She was down there a long time fighting the conch. But, G, the way she came up. Like she had taken back something that was hers. Like it was a…' Nina shook her head, still at war with the memory.

'I can tell you one thing. That conch shell lives. My friend's parents have both passed. Even my friend's gone. One of her brothers has the homestead now. It's there, on the mantelpiece, set apart from the figurines and knickknacks. All on its own, its underside pink and shining. If you put it to your ear, you can still hear the sound of the ocean.'

'Whatever Rosie says, that conch thing needs to be one of the stories for my project, Nina,' Genesis said.

The drumming of tiny fingertips of November rain provided the only accompaniment as they crossed one bridge after another, making their way to St. David's Island and to Rosie's house.

Rosie

Despite the rain, Rosie was out in her yard working.

The house and yard seemed poised between order and neglect, like their owner, wearing a battered felt hat, bent over, snapping off dead blooms from a clutch of rose bushes. She had not heard the car's approach and when she became aware of footsteps, she straightened up a little too quickly, so the first thing Genesis saw on Rosie's face was a grimace.

'How's Rosie today?' said Nina, embracing the old woman. 'Working in the garden in the rain? Dr. Butler wouldn't approve.'

Rosie raised a single eyebrow at Nina before looking away. She wiped off soil and debris onto the outermost layer of the slips, dresses and aprons that she was wearing, then reached up and took Nina's face between her rough hands.

Genesis looked around. She took in the roses, the beds lying fallow awaiting the planting season, the rusting bicycle frame, the compost heap, the dilapidated garden shed, the immaculate fork and shovel, the cottage with its newly painted roof and walls but peeling shutters. And, hoisted on dry land, a small rowing boat, with its two oars in positions of readiness.

'So! You brung the girl!' Rosie said, advancing upon Genesis. Genesis hung her head. 'Come on, girlie! Give me that arm. I'm ninety-two, you know.'

Genesis extended her arm and ushered Rosie Fox into her home where she disappeared behind a faded floral curtain to take off the outermost layers of clothing, leaving Nina and Genesis in the cramped living room. 'Girlie!' Rosie's voice was muffled as she drew a housedress over her head. 'You know how long I been here?'

'No, Miss Rosie.'

'Who in the hell told you call me Miss Rosie? I'm Rosie and that's it!'

There was a discreet cough on the other side of the curtain.

'I been here seventy-one years. Came here as a bride. My husband's name was Johnny. And he brung me here.'

'That's nice. Rosie.' It sounded like Genesis was tiptoeing across every word.

'That's my Johnny working on his boat. The picture in the black frame. See it, girlie? The other one's my Dee, the day him and Nina got married. The one in the silver frame. And you know what?' As she wrestled with her garments, Rosie chuckled. 'When I came, I walked from my own people's place – the Lambs – just down the road. White dress and all. Back in them days, the bride was s'pposed to look all miserable when she left her family. She was s'pposed to cry and carry on. That was the way, back then.' The chuckle was expanding into a throaty laugh. 'But not me! Nossuh! I couldn't wait for the Fox to lie down with the Lamb!'

'Honestly, Rosie! That tired joke again! You told it the very first time Dee brought me here. And you know how prim and proper I was back then!'

'What you mean "back then"?' Peals of laughter on both sides of the curtain.

Rosie finally came out, still bulky but now dry. 'Well, we better get a move on,' she said.

'Where to?' Nina asked.

'Girlie here wants to find out about the day they lifted Dinah Smith off her porch in Tucker's Town. That's what you told me on the phone, weren't it? We need to go where we watched it happen.'

They went back out into the late November afternoon. The rain had stopped but a heavy pall of cloud pressed down. From the car park, they looked up at St. David's lighthouse. Its red and white tower seemed to be in the clouds. They looked across at misty little islands, bridges and points of land, surrounded by restless grey water. Clearly visible despite the haze was the peninsula, Tucker's Town.

As they started the slow climb up the hill, Nina and Rosie spoke of who had died, who was building a house where, whose child was in trouble. They seemed to forget about the girl.

It was Rosie who put the interview on track when they reached the top of the hill. 'Well, girlie, you gonna ask me questions or come back to the yard and help me pull weeds?'

Genesis switched on her little cassette recorder and cleared her throat. 'How old were you when the last person was forced out of Tucker's Town?'

'Eight. Or nine. No! Nine. Because I'd just started school. But I knew about it, all right. I was a pain in the tail even then. Always up into big people's business. When they thought I was playing or swimming or doing my chores, I was listening too. Always liked listening to the old people.'

'When did the grownups start talking about it?'

'From when it started, of course. It took them one maybe two years for them to do it all – get the Americans interested, get the local boys involved – them Forty Thieves could smell money...'

'Who were the Forty Thieves?'

Rosie looked at Nina in astonishment. 'What they teach these children at school?' Turning back to Genesis, she said, 'They owned everything... Yes, as I was saying... Yes. The local white boys wanted to make a place for the richest of the rich to play and stay, where they didn't have to be bothered by no stinky natives. Them Forty Thieves! They passed a law in Parliament. Because...' she slapped her thigh for emphasis. 'They owned Parliament too! All they didn't own was the land. But that didn't last long.'

They arrived at the bench in front of the lighthouse. Rosie was about to sit down when Nina sent Genesis back down the hill to fetch towels from the car. While they watched her speed down the hill, Rosie slid her hand along the back of the wet bench. 'She don't know much, does she?'

'Well, school is very different from when Dee and I were there.'

'Don't mean that,' Rosie said, wiping her hands on her dress.

'She don't know how to live at peace with her soul-case. Scared. Hiding. Always ready to make off...' She raised her cat's eyes to the tall figure of the girl coming back to them, passing a thickly wooded area at the base of the hill.

'Nina, look at her. Walking right by Dark Bottom not knowing what it is.'

Nina shook her head and said nothing.

With the bench wiped down and dry, they sat down and Rosie settled into her story.

'My Uncle Dennis was the lighthouse keeper and used to live in this house right behind us. We children used to be swarming all over here, especially during the summer. Come to think of it, I remember that Tucker's Town thing over two summers. We could sit here and watch what was going on across the water. Couldn't see everything but we could see them fine horse and carriages rolling into Tucker's Town. Said they was coming to "talk to" the people who lived there. But in Parliament, they called them people backward with no morals. That's what got my daddy vexed. He thought they shoulda been offered more for their land. For my mama, it wasn't the money. Mama was all about what's right. And it was wrong that they didn't have the right to live in a place they'd called home for generations. Sometimes of an evening, my mama would come right up here with we children and watch the lights as they moved about over there, across the water. She took it hard. Real hard. Thought it was just wrong.'

Genesis checked there was still room on the cassette. 'What about when Dinah Smith was evicted?'

'She was the last one. Out of four hundred. She stayed alone in her house for months. Maybe longer. They worked around her. I believe they finished building the golf course while she was still there... Every time they tried to come and bully her, she would snap and spit and carry on at them like some terrier with a bad case of fleas. In the end, girlie, they were too much for her.

'Did they kill her?'

Rosie examined her hands for a moment. 'Kill? They didn't put a gun to her head, if that's what you mean.' She dropped her hands into her lap. 'All kinda ways to kill... When they came and found her sitting on her porch, still refusing, still spitting, they picked her up, her and her chair, put them in a carriage and that was it.' Deep sigh. 'Tucker's Town was theirs.'

'Did you know her?'

'No. But one time, years later, Johnny and me drove past Dinah Smith's house, the new one. There she was, on the porch smoking her pipe, just like we'd heard, looking straight ahead, just like we'd heard, singing the song that made the Forty Thieves turn purple.'

'Do you remember it?'

Rosie gave the girl a steely glare. 'One thing you have to learn about old people. No matter how old we get, we never forget the big things that happened to us. They never disappear.' She got to her feet and in a wobbly voice, sent her song out across the water, to any of the Forty Thieves who might still be alive and listening:

Goodwin Gatling is a thief
And everybody knows it.
He carries a whistle in his hand
And Stanley Sterling blows it.

They stayed on the lighthouse grounds until Rosie sniffed the air and predicted that it would rain again in five minutes. As they turned to go, Genesis gave a wide smile and tapped her cassette recorder. 'Thanks, Rosie!'

Before getting in the car, Rosie veered off towards the area of bush and dark, tufted trees.

'Where's she going, Nina?'

'Don't ask.'

Within moments, Rosie was back clutching something.

They arrived back at Rosie's house just as the first fat drops started drumming on the roof.

'Tank rain,' Rosie declared. 'Time for hot tea.' She emptied what was in her hand into a battered tea canister on the window ledge and then trudged down the steps leading to her kitchen. As she assembled the tea things, Rosie knew by the groaning of the floorboards overhead that Nina was explaining certain things in the room to the girl. She amused herself imagining what Nina was saying. All she knew for sure was that there was lots of talk and muffled laughter, so much so that when she mounted the final steps, they were too deep in conversation to hear her arrive.

'Looks like dirt,' Genesis was saying, peering inside the tin canister.

'It is,' said Nina. 'Special dirt.'

'Anyone for tea?' Nina and Genesis leapt apart, almost spilling the contents of the tin. Nina sat down in the chair nearest where she stood while Genesis retreated to the farthest corner of the room. Rosie set down her tray, poured the tea and added generous helpings of condensed milk to the strong brew. The room grew quiet, except for the appreciative slurping of Rosie drinking her tea. 'Girlie,' she said, 'that soil's from Dark Bottom. Every time I pass there, I pick up a handful and bring it home. To let them know I've been.'

'Them?' The girl's eyes were wide.

'Them. The old people. Those Indians from America. That's their place. Long time ago, when the whole hill was covered in cedar. It was a sacred place then. Where they used to go to sing. To drum. To pray. It's still their place.'

'Don't scare the girl with that kind of talk,' Nina begged.

'You scared, girlie?'

'No.' Without looking up, Genesis added, 'Yes.'

'No need. For me there's no difference between today and yesterday. It's all the same.' Rosie drained her cup and fixed Genesis with her tiger's eyes. 'I might give you that tin one day.' She sank back into her one good chair and turned to Nina.

'Now! I'm done enough talking for today. Turn on my TV, Nina. Time for *General Hospital*. Gotta see if Tiffany's going to marry Blade again. You all better be on your way.'

Nina and Genesis stood obediently, Nina switched on the television and they said their goodbyes.

'Girlie!' Rosie called. 'Remember what I said about old people. We remember what counts.'

As the growl of Nina's car became a distant purr and the theme music of the soap opera swelled, Rosie turned the television off.

This talk about the old days had filled her to the brim. She needed nothing further.

CHAPTER 5: THE PROJECT

Tess

At the doorway, Tess watched as Shauna Williams pushed her stroller into the fading light. She returned to her desk and pulled out a reference form that had CONFIDENTIAL stamped on the top. Shauna's details had already been filled in. There remained three unticked boxes: from left to right, Highly Recommended / Recommended / Unsuitable. Tess's pen bypassed 'Highly Recommended' and hovered between 'Recommended' and 'Unsuitable'. She ticked the middle box, knowing that this reference would probably succeed in getting the one-bedroom apartment Shauna desired. Whether it would keep her baby's violent father at bay was another matter.

Tess tried to put aside the tensions of the past hour – the demands, the accusations, the frustrations, the hard truths, the tears and the toddler dozing in her mother's arms. She looked out of the window. Soon be dark. Every tree, every cloud, every puddle announced the imminent arrival of December. Hers was the only car left in the car park. She had the whole place to herself. After a cup of coffee, she took a few moments to survey her domain. Tidy shelves and cabinets, maidenhair ferns flourishing on the sill, public service awards on the walls. There was nothing of herself here. The business of the National Council for Children was the protection of children, and their clients were young women like Shauna. She was its respected director. This gave her immense satisfaction. The family wisdom had been that the only job she was born to do was to bag a rich man. She'd shown them! The fact that Richard was rich was not relevant. He hadn't been when she'd married him.

She set about her final task of the day – to make copies of her grandfather's diaries for Genesis and her Tucker's Town project. She opened a drawer and took out four slim volumes, each bound in black sealskin and embossed in gold with a year between 1920 and 1923 and the letters 'NTD'. Nathaniel Thomas Darrell.

She opened the first book. It was not the even, slanting handwriting that brought the memory of her grandfather, the patriarch, with the thick white moustache and the soldier's bearing. It was the odour that wafted up from these pages which probably had not been read since his death over forty years ago. At twenty, Tess had been brought home from university for his funeral and, even in those early days, there were members of her family who thought she was becoming a dangerous radical. She'd come home prepared to be critical of them all. But during those days of public farewell to this long-standing Member of Colonial Parliament, pioneer in the business of tourism and stalwart of the Anglican Church and the Yacht Club, what she had actually felt was a keen sense of loss. This was the grandpa who had taught her to sail and to play chess, and with whom she would sit, playing quietly, when he went through the daily ritual of writing up his diary. She had been one of ten grandchildren but had always felt special. He had taught them all how to sail and to play chess. She alone had been allowed to be in the library with him when the sun was going down, the only one he would sometimes take on his lap and show the blotter and the India ink and feel the smoothness of the cover, the only one for whom he would flick through those pages covered in what she had thought of as mysterious symbols.

Some memories of her grandfather were not welcome. When Genesis had asked her whether there was any connection between her family and the Tucker's Town story, she had considered saying no. But she knew that her grandfather had been involved, perhaps not in the front line, but not in the background either. She also knew that from the inception of the Tucker's Town project until his death, her Grandpa Nate had been among those who in private considered themselves to be the architects of the 'Bermuda Miracle', the transformation of twenty-five square miles of limestone rock into an affluent centre of tourism and commerce. Tess had to remind herself that almost a century had passed since Tucker's Town's original inhabitants had been forced to leave, that her grandfather had been a product of his time and that times had changed. As long as she could maintain some distance between herself and the events of the early 1920s, everything would be fine. She owed it to Genesis, to Shauna and to all the people at the heart of the work she did, the work that made her who she was. She owed it to them to show that she was not afraid of digging up history.

An hour later, Tess was in her car, beginning the ride up to Sweet Airs. Her temples throbbed with the words of her dead grandfather. She had copied pages from three different diaries showing how, over the days, weeks and months stretching between 1920 and 1923, Nate and a handful of others had reconfigured an unkempt but pristine backwater, making it into a luxurious zone of exclusion, fit only for the wealthy. She hesitated when faced with these entries, driven as they were by phrases like '*for the progress of the colony*', but took a deep breath and printed them anyway. Then came the May 31, 1921 entry. It was written soon after the people who'd always lived in Tucker's Town – poor, black and ignored by all – started marching on Parliament, brandishing petitions. Fighting to stay in their homes. Generally acting up. In his diary Nate had called them '*dissolute, immoral, ignorant fools*' who didn't understand that '*what is good for the Bermuda Development Company is good for Bermuda.*'

So unlike Grandpa!

That entry didn't make the cut. Tess couldn't do that to her grandfather, who'd been courteous to all who crossed his path. She was giving Genesis more than enough for her project. '... *immoral... ignorant fools...*' She would not have Nate's name besmirched by this uncharacteristic lapse.

She was on autopilot as she drove home, her mind on Nate. She hadn't thought about him for a long time, but whenever she did, gratitude for his overwhelming decency bloomed in her chest, setting him apart from the rest. Money and status – these were the living breath of her mother and father, her brother, her uncles, her grandmother Lottie, all of them. But not Nate. Always thoughtful and measured, he swam against the tide, trying to navigate between privilege and righteousness.

Only once had she seen him out of control. His icy rage had lasted four straight days.

She and her brother, then nine and eleven, had exhausted all the possibilities for wild play in their grandparents' house and yard but were still hungry for excitement.

'Let's go to the cellar!' It had been her idea.

'You crazy? Grandpa will cut our tails!'

'Not if he doesn't know.'

They'd sneaked past Maisie, busy getting dinner, entered the pantry, found the peeling door to the old cellar, fiddled with the ancient latch and pulled the door quietly behind them.

They crept down the rough stone stairs in the absolute darkness, a ferment boiling in their minds, their bodies, robbing them of speech. This was adventure!

When they reached the bottom of the stairs and stepped on soil, the adventure stopped. They couldn't see their hands but could hear something. Something squeaking, groaning. Was that Maisie moving around in the kitchen above? And the smell! Like the stale breath of monstrous living creatures that they could hear, smell and feel!

In a flash, her brother was back on the steps again, with Tess trying to grab hold of his shirt tail as they scrambled up. But the door wouldn't open, no matter how hard they tried.

'It's the latch!' her brother said. 'We're locked in!' He started pounding on the door.

'Help! Help! Help! Maisie! Help!'

Their voices were hoarse before a series of heavy footsteps approached the cellar door.

'What the devil...' Maisie said, swinging the door open and yanking them into the kitchen. 'You children crazy or what?' She grabbed them by the shoulders and started to shake them.

'Maisie. Stop.'

From the far end of the kitchen, Grandpa Nate's voice was not loud but crackled with electricity.

'Bring them here.'

Maisie ushered them forward, her head cowed but her arms protective.

'That will be all, Maisie.'

He said not a word to them until Maisie's footsteps could no longer be heard crossing the kitchen tiles. Only then did he look down at them. Tess remembered the rigid moustache. The hard blue eyes. He did not raise his voice.

'Did I or did I not tell you never to enter the cellar?'

Tess, who ordinarily might have been foolhardy enough to hazard a reply, was struck dumb by the stony face, the chilling tone. Her brother shook silently.

'If you ever go to that room again, you will never set foot in this house again. Ever!'

He'd spun on his heel and walked away.

Tess poured herself a neat whiskey. That incident had thrown the house into uproar. The way kindly, soft-spoken Grandfather Nathaniel had fixed them all with murderous eyes became the stuff of legend. After weeks of hand wringing, Maisie realised that she would not be fired. There followed many embellished versions of the incident, especially as part of Maisie's induction to any new domestic help, under the general heading of 'Don't get on his last nerve'. And it took years for Tess's mother and father to lose the fear of being written out of Nate's will.

But Tess alone had been privy to the sequel to Nate's cold fury.

On the fourth evening of abject misery, Tess had climbed the gate separating her parents' house from Grandpa Nate's and slipped inside. No-one was about. She tiptoed across Grandma Lottie's 'drawing room' towards the library. Usually, the door was wide open but this evening it was shut.

From the other side of the door had come the sound of somebody choking. Tess wondered where her nine-year old self had found the courage to push that door open.

He was not in his normal place, seated at his desk, pen in hand. He was in profile, standing. His body seemed to be buffeted by an unseen wind while his eyes were trained on the open door of the wall safe. The choking sounds became words.

'Show 'em who's boss… I like 'em young, black and shiny… This is how it's done, boy…'

She had been fused to the spot.

'See… like this… Rough… Make 'em holler… here… In the … In the…'

Something seemed to stick in his throat.

'In the...'

'Grandpa!'

He whirled around at the shrill sound but his eyes swept across her unseeing, and came to rest on a piece of rolled canvas lying on the floor.

'Get out!'

His eyes were blank. He didn't know who she was.

She'd turned to run.

'Stay!' The tone and the gesture were loud and clear.

He lowered himself onto the sofa and reached for the canvas. With trembling hands, he unrolled it and started to mumble again. Looking at the image, he said, 'Break 'em young, you said. The younger the better, you said... The rougher the better... In the... in the...'

Everything Grandpa Nate said entered Tess's ear like a terrifying, foreign tongue. But the sight of his heaving chest and glistening tears proved greater than her terror.

She ran to him.

In the fragment of a second before she reached him, before he looked at her and recognised her, he'd completed his thought.

'In the breaking room!'

As she drained her glass, Tess heard the four words from that evening long ago. At last, they were in a language that she could understand. She replayed the whole scene from hearing sobs on the other side of the library door to taking his hand and listening as his pain came pouring out, the pain that the bad man on the canvas had bequeathed him. The bad man was his father and the breaking room was the cellar. Those were the only details that stuck in her memory.

As she climbed the stairs, Tess felt like an old woman, her limbs slow, her mind sagging beneath Nate's broken words. Then she remembered the last thing he'd said to her – after he'd returned to his normal self, after he'd asked her to forgive his unseemly behaviour, after he'd put the rolled canvas back in the safe.

'Forget tonight, Tessie,' he'd said. 'Drown it. Then get on with your life.'

I've done what you told me, Grandpa, she thought, just before sleep claimed her. Drowned, buried every grief, every blow, then carried right on. But they always come back.

Genesis

Nina has an early meeting this morning, so last night I told her don't worry, I'll catch the bus to school. She gave me her look and I started to laugh. Then she started and carried on until she had to wipe her eyes. Didn't say all the things she would of said two months ago, like how will I know you'll get up on time, have your bag and your uniform ready, how will I know you won't miss the bus... She didn't say anything. Just carried on laughing. She knows I'll be in school on time. Especially today.

Seven-thirty at the bus stop. The first bus is empty. Good! I don't want to be around any loud schoolchildren this morning. Take a window seat. It's a pretty day. Cool but sunny. I squeeze my bag tighter against my chest.

Wonder how many hoops she'll have to jump through to give it the mark she knows I really deserve. Yeah. Stick-woman Powell grades the person, not the work. But it's gonna be hard for her to do it this time because the work is good. Damn good!

There I go again. Hope nobody's watching me, the way I keep touching my bag to make sure the folder's still in there. I like the folder Tess got me. Plain. Professional. Like her office. When you got a boat and a house with a library, you don't have to show off.

I never knew it would of been so much work. Trying to get it to make sense, to go from one point to another in the right order. To show that it's not just what's in books that makes history. What real people remember, that's history too. I never thought about that. Never knew much of anything before. Got to give it to them – those three really stepped up. I'd start making off about how I'd never finish and who gave a rat's ass about it anyway and they'd leave me to it and when they came back, they'd just ask what the problem was and I'd show them. But each of them came up with something great. There was Rosie, of course, keepin it real. Nina, with her story about the conch that had more rights than the people. And Tess – who asked me to forgive her for some of the things in her grandpa's diary. She was very quiet when she said that.

So was Lizzie. Quiet. I know she's been in competition with the others – to see who could help me the most – these are some crazy bitches... The day she came with the picture of her grandpa should of been her moment. The only picture of the actual event! But, no. She handed it over with what her grandma had written and said she had to go to work. What she needs is a grease job, I swear.

Have a Bermudiful day, the bus driver says as I get off. What he think I am, a tourist? But even that can't stop me from feeling the way I do. Town isn't completely awake, just yawning and getting ready for another day's business. This morning the sun is brightening up everything and it doesn't seem like December is only a couple of days away. Left my Walkman on the kitchen table. Doesn't matter. So many sounds that I usually don't hear...

Man! That one's loud. Some bike's got muffler problems... Coming closer... What the... I swing around... Uriel. With this smile all over his face.

'Hey, G!'

'Hey, U!'

No matter how long it's been since we last saw each other, that's how we always start. I feel so good when I see him. He's got this kind of a... glow.

'Boy, you better stop creepin up on people like that.' I can feel my cheeks stretching out into that smile I only give to him.

'People don't see you no more. Now you're up there with those white folks...'

'Nina's not white.' I suck my teeth.

'...those rich folks, then.'

'Nina's not rich.'

'Anyway. We don't see you.' He's still got that smile but there's darkness around his eyes. 'Well, what you standin there for? Show me some love.'

I lean in and give him a hug. But, wow, he does not smell good! 'What you been up to? Diggin ditches?'

'Like I would,' he says. 'No'. He looks away. 'I been doin some... business. Goin home to my bed now.'

'Don't like the sound of that.' I feel like I'm older than him.

'You always was a bossy little somebody. Even back in de day.'

Back in de day for Uriel Caines and me. From our time in the playground of the primary school when they teased us about our funny names. From then. Always in the same school until he dropped out. Twice with the same foster parents. Together in the Robinson Home. When he wasn't having his own ass kicked, he was looking out for mine. We both laugh. A quiet kind of laugh.

'What you got in there,' he says pointing to my bag. I feel it against my chest. I'm holding it like my life's in there.

'Work,' I say, and see he's waiting. 'Okay. It's not just work. It's something different. Special.'

'Let me see it.'

Don't know why but I don't want to take it out of the bag. It's not U. But maybe a high wind will come and blow it away. Maybe it'll fall into a puddle. Maybe...

'What's it about?'

'My social studies project. About what happened in...' His eyes start to glaze over. 'I need it to graduate.'

'What's the big deal? You're smart! Always were!' He's really staring at me now. Serious. Then the light comes back into his face. 'Why don't we have breakfast? I could take you to where I stay.' He's on a roll, talking fast. 'All right! You don't have a helmet – but it's just over the hill – and too early for Babylon. I'd get a shower, we could pick up some food then go and sit off on the rocks. Shootin the breeze with you after so long. For me, that would be a good time.'

He stops.

I feel a pain in my chest but I say it anyhow. 'Uriel, you need to get a job.'

He smiles and adjusts his helmet. 'Miss Genesis Smith, I will check you later.' He's making a big deal of talking proper.

'I mean it, U. What kind of bullshit business are you in that keeps you out all night?'

He's laughing now but he says, 'Better watch it. You're startin to sound like one of them.' Then he horses his bike up on its back wheel and roars off, kicking up a cloud of dust.

I squeeze my bag and try to control the throbbing going on underneath it. Why did I have to see him this morning? Uriel. Flashing on and off in my life like some messed-up light bulb.

Never really there but never really gone either. The nearest thing to people I'm likely ever to have.

Don't know how long I stand there, hearing the traffic wail past, knowing that students are walking past me on the way up the hill to our school. Then I pull out my folder.

S4 Social Studies Project: Genesis Smith

The Tucker's Town Clearance

Four Witnesses to History

I straighten my back and begin the long climb.

CHAPTER 6: DANCERS

Nina

At Salt Cay, Boxing Day, about twenty of Nina's blood relatives lay defeated beneath the weight of their second gigantic meal in less than twenty-four hours. Throughout the house, conversation had petered out; even the cackle and banter in the kitchen had degenerated into a listless murmur.

But movement came. In the corner of the living room where he appeared to be sleeping, Uncle Jack sat up. From the doorway of the kitchen, Nina watched him lean in the direction of what sounded like a soft and distant pulse. Nimbly, he was up and moving to the front door. Genesis, who had been sprawled out next to him, heaved herself up onto her elbows, as though coming out of a dream.

'Mama... what's that?' a little boy asked, his new toy forgotten.

Sound was snaking through the air, gaining substance with every moment, nudging every living soul awake – the overindulged, the overworked, the overfed. First a heavy drum, a metronome, echoed the beating of the heart. Next an explosion of quick anarchic rhythms insinuated into the space between the heartbeats. Flying above these was the shrill treble of whistle and fife. And, as though in slow motion, the young and the old and all those in between put aside their indolence and waited for Jack to give them the sign.

He threw open the door and in rushed the sound on the breath of the evening. Punctuating each measure came a chorus of rough and happy voices.

'Ay – O!'

'Ay – O!'

Still Nina and her people watched and waited. Jack stepped

outside, a dark outline against the gold of the setting sun.

'They're comin, Mama!' As one body, the children hurtled forward at the command of the drums.

'Sounds like they're turnin up Cobbs Hill…'

'We can catch 'em…'

Parents and grandparents dashed towards the door, ready to follow their children and Jack. They were already at the roadside, joining the throng that trailed behind the music like the long tail of a flamboyant buzzing kite.

Only three people remained inside – Nina, with her Christmas apron on, Rosie, clutching something in her lap and Genesis, still in the corner where she had been sprawled.

'Didn't know… that people like you…' Genesis faltered.

'Girlie!' Rosie said. 'What you waitin for? Get out there!' She turned to Nina. 'What? Too dicty to follow them…' Before she could finish, Nina was in pursuit of the girl's retreating form. At the door, she swung around.

'Aren't you coming?'

Rosie settled back in her chair. 'Leave the door open. Long as I can hear 'em, I can see 'em too.' She tapped her head with a crooked finger. 'Besides, I want to look at me and my mate!' She smiled down at the framed photograph that Nina had given her. It was of Rosie and a handsome young man dressed in full Native American dress. It had been taken a few months ago when, after centuries of separation, her St David's Island people and some of their North American cousins had reconnected and celebrated with story, song and dance.

Gratified that the present was appreciated, Nina whipped off her apron and followed the sound.

Gombeys!

It did not take Nina long to find Genesis out on the road. She was taller than most and darker. But it was her dancing that set her apart. Not the mechanical tramping of those who had been following the music for hours nor the frenzied gyrating of those who had recently joined in. She was bent forward, her arms stretched back into wings, her waist the axis from which all movement flowed, her feet skimming the road with a light, minimal step.

Nina pushed through the crowd until she was level with the girl. When she saw her face, naked, abandoned, unseeing, she was suddenly afraid.

'G!'

The girl blinked twice, gave Nina a luminous smile and grabbed her hand. 'Let's get up front where Uncle Jack is... Too far away from 'em here... They're gonna stop soon...'

Nina was dragged along as Genesis bulldozed through ranks of strangers, friends, family, all faceless in the fading light, all reduced to their shuffling feet and their voices crying in unchanging rhythm, '*Ay – O! Ay – O!*'

The drumming was getting louder and, high above the heads of those in front of her, Nina could see the swaying tips of the dancers' headdresses, sometimes bowing out of sight only to appear again, blazing like tiny fires in the last rays of the sun. The crowd wasn't surging forward anymore. What had seemed like a kite's tail was slowing down, spreading out into a untidy ring, as the members of the procession jostled to catch sight of the spectacle that went with the sound.

Surrounded by hot, chanting bodies, Nina could no longer see Genesis, could only feel the powerful clasp of her hand. A wave of panic swept over her. She had felt this way before, but never so vulnerable. As a child, Uncle Jack or her father would look after her. Later, Dee would shield her, always keep her on the fringes of the crowd. How could she have allowed herself to be carried along by this feverish throng, by this unleashed teenager?

Genesis was suddenly in front of her.

'What now? Look. I don't like this...'

Genesis turned her back on Nina and waited. Shaking her head, Nina put one hand on the girl's shoulder and the other around her waist. The girl ploughed forward, shouting 'Keep your head down and hold on!'

Nina squeezed her eyes shut and felt rather than saw the crowd part to let them pass. When she opened her eyes, she and Genesis were on the inner fringe of a tumultuous circle.

In the centre were the Gombeys.

They banished the night in the pool of brightness in which they danced. They were giants in their tall crowns of peacock feathers, inscrutable gods behind their painted masks, irrepressible popinjays in their fringed trousers and overskirts, in their beaded, swirling capes. From the smallest dancer just mastering the steps to the fearsome Captain dominating his troops with his whistle and his whip, all were creatures reborn. Their element was colour, their song was movement, their master, rhythm.

'There's Uncle Jack!' Nina was astonished at the way Genesis could make herself heard. She looked in the direction of the pointed finger and saw Jack right next to the drummers. 'Where all the action is!' Genesis laughed.

'Look at him,' Nina called. 'He's reliving the good old days when he was a Gombey captain!' She could see the light in Jack's face. The rest she could imagine. The old black skin glowing with sweat, the eyes half-closed, the mouth half-open – like the drummers beating in a trance beside him, beating out the rhythms of Africa.

The circle had spilled across the entire street. The revellers were giving their tired feet a rest, contenting themselves with moving on the spot, the chanting dying on their lips. Nothing could compete with the drums as they summoned the spirits of the night.

The Captain – ten feet of brilliant menace – gave a shrill blast on his whistle and spun around, a thousand lights bouncing from the tiny fragmented mirrors on his immense tasselled cape. Never missing a step, he faced his troops, his dangling leather whip an active threat. They leapt to attention and formed a circle around him. He blew his whistle again, cracked the whip and brought crowd and dancers under his control.

As the Captain moved from one foot to the other at the centre of the circle, his dancers began running around its circumference, each clutching a painted tomahawk. As the circle became more defined, the dancers – twenty, maybe thirty of them – became warriors, fierce, dazzling, each following the man ahead of him, each tailoring his movements to maintain the perfect circle, each on the alert for a sign from their leader. Another blast of the whistle and they broke the circle and, bending low and spinning, their peacock crowns parallel to the ground, their capes flying out around them like rainbows, they formed a straight line in front of him. Ordering them to stay with a stab of a single gloved finger, the Captain turned towards the drummers and, covering the space separating them in a sideways motion, made the many layers of his fringed costume shiver with every tiny step. The drummers pounded out their welcome. Off he went again, flowing sideways like a wave, this time ignoring his troupe, who were still awaiting his command. He headed instead towards the onlookers in large, jerky strides, falling but always catching himself in the nick of time. With one arm outstretched, the other brandishing the whip, he lunged forward and reared up, monstrous, in front of the crowd.

People scattered, screaming.

Amid the pandemonium, Nina realised that she was no longer holding Genesis's hand. The girl was nowhere to be seen. The drumming swelled and something told Nina to turn around.

Genesis was in front of the Captain, one foot planted on the ground, the other raised in challenge, one hand on her shoulder clutching an invisible tomahawk, the other arm outstretched, ripples of movement emanating from the middle of her body. The Captain continued to tower over her, brilliant, dangerous, like a shaft of lightning touching the earth. But Genesis did not back down.

Nina jumped forward and yanked the girl back into the crowd that had reformed and found its voice again.

'Ay – O!'

'Ay – O!'

Words of reprimand died on Nina's lips when she looked into the girl's shining face.

'I always wanted to be one... It's so unfair... Only guys...' Nina shook her head, squeezed the girl's hand tightly with one hand and reached around her waist with the other.

More than anything, Nina had wanted to give Genesis the feeling of belonging to her family. In every massive grocery expedition, in every present wrapped, every old person visited, in every carol sung, in every long hour spent with her in the kitchen, there it was, her desire to make something happen. To make the girl lose her mask. To make some great feeling come into being, to be born in Genesis, like the child in the manger.

Despite her best efforts, it hadn't happened.

Nina turned to face the circle. The warriors were on the move again, dancing in a line towards the Captain, then tripping lightly backwards, their capes bobbing and swirling. Red green purple yellow black blue orange violet – they trembled and clashed against each other. Nina closed her eyes and behind closed lids, she saw the costumes break into a whirling kaleidoscope. When she'd left her house, she'd so much wanted to teach Genesis about these dancers and their dance. She sighed. There would be no teaching tonight. Only dancing.

'Over there! The Wild Indian!' The girl's voice was high and sharp. 'Let's get closer!'

She grabbed Nina and started pulling her along the periphery of the circle, towards the drummers.

'G! Now look...' But the exasperation in Nina's voice was absorbed in the bedlam.

Genesis came to an abrupt halt. Centre stage was occupied by two dancers facing off against each other: one in yellow carried a small bow and arrow, one in blue, a rope. Each time blue made his approach, yellow retaliated with threatening gestures of his bow and arrow. Close enough for their headdresses to touch, they strove against each other, bobbing and weaving, feinting and dodging, attacking and retreating. Blue against yellow. Yellow against blue. All the time dancing, stamping the earth, flying from it in leaps and falling to it on their knees.

In a daring move, blue all but managed to loop the rope around yellow's waist. But yellow was like a ball of mercury. He wheeled around, his cape spinning out like a golden cloud, leapt high into the air and landed in a perfect split, was on his knees again, then sprinted away. The crowd roared and rewarded the duellers with a hail of coins.

'Do we have any, Nina? Do we?'

Nina felt a disapproving sigh making its way up her chest. Halfway up, she dismissed it. Enough! Enough of being the world's biggest bore, the world's biggest spoilsport. Nina had no money but knew who did, who always did. She ran past the drummers, braving the thunder of the bass and the rattling of the snares.

At first, he didn't recognise her.

'Can you give me some money, Uncle Jack?' Nina spoke normally, but she heard the voice of a five-year old, excited, frightened, but knowing she was safe. Slowly, his hand searched one of his roomy pockets and reappeared full of silver. He gave her the toothless smile that she loved so much and handed over the money.

Genesis was right beside her.

'Here.' Nina slid coins onto the impatient, outstretched palm. Closing her fingers into a fist, Genesis threw her arms around the old man and ran straight into the middle of the circle, in between the two combatants and cast her money down in front of the one in yellow. For a moment, they danced a duet, Genesis and the Wild Indian, jumping and spinning and falling to the ground, before the Captain bounded towards her wielding his whip.

She ran back and collapsed, laughing, into Nina's arms, as the Wild Indian bowed and the crowd cheered.

'You know him?' Nina blurted out.

'Does anybody know a Gombey?'

The Captain sounded his whistle, a woman came out of the shadows to pick up the money and they were off again, in a snaking line, finding an opening in the crowd, passing through it, out into the dark, onto the road ahead, pulling the revellers with them, behind the hypnotic drums, pulling them out into the night.

Uncle Jack fell into step behind the drummers, Nina and Genesis behind him. Catching herself, Nina stopped.

'It's time to go back now.'

Nina saw Genesis flinch. 'But Nina...'

'No, really. It's late. Time to go home.' The sudden drooping of the girl's shoulders stiffened Nina's resolve. 'These guys are just getting going. God knows where they'll end up.'

Genesis stood saying nothing with her head down as the crowd surged around them. In that instant, Nina saw the whole horrific cavalcade of possibilities. A young girl turning the corner, but not there yet. A good student now, but not yet stable, out in the street on a night with rhythms and sights whose purpose was to mesmerize, to intoxicate... This night would make her deaf to that still small voice that Nina was so desperate for her to hear.

At last Genesis raised her head and looked straight into Nina's eyes. A no-bullshit look, direct and honest. 'Please.' Again, the girl's uncanny ability to make herself heard above the din.

Nina felt like she was wrestling with someone. A gombey? An angel?

'O.K.'

'What?'

'I said O.K.'

But before she could run off, Nina grabbed her. 'On one condition!'

'What...' Genesis looked at the raucous, dancing throng who moved around her and Nina like water around rocks. '...condition?'

'Find Jack and stay with him.'

'Find Jack!' she said and vanished into the crowd.

The people were singing again. *'Ay – O! Ay – O!'* Nina stood unmoving as the river washed by her, listening as their voices became more and more faint. Eventually all she could hear was something high and diffuse flying over the pulse of the mother drum.

On her walk home she berated herself for not standing strong. Had she really entrusted the girl to this senile and certifiable sufferer of Old-Timer's disease? He'd hung up his captain's cape, but could he bring her safely home?

But as she turned into her driveway, it struck her that what she had wanted had happened. The birth of the great feeling, the child in the manger. The opening of a heart to love.

She had wanted it to happen to Genesis.

But it had happened to her.

Genesis

'Where do you want me to drop you?'

'By the bus station.'

Our helmets bump into each other.

'Gotta get something in town. For back to school. Then I'll get the bus home.'

We're talking loud. The only way we can hear over the bike

engine. Even as I shout, my voice wobbles. *Shit*! I used to lie like a pro.

It's not just telling expat boy that I'm getting something in town when really I'm meeting U. This whole scene is weird. Me on the back of his bike, holding him round the waist. Trying to sit up, not lean into him. Got to keep that space, but something keeps on pushing me into him. I can't *not* feel my boobs against his back, can't *not* look at the back of his helmet with a few bits of his hair straggling out. His neck. A band of bright, pink skin.

Let this ride be over soon. And let U be waiting.

Found him the day after I saw him dancing on Boxing Day. Said we'd meet last Saturday. But he never showed. He had me waiting an hour. Didn't he know how much I wanted to see him? What a pain in the ass! I swear to God, if he doesn't show this time, that's it. I won't waste my time on him. Done with that. Done with him. Who am I kidding?

I always forgive him. Don't know if I can forgive myself for not recognising him though. Took me days to get over that! Didn't look like him until I saw those red feathers dangling from his bow. Same ones I glued on when we both started at the Robinson Home.

He doesn't get the risks I'm taking. If one of them bitches or someone from school sees me, I'm so screwed. Tess's Christmas present to me is in danger. It's been a week and Nina's still pissed at her. *A cell phone… Such an expensive gift… Isn't it too much… too soon?* Tess only got away with it by tacking on a set of math classes – given by expat boy himself.

This looks bad… The world's most clapped-out Scoopy and the nerdiest-looking whiteguy on earth. Seriously, U, you'd better be there.

He will. I did his homework for him; he taught me how to dance. How to run. We go back.

Town traffic's at a crawl. My face is right into that pink neck. Sweat? Shampoo? We stop. Finally.

I hit the ground running when expat boy shouts, 'Genesis!'

'Oh, sorry… thanks for the ride.' Hope my voice sounds sorry. He stands holding his bike. Looking. 'Thanks a lot.'

I take off, flying. Just round the bend I feel the air shaking.

Gotta follow where the vibrations lead me... A brand-new BMW with shiny chrome rims.

'Hey, G!'

'Hey, U!'

I climb in and we roar off, the bass of his music pounding in my head. I stand it for about a minute.

'Turn it down.'

'Say what?'

'TURN THE FRIGGIN MUSIC DOWN!'

Even when I was a kid, I couldn't stand music that loud. I glare at him. Pretending to make a face, he turns it down.

'Who they belong to... the wheels?'

'My ace-boy... you wouldn't know him... lives Loyal Hill... Gotta get it back to him later...'

'Is he a doctor or a lawyer?' I shout. 'Cause only one of those can afford one of these.'

'A businessman. He's a businessman.'

His voice is smooth and he's looking straight ahead. That profile... Like somebody carved it. In some kinda gold, light-brown wood. Skin pulled tight across his bones... Always that glow. A little smile. Kinda satisfied.

I take a deep breath. 'I think I found a job for you.'

He glances at me, then starts laughing so hard he has to swerve to miss somebody crossing the road.

'You? Found me a job?' He's off again, cracking up, letting go of the steering wheel to wipe his eyes. I fiddle with the heating knob. It was cold on expat boy's bike. The laughing stops. Eventually.

'Yes. You heard right. Me! Who do you think? You think I don't know you? I may be the only person in this island who does. You may be older than me, but wiser? I don't think so! O.K. You hauled my ass out of the fire a lot of times. Now it's my turn.'

He turns his head, just a fraction.

'My ass is not on fire.' His voice is cold. I turn away from him, don't want to see those eyes. They look like they're sorry it's me they're looking at.

'There are a couple of options...'

I hear myself. It's unbelievable!

'G! G!' He's deadly serious. 'What happened to you? You sound like one of them...'

'Give me a break, Uriel.'

'Yes. Uriel. I know my name. Know yours?'

'You talk some tired shit, you know! What? Can't think of anything to say?

He shrugs, adjusting the mirror. Finding something else to do.

'Didn't think so.'

We're right there already, just like I knew we would. Him saying I'm somebody else. Me saying I'm not. There's ice flowing through my veins. The car enters Blackwatch Pass and suddenly it goes dark. Limestone walls press in on us. Striped, grey, rough, tall. Looking like they could crush us both.

I clear my throat. 'One of the three women the Court gave me... Well, one of them, Tess, she's richer than God. I'm sure there's some job you could do for her. Between the house and the yard and the boat... There must be something.'

Silence.

'There's this guy called Simmons. Does everything up there. Looks like he could do with some help. And today, an old guy comes up to Tess's house when I'm doing my work with my... tutor...'

'You mean the white guy.'

'Well, yeah.' *Him.* I'm not going to talk about *him*. 'Anyway, when I was doing my work, this man comes up Tess's house.' I rest my hand on his arm. He moves it away and puts his hand back on the wheel.

'This guy is old but real famous. Goes out to the reef and dives up treasure. Says he's gonna need somebody to help him on his boat come March. The person who was doing it before quit. So there's a definite possibility of something for somebody like you who likes the water... I think I would just have to talk to Tess...'

More silence. I make one final effort.

'Your ass might not be on fire yet. But it soon will be, long as you hang with whichever *businessman*... owns this car.'

He cranks up the volume and we thunder down the road. I close my eyes, shutting out those dark stone walls. Keep them shut until the car slows. I open them and what I see tugs at my chest. *Back in de day* our special place. *Our* place for the best games, best picnics, best camping and, for U, the best swimming. I don't say anything. He kills the engine but doesn't look at me.

'G,' he says finally, 'I know what you're doing. And it's cool. You're someplace new and you think I should be there too.'

He's still turned away from me. In my mind, I can see his eyes. All light sucked out of them, like before, when some grown-up had cut his tail. When that happened, I used to go hide out with him, cry like it was me with the welts on my ass.

'I don't want nothing bad to happen to you!' Words burst out. It's got hot all of a sudden. Heater pumping air. Sweat creeping under my arms. 'I don't want us to be like those sonsabitches who put us here. Our daddies? Who knows who they are?'

I suck my teeth. Why am I bothering? He won't even look at me.

'And our mamas... Yours, drunk, disorderly, strung out, always inside doing time. Mine, seventeen and pregnant then twenty-one and dead... stupid. Stupid!'

I grab his chin and force him to look at me. 'We don't have to be them.'

Nothing. Then suddenly... that smile.

'Relax, Miss G. I'm a free man. Nobody tells me what to do. I lay off when I feel like it. And hustle when I feel like it. Nobody owns me. It's not what you think. This car? On loan from a friend.'

We get out and start walking. Not a word. We duck from the spray off the rocks. The rusty old railway bridge is still there, still dead in the water.

'That musta been something once,' he says.

'Not much left of it now...'

He's found something in the bushes.

'Catch!'

'Over here!'

'Throw it back!'

'Kick it!'

'Pass it!'

Forgot how much fun playing ball with U could be. And how intense. A day at Pontoons meant we were happy.

'Enough, Uriel! Enough! You win.'

I flop onto a bench to catch my breath. He sits next to me. He hasn't even broken a sweat.

'Damn! Look at the time.'

'Soon. Comin right back, G.'

He walks away. An athlete's walk. Strong. Graceful. Before he gets to the car, he does the tomahawk move. Just for me. My Wild Indian...

I zone out. Everything's calm. The only sound is the water lapping against the rocks. Safe. His footsteps are coming near but I don't feel like opening my eyes yet. Then... the scrape of a match, the long breath and the ganja cloud filling my head. I start to cough and laugh at the same time. I laugh to stop myself from coughing, from crying. Why didn't I know he'd be getting a spliff? He's right. I am becoming somebody else.

I open my eyes. What he's offering me is slim and ladylike in comparison to what he normally smokes. Monsters thick as cigars... I don't hesitate.

'Five more minutes. Then you have to take me back.'

Five minutes later, we're in the car. Five minutes after that, we're in some crowded yard where a guy – not the businessman himself, of course – is waiting to pick up the car. Then it's onto his bike and the ride to Nina's house.

Things go by fast. First gloomy Blackwatch Pass, then the tall cane grass of the marsh, then houses stacked against each other. The bike winds through Back-a-Town, over Till's Hill onto the street that used to be my hangout spot, our hangout spot. Past Swinging Doors, Spinning Wheel, Zaki's Caribbean Food Mart, Digicel, Dub City, Rotis, passing people on their way home, to work, to get food, passing people who are there to sell, to score, to make a deal. Looks familiar but different too. Even babylon cruising in their cars look different. I shut my eyes. We're flying.

My arms are holding him tight and his lean body's carrying me. I can see him with my eyes closed. Running for the ball, diving for it at full stretch. The gombey with the bow and arrow jumping and spinning and never getting caught. An athlete. A dancer. He could be either but he doesn't know it... he doesn't. I learned I could be more than I was with my Tucker's Town project. I want him to feel like that. To know he can be so much more than someone running around Pontoons, so much more than the Wild Indian. So much more.

The wind is cold on my face.

'Stop at the next bus stop.' I get off. His eyes look empty. 'You can't take me right up to the house. You know that. I'm supposed to have spent the last hour coming home by bus.'

I can't leave. 'I want to see you again soon. I'm serious, U.'

He revs up the bike but I plant my legs on either side of the front wheel.

'So I'll call you on this cell number?' I have my cell phone ready.

'Better not,' he says. 'My ace-boy what owns it is coming back from the States tomorrow. I have to give it back.'

'How will I find you?' I shove my phone in my bag. 'Do I have to go to your place?'

'Better not, G. Probably be moving soon. Place belongs to the same guy who's coming back.' He's laughing as I shake him by the shoulders.

'You don't know how lame you sound, Hugh...'

He takes off his shades and looks at me hard. 'G. You know how weird *you* sound?'

My hands fall to my sides. Why am I the weird one all of a sudden? I step away.

'If you need to, you'll find me.' In a puff of smoke, he's gone.

I stand there like a fool. He's right. I'll find him when I need him. I start walking.

Salt Cay coming up. Gotta get my head together. If Nina's home, one look at me is all it'll take. Gotta be ready. She might still be out doing her visitations to the sick and the shut-ins. Then again she might not. The soldier tree at the gate... No car in the driveway. Light's on in the house. That can mean only one person. Uncle Jack!

Making it back before Nina... I turn the door handle. The smile on my face lasts a second. It strikes me right behind the knees. Why U called me weird.

The expat boy. His name. I called U by his name.

CHAPTER 7: SALT

Hugh

'What's that definition again?' G's tone was halfway between interest and petulance.

'You can add radicals,' Hugh said, 'if they have the same index and the same radicands…'

'Bla bla bla…'

'I thought you said you wanted to learn something.'

Genesis looked at him. 'Speak English, Teach.' The sternness around her mouth was not convincing. 'O.K. That definition. Lay it on me again…'

Hugh took a deep breath and looked outside at the quiet February day. Why did she suddenly change his name? One day, Hugh. Now, Teach.

'You can add radicals,' he resumed, his voice deadpan. 'Wait.'

He turned towards the white board. Halfway through the equation, he felt her eyes on his back. Did his t- shirt have a hole? It was short and he wasn't wearing a belt to keep his jeans up. Were his underpants showing? Was she, as she would say, checking him out?

There was a knock and, through the screen door, the outline of a stout figure topped by a thatch of white hair. He was saved.

'Buddy! Come in!' Hugh opened the door, all smiles.

'Oh,' Buddy said, noticing Genesis. 'Got your mate here again?'

'Yes. Yes. Genesis, you remember Mr. Darrell.'

'Hello, young lady.'

Genesis gave a nod in the old man's direction and slumped back into her chair.

'Yes. Maths lesson… or should we say… torture…' Hugh

threw a glance towards Genesis. 'Every Saturday afternoon… Buddy, good to see you!'

'Yah. Thought you might like to know how things're going.' He was about to sit down but hesitated. 'Look… I'll come back when you're not so busy.'

'No! Give me a minute.' Hugh hurried to complete the solution on the board and told Genesis, 'Do the next five, using this model.' He drew up a chair and gestured to Buddy to sit. 'Now! What's the score?'

'Seven thousand.'

'Unbe-bloody-lievable! Seven thousand years! Seven thousand… We thought four, five. Six at the outside… But seven thousand!' Hugh slapped the old man's shoulder.

'Yah.'

Since coming to the island, Hugh had started drawing again, and even in this moment of delight, he found himself observing the old man, as though preparing to make a sketch. A disparate, somewhat contradictory set of features – straight white hair, plump waist and muscular arms, salt-roughened hands, round, brown-speckled pink face, a beatific smile, and the sharp blue eyes that missed nothing. Individually, not out of the ordinary. In combination, remarkable. Then there was what accompanied Buddy wherever he went… the tang, the essence of the sea.

'What's going on?' Genesis started closing her books. 'Got an assignment to hand in on Monday… thought you were supposed to be helping me.' She stood up suddenly. 'Maybe I should bounce. You guys are too busy doin… whatever…'

Hugh heard the affront in Genesis's voice and rose, standing between the girl and the old man. 'Sorry, Buddy. No. Don't get up.' He turned to Genesis. 'Here's the thing. Life's not always about you. At this moment, it's not. The maths lesson is over. You're quite capable of doing those remaining questions on your own. However, if you want to learn something else today – something important – you're welcome to stay.'

He crouched down in front of Buddy, offering Genesis his back.

'Exact figure is seven thousand, one hundred and forty-three years.'

'Carbon dating!'

'Yah. Seven thousand years ago, that cedar was breathing in the open air, just like we are right now.' Buddy turned to include Genesis but she had reopened her book and was apparently studying it. 'It was already dying. The sea was rising and the salt was attacking its root. Trees're no different from people. Don't know what the hell's going on. Till it's too late.'

He stood up. 'Anyway, Hugh, thought you'd like to know.' He took a few steps towards the door. 'Almost forgot. Brian's coming next month. Bringing another scientist. From Massachusetts. They want to scout around the reef some more to prepare for their visit in July.' He paused. 'Want to meet them?'

'Do I...' Hugh's face flushed with pleasure. 'Of course!'

'Buddy, before you go, I have something to show you.' As Buddy hesitated at the doorway, Hugh was all activity – logging on to both his laptop and his pc, scrolling through a mass of files on each computer, pulling up a chair and beckoning Buddy to sit.

'Look,' Hugh said, pointing from one screen to the other. 'Someone from work sent me these yesterday.' The two images were like siblings – they shared everything – ancestors, life blood... But they were different.

'Oh. The Hurd Survey.'

Of course, Buddy would know about this!

Buddy drew closer. 'I never saw this aerial view before.'

'Yes,' Hugh said, with renewed enthusiasm. Instinctively he twisted around and beckoned Genesis to come closer. 'This chart shows the reef line surrounding the island. Drawn in 1797. Over here, a shot taken from a satellite. In 1997.'

Genesis shuffled over reluctantly and they gazed at two versions of the island, one drawn painstakingly by hand, the other captured by space-age technology. They were pictures of land and water, the land above water – the island – and land beneath the sea – the reefs that gathered in a protective ellipse around it. Each made visible the rim of the crater of the great, extinct, undersea volcano. The original drawing, in tones of sepia and old ivory, looked like a faded lace doily, with its scallops and fluted edges; its modern equivalent was in living colour. In it, the island was a black fishhook with a fine line of white along its southern flank. The South Shore beaches. The rest of the photograph was in shifting shades of blue and green, the peaks and undulations of the crater clearly visible, sometimes lightening into tinted translucence where the reef lay just below the water's surface. Beyond the island and its reef, the sea darkened into deep violet.

'There,' said Buddy, pointing to the colour image. 'That's where we got our cedar root. Right there. Thirty feet down.' His finger moved to a cluster of rocks on the earlier chart. 'Yah. There's Gurnet Rock.' Buddy sat back and sighed. 'Those guys really knew what they were doing back then.'

'You mean Admiral Hurd?'

'What Hurd?' Buddy laughed. 'I mean Pilot Darrell and them other two. They were the ones who made this map. Hurd just did what you English do best. Supervi...' He caught himself before Hugh could protest. 'Not *you* English. *The* English. Very different from *you Welsh.*' Hugh responded with a grudging smile. 'Hurd was great at supervising. But it was Jemmy Darrell and his two mates. They had every nook and cranny of the coastline in their heads. And a knowledge of the water we lot today can't even imagine. Those guys rowed out in their wooden gigs and sounded that ocean with nothing but their plumb lines...'

'How did they measure the depth? Was the rope marked?' Hugh asked.

'In a way, yah. It was tied at intervals with different kinds of material, in different colours, each one representing a number... I remember seeing a rope like that when I was a boy. Tied with bits of leather, serge, calico. White, blue, red. Cloth and colour. That's how the measurements went. In fathoms – like this...' Buddy stretched his arms out wide. 'Numbered fathoms. White calico was two fathoms, blue serge was three. And so on. 2, 3, 5, 7, 10, 13, 15, 17, 20.'

'It would have been better without 10 and 20.'

'What?' said Hugh, dragging his eyes away from the screen.

'Without 10 and 20, they'd of all been prime numbers.'

Hugh and Buddy stared at Genesis.

She said with a smirk, 'What, Teach? Thought you told me prime numbers were kinda permanent. Special. Even in a bullshit... in a... old-school story like this.'

'This is no old-school story!' The colour was rising in Hugh's face. 'This is the truth.' He glanced at Buddy then turned back to the girl. 'I don't understand. What have you got against learning something? What have you got against the truth?'

'Easy, boy. Easy. What's true for some ain't true for others,' said Buddy. He walked towards the door but stopped as he drew alongside Genesis. 'One thing I know is true, though, is that Jemmy Darrell knew what he was doing when he sounded the ocean. Knew the ocean and respected it. At the end of the day, that's what got him his freedom.'

His hand was on the doorknob when Genesis was at his side.

'This pilot of yours... was a black man?'

'Of course. All the pilots were.'

'And he was a slave while he was doing all that stuff with the rope and the colours... making that map?'

'Yah.'

Before Hugh could do anything, Genesis was barring Buddy's path, her face a confusion of emotions.

'Darrell. Didn't you say his name was Darrell?'

'Yah. James Darrell.' Buddy's eyes were calm.

'Darrell. Like your name. Darrell. Like you!'

'Not many names around in those days. We had to share them.'

Hugh stood watching, unable to move, to speak.

'So. Your family *shared* your name with his family.'

Buddy let out a sigh. 'Hugh. Young lady. I'll be seeing you later.' His eyes locked with the girl's for an instant. She stepped aside and let him pass.

A heavy silence hovered in the air.

'How dare you?' Hugh's voice was ice. 'How bloody dare you talk to him like that?'

'How dare I? How dare I?' Genesis started stamping around the room, circling Hugh. 'He's the one who couldn't friggin admit that his people owned slaves and that his friggin pilot – the one he's biggin up and calling a hero... He was one of them. A slave!'

'What's Buddy Darrell supposed to do about what happened two, three, four hundred years ago?'

'He could admit it!'

'Admit what? Slavery existed. It's a fact. It can't be undone.'

Her face shimmered with rage.

'What could he do? Apart from admit it?' She went up to within inches of his face. He backed away. 'He could make sure people know about that... that bleddy pilot. The black one! And what about your friggin root! What about that! Only you people know about that! Why don't you and your friend tell people about that? Why?'

'What are you talking about?' he said, truly bewildered. 'People do know about both of them! They're in the public domain!'

'Public friggin domain! For your people... not mine! Why do your people keep things from my people! Tell me that!'

'Genesis, you may think that there are only your people and my people. Think what you like! It's pointless trying to persuade you otherwise. Not in this island! But there's only one science. One knowledge. And it's for everybody.'

'Oh yeah? If it's for everybody, why isn't this stuff... this pilot, this map... your goddamn root... Why isn't it in schools? The schools where people like me go. Why isn't it there?' Amidst her anger, Hugh heard what sounded like an appeal to him, to understand her at last. But why the hysteria that had taken her over? It was his turn to force her to understand.

'Knowledge is for everybody. But people have to want it. To use it.'

Genesis stopped dead in her tracks.

'So it's our fault that we don't know shit!' She raised her eyes to the ceiling. 'Whose side are you on anyway?'

'What?'

'Whose fucking side are you on?'

'Side?' Spittle leapt from Hugh's mouth. 'There always has to be a side for you, right?' He gripped the back of his chair and willed himself into silence.

'Stupid bitch. Letting yourself get taken in. Teach, explain this,' she simpered. 'Teach, show me that. And you...' She threw him a withering glare. 'You! Acting like you think I can be something. Somebody! But all the time... Just like them. Like all of them... We're nothing more than something to use. Like that poor bastard who doesn't even have the map named after him – when he did all the work!' She was breathing hard. 'And where does that fool get off barging in on my time... My time!... the one time in the week when... when...' With a furious hand, she swiped away a tear, clenched her fists and with her chest heaving, threw him a look that could kill. 'I... I...' She couldn't get the words out so she bent forward as though to attack him.

'Genesis! Calm down!' He blocked her, his arms extended, his open palms gesturing halt.

She stopped, struggled with her breath and said, 'I... I'm... so... angry! All the time!' One of her hands was waving about. 'And once in a while...' Her gaze dropped to his. 'I know why.' She struck her chest. 'Like now!'

'Calm down, G!' He stepped towards her.

'Keep away from me... Don't touch me!'

'I only wanted to...' he said, retreating.

The phone rang. After the third shrill ring, Hugh answered. 'Yes. She's here. I'll tell her.' He looked uncertainly in the girl's direction.

'That was Tess. Something's come up about this evening. Some change of plan.'

Genesis snatched up her things. 'What bullshit does she want? What bullshit this time...'

When she was at the door, she turned to Hugh, her face still ablaze. 'To think that I wanted U to work for that Buddy Darrell!'

'What do you mean you wanted me to work for Buddy?'

'Not you! U!'

She stomped out.

'You missed 15!' Hugh shouted at her retreating back. '15's not a prime number either!' He slammed the screen door so hard it quivered on its hinges.

Tess

Genesis crossed the patio, fists still clenched and eyes down. Stationed at one of the sliding glass doors, Tess watched her coming. She felt as if a blowtorch had been searing random patches of her neck and face. She hoped Genesis would not notice.

'You'll never believe it,' she said, pulling the girl inside. 'He's picking me up in the PJ and we're going directly to Provo.'

Genesis didn't raise her head.

'I was supposed to meet him on Monday. One call and now… all bets are off! Well, come on! You've got to help me. Paulina's got the day off and I have too much to do… Have to be at the airport in… Less than two hours! Oh. My. God.'

She sped away in the direction of the grand staircase like an overexcited child. On the third stair, realising that she was alone, she turned round. Genesis had not moved from the door.

'G! I need your help. I can't get it all done in… next to no time.' Seeing no reaction, Tess took her voice down a notch. 'Calls. Emails. Texts. Packing. Packing!' Her voice started to climb again. 'Paulina was coming in specially to do that tomorrow but today she's at some… Filipino event…'

Genesis shrugged. Tess swept her hair back with a trembling hand. 'Are you going to help me?' Her voice almost resembled its normal tone.

'Only if you stop being weird. And stop talking like I know what… what Provo and PJ mean.'

'Sorry!' Tess grasped Genesis by the shoulders. 'Sorry.' Her hands fell to her sides as she tried to summon the image of herself that the world knew. 'Provo is short for Providentiales. Means something like Under God's Protection. One of the Turk's Islands. The resort island.'

'Hold on… Turks… The place Nina's people are from?'

Tess nodded. 'And PJ is short for… private jet.'

'Are you…' Unable to finish, Genesis doubled over in waves of laughter, managing every now and then to blurt out the odd word or phrase. 'PJ… Not pyjamas! Provo… Gotta find a new resort… or invent one… Bermuda's too ordinary… PJ! Provo!'

Tess had to wait it out until the girl was finally silent. She tried again. 'You know…' Her voice was almost steady. 'I'm sure I told you that every year, Richard and I take two weeks together. For twenty years – since we bought the place in Provo – it's been the only thing I can set my clock by. Over the years, he's missed Christmases, birthdays, anniversaries… Wall Street, you know. And I refuse to live anywhere but Bermuda! But the last two weeks of February are always ours. No business. No family. No calls. No emails. Just us.'

'Wow!' Genesis sounded interested. 'You're saying he bailed on you?'

'No! Not at all! No! He's made it two days earlier and has changed around what we always do. Meet in Miami. Overnight at the Four Seasons. Travel together the next day. Always the same. Always. Until now. Sending down the private jet to get me.' She looked intently at Genesis. 'Why would he do this?'

'Tess. How you could ask me a question like that? I'm poor-ass and not even eighteen.'

'Yeah but you're no ordinary seventeen-year old. You've got an old head.'

'No I haven't! Seriously. What do I know about marriage?'

'That's just it! Because you don't have any romantic... preconceptions... You might be able to see things in this situation that I can't.'

'I don't see anything in it. Maybe he changed the routine... to show off... A Valentine's present.'

'You think? But I don't understand the haste... And the... the...'

'What, Tess?'

'The... elaborate gesture.'

'How long you been married?'

'Thirty-nine years this September.'

'Geeze! I don't expect to live that long...' She paused, then declared with a bright smile, 'Maybe ya-boy decided it's time to take you on a date!'

'You think?'

'Sure.' Genesis started walking with Tess towards the stairs. 'Or maybe he's feeling guilty...'

'You think...' Tess stopped in her tracks. '...he's having an affair?'

'It was a joke!' Genesis shook her head. 'Come on! You're both too old for that kind of crap.'

Tess looked relieved and attempted unsuccessfully to swat Genesis on the shoulder. They both laughed and carried on up the stairs.

'What you want me to do?'

'One load of laundry. No, two. Fold the clothes I'm taking.'

Tess started climbing the stairs, issuing instructions while mentally scrolling through her own list of tasks. 'Then iron my travelling outfit.' She looked around and found Genesis had stopped. 'What's wrong?'

'So… this is me being Paulina for a day.'

'Is that how it sounded?' She replayed her last few sentences. *Do the laundry. Fold my clothes. Iron my outfit.* Not just the orders but the casual arrogance of their tone and their expectation of immediate action. Her normal self would have been horrified. But with her head in a jumble and time pressing, all she could say was, 'No. You're one friend helping out another.'

'That's it?'

'Please.'

Genesis stared straight ahead and did not move.

'All right, G. I'll pay you at the hourly rate that I pay Paulina. That's fair.'

'I don't want your money.'

'What do you want?'

'I want to stay here tonight – like I was supposed to. Before the change of plans. OK. There won't be any poker or any of your tired-ass music. No stories about being a hippie.' Genesis looked directly at Tess. 'I want you to let me spend tonight here in your house on my own – like you trust me. And I don't want you to tell Nina.'

'I'm not sure…'

'If I can stay, I'll wash and iron and pack for you. I know how to do those things. The one thing I learned in foster care… I'll cool out here tonight and be back to Nina's in the morning. In time for Sunday brunch.'

'Fine.' Tess's tone was decisive for the first time since her husband's phone call. 'The dirty clothes are in the hamper.' With that they set about their tasks, crisscrossing each other on the stairs, the laundry room, the library, the bedroom. Ten minutes before the taxi was due, Tess was packed, dressed and waiting.

'Madame looks good.' Genesis gave a little curtsy.

'Don't I always?' Tess tried to sound flippant but she was pacing around the entrance hall beneath the sunflower skylight, obsessively fingering the heavy bangle on her wrist.

'I always feel... I don't know... edgy... before this February trip. Don't get me wrong. I look forward to it. It's our time! It's the place itself. Not Provo. Provo is almost... blank. The sun is hot. The sea is blue, though not like ours. The sand is white. The villas are high-spec. You can't have a feeling about it. I guess that's why Richard likes it. The opposite of Bermuda. No ties for him, but there are for me! Twenty years ago, I was in Grand Turk selling the last of the family land. Richard happened to be with me and that's when he discovered Providentiales. It's the closest thing I've ever seen to him falling in love with a place. It was different for me, though.'

'Why?'

Tess stopped fidgeting with her bangle. 'Because of what we did there... Didn't Nina tell you?'

'Tell me what?'

'Part of my family owned property there. Like most of the big Bermudian families a couple of hundred years ago.' Tess's hands were still. 'Didn't you know that?'

'No. I thought that only black Bermudians came from there. Like Nina's people.'

Tess shook her head. 'Our lot took your lot down to rake salt.'

'Is that why Nina's house is called Salt Cay?'

Tess sighed. 'I guess... It was all about salt. That's what changed my family from poor whites into...'

Outside in the gathering darkness, a taxi horn sounded.

'Wait a minute. Before I go...' Tess disappeared into the library, brought back a slim paperback and handed it to Genesis. *The History of Mary Prince A West Indian Slave Related by Herself.* 'This'll tell you what happened.'

With her back to the girl, Tess said, 'I go to the Turk's Islands to be with my husband. If it weren't for that, I wouldn't go. It's too bleak. Too arid. I guess it was making all that salt.'

Tess stood motionless for a while then picked up her suitcase. 'Goodbye, Genesis. Make sure you put the alarm on when you leave.'

'Have fun in the PJ!'

Genesis

I listened till I couldn't hear the taxi's engine. Opened the book. Read it in one go. Thirty-five pages. A first.

The opening sentences got me. '*I was born at Brackish Pond, in Bermuda, on a farm belonging to Mr. Charles Myners. My mother was a household slave; and my father, whose name was Prince, was a sawyer belonging to Mr. Trimmingham, a ship-builder at Crow Lane...*' Those names – Myners... Minors... Trimmingham... Crow Lane... So familiar... '*A sawyer belonging to...*' Sawyer. What's a sawyer? *Belonging to...*

And Mary Prince... Tough, no shit Mary. Took on people bigger and stronger than herself. And even if she didn't win, she didn't lose either. If I'd of had a grandmother, she would of been like that. If I'd of had a mother... But I didn't. Just that stupid girl, knocked up, a mother and dead by the time she's twenty-one... Not like Mary. Not like Mary.

Too much! I have to put this down.

What am I going do in this big house for the next twelve hours? Sweet Airs. Nothing sweet about this place. Seems like it grew out of the rock. That hard. But I like being here. Like giving the finger to all those guys hanging on the wall, with their beards, those big old moustaches, those medals on their chests. Some of them around in Mary Prince's time. Think I can hear them cussin. Get that coloured gal out of our house... Sorry, guys. Your daughter gave me permission... Hear me? I got PERMISSION to stay!

Why'd I make that deal with Tess? But I had to do something! Couldn't let her get away with making me into her maid. If she'd of been in her right mind, she'd of never agreed to it. She'd of been like, I have to call Nina... But she was so out of it, all she could think about was her screwed-up marriage.

If only I had a number for U... we could chill out up here for the whole night. I'd love him to see this place. It would blow his mind. Let me try that old number anyway. Can't hurt.

'Yo.'

'Back at you.'

'Who's this?'

'I'm looking for U. Uriel.'

'So why you calling me? Hey! Forget U. You as fine as you sound?'

'Can't hardly hear you... What's that racket?'

'GOOOOOOAL! Just five minutes into the game!'

'Look. If you see U, tell him his ace-girl called... Hello? Hello?'

Well, that's it. Football. Won't be hearing from him! Just me rattling around this house until morning. Might as well flick through the book again... Mary in Turks Island, where Tess is going... raking for salt, standing in salt water, watching the blisters rise on her legs, diving for stones for the master's house... Nothing but whippings and psycho owners... And work! So much work! OK. That's enough. Enough, Mary.

My cell... 'Hello?'

'Hey, G!'

'Hey, U!'

We shout over the screaming of the crowd. A few minutes later there's a plan. U won't be coming up here. I'll be meeting him in town. Going to be tight. The ferry'll be leaving in fifteen minutes. Think, G, think! I don't have a key to this house so once I'm out, there'll be no going back.

I change into the clothes I brought for my sleepover with Tess. That pisses me off. A night out in town and I'll be wearing the scrubs I brought to knock around this house in. But got no choice. If I walk into Nina's house tomorrow smelling of smoke and God knows what, I'm so busted. Woman's got a nose like a bloodhound.

I borrow Tess's red leather jacket. Too small for her. Perfect for me. Oh yeah. I'm ready. Got to run...

I get on the ferry, feel that dark water rolling underneath me. I hate the water! Shit, it's cold!

On our way. The sound of the engine is kinda soothing and I try to relax. Twenty minutes. Should be able to manage that. I look in my bag. Two books. Mary's. And Teach's algebra book. No way will I touch that. Let him and his mathematics eat dirt!

The smell of the night water comes in through the window and I feel the ferry rising and falling. That's what I hate about the ocean. Nothing steady. Nothing stable. I turn away and reach out for something to hold on to. Mary's book stares up at me.

I open it again and the words are like black water pouring all over me...

I was bought along with my mother... Black words. Some I don't understand and some I do. Somebody bought Mary, bought her, like a piece of meat, a chair, a yard of cloth. *Bought* her... How did that feel – to the person who was bought and the one that was buying? How did it feel? *Along with my mother...* Mary had a mother until she was grown. Hmmm. Mary was bought but she had a mother. Who tried to protect her. Mary was bought. But she was never an orphan.

The words roll over me. Her master is in the bathtub ordering her to wash him. *I would not come, my eyes were so full of shame.* Oh yes. Mary and I both know about that. Runnin from that. All those years in foster care, I been runnin from men like that, men who thought I was their toy and women who turned a blind eye. Runnin from how they made me feel. *Shame.* People don't even use that word no more. Like it don't exist. But it does.

The words. Mary's words in Turks Island as she dives for stones in the deep water. *This was very hard work and the great waves breaking over us continually made us in danger of being drowned.* My hard work isn't raking salt or diving for stones or studying at school. It's runnin from feelings. Cause if they catch up with me, they'll be like the big waves on Grand Turk. They'll pull me under.

CHAPTER 8: GOING HOME

Genesis

U's at the ferry terminal waiting. Oh God! I throw my arms around him and squeeze him tight. My whole body is trembling. From the book and the cold night air over the water.

'You OK?' His eyes are soft.

'Sure.' I laugh for no reason. 'Sure.'

'Good.' He hands me a helmet. 'Put this on. We gotta bounce.'

'Where to?'

'Back to the game. Gone into extra time.'

Five minutes later, I'm getting off U's bike and putting my feet on solid ground. Nothing but people hollering, whistles blowing. A flood of white light glaring down on the pitch. There's dreads on both sides and when they run, their locks flow out behind them.

I never did like football. Not the way U wanted me to. Something in my brain didn't click. All the other things he taught me – basketball, cricket, track, gombey dancing – I wasn't just good at them. I was great! But football... When I could finally explain the offside rule, he took me to a bar and bought me my first drink. But tonight, none of that matters. I love football. No. I love being at a football game under the lights on a Saturday night with U, surrounded by the people Tess and Nina and Lizzie would call loud. Uncouth. My kinda people.

U and I are sitting with the rest of the Town fans. When he leans forward, I lean back and let the whole night wash over me. I'm not following the game. Can just about see the players. Brown and gold pushing in one direction. Red, gold and green pushing in the other. Up and down the field they go and I'm here smiling. This feels so good. This smells so good. Heineken. Fries.

Chicken. Mayonnaise. It sounds so good, especially the cow bell clanging big time because Town is one up.

The players are tired. The more tired they seem, the louder the fans get.

'What you b'ys doin? Tryin to walk de ball into de net?'

Near us a group of seniors start carrying on. They're pretty tanked up already and not impressed with what they're seeing. 'Take dat b'y off de field! Dat number nine.' His mates join in. 'None of dem b'ys know how to play. Not like when we b'ys were out dere...'

There's a huge 'Oooooooo!' as a shot from midfield narrowly misses the Town net. Things settle down but even I can see that they're in trouble. Town's energy's all gone. Their fans shout out encouragement that sounds like insults.

'Get dat ball! What you waiting for?'

'I bet you a twenty we go to penalties...'

'Left foot, b'y! Left foot... Didn I tell you left foot?'

'Down de wing! Down de wing! What's wrong with you?'

There's a woman with a voice like a dentist's drill. People living way down the road must be able to hear her. 'Hey, ref, are you blind? Don't let me have to come down dere...'

'Memba de time dat b'y kicked your son! Dat time you went upside his head with a umbrella. Member dat?'

On and on it goes. I'm not watching. Just happy to be back after a long stretch away. Time is running out. The words 'penalty shoot-out' are moving through the crowd like a wave. People are mumbling, sounding scared for dem b'ys on de field. Even the cow bell is silent.

I open my eyes and see it. A tangle of bodies. Someone on his own finds strength, draws back his leg and sends the ball towards the Blazers' net. It travels in slow motion. But the line is straight and it explodes in the corner of the net like a rocket at liftoff.

The whistle blows.

U leaps up first. Then everyone else – umbrella lady, half-cut seniors, football commentators, mayonnaise eaters, gamblers, cow bell ringers... All of them. Up in the air. Celebrating. Victory for Town.

Half an hour later, we all burst into the club by the harbour where the best DJs are. From white floodlight to the white ball spinning in the dark, breaking up the light and sending it in a million pieces across the crowded room. From one kind of noise to another. Inside it's a sound that you feel. It comes through your ears and ends up where your heart is. Coming from monster speakers on the platform up front. From the DJs as their hands glide from one turntable to the next, mixing the sounds, working the crowd.

Everybody's jumping. Jumping and sweating.

Heaven!

U and I push our way right to the front. I give one of the DJs my bag and my jacket. The night belongs to me. I can feel my body being taken over by the beat. Feel the sweat collecting on my scalp as I jump at the command of the DJ.

'Make some NOISE!'

We jump in the air with one arm up, our fingers splayed, our arms pumping in the direction of the DJ. He calls out to us. We answer. The music changes to dancehall and I'm one of them bad girls right up front who bend forward and present the DJs with a back view. In and out. Up and down. Round and round they go. We look over our shoulders at our backsides like they don't belong to us. Like we're just watching some slammin BET video.

U comes and goes. He brings me a drink which I throw down in one gulp. He does the same. In the middle of the dance floor, a thought sneaks up on me. I can hold my liquor. U can't. Then the DJ calls, 'Somebody say Fire!' And we all scream, 'FIRE!'

In the middle of the Black Chinee song, U reappears and we start winding up on each other so bad that people make a space around us. Belly to belly we flow. Like music. Like fire... Never danced like that with U before. As the song's ending, when we're doing some sweet grinding, when it's feeling so good, here comes another thought...

Something's wrong.

'Gotta pee!' I shout.

I push my way through to the edge of the dance floor and run to the bathroom. Part of me's scanning the place with the Nina that now lives in my head. No soap. Damp bits of toilet paper collapsed in clumps on the floor. *Dir-ty*. That's how Nina says it. Dirt never bothered me before... But much more than that, I'm trying to wrap my head around that dance with U. No! It wasn't right! Not with U! It's not supposed to be like that...

I sit on the toilet seat sweating, trying to work it out. I vaguely hear somebody come into the bathroom but all I'm thinking about is how come I let myself dance like that with U. Even for a second. Not U, the nearest thing to people I got. But I did pull myself away. I shut it down before it went any further.

I'm still flustered when I go to wash my hands. But by the time I'm turning the tap on, I'm starting to cool off. Then I look into the mirror and behind my shoulder there's this face staring at me. All dark hair and big eyes.

'Lizzie!'

I don't turn my head. Just keep looking at her reflection. What the ass is she doing here? You can never tell which Lizzie's gonna turn up. Corporate Lizzie. Cosmo Lizzie. Catholic Lizzie... And now – Slummin Lizzie.

She moves from behind me, leans into the other basin and slowly applies some lipstick. She smacks her lips together and puts the lipstick in her bag. Only then does she glance at me.

'Gen,' she purrs and swishes out.

It's all over! Nina's gonna find out. Lizzie's probably makin the call right now. I'm so screwed!

But no! I take a deep breath. Lizzie won't say a friggin word. She'll go to her grave before she'll admit to Nina that she was at this club!

I dash out of the bathroom, bursting to tell U about creepy stalking Lizzie and how she'll never tell. Not only is it a good story but it will get U and me back to where we belong. Best friends. The ones who say Hey G, Hey U every single time...

I catch sight of U before he sees me and all the joy drains out of me. It's the way he's moving. I've seen it before. He shouldn't drink. It makes him crazy. I know the signs. He's not there yet. Still holding back. But everything's different. When he comes over, I don't tell him about Lizzie.

He asks me to dance and I say I'm tired.

He offers me a drink.

'What's in it, U?'

'Coke.'

'That's it?'

'Yes. Mama.' His words are still pretty clear. The glow that I alone can see is still there but has become dull. He's on a slippery slope. 'Got to keep my head straight,' he says. 'We got a long ride up to The Nice White Lady's house.'

'What?'

'The Nice White Lady's house!' We have to shout over the noise.

'We're not going there, U. I don't have a key!'

He doesn't say anything for a while. Still having to shout, he says, 'Not the White Lady's house. Not the Black Lady's house either. Where are we... you... going to sleep?'

'Your place!'

Nothing.

'Come on, U. You do have a place...'

'How come you didn't tell me this before?' He stumbles over his words.

'I did! I told you on the phone. I said... I thought I...'

'I'm kinda living between places right now, G.'

'So, where the hell do you sleep?'

'Well, a room a guy's been letting me use...'

'We'll go there.' I look at all the people having good time. 'You need to get me to Nina's house first thing tomorrow morning.'

'Right.' He moves off, shoulders hunched, head down. His walk says it all. Something inside me breaks.

We stay at the club until it closes. By that time, U has passed the point of no return. He's not mean, doesn't want to fight or cuss. But the light in his face... it's gone.

I don't feel good about getting on the back of his bike but I do it anyway.

'Where we going?'

'Princess Street. But I have to pick up something first.'

His riding is pretty OK, but I'm hearing voices telling me to get a taxi and go home to Nina, telling me not to get on the back of the bike of someone who's drunk, telling me not to spend the night God knows where.

But it's not 'someone'. It's U. And he's looking so sad.

We stop at a bar that has doors like the saloons in those old movies. All the feeling of being home is gone. Was home always like this place? Nothin but raggedy whores, fall-down drunks, desperate crackheads, the steady cussin of two old guys with their arms around each other – looking like they're fighting one minute, hugging the next.

U puts me in a chair next to the door and goes to talk to the man behind the bar. Don't like the way people are looking at me so I pull my bag to me like a shield. My hands feel clammy. I rub them together and put my finger to my lips. Salt.

The twelve hours gone past rush at me. All the things that I'd forgotten at the game and at the club. They're back to torment me.

The house where we're going to sleep is around the corner. U fumbles for the key. He doesn't look at me. Not once. I can't see much as we walk down a dark hall but I hear sounds – snoring, a child calling out in its sleep, some low, agitated talking. We get to the room. U's room. I can see the outline of a mattress on the floor and head for it, knocking over what sounds like a can. The covers of the bed are all in a heap. I lie on top of them, holding my bag, grateful for the jacket – cause I'm not going to be lying under none of those filthy-ass sheets.

U lies down next to me. We lie on our backs like statues for what seems like forever. Even in the darkness of this nasty room, in my head, I see U's glow. In the playground, in the ocean, in the street, on the field, at the Home – all these places where his feet and his arms and his heart effortlessly show his brilliance. The only place it didn't exist was in the classroom. There he was the dumb boy. He didn't make trouble but his mind was like lead. The alphabet was his enemy. The simplest word became garbage as soon as he approached. And nobody helped him – just passed him along, from one year to the next, another piece of garbage, like the words he could not unlock. Till he got tired and headed towards the fun and the friends and the street.

U turns on his side mumbling something. Sorry, I guess. I feel sorry too. Sorry that I can read a book in a couple of hours and he can't; that I can understand words and ideas and he can't; that I'll find a way to get off this rock and he won't.

No. I don't feel sorry.

I feel sorrow.

In the gloom, I see there's a window. I stare at it and wait for the moment when that black rectangle turns grey.

At first light, I'm on the road, walking the five miles to Nina's house. I don't bother to change my clothes like I planned. It's about eight o'clock when I reach Salt Cay. I walk straight into the kitchen and find Nina with her hands flaking cod fish. She sees me and stops short.

'I... I spent the night in town... with an old friend.' I hear her gasp. 'But I came home.'

*

Help! Help me! Uriel!

Them big boys chasin me! All down the beach. They want your ball! But you told me to hold it for you. I been runnin like you taught me. But I'm smaller than them so I start dodgin like you taught me.

I'm in the water. Dodged straight into the water. White and bubblin all around me. Don't have the ball no more. It's floatin right to them. They not lookin at the ball. They lookin at me!

They comin in the water shoutin. Goin teach you how to swim, lil girl! Goin teach you a lesson! Laughin... laughin.

Uriel, where you gone to? Where?

Stumble and fall back. Get a mouthful of sand, water and salt. Everything round me movin. Water just won't stop movin... takin me out... pullin me under... Help me, Uriel! Like you promised.

I'm tryin to get up. Legs turnin to jelly. Water rushin round my shoulders. I see you! You're comin! Runnin real fast across the sand... I'm gulpin water. Uriel! Help me!

I'm bein pulled out. Towards those big waves with the white teeth ready to swallow me. Can't stand. Can't think.

Undertow!

I look back. To the shore.

One of them boys is lyin face down in the sand. The other's bent over coughin, holdin his stomach.

You're divin in!

Comin for me.

Comin to get me!

Two hands are grabbing my shoulders. Them boys again! I start to fight.

But it's not them.

It's Nina. I'm in my bed and my pillow is wet. I look into Nina's eyes and start crying all over again.

Nina

'Tess?'

'Hi, Nina.' A slight pause. 'Did I give you this number?'

For almost a week, Nina had been rehearsing what she would say to Tess. Now that Tess was on the phone, she didn't know where to begin.

'I told Paulina to give it out only in an emergency. Has something happened?' The worried tone in Tess's voice intensified Nina's fury. But still she could not speak.

'Did something happen to Genesis? Is she in trouble?'

Hearing Tess say the word Genesis unlocked Nina's tongue. 'Letting that girl get mixed up again! With... with...'

'Tell me what happened! Is she in jail?'

'With drug dealers, whores and Christ knows what... the ones I'm trying to protect her from...'

'Nina!' Tess shouted. 'Is she in jail?'

Nina glared at the phone. 'No.'

'That's a relief.'

'No thanks to you.'

'I don't appreciate your implication, Nina.'

'Not implication. Fact! You sent that girl right back to those...'

'Stop, Nina! Is she hurt?'

'...creeps... addicts... child molesters...' Nina's unsteady spurt of words ended in a simple 'Yes'.

'What happened?'

With her stomach heaving, Nina found clarity. 'You gave Genesis a night off. From responsibility. She took it. Went to all the places that we've been trying to keep her away from. All the people. Like offering a bottle of black rum to a recovering alcoholic. Yes. She took it. Ran wild. Got up to God knows what... Spent the night with some boy she used to know.'

Tess paused. 'Did he rape her?'

'No.'

'Did he beat her up?'

'No.'

'Get her high?'

'No.'

'You said she was hurt!'

'She was. She is. Very. Took three days to stop her crying.'

'I don't get it, Nina.'

'You wouldn't. By the way, Tess, how's the vacation? How's the resort? How's Pro-vi-den-tia-les.'

Silence.

'You haven't got a clue what the last week's been like.'

No reply from Tess.

'*I spent the night with an old friend*. That's what she said when she came in... Then the worst kind of crying I ever heard. I had to grab her instead of going upside her head. Had to hug her and smell all the smoke and booze and God knows what else on her. Had to hold on... All she kept saying was how I have to help this boy. This boy she grew up with and all I kept saying was no. I won't help him. No. You can't either if you want to save your life. You have to choose between his life and yours...'

Nina took a breath.

'Three whole days of this! Up and down, with me going on and on about how she has to leave her old life behind. How there's no turning back. If she does, she'll lose everything she's gained.'

Through the phone Nina heard the clinking of ice cubes against glass.

'Everything! She'll lose everything, I tell her. But she won't give up. He's like a brother to me, she says. On and on. She tells me, I want you to get to know Uriel... Don't tell me his name! I want you to meet him, she keeps saying. Meet him! I scream that she will bring that boy into my house over my dead body.

'It's been awful. Every day when I came home from work, I expected to find her gone. I didn't. But she looked at me like I was the most evil thing she'd ever seen. The fourth day, she was waiting for me with her promise. I won't see him again. Her face! I had to turn away...'

Tess cleared her throat. 'I'm so sorry, Nina. I can imagine what it must have been like…'

'She's been having terrible nightmares,' Nina said. 'Every night. Keeps screaming *Help! Help me!* When I try to hold her, she lashes out. And when she wakes up… sobbing… sobbing…' Nina's voice broke. 'You have no idea.'

'You need to be grateful – we all do – that nothing… irreparable… happened. When given a choice, she chose to come home.'

'That's just it.' Nina's strength returned. 'You shouldn't have given her the choice. It was too soon.'

'Come on, Nina. She'll be eighteen in less than two months. In the eyes of the law, she'll be responsible for her actions! An adult. We need to start letting her be one.'

'We? Who's we?' Beads of sweat stood out on Nina's forehead. 'Who the hell is we?'

'Now hold on.'

'No. You hold on! And think about this girl. This one girl! The one with… nothing. Who had to bring herself up. This is not somebody who was a Brownie, who was sent to Sunday School, somebody with a mummy waiting at the school gates. This is Genesis. Who needs time to learn… everything.'

'Nina, you are upset. I understand that.'

'Don't do that! Don't you talk down to me, like I'm one of your clients…'

'As I was saying. Before you interrupted.' Nina could hear the rasp of Tess's breathing. 'Whether you like it or not, she'll soon be on her own. We need to give her practice in making choices. Good ones. Like the one she made the other night. Instead of going off on me, you should be congratulating yourself on what she did. And what you've done. What we've all done. Yes, we! A well-timed intervention – like we've done with Genesis – can have positive and long-lasting results.'

'She's not a statistic. Despite all your good works, all your awards, your so-called professionalism, you don't understand the first thing. She's not part of some group called… Tess Alexander's Success Stories! You hear me? Not! If you don't know that we have to fight for Genesis every inch of the way, you don't know a damn thing!'

On the other end of the line there was the faint sound of knocking. Nina pictured Tess in her island resort. The chambermaid bringing fresh towels? The chauffeur ready to take her to town?

'Your problem is you think you know everything. Because you've always owned everything!'

She stabbed the OFF button and threw down the phone as though it were burning. She stood in the middle of her kitchen trembling at the words she had just spoken, remembering how Dee had once said the same thing many years ago. Reminded of this ancient grief, she collapsed weeping into a chair, overcome with a sense of Dee's presence and of a night she hadn't thought about in many years.

At dawn that day, two men convicted of assassinating the English governor had shuffled towards the death chamber. By the time their bodies hung lifeless from the gallows, black rage had broken out and set the island on fire.

Since the arrest of the two men, she'd watched the slow transformation of her husband. They had always been on the same page. He'd been proud of her when she'd gone off to study at St. Giles Hospital, south London, and until the day he died, one of his favourite photos was of her wearing her crisp white cap bearing the thin black band. State Registered Nurse. Up till the day of the hangings he had never felt less than a man because he worked with his hands; he had never questioned 'the way things were'.

Now, for the first time in their marriage, she and Dee were openly at war. After only a few minutes at home from work that evening, he'd headed for the door.

'Where you going?'

'Out,' he said, without looking back, and roared out of their yard on his motorbike.

Nina had paced up and down in their small apartment, alternating between fury and tears. She knew where he was going. In the months, weeks and days leading up to the trial, sentence, appeal and execution, she'd watched the mutation of Dee's tranquil spirit from bewilderment to frustration to outrage. With death in the air and flames in the streets, she felt a hot wind blowing her husband towards action. She'd tried to block out the sounds of mothers gathered outside, begging their children to stay home, then cursing them when they kickstarted their bikes and hurtled towards the fire and smoke of black islanders' rage. She felt paralysed. It was only when she smelled smoke – not from town – from her own kitchen and she saw that she had burnt the dinner that she acted.

She had pulled on her long denim shirt against the cold December night and headed towards the smoke. But her mission was not to change the world. Hers was to change Dee. To change his mind. To pull him back.

She could not let Dee get involved in this violent night. When she'd looked into his eyes just before he'd left, she couldn't find him. Or even his good, kind father whom he so resembled. All she could see was his mother. Rosie, hard-core when it came to right and wrong.

Damn Rosie!

Hurrying down the winding lanes, she replayed Dee's and Rosie's conversations as the trials ground on. The talk always ended with his father, Johnny, dead over a decade before. He'd never voted. Had died before one person, one vote. The only Bermuda that Johnny knew was the no-blacks-in-hotels Bermuda, the no-blacks-in-the-Civil-Service Bermuda, the no-blacks-in-restaurants Bermuda, the no-blacks-occupying-certain-seats-in-movie-theatres-and-churches Bermuda, the no-blacks-contaminating-white-schools Bermuda. The segregation-without-end Bermuda. This was what was pushing Dee, the weight of his dead father and all who'd gone before him.

As she carved a path towards the sounds of crackling and shouting, what drove her was a fear of what the attempt to right the wrongs of so many generations would do to her man.

Suddenly, she stopped short. In front of her was a liquor warehouse. One side was engulfed in flames. Figures were moving in the darkness, brisk, bent over. The air reeked of kerosene. A lighted bottle flew, shattered a window and was devoured by the burning building.

A tall man stood up, a bottle in one hand, a lighter in the other.

'Dee!'

He saw her. She ran to him and grabbed the hand holding the lighter.

'Go home, Nina!' His voice was like gravel, his eyes hard and staring. 'I can't be the only one not doing something.' She moved closer.

'Stay where you are!' Dee barked. 'They'll always keep us down because they know everything.'

'You don't really believe that!' Her erratic breathing made it sound like a question.

'No!' Dee shouted. 'But they do! They think they own us because they've always owned everything. And that ends here!'

Nina stepped between his outstretched arms and slid hers around his neck. She ignored the whoop of joy from behind them as another Molotov cocktail sent a plume of flame up the side of the building. Her eyes were wide and luminous in the darkness.

'Before you become part of this…' she said, 'I want you to think of the children we're going to have one day. Yes, we will. Will you want them to know that their father did this?'

'I'll want them to know that their father stood up for them.' His voice soared above the shouts of the rioters and the crackling tongues of fire. 'That he stood up for what is right!' There was a sharp click as Dee ignited the lighter and, with both arms outstretched, one holding a bottle, the other a lighter, he locked his body into a crucified position.

The flaming lighter served only to heighten Nina's urgency. 'Like this? There are better ways. To be a father. To be a man…' She held him tight and would not let him go until she felt his resistance draining away.

'I'm so sick of this.' Anguish thickened his voice. 'Sick of the way things are.' His shoulders sagged and his arms went around her.

There was a smell of burning.

Close to them. Too close. Not the warehouse. Closer.

Nina screamed.

Her shirt was on fire.

Dee dropped the lighter, hurled the bottle away and ripped the shirt off her shoulders. Nina smelled scorched skin. It wasn't hers. With a single-minded ferocity, he stamped out the fire from the burning shirt, reducing it to smouldering shreds.

'You all right, Dee? You all right?'

'Yes. I think so... I think so... You?' Nina felt Dee's frantic hands running over her head, her arms, her back, then took her in his arms to quell her violent shaking. When she touched his hand and heard him cry out and smelled his seared flesh, she pulled him away and he didn't resist.

To the sound of shouting, the crackling of burning wood, the shattering of glass, they turned their backs on the riot and the incandescent beauty of the sky aflame.

★

Nina wept as the brilliance of that night's memory began to fade. She wept for Dee and having to grow old without him. She wept for herself, the woman who had stood between him and his need to act and wondered at all the decisions she'd taken since that night when she'd played it safe.

She wept for Genesis and the road ahead. She thought of Tess Alexander and all her good works.

'I should have let you throw that bottle, Dee!' she cried out, her muscles clenching. 'I should have thrown one myself!'

CHAPTER 9: SEA CHANGE

Lizzie

Lizzie awoke early on Holy Saturday, her head still throbbing. Yesterday, she had pitched too many kites. Eaten too many fish cakes, too many hot cross buns. Drunk too many glasses of wine.

Good Friday had left her feeling both sluggish and empty.

When she stumbled out of bed and onto the verandah the clouds overhead were brightening as the sun threw a net of light over the ocean.

'Oh my…'

She ran back inside and grabbed her binoculars.

'…God!'

Lizzie's mouth stayed open but her fingers worked hard to get clearest magnification.

Beyond the breakers, the ocean boiled white as a pod of whales passed by on their way north. There was a clear view of them in the morning light and for at least ten minutes, she watched as they churned the water – blowing fountains into the air, showing off the white underside of their flukes, swimming upside down with flippers slapping the waves, diving down then surfacing like living submarines. Even at a distance she saw they swam as a group. As they disappeared from sight, one of the whales heaved its tremendous bulk clean out of the water and for a moment, seemed suspended in midair.

This was a good omen. Her first weekend in her own place. She hummed to herself as she reached for her new coffee-maker. In a few minutes, she was back outside with a coffee, pulling her wrap around her shoulders. The ocean stretched out before her, its dark navy retreating before the advance of variants of blue from turquoise to cerulean.

It was an unfurnished rental, with the option to buy later. She gave herself five years – max. Then the cord would be cut for good. Crisp. Sharp. No clutter. Nothing to remind her of the place she'd always called home.

For several minutes she stood thinking about the whales, before deciding on her next move. Town. She would go shopping for a memento of the sighting.

After some aimless ambling about town, she headed for an upmarket tourist shop where she bought a small watercolour of a whaling boat and immediately took it to be framed. She remembered one of Avó's stories she'd heard as a little girl. It was about Pedro, their earliest ancestor, who had arrived on the island over a hundred years ago. *He would cry Baleia! Baleia! So loud the whales could hear him.* It had been so long since she'd heard those words... She retraced her steps and bought another print of the same picture.

That night, she thought about the coming Easter Sunday, with everyone dressed to the nines, the high resurrection mass and the endless feast at her older brother's house. She would find a moment to give her grandmother the picture. A thank-you for her help with Genesis's project, and a moment to connect with the one family member who, like her, was consigned to the fringe of everything.

Genesis. She still hadn't processed the image of herself and Gen wearing a red leather jacket in the mirror at the club, music booming from behind the cloakroom door. Why had she felt so furious when she'd seen that vivid face, no longer the grateful child she'd taken for ice cream when she'd been her Big Sister? But she looked better. Much better. Nina's insistence on good food and eight hours' sleep had paid off. That dark skin was clear of pimples and the beanpole frame had added a pound or two. She had lost the tacky wigs, extensions and weaves; her hair was cropped short, showing off a perfectly shaped head. Now she could attract respectable men, not just trainee gangstas. Was it that had so upset her? That she'd grown beyond her? All she had managed to say was 'Gen'.

No need to be upset. Gen was on her way up. Up and out. What about her – Elisabete Moniz Pereira? The new apartment was a start. But wherever she lived, she was still in her mother's house, which looked 'normal' to the world outside, but on the inside, it wasn't like any other house she knew. If she lurched from one extreme to the other, it was because of that house. She carried it with her. She would walk away from it. Little by little she would.

Easter Sunday rolled over her with its usual mix of suffocating familiarity and isolation. At last, when things were winding down, she offered to take Avó home. Avó was tired and she still had unpacking to do. Before they left, Lizzie pocketed a handful of candied almonds, flashed a big smile and called, 'Amêndoas. Love them!'

Avó said nothing during the drive, although she seemed more relaxed than at the dining table.

'Thank you, Elisabete,' she said when they arrived. She wavered at the door. 'I see you soon?'

'No! I'm not going yet. I have something for you. Would you like some tea? Let me make you some tea.'

Avó nodded and started walking towards her room.

'No, Avó! Let's have it right here.' The old woman seemed confused for a moment but then gave Lizzie a conspiratorial smile. It had been years since she'd occupied the main part of the house at a times other than those prescribed by Ines.

It was awkward at first. Lizzie made heavy weather of the tea-making while Avó sat at the kitchen table with one eye peeled on the door. But by the time they were sipping their tea, Avó had begun to talk about what Easter was like in Açores, where they were in church every day of Holy Week from Palm Sunday to Holy Thursday. Then Good Friday with all the stations of the cross... Not like in Bermudas, when the holiest, most terrible day of the year was like a party.

When there was a pause, Lizzie passed her a manila envelope.

'What is this?'

'Open and see.'

Avó carefully pulled out the picture. '*Baleia*,' she murmured, tracing the line of the boat with her finger.

'That's what I'm going to call my new place.' Lizzie gave a nervous laugh.

'*Obrigada*, Elisabete, *obrigada*.' Lizzie felt her grandmother's eyes searching her face. Finally, Avó said, 'It is good that you have gone to live in your own house.' How different from the tears and predictions of doom from Ines! Lizzie reached out and took the old woman's hand.

'You are finally grown,' Avó said. 'You have reached your... *maioridade.*'

'But, Avó! I'll be thirty-one next month!' Lizzie smiled indulgently. Avó did not smile back.

'It is only now that you are grown.'

'I've been grown up for a little while.' Yet another smile that was not returned.

'Only now.'

Lizzie frowned. 'What about the years studying and working?'

'Before, when they sent you away, you were a child...'

'I wasn't!' Lizzie leapt to her feet, her face burning. 'I was seventeen years old. Bright for my age. Ready for college!'

'A child. Then, you could not choose, could not choose your life.' Avó's movements were slow and deliberate as she walked to her room. 'Only now. Only...'

Lizzie was already out the door, revving up her engine, stepping on the gas... Getting away.

'Jesus Christ! She knows!'

Tears coursed down her cheeks as she swerved and overtook recklessly on the winding roads. Only her mother was supposed to know what had happened when a little scrap of life had been snuffed out so that the family could live without shame.

Even now, over a decade later, Lizzie felt torn apart when she thought about it. So glad that with that one act, she had been able to open her world to more possibilities. So haunted by the loss of someone she might have been able to love.

Nina

A week after Easter, Nina and Genesis entered the Seahorse Grill and found Tess waiting. They had barely sat down when Genesis said she had to go pee.

'As it's her birthday, I'll have to let that pass,' Nina said.

'What's wrong with her saying she has to go pee?'

'Because...' Nina could feel heat rising along the back of her neck. 'Because... it's crude.'

'Nina, do you pee?'

Nina straightened up. 'No, Tess. I urinate.'

'Oh,' said Tess, flicking away a stray hair. 'Wearing white gloves and using silk toilet paper?'

Nina glared at her but said nothing. She would not let Tess push her beyond breaking point again. She'd lost control. Once was enough. Never again.

The restaurant verandah was right by the harbour. She took a slice of bread and tossed it overboard. For a moment, the sea erupted with the thrashing of fish.

'I wonder why she chose this place,' Nina said. 'For tourists really. I don't understand...'

'I do,' Tess said. 'She told me. When she was in primary school, one of her foster parents won a raffle and the prize was dinner for four. At the Seahorse. It was the first time she remembers being taken out for dinner.'

'She told you that? That's funny. She didn't tell me. She never talks about...'

'What's going on?' Genesis asked, appearing in front of them. Nina tried to rearrange her face but was saved by the arrival of Lizzie, bearing a large white cake-box and sporting a short haircut and rhinestone-studded shades.

'Check Lizzie! Check the hair!' Genesis reached over to feel the glossy curls. 'You look wicked!'

'Like I'm supposed to! What's everybody drinking?' Lizzie's smile grated on Nina. But despite its inauspicious beginning, the lunch passed off without further incident. Tess and Lizzie doled out advice on what it meant to be eighteen – from getting a credit card, voting, getting married, practising safe sex.

Nina sat back and listened, feeling detached. What was Genesis making of it all? She was laughing a lot at Lizzie's Cosmo advice, but you could never tell... Then came the arrival of the confection conceived of and organised by Lizzie – seventeen small, iced cupcakes in a circle with a big one in the middle bearing the letter G, spelt out in candles. They sang happy birthday and Genesis blew out her candles. Lizzie flirted mercilessly with their Italian waiter, but he was more than a match for her. By the time he took the photo of them all, everyone in the restaurant was laughing.

They spent the rest of the afternoon playing tourist, taking in the sights of Ye Olde Towne of St. George, walking along its cobbled stones, shaking their heads at the nagging wife as she came up spluttering and kicking on the Ducking Stool, taking pictures of each other in the Stocks, walking down Featherbed Alley and Old Maid's Lane. Admiring the aged cedar beams of St. Peter's church.

It was a good day out. When they arrived home, Genesis thanked Nina and went to bed early. Alone in her kitchen preparing for Sunday brunch, Nina thought about the commitment she had made to work with those two other women. It was holding, but only just. She could not trust Tess again after letting Genesis run wild that night. And why would G tell Tess about when she was in foster care? She'd never spoken about that time! Then there was Lizzie. Mostly she just seemed immature, flip-flopping all over the place. Was there something more? Something she was hiding?

Nina continued mincing onions and parsley. She was only interested in Lizzie inasmuch as she affected G, and these days G seemed to be enjoying Lizzie's company. She threw the onions into the bowl of flaked codfish. If Lizzie was on the whole a good influence, then she could stay. But if the unstable outweighed the good, she would find a way to ease her out of G's orbit.

Genesis

'That's it, Genesis,' he says. 'You've just solved the last problem. Of the last class.' He looks over his glasses.

'Yes. Monday's the exam. I think I'm ready. Thanks.' I wish I could say thank you properly… like I meant it, which I do.

'Don't mention it.'

The way he says it proves my point. When I say thank you, he hears thank God it's over. I want to say something to fill the big space in the room.

'Yeah. But it' not over for me. I need to do my SATs again in July…'

'Do you need any extra help for that? I don't mind...'

'No. It's OK. I'll use the workbooks... If I get a higher grade in math, I'll be able to get into this college they want me to go to.'

He doesn't say anything.

'What?'

'Isn't it time...' he says in his "this-is-important" voice, 'you started making your own decisions?'

'Excuse me? I always make my own decisions.' I glare at him but we both know it's not serious. 'I said I wanted to go to college. I was busy with my exams. So they did the research. Tess mainly. Showed me everything on the website. Looked cool.'

Again, silence.

'Tess said she'll pay.'

'Good old Tess.'

He's starting to piss me off. 'Yes! Good old Tess! You think I could even buy toilet paper without her?'

Then I remember the thing in the bottom of my bag. 'Here.' I pass him the package. He goes red, all butterfingers as he opens it.

'It's...'

'You like it?'

He doesn't raise his head. All I see is his hair falling over his forehead. And his hand moving over the blank pages of the book.

'Tess helped me choose it.' Talking fast. 'Now you can do all your drawings in it. Instead of messing up your place with piles of these!' I take a drawing from his desk – a view from his window. The words come out slowly as my finger traces lines on his drawing, appreciating it. 'I used to like to draw. Until somebody said it was...'

'Said it was what?'

I want to kick myself. 'Nothing.'

'What did they say? Tell me.'

'I'd never liked drawing before, then I did and used to do it all the time. One night the lady I was staying with wanted me to go to bed early... But I wanted to finish my drawing. She picked up my picture, said it was stupid and tore it up.'

When he doesn't say anything, I feel stupid again. Like all those years ago.

'Genesis, you're the most un-stupid person I've ever known.'

I begin to laugh. 'Un-stupid? That's supposed to be a compliment?' That serious-nerdy look in his eyes disappears and by the time we reach the door, he's laughing too.

'By the way, I'm starting what you said I should do.'

'What's that?'

'I'm going to write an article about what the finding of the Gurnet Rock cedar root means. Like you said I should.' And then with a chuckle, he says, 'Not very politely, if I recall.'

'What are you going to do with it? Put it in the paper?'

'Maybe.' He's looking at me, smiling.

'But, Teach, that's not what I said! Not some big-word article that nobody will read. You need to...' I'm working out what I want to say while I'm saying it. And working out whether I'm angry or not. 'It has to be for kids! Kids like me. Like I was. Has to be something they can see. With pictures. If you do it right, they'll understand! They're... un-stupid. Like me!'

He doesn't say anything but looks down at the notebook I gave him, turning it over and over. 'You're right. You're right, Genesis.' He holds up the book. 'It's beautiful, by the way. Thank you.' My cheeks start burning – the way he said it.

Suddenly all his attention switches to something floating in the water. Looks like a branch to me.

'Here.' He pushes the journal into my hand and starts stripping. Glasses, shoes, shirt, vest. Keep going, keep going... He stops. Damn!

'If it gets over there, we've lost it...'

Next thing I know he's running along the dock and I'm trying to keep up with him.

There he goes. A running jump overboard. It's a whole month before the twenty-fourth of May holiday – a month before any sane Bermudian goes into the sea. Doesn't he know? How could he? Look at him. Teach thinks he's some sort of Superhero... And what's he rescuing? An oar! Might as well sit down and watch the show.

Hmmmm! Damp. And splinters? Tess, you really need to do something about this dock. Looking down between the boards is scary. Deep water... Where is he? I hate it when they dive and stay under so long! Hate that shadow moving under the water. There! He's coming up for air, then away again. One arm up and over, the other one up and over... Head down, arm over, head to the side. Makes it look so easy...

U used to swim like that. Used to. I guess he still does. *He* won't be in the sea yet. Funny the kind of things he was strict about. No swimming until May twenty-fourth. No weed until five p.m. He was... how would Nina say it... *intransigent*. Yes. He was intransigent! Was? He still is everything he always was. Just somewhere else. Where I don't get to talk to him. Or see him smile... Can't go back there. Nearly lost it that night. Nearly lost everything. Nina's right. Prospects! That's what I have now. I'm going somewhere. Where I'm going, U can't come...

He's got it! *Yay, Teach!* He must think why's she waving like a fool... He's got hold of the oar and is hauling it back to land. Boy's got some serious muscle. Can see it from here. Different altogether from U. U's strong, too, but doesn't look it. Looks skinny but you touch his arm and you're touching iron. That night when we were dancing, I could feel the iron running the length of his body, but mixed with something really soft, something that *gave* when you moved close to it... You're one crazy bitch. Crazy to dance with him like that. Not U from down the hall at the Robinson Home!

No splash, just a couple of ripples as he moves towards the place where the water's suddenly light blue. Where his precious punt is. Punt. You have to be careful how you say that word. Truly. It's a real Teach kinda word. Straight and weird at the same time... So why does he keep asking to teach me over the summer when today is supposed to be our last class?

I shut my eyes. Oh, the sun feels good. A red blur through my eyelids.

Can't explain what's happening. Where did that business about Miss Audrey tearing up my picture come from? Haven't thought about that for years. I don't think about these things. Or I didn't. Seems like I do now. Not so long ago, I told Tess about when those Tuckers took me to eat at the Seahorse. That same night Old Man Tucker tried something with me... I've seen all those people who messed with me when I was young. Seen them lots of times in town, on the bus, all over. It's like I never laid eyes on them before. They've been so gone from inside me. Until now. Any idiot – Tess, now Teach – anybody can just tap me on the back and out comes this stuff I'm not supposed to remember...

Red mist in front of my eyelids... Peaceful. I can hear a little splashing sound moving in the direction of the strip of sand where the punt is. Teach. He's not that bad. Truly. But I can't let him start getting into my business. That can't happen. And... he's starting to give me that look. A few minutes ago, I swear I saw that look. Like he's seeing me naked. He never used to look at me like that. No. That's all I need...

I open my eyes and see him pulling the oar across the sand. He looks back and sees a white plastic bag floating in the water. Boy Scout goes in to get it and I close my eyes again. A cloud must've gone over the sun because the red mist is gone. All I can see is that white plastic bag floating on the water. I feel my stomach getting tight. Tighter... A knot that's hurting me. The plastic bag looks like white fabric floating on the water... and underneath the water there's a shadow...

I gasp. Jump to my feet and almost lose my balance, almost fall in. What the fuck...? I look out again, knowing it's just a plastic bag. Teach is back in the water again, swimming towards the dock. I'm so glad to see him! He's real. Not some crazy thing in my head. I wave to him and when he gets to the steps of the dock and sees my face, he does a giant belly-buster and wets me up completely – including my hair – then starts swimming up and down in front of me. He's on his back, beating his arms like they're flippers. Dives down so all I can see are his white heels, rolls over like a dolphin...

Every now and then, his head comes above water and he shouts out, 'I can teach you how to do this!' Then down he goes.

I keep telling him he's one crazy fool and every time I say this, the tightness in my stomach starts to loosen. He keeps going, splashing me whenever he can, disappearing for a moment, then up he comes again. 'I can teach you. Maths. Swimming. Anything you like.'

Gone again. Up he comes, his hair plastered to his head, a serious-funny look on his face. 'Say yes. That's all. I dare you.'

He goes under one last time, streaking away from the dock. I don't feel good until I see him come up again, see him turn and head for the dock. He does this big act of being too tired to get up the steps. I go over and stretch out my hand. He takes it. I try to pull him up but I can't move him.

'Not until you say yes.' Our hands are pulling in opposite directions. A little more effort from him and I'll be going overboard. But he doesn't. He waits.

The sun comes out from behind the clouds and I feel it go right through my body.

'Yes.'

'I can't hear you!'

'Yes!'

CHAPTER 10: FULL OF GRACE

Hugh

'When will we get there?'

The question dragged Hugh from thoughts of Genesis and made him look around. Behind him lay the island, still visible, ahead, an empty blue horizon. He looked to see what the other people on the boat were doing. Simmons, of course, was at the wheel. But, as a moving part of *Miranda*, he hardly counted. It was the two children who caught his eye. One aloft on the bridge, a small burst of electricity next to the stolid figure of Simmons; one astern, having just come to sit by him. One, the grandson of the person who steered, moored, swabbed, scraped, painted and polished the boat. The other, the granddaughter of the person who owned it.

School was out and by the end of June the boy needed looking after by his grandfather until summer day-camp began. The girl, on holiday on the island, was being looked after by Tess while her parents spent the weekend in New York, seeing a show. Both eight years old and keeping as far away from each other as possible.

'Will we get there soon?'

Hugh looked down at her wide-brimmed hat and felt a surge of annoyance. It really was too much! As usual, this babysitting gig for Tess had been a last-minute thing. For the past week, he had been busy with work and evening swimming lessons with Genesis. He had been only vaguely aware of the dinners and the outings laid on by Tess to entertain her first-born, Charlie, visiting from London with his family. The wife – whom Hugh had identified as high-maintenance – had decided she wanted to see the Broadway revival of *Nine* and that was that. They would spend the weekend in New York and Grandma Tess would look after Isla. He'd become involved when the phone had rung before seven that morning. Tess. She had to spend the day raising money to prevent one of her clients being hauled off to prison for non-payment of bills.

'Please, Hugh. Help me out. I trust Simmons completely and Isla is a good little snorkeller. But she's shy and she'll feel more at home with you.'

A glorious Saturday and a swimming lesson with G down the drain. Added to that, children made him nervous.

'Soon,' he said to the child. 'We'll get there soon. Fifteen, maybe twenty minutes...'

A pair of grey eyes looked Hugh squarely in the face. He shifted in his seat, trying to hide his surprise. Everything was so familiar – the light brown tendrils escaping from the hat, the determined mouth, the pale arms and legs... The voice was different, with its clipped accent and without the Welsh music. But the child undoubtedly reminded him of someone else. Someone from the past. Kate.

'You're not scared, are you?' he asked.

'No,' the little girl said. 'Daddy brought us out here last summer. I remember seeing the fish.' She frowned as she took her mask out of the bag next to her. 'I... don't remember going... so far away from land.' She fingered the bright pink band around the back of the mask. She added, 'Can hardly see it.'

Hugh glanced back and saw the receding contours of the island. He slid along the cushion until he was only inches away from her.

'You liked the fish?' His tone was kind.

'Yes.' Her head was down, her voice a whisper.

'Well then...' He bent over, getting next to her ear. 'You won't see the best fish when you're close to land. You have to go out far – to the reef.'

She looked up and gave him a triumphant smile. 'I'll tell Daddy that!'

Hugh was powerless against that smile.

'Want to see my things?' She upended her bag and passed her pink snorkel and flippers to him for examination. As she rambled on, without needing him to make any response, he thought of Kate, his first love. His first heartache.

Best friends who'd blossomed into childhood sweethearts in a rainy Welsh village and beyond. It had seemed an obvious truth that they would grow old together. It had been a long time since Hugh had thought about her in such a concrete way. Usually, it was an involuntary tightening of the chest, a feeling without either shape or name... So much life had intervened.

The noise of the engine changed and Hugh felt rather than saw that the boat was no longer chugging along but was involved in slow and subtle manoeuvring on the smooth immensity of water.

'Hey, Doc. Put her in reverse!'

Only Simmons called him Doc.

Hugh hustled towards the steering panel. On his way, he bumped into the little boy, flying down the steps. The child's explosive energy made Hugh stop short. He had what Hugh considered 'that island look' – eyes a mixture of green and gold, rusty brown hair halfway between curl and kink and skin the colour of fresh brown bread. Without actually pushing Hugh aside, the boy streaked into the cabin in a whoosh of turbulent air.

'Come on, Papa!' he called, reappearing with his mask and one flipper on. He flopped down on the rear seat to put the other one on. Isla beat a hasty retreat to the far end of the seat.

Simmons came and gave Hugh instructions. The time would be divided in two – Hugh would go in with the children for the first session while he kept the boat parked nearby, then they would make the switch. Hugh took his place at the back and leaned over. They were in very deep water, calm, dark blue. A few meters away lurked the shadow of the reef.

They dropped into the ocean, first Hugh, falling in, almost with a sigh; then the girl, in a flurry of pink flippers; finally, the boy, making a huge splash.

They were immediately surrounded by long grey fish, shadowlike, on their way somewhere. Swift and fearless, they moved about the boat and the swimmers, seeing but not acknowledging them, focused on their unseen destination. Within moments, they were gone. At that first contact, both children made a rush towards Hugh, the boy bumping up against his left flank and the girl grabbing his right arm. He shut his eyes and counted to twenty and when he opened them, the children were doing as he had hoped – bobbing in the water and getting used to the new reality.

He took the lead, flippers moving gently, his snorkel a periscope. The children swam on either side of him, while the dark, indistinct shapes of the underwater mountain became more and more clear.

At first the reef seemed made of hard rock but Hugh pointed to soft round domes, crowned by frail, brilliantly coloured arms waving in the current. Spread out beneath them like the canopy of a forest was a patchwork of forms, sometimes linked, sometimes separate, punctuated by wide, fathomless sand holes. The children started pointing to the weird shapes and textures in every colour imaginable – green, yellow, brown, pink, purple. Soon they stopped pointing as school upon school of fish came to call. At one point, the boy seemed obliterated by an undulating curtain of electric purple that fell before him, each fish as tiny as his own thumb. A family of orange and black clownfish danced around the girl, before carrying on their way. Hugh was trailed by a solitary angel fish whose translucent fins made a faint fluttering along his thigh.

They could hear the comforting hum of *Miranda*, always there, sliding back and forwards on the slight swell, keeping close, keeping them safe. When the horn sounded, they swam back to the boat. Hugh climbed aboard while the children bobbed in the water. Simmons put on his own gear. The children talked in excited voices.

'Three parrot fish followed me. Great big ones. One blue, one green, one pink. They was wicked!'

'Bet you didn't see that big jelly fish...'

'What you mean? Sure I did!'

'And what about them co'pollies! Never seen so many...'

'Co'pollies? Which ones are they?'

'Yellow and black striped. They was all around you.'

'You mean the sergeant majors!'

'Sergeant major for you. Co'polly for me!'

'Enough!' Simmons said with a laugh. 'Give us another half an hour,' he told Hugh. 'Man overboard!' Simmons cannonballed into the water. When the children stopped squealing, they swam to the reef in formation.

Hugh put the boat into a gentle reverse and positioned it so that he could see the others with ease. They were now over the reef and he could tell that the children now felt part of the underwater world. He moved the boat forward as the swell, as slight as it was, drifted it away. Keeping the boat just at the lip of the reef was all he had to do. Now that he had no children to look after, his thoughts wandered to something he had seen below, out of the corner of his eye. It was far down, emerging from an immense fissure in the rock. At first, there had only been a shiver in the sand. Then it appeared, a great, dark winged creature, flying slowly through the water. Majestic in its black cloak, with a hint of danger. A manta ray. Monarch in the kingdom of grace.

He looked at his watch and sounded the horn. Simmons and the children headed for the boat. All of a sudden, the boy started to gesticulate wildly, pointing at something below. The children shot forward churning the water with their flippers, as if to overtake Simmons.

'Shark, Papa! Shark!' the boy cried, ripping off his mask.

'Shark?' echoed the little girl, her voice full of excited panic. She glanced over at the boy. 'Shark!' This time, the panic was real.

Simmons turned. 'Okay. Okay, Akeem. Calm down.' Simmons reached the stern and grabbed hold of the steel steps.

'Doc!' Simmons called, grasping the girl by the waist. 'Give me a hand!' Hugh leaned over, caught her under her outstretched arms and bundled her in. Then he hauled up the boy.

Simmons heaved himself onto the deck. Panting and streaming with water, the children threw their arms around him and would not let him go until their breath had returned to normal.

Hugh handed out towels and Simmons started to rub down his grandson. 'A shark and a rockfish,' he said gravely. 'Better learn the difference.' With a smile, he turned to the girl. 'Both of you.'

It took an hour for *Miranda* to get back to the dock at Sweet Airs. Hugh's babysitting duties were over for the girl was now aloft, sitting between Simmons and the boy. There was plenty of chatter and laughter up there. At the stern, Hugh was content to sit and contemplate the retreating blue world. Each time he entered that world, it was a revelation. He remembered the day he and Buddy had gone out far beyond today's reef, to a place where yet another seamount fell sheer into some of the deepest ocean in the world. The water there had been warm, like today's, of a perfect clarity, a deep cobalt blue, and bounded only by the sky.

He thought of Genesis. How wonderful it would be to swim with her in water like that.

The altered drone of the engine told him that they had reached home. Tess was on the dock to greet them, full of embraces and exclamations at the adventures of the day.

Hugh turned to take his leave.

'Bye, Hugh,' the little girl said as she took her grandmother's hand.

'Bye, Isla,' he replied.

Under the shower in his apartment, he thought of the little drama of pulling the children up into the boat. What was it that he'd seen in that bright sunlight? There was something... He chuckled. It was Isla's arm. It bore the birthmark. The family brand.

Nina

On the last Sunday morning of June, Nina found Genesis sampling some of the dishes ranged along the kitchen counter.

'Morning,' Genesis said, licking her fingers. 'You're early.' She pointed to the clock: eight-thirty. 'All dressed and going to your... mystery place.'

Nina laughed. 'No mystery today. I'm going to Sharon's baptism.'

'Which Sharon?'

'My niece Sharon. Janet's oldest.'

'Isn't she... like... in her forties?'

'Thirty-nine.'

'Not too old?'

'Not for this. A baptism. Not a christening.'

Genesis shrugged. 'All this Christian stuff... I don't get it.'

Nina propped herself on a kitchen stool. 'Listen. I'm telling you this as someone who's been in this Christian stuff, as you call it, all my life. Who's been completely sure... until... These days I'm not as sure as I used to be.

'Anyway, here goes. Sharon is being baptized with water and the Holy Spirit because she has taken Jesus Christ as her personal saviour and wants to be born again in his blood.'

'Right.'

'She wants her life to be different. You can see why.'

'Sharon. Isn't she the one with the three kids?'

'And three fathers and no husband and a job at the checkout counter. That Sharon.' Nina sighed. 'She's tried a lot of things to get her life in order but since she joined Elder Zuill's church, she really does seem a lot better.' She stood up. 'That's why I'm going. For her and my sister.' She picked up her keys. 'When they baptise her, I want to be there.'

She was at the door when she heard quick footsteps behind her.

'Can I come?'

Nina was taken aback. Months of invitations to religious services of all kinds had been politely and not so politely declined.

Fifteen minutes later, Nina and Genesis were following a group of people through windblown shoreline bushes onto a beach, removing their shoes as they walked.

The white glare of the sun struck their eyes as they emerged from the undergrowth and saw the sea before them. The air was already hot but the sand was still cool underfoot. A line of worshippers headed towards an escarpment that rose out of the sea, providing an emphatic fullstop to the beach. There was an opening in the limestone spur and when Nina and Genesis ducked through it, they found themselves in a space very different from the bright blue water and broad curve of pink sand behind them. A fragmented circle of rock surrounded a tiny bay. The congregation stood on the sand and looked out at water so protected from the open ocean that it rose and fell as though barely breathing, while a wall of boulders broke the back of the ocean waves before allowing them to slip into the cove. There was no glare here. A filtered light placed the water at the green end of aquamarine.

'They're wearing white,' Genesis whispered.

'Yes,' Nina whispered back. 'The saints wear white.'

'The what...?'

A couple of women behind them started humming. As the humming grew louder, those in white took up position by the edge of the water, then formed a double line on either side of the entrance to the cove. Those few wearing colours – which seemed outlandish in this setting – slotted themselves in where they could.

'Nina! this way!' The girl's voice was urgent. 'I want to see!' Genesis dragged Nina to a place just beyond the water line that would afford them a good view.

The saints began to sing and in the natural amphitheatre formed by the rocks, their voices hung clear and sweet above the pulse of the surf. Nina closed her eyes and saw herself holding her own mother's hand on another beach, at another time, hearing the words of the same song.

Take me to the water

The voices were accompanied by slow, rhythmic clapping.

'They're coming!' Genesis whispered. But Nina's eyes were already on the group moving between the double line, led by two women of God in white garments. Their powerful voices amplified the sound echoing around the circle of rock and water.

Take me to the water, Jesus

Then came Sharon's three children, two looking shy, one wearing a beaming smile, followed by their grandmother, Janet, her head slightly bowed. Nina took a deep breath and joined in the singing.

Take me to the water

The Elder was next in black vestments. When he raised his arms, Genesis thought of the outstretched wings of a large black bird. After him came Sharon, wearing a white robe, her head tied in a white cloth. Her shoulders were shuddering, as though her head was too heavy to raise.

'Why is she…?'

Nina took her hand, squeezed it and carried on singing.

Take me to the water and baptize me!

The voices of the saints filled the place. The Elder raised his hand for silence.

'Let us pray. Father God, we gather in this your holy place this morning to praise your name, Amen, and glorify your Creation, Amen. The sky over our heads, Amen, and the sand beneath our feet,

Amen, and the great ocean that girdles your entire world. They all proclaim the glory of your holy name, Amen. But even in the magnificence of your works, Amen, you are a God of compassion whose eye is on the sparrow. The sparrow that is about to fall! You lift her up in your everlasting arms. You do not let her fall. As we come here this morning, Amen, we ask your blessing on your servant, Sharon, as her old life drowns and is gone. As she is born again into the sanctified life of the spirit, through blood and water, Amen, and through the fire and spirit of your only Son, Jesus Christ, our strength and our redeemer. Amen.

'Let the congregation say Amen!'

'AMEN!'

The Elder handed his bible to one of the saints, entered the water and walked until he was in waist high. He motioned to the others.

The humming started again and the circle tightened at the water's edge. People, eyes closed, began swaying. Now the clapping grew louder, faster. A feeling that Nina hadn't felt for years stole through her body and she too closed her eyes and started to sway.

The two women attending Sharon took her by the hand and led her in. With every step towards the Elder, the shuddering of her shoulders lessened. The cove rang with the clapping and the singing of the saints. By the time she reached him, she was calm.

The Elder raised both arms and stillness replaced song. 'Daughter, do you love the Lord and take Him as your personal Saviour?'

'Yes, I do.'

'Do you believe that by this water you will be saved and all your sins washed away?'

'Yes, I do.'

The Elder put one arm around Sharon's shoulder and each woman placed one hand in the middle of her back. Sharon held her nose and closed her eyes. On the shore, Nina saw Janet restrain one of her grandchildren.

'In the name of the Father, Son and Holy Spirit...' Sharon looked towards heaven and leaned backwards onto the supporting arms. 'I baptize you.' She disappeared beneath the water, her white gown floating out around her.

Nina felt fingers digging into her hand and saw that Genesis had turned her face away from the water.

'You all right?' Nina asked. Genesis had turned back to watch wide-eyed as Sharon's streaming head and shoulders broke the surface of the water.

'Drowned with Him in baptism. Raised with Him in eternal life!'

The saints burst into praise-song, a host of arms reaching for the sky. Sharon embraced the man and women who had baptized her and began to walk towards the shore, the water pulling her back, making every step an act of will. Her face was like another sun, dark and radiant. Her youngest child broke free of the restraining arms and ran towards her. Sharon was crying again, crying and laughing at the same time, hugging her children, her sobbing mother and as many of the saints as she could, as many who didn't mind getting wet.

Nina waited her turn, then took her niece into her arms.

'A new life, Sharon. Never turn away from it.'

Nina sensed Genesis hovering at her side. She turned and saw that the girl's face was streaked with tears.

'My goodness,' she said gently, stroking the girl's cheek. 'This is what happens, G. Sometimes the spirit just gets you.'

'No!' With her face still wet, Genesis looked Nina squarely in the eye. ' Not the spirit. Allergies! It's that time of year.'

Nina watched as the girl strode rapidly out of the baptismal bay.

Genesis

I thought... I thought... it was goin to be a christening...

I been to one christening before. Somebody took me – can't even remember who. But there was a baby in a frilly dress and a pastor and a few drops of water from a bowl. That's it!

I thought it would be like that. They would just have it here on a pretty beach, a nice background and someone would get a bowl of sea water and put a few drops on Sharon's head... take pictures.

Then I saw that preacher walkin into the water, walkin like

Uncle Jack does early in the mornin, with all his clothes on, walkin like he can walk right out to the horizon. Then the preacher's callin to Sharon to come.

Didn't think they would try to drown her! I woulda never gone I woulda never gone... And Nina's all spaced out, like I'd dropped out of the universe for her... Singin and hummin and swayin like a crazy person.

I can't look! Can't look at that white robe goin under.

Suddenly, outta the corner of my eye, I see him. Her child. The only other one, like me, who thinks she won't come up outta that water. He wants to run, get Sharon, but he's too small and someone's holdin him back, something's holdin him back. I can see him cryin and I can feel him cryin because he can't go and get his mama...

Then it's over. Sharon didn drown and everyone's makin a pack a noise. Everybody's happy, even the little boy huggin his mama. And Nina's she's... talkin her stuff.

I think Nina'll be mad at me. Or sad. But I can't help that! She didn protect me today, just when I thought I could trust her. She didn protect me!

Lizzie

Avémariacheiadegraçaosenhoréconvosco...

The high summer sun beat down on the faithful. Lizzie could hear Avó quietly intoning the familiar undifferentiated string of sound as they crossed the square. Despite the scrape of shoe leather against cobblestones, despite the murmur of Portuguese rippling through the crowd ahead of them, she could still hear her grandmother's voice.

'...among women. Blessed is the fruit of thy womb...'

As they entered the narrow lane, Avó stumbled; Lizzie steadied her, saw the look of gratitude but her lips still moving without the slightest pause.

Lizzie gripped her grandmother's elbow and guided her forward, passing the white stone Madonna and child gazing out on the line of trees that separated them from a view of the sea. She couldn't believe she was really there – publicly identifying herself with her community, going to church when it was not strictly required by family protocol, taking on the role of her grandmother's protector... It was not like her at all. But then, events had conspired to bring her here, walking with the faithful.

The rest of the family – who would usually have been conspicuously celebrating one of the great feast days – had been at the hospital from the moment they'd received the call that her brother and his wife's baby, the first grandchild of João and Ines, was on its way. Lizzie had been roped in to take Avó to the feast of the Holy Spirit. *La festa do Espirito Santo.* She had not resisted. She preferred the heat of July to the labour ward.

And, besides, after the conversation on the way to the *festa*, everything was different between herself and Avó...

★

In the car, Avó had been more talkative than Lizzie could ever remember. Memories of the Holy Spirit *festas* in Açores and her observations of life in Bermudas over the years.

'Now we have our *festas*, we walk with our banners, we do our dances in the square... Not like before.' She paused. 'Before,' she said in English and bent her head forward. 'It was head down.' She leaned further. 'Forget Açores.'

Lizzie remembered their last real conversation, before she had run out of the house on Easter Sunday. Could she raise the subject of what had happened to her when she was seventeen?

'It's true. It's official. We exist. Avó, back then, when you were young, were we... the families... the neighbours... were we as scared of... scandal... as we are now?'

Avó's animation subsided and she seemed preoccupied with her hands.

'We always fear scandal, Elisabete.' She raised one hand. 'Since ...' The hand waved backwards, to the beginning of time.

'What happened to me back then...' No time to weigh her words or even know if her Portuguese was correct. Her heart was thumping. 'I was seventeen... and pregnant.' She stopped dead. 'The scandal would have killed my mother.' Lizzie's hands were sweaty on the steering wheel as she cornered. '...And my father. Would have destroyed us all.' She gave Avó a wan smile. 'But I turned out OK, didn't I?'

Silence again as the car skirted a bright lagoon.

'How did you know, Avó? I'm sure my mother didn't tell you.'

'No. No-one told me. Not even my son.' Her head shook slightly. 'But for a week, there was something… heavy in the air. I heard Ines crying. I heard you throw up twice. Your father didn't come to see me for three days. Then you and your mother were going on a trip. Your father said you were going to see a school. But he wouldn't look me in the eye when he told me.'

'Poor Dad!'

'But I only knew for sure when you came back a week later. The laughing Elisabete – the bright light in the family – was gone and someone else had come back in her place. That's when I knew.'

Lizzie's hands tightened on the steering wheel and she counted backwards.

'But, in the end, it was for the best,' she said. 'I was too young to be a mother, Avó.'

'I had my first child at sixteen.'

Lizzie had expected that. Talk of the sins of fornication and murder. But she knew she had to talk to somebody.

'Things were different then, Avó.' Feeling a little calmer, Lizzie pushed on. 'But scandal. That's still the thing we fear most. You said so yourself. And the boy. He was not one of us.'

'He was *negro*?'

'No.'

'I always thought he was *negro*!'

'Well he wasn't. He wasn't Portuguese. He wasn't Catholic. He hadn't done a day's work in his life. He wasn't one of us.'

'And he wasn't *negro*!'

Lizzie almost laughed at how amazed Avó was.

'His parents were rich and he got anything he wanted. Including me.' Lizzie slowed down as she approached a pedestrian crossing. 'I tried to be good, Avó, but the night when it happened, was the night before he went away to college. It was really exciting!'

Avó made three swift signs of the cross and kept her head down.

'I was punished all right. That night was the beginning and the end. End of the boy, who never came back to Bermuda. And end of the excitement.'

'Because the boy didn't come back?'

'No. The end of feeling anything. With any man.'

Avó made another sign of the cross, this time slowly, her hands trembling, not able to look at Lizzie's face.

'I could never separate having…' Lizzie caught her breath. 'Having sex with…' She heard her grandmother gasp but she kept going, 'With the… the abortion and everything I went through after that.'

Lizzie pulled over into a bus stop, glancing in her mirror to check a bus wasn't coming. She faced Avó. 'You know what it's like in that house. I am guilty whatever I do. Half of me believes it was the right thing to do. The other half, the half that doesn't believe in God…' Lizzie forced herself to look at her grandmother when she said this. 'The other half thinks that I lost a part of myself that I can never get back.'

Avó was holding her rosary beads, her eyes fixed on them.

'The last half thinks I'll go to hell. What do you think, Avó?'

'I'm not a scholar, Elisabete, but I think there are too many halves!' They both raised a smile. 'The Church is clear about these things. No "sex"…' She whispered the word in English. '…except when you're married and no "abortion"…' Also in English. 'Ever.'

Lizzie sat motionless.

'The Holy Father tells us this and he is next to Saint Peter, in a line straight to God.' Avó sat back. 'But, you know, I have spent so many years in that house, in the house of Ines, and have had plenty of time to think about things. I was seventh of thirteen children. One day, when our mother was just too tired to wake up, she just didn't. And I remember little girls, twelve years old, who died bearing the children of grown men, important men of the district.

'When I have been in my little room thinking of these things, I say to myself, Sao Pedro and the Holy Father, they are men.' Avó stretched her spine. 'What do they know of us women?'

Lizzie looked across at Avó, wide-eyed. Her grandmother was a subversive!

★

When she entered the church with Avó and the crowd of worshippers, she expected a dark cloud to descend upon her as it usually did when she went to mass. But this time she felt an easing of the tightness in her chest that had stalked her for years. The familiarity of the ritual was soothing. She didn't ask herself whether she believed in it or not, just accepted that it was part of her.

Outside, Lizzie placed her hand on the stone Madonna and followed her gaze through the curtain of trees to the open ocean. She would have been able to see the whales when they passed in springtime; she would have heard her great-great-grandfather call out *Baleia Baleia* in the early morning. Lizzie smiled at Avó as she settled her in a shady spot and ran to join the procession.

The scarlet cloaks, the little girls clutching their flowers, the undulating silken banners, the crowned child, the glittering sceptre, the marching band... they pulsated around her as she moved with them through the lanes and alleys of the old town. The sights and sounds entered into her and nudged away her pain.

In the town square, she was part of a large crowd applauding dancers on a wooden stage. Someone was singing a haunting melody while the dancers performed. Women wearing coloured headscarves and white embroidered blouses held out wide, aproned skirts as they spun. Men, sober in black and white, stayed close to their partners, sometimes clasping their hands behind their backs, sometimes raising their arms, sometimes clapping. Occasionally, a man proffered his shoulder for a woman to place her hand on. Lizzie smiled at the courtliness of the gesture. When she saw it again, her hand flew to her chest. The light touch on the shoulder. So intimate!

She looked across to see Avó sitting on the other side of the square, talking companionably to some other old ladies. Their talk in the car had been so rich, so revealing – so overdue. She passed through the crowd, glad to be among them, glad that she had been made to learn the language. She was rehearsing what she would say to Avó: *So you want a woman Pope. But beware! I know who would put herself forward*. She would pause for five seconds. *Ines!*

By the time she reached Avó, she was laughing so hard she couldn't say anything.

'She's back,' Avó said softly. 'The laughing Elisabete.'

CHAPTER 11: TREASURE

Hugh

With one hand, Hugh cupped it and felt its weight; he trailed the fingers of his other hand along its grooves, ridges and valleys. The most perfect specimen of brain coral that he'd ever seen. None of the other things in this room – the gems, the fragments of pottery, the bits of ballast, even the photograph of a fabulous jewelled cross, all plucked out of the sea by Buddy – none of these had the same effect on him as this did. Every visit to Buddy's house, he found a moment to marvel at this coral, the remains of a community of living creatures but to the unschooled eye, a stone.

Buddy had gone to take Brian and the other scientists visiting from Boston back to their hotel. 'Hold on till I get back,' he'd said on his way out. Seemed like Buddy wanted to see his first attempts at animation... He was sorry he'd mentioned it. Now that Buddy knew about it, there would be no going back.

With the coral still in his hand, Hugh stepped out onto the verandah. It was almost nine o'clock, the light was starting to fade but he could still see a few stalwarts taking their last swim in the bay. Buddy's boat, 'Miss Molly', rocked lazily by the dock. His mind wandered back to when, in a homemade costume in front of the assembled school, he'd held a plastic skull and mangled some famous lines from Hamlet and prayed to be spirited away to the science lab. So long ago!

When he looked out again, it was utterly dark. The swiftness of it still took him by surprise. He sat in a chair, closed his eyes and waited for Buddy to return.

His thoughts drifted towards Genesis. Her first lesson in the water was over a month ago. This is how you float. Put your head back. Relax. The water will keep you up. All he could see were her eyes. Her face seemed swallowed by them – wide open, pleading, trying to overcome her fear, failing, giving up, trying again. All he could feel was her skin as she lay in his arms just at the surface, her skin like silk, cool like river water, a river of black silk.

Hugh shifted in the chair and forced his thoughts somewhere else. A different face. A different pair of eyes. Grey. Untroubled. Encouraging, even after his disastrous Shakespeare performance in front of the school.

Kate had moved into his neighbourhood when they were both eight and from that moment on his place as top of the form was no longer assured. At first people thought they were fierce rivals but soon saw that it wasn't a real competition – just mutual pleasure in the same things. They helped each other on the rare occasions when they were not in sync – she loved Shakespeare and hated French, the opposite of him. But their hearts lay in science and when they decided to go to the same university, family and friends on both sides assumed that it could only end in marriage.

Their futures seemed assured. They had their work. They had each other. They'd grown up together; each had been witness to the other's changing body, developing mind. When their friendship entered a new phase, they were shy with each other and very tender. It was as it was supposed to be. As Hugh thought about those times, he felt an ache in his chest.

Five months into their final year, Kate met Max, the wild man of the campus. Rich, posh, charming. A womaniser, a boozer, an experimenter with mind-expanding substances, an indifferent student... In a cataclysm of passion, rage, amazement, class warfare and tears, Kate had fallen from grace into the arms of someone who, six years later, Hugh still thought of as a predator.

He'd only seen her once since then, a week before he'd left for Bermuda. She was married – but not to Max. She had got back on track academically and was working as a researcher for a pharmaceutical company. She'd confided to Hugh that what she and her husband wanted most was to start a family. He could see she was happy and was glad.

He looked out into the dark. The chorus of whistling frogs swelled around him, drowning out the lapping water. It astonished him how creatures so tiny could fill a whole night with their music.

It all connected to Genesis. The darkness. The fragrance. The mystery... He didn't want what had happened to Kate to happen to him. To be overwhelmed by some irresistible force. To lose everything you thought yourself to be in some... madness. He thought of Max and the tales of his legendary prowess – and his own tentative and inexperienced lovemaking with Kate. There'd been such unbearable sweetness. When the first shock of Kate's defection had worn off, he had grimly set about rewriting history. No pleasure there, just a necessary exercise to staunch the wound. It would take time for the trauma of Kate to retreat. A few years and relationships later, he felt like a man again. Until now.

Was she a female version of Max? Without the money, of course. The way she walked... All bounce and uncorked energy. As graceful as a sleek black cat. At home in her body. Unaware of its power. Or was she?

'What you doing out here in the dark?'

'Oh, sorry, Buddy. I didn't hear you!' Hugh scraped his hair back off his brow and tried not to look flustered. He picked up the coral, as though for protection.

Buddy leaned on the railing for just a moment. 'Pretty, eh?' Then he turned his back on the bay. 'Let's see the thing you did on the computer.'

Seated at the large dining-room table, Hugh opened his laptop and clicked on an icon. The title page appeared: *The Day the Cedars Drowned*.

'Like I said, it's just an outline... An unfinished outline.'

'It's all right. It's fine. Just get it going.'

'OK.' Hugh's finger hovered over the mouse. 'As I said when the guys were here, the voice in the voice-over can't be mine. Can't be Welsh... obviously... Has to be a local voice. It's nowhere near being finished...'

Buddy put his hand on Hugh's shoulder. 'Stop apologizing.'

The screen filled with the image of a tree.

The Bermuda Cedar tree. This tree is endemic to our island. That means there's no tree exactly like it anywhere else and that it's been here for many hundreds of thousands of years. I'm sure you recognise it.

The single tree morphed into a stand of cedars.

You may have seen a group of cedars like this, near your house or on your way to school.

The stand multiplied into a grove.

You might not have seen as many as these unless you've been on a boat ride around the Great Sound and seen one of the few remaining cedar groves like the one on Gibbet Island.

The grove blossomed into a forest which filled the screen.

Even the oldest living person in Bermuda has never seen this – the cedar forest which used to cover the island from north to south, east to west.

The next image was of the island, seen from above, with no white roofs, no roads, just a green fish hook lying in a blue sea.

'Good... The last two are ...'

'Digital.'

'Of course. Straightforward intro. Something that kids can understand.'

Moving images now occupied the screen. *Miss Molly* was steaming across the Sound. Buddy gave a belly laugh as he saw himself at the helm. 'You never told me Brad Pitt would be starring!'

In 2002, Buddy Darrell, Bermuda's own famous marine scientist and treasure-hunter, made a great discovery...

'I think you should take out *scientist*...'

'Definitely not. Why do you think these guys from top universities come to see you? Because you're not a scientist?'

'Strictly speaking, no. Not like they are. Left school at sixteen... Can you go back?'

Hugh hit rewind.

...a great discovery. Thirty feet below Gurnet Rock, just beyond Castle Harbour, he found this strange-looking object.

The footage showed Buddy diving down and wrestling with something that looked like a great spider attached to the reef. It finally let go and began to rise to the surface.

'I always find this moment... spectacular.' Hugh's voice was hushed as he watched its eerie ascent. 'The past rising...'

'With all its secrets,' said Buddy.

The scene shifted to *Miss Molly* with the spider looking almost alive on deck.

It was the root of a cedar tree that had once flourished like the ones that you see on your way to school. Before it was covered up by the ocean.

'I'm not sure about this bit,' Hugh said. 'Don't think the transition into the science is smooth enough.'

I can hear you ask, 'How did that happen?' and maybe 'Why did it happen?' Let's try to answer the first question – how did it happen.

Hugh shook his head and looked away but Buddy Darrell seemed riveted as a hand came on screen.

Here is the underwater mountain – or the seamount – that we call Mount Bermuda. See how it's covered in cedar forests.

The hand drew a picture of a broad-based mountain coloured entirely in green.

And this is the Atlantic Ocean.

The hand drew a horizontal line and, in a flash, the base of the mountain was covered by the blue sea.

Now look what happened thousands of years later.

The hand took the blue pencil and moved it upward. All the green in its path was washed away by the rising water.

And look. It happened again.

The blue water mark ascended covering another slice of the mountain.

And again. Just over seven thousand years ago.

The blue pencil continued its march, obliterating more of the mountain until only a tiny green peak remained.

'Stop there!'

Buddy studied the image on the screen: the great seamount traversed by four blue lines, with the coral island at the top.

'Keep going.'

Seven thousand years ago, the reef at Gurnet Rock was land...

Here there was a shot of Buddy in his wetsuit trying to pry the root out of the reef...

And the root that Buddy Darrell pulled up belonged to a cedar tree growing in the open air.

...followed by a shot taken from the reef showing the distance between it and the hull of *Miss Molly*.

Hugh clicked on exit, returning to the screen that announced *The Day the Cedars Drowned*. He looked disconsolate.

'I told you it wasn't finished,' he said at last. 'Didn't even get to the bit about climate change... or how trees drown... or the three submerged coastlines you've found…' Hugh got up and started pacing. 'Or to the picture of Horseshoe Bay now and in a hundred years' time… I want to make it interactive so they can click a button and make the sea rise and fall…' He made a small helpless gesture with his hands. 'That's what I wanted! I'm doing the technical bits, like the animation, the hard way – trial and error…'

'Didn't I tell you to stop apologizing?' Buddy stood up and stretched. 'It's good. Or it will be good when it's finished.'

Hugh sat down again, hunched over. Without looking at him, he said, 'I'm not sure, Buddy. You don't have to be kind…'

'Nobody's accused me of that before.' He drew up a chair, chuckling. 'What you are trying to do is wonderful. It's all very well having wine and cheese parties to get people to come to the museum to see it…'

Hugh snorted, remembering the well-heeled crowd at the unveiling of the root.

'What you're doing is going out to children and explaining it to them. In a way that they'll understand. We need the children – not just in the $15,000 a year schools…' Buddy stabbed the table with his finger. 'All the children. They need to understand their world. If we can't get it through their parents' thick skulls, we can try with the children.' Buddy leaned back again. 'I think it's a fantastic idea!'

Hugh smiled. 'It kind of is, isn't it?' They both laughed. 'It wasn't mine, you know. It was G's.'

Buddy raised an eyebrow.

'My maths student.'

'That young lady?' Another chuckle. 'Yah. She was sharp, all right.'

Hugh collected his things and started towards the door. 'I'm still glad Brian and the others didn't see it. They would have seen it as dumbing down science.'

Buddy didn't answer straight away. 'You were that kind of scientist when you first came here.' Buddy fell into step beside Hugh as he moved towards the door. 'I really thought you were.' He paused. 'But you've changed. Yah. You have.'

'I have?'

'Wait a minute. I have something for you.' Buddy bustled back into the room and returned with the coral.

'Here.'

Hugh felt a deep heat rising along his neck. 'I can't possibly. Didn't you say that you and your father found this when you were a boy?'

'Take it.' Their eyes met for only a second. 'Anyway, if the police were to come here, they'd have to arrest me. It's illegal to even possess them. Less likely to harass an expat.' It was Buddy's belly laugh that Hugh heard as he walked into the night, clasping the coral to his chest.

Genesis

I'm going... If I asked anybody on this bus how many times they been away, they'd say four, five, ten times... The only person I know who's never been away is me.

I'm going! To Tess's old school. In six weeks' time, I'll be there! With a lot of girls who never did a day's work in their lives. I get it now. Go into their temple and take what you need. But don't let any of them rich chicks mess with me... Still got a good left hook.

Feels good in here. Cool. Bus almost empty. Can't stay over Rosie's too long...

St. David's Road. US base gone. MacDonald's gone... So is the St. David's Rosie talks about. Says in the old days it was a separate island. Still feels different. Guess it always will, long as there's people like Rosie around. Rosie. She would have made a slammin grandma. Shame Nina and Dee couldn't have a baby... If I could choose a grandma, it would be Rosie... Can't wait to see the look on her face when I tell her!

My stop.

Oh God.

It's U.

U!

He's stopping. Haven't seen him since that night. At the football game. At the club. In that nasty room...

'Hey, U!'

I put my hands on my hips and tap my foot. He's coming back. Pulls up beside me.

'Hey G!' Hardly hear him, his voice is so low.

'What took you so long? I been here for hours.' I can feel my face break open in a smile but nothing's coming back in my direction. 'Well?'

'Sure you want to see me? Or be seen with me?'

'What I want and what you need is this.' I give him a slap upside his helmet and he lets me take him by the shoulders and wrestle him a little. 'Come on. There's someone I want you to meet.'

'I'm supposed to be meeting somebody.'

'She'll have to wait!' I start walking but he's still hanging back. 'Come on! It's just around the corner.'

Rosie's back is to us when we reach her gate.

'Here?' I see him checking out Rosie's yard. A mess, as usual. The rowboat is there ready for action. But the bicycle frame is gone. Somebody's painted her shutters but her roof looks like it could do with a coat. I don't think U's seeing any of these things. The growing things – that's what he's staring at because they block out everything else. All that green with bits and pieces of colour. Her corn is almost up to my waist. Her tomatoes, all staked out – I helped her do that a few weeks ago. They're bearing. So are the peppers. And her bush garden is full of all kinds of strange looking plants.

She turns.

'Hey, girlie. How goes it?'

I run over and give her a hug. She smells like soil and cinnamon. I pat her around her middle and start to laugh. 'Still wearing everything you got?'

She cuts her eyes at me then spots U, standing at the gate like a statue. 'Whoever you are, better come in.'

Timid. That's the only word to describe how U looks walking towards Rosie. Like a little boy.

'Who's this?'

I need to help him out. I remember when she put those green eyes on me the first time. 'This is my friend. His name is...'

'My name is Uriel.'

Rosie doesn't let go of his eyes. 'Who's ya people?' She steps closer, examining his face. 'You from round here?'

'No. My mama's a Caines...'

'You look like my Johnny... Who's ya deddy?'

'My deddy was... a Pitcher. I think.'

'What!' Rosie throws her head back and laughs. Looks like she's had a few teeth taken out. 'A good St. David's name! Ya from round here, boy – whatever else happened. That's why you look like my Johnny.' She holds out her arm and waits for U to take it. 'Uriel. Another funny name.' She looks at me, then back at U again. 'Anyway, I can't remember nothing no more. I'll just call you Mister.' She takes a step forward. 'So come on, Mister. Work to do.'

'OK. Break it up.' I shove U's arm away. 'Because you got a good-looking young guy now, you forgot all about me?' I talk that way to Rosie these days. She likes it. I turn her by the shoulders so she's only looking at me.

'Rosie.'

'Yes.'

'I'm going away.'

She's looking worried all of a sudden. 'Right now?'

'Of course not! Soon, though. First week in September.'

'Well, you need to tell me! People's always coming here just before they go to the airport.' She starts shaking her head. 'Where ya goin?'

'College. In the States.' I'm taking my time. 'Got the best grades in my class!'

'College.' She says it real slow rolling it around in her mouth. Then, there it is. The look I been waiting for. And the smile. Her finger raising my chin, then the long hug. This time she smells of ginger. The ginger makes me sneeze and I can't stop and the sneezing messes up my eyes and I start to cry though I'm not really crying it's really just the ginger and Rosie offers me one of her layers to dry my eyes with and when U sees her other dresses his mouth drops open and he starts to laugh and in the end the three of us are laughing until we can't laugh any more.

'I won a prize at school once. A cup,' she says. 'Penmanship.'

'What's that?' Really. U is sometimes so embarrassing.

Rosie looks at me. 'What? They don teach you how to write no more?'

'Of course.' I glare at U. 'Handwriting.'

'But...' she says, retying one of the tomato plants, 'what I really wanted was the arithmetic prize.' She makes sure it's just right before moving to the next. 'But Glendon got it. My brother. He could add up, subtract, multiply and do long division in his head. For the next fifty years. Never needed no machine. Nothing. All in his head.'

'Then what?' I look at U. It's like he never talked to an old person before. Like he doesn't know when to keep his trap shut. 'He died?'

'No,' says Rosie, moving along the row. 'Didn't die for another twenty years.'

'What... just got old?' says U. I'm looking hard at U. How he get to be so ignorant? He's got this intense look on his face. He really wants to know.

Rosie straightens up. 'No. He stopped. The day he stopped drinking black rum was the day he lost his gift.' She goes back to work. 'After that, couldn't add up for shit.'

We spend some more time walking round Rosie's yard. Because we're young and 'ain't got the rheumatism', she makes us move some branches from one corner of the yard to another. U keeps asking questions that make me want to slap him. Rosie answers with a look on her face like she kinda pities us.

'Time for some ginger beer...' We trail along behind her into the house.

First thing she does is pass U the picture of her Johnny when he was young. It's true. They look alike. Could be brothers. Or father and son. I wonder what U's feeling, seeing his face in a guy been dead fifty years.

She disappears down the steps to her kitchen and comes back panting because she's got this heavy tray with a giant pitcher of drink and big glasses full of ice. Makes me pour, then makes U get up from her special chair – I knew she would. The drink burns but it's good. Sweet and cold. U gulps it down and tells her he never knew people actually made ginger beer. In their own houses.

There's that look again. Rosie does feel sorry for us!

U goes over and picks up the picture that Nina gave her for Christmas. 'Who's this guy you're with? And what's with the feathers? And the plaits?'

Once again, I feel the urge to go punch U out. Then again I'm glad he's talking like this. So not like him around strangers. Shows he's not scared of Rosie. It's like he's known her all his life.

'That's Tall Oak's boy.' She slurps down some more ginger beer. 'What?' She looks at me. 'You didn tell him, girlie? What kind a friend are you?' She levers herself out of the chair and goes and tests the fishing line disappearing out of the window. 'Looks like I'm gon have to open a tin of sardines tonight.' With her back still to us, she says, 'That was taken when a group of Pequots from the States came here last year – around this time. They came here and showed us St. David's Islanders that we was the same people. From way back.'

U is looking hard at the picture. 'He's got a tomahawk in his hand. Like in our Wild Indian dance.'

'You a gombey?'

'Yes, ma'am.'

'You shoulda seen it that day – when we celebrated with them – when he danced with the gombey. One from Africa. One from over Stateside. Shoulda seen them, Mister. Like brothers they was. Same mama. Different deddy. And both... like they knew each other.' Rosie does a turn around the room and U picks up his arm and does some steps around her and I'm feeling something big rising in my throat.

She stops.

'Time you all went about ya business.' She starts going down the stone steps. 'Come on! There's some stuff you need to take.'

U and I go with her to the kitchen. I've been down here enough times but it still feels like I'm stepping back in time. Like the yard, it looks like a mess but there's some order too. Nina's tried to replace the tins and old containers with glass canisters with fancy stoppers but the beat-up tins are never thrown away. Always full of Rosie's leaves and potions.

There's barely enough space for the three of us and Rosie keeps swatting us away as she gets our plastic bags ready. Four ears of corn each. Some tomatoes. A few sweet peppers and a handful of bird peppers. Then the herbs.

She looks at me. 'Need some more aloes?'

'No, Rosie, I'm good.'

'Sure got rid of all them nasty pimples on ya face. I'm putting some in. Mash em up good, now. Like I showed you.' She pushes down three thick spiky leaves in the bag. 'Put some in ya hair too. What's left of it... And take some Father John to Nina. Sounded like she's comin down with a fresh cold.' In goes a whole clump of leaves that I swear are weed – except for the white stripe down the middle.

She gives U a good going-over with her eyes. 'I don know where to start with you. You don sleep. You don eat good. You better come back another time. For now, just take this.' She hands him a whole bag full of leaves the size and shape of saucers.

'What I'm goin do with these?'

'Eat em!' She gives him that look. 'Tonight when ya makin ya supper, just wash these off and eat em like a salad. Nasturtiums make you feel good. Great for ya bowels too.'

Now that's done, she's pushing us up and out. Time to go. Out in the yard again, it's like she's not quite ready for us to leave.

'You know, when Tall Oak and his people came here last year, it was real nice. To know about his tribe and how we're related. I knew that the whole world was runnin around in my veins.' She holds out her arm and we can see those blue veins underneath her skin. 'The African woman gave me my mouth and something comfortable to sit on. The Scotch or Irish man – don't know which, but he was one of them prisoners who spent his last days on this rock – I know that much. He gave me these eyes. And now, the Native.' Rosie's voice is a whisper. 'It's like... the circle is complete.'

Just when I'm starting to get scared, she turns to us and smiles, the sun coming right through it. 'You know...' Her voice is back to normal. 'I got a fortune here. I'm a rich woman.' Her arm goes out and takes in her house, her yard, the rocks and the water.

U is rooted to the spot.

'What's the boat for, Rosie?' I ask.

'Nothing. Not no more. Johnny used it to row out to his brother's fishing boat. But mainly he and I would get in it and go driftin off over there of an evening.' She's pointing towards some calm water just past the rocks.

'He made it himself. That's when there was a lot of cedar

around.' She gives a big sigh. 'That man was sure good with his hands.' She looks straight at us. 'And he was a pretty good carpenter too!'

She doubles over cackling and pushes us out of her yard. Even after the bend in the road, I can hear her calling, 'Gotta tell Nina that one!'

U pushes his bike and I walk next to him. Nobody's talking. My head is full of Rosie. When we get to the bus stop, he opens his mouth and before the words come out, I know it all. What he's going to ask and what I'm going to say. And why. All in that one moment.

'Want a ride home? I can take you home.'

'Thanks, U. I'll catch the bus.'

'Cool.'

He hangs around without saying anything else for what seems like forever. I'm wondering why I said no and I go back to the instant that he was going to ask me when it all came back to me – our last night together and the promise I made to Nina. The promise I made to myself. I feel my heart breaking when I think about Rosie, her yard, her house. We were like children again with the kind of childhood we could of had but didn't... But I can't go back.

Won't.

'I'm catchin the bus.'

He doesn't say anything but I know it's not over. He comes closer to me, real close to my face. 'How come?'

'I'm going swimming.'

'Swimming... You!' He gives a laugh that doesn't sound like a laugh and looks up to the sky, like he's searching for something. 'Who with?'

I don't wait a second. 'With the expat guy. He's teaching me.'

I blow a long breath out, feeling like I just ran a marathon.

U puts his helmet on and revs up his bike. He nods and takes off. Then he's back. He says something, with his bike so charged up it's like it's about to take off without him, front wheel off the ground, exhaust smoke everywhere. It's hard to make out what he's saying over the noise and the fumes. Then he's gone again at such a speed that the bag Rosie gave him splits open and there's a cloud of these round green saucers flying everywhere then crashing to the ground.

My bag of corn and aloes grows heavy on my arm. I see the bus. Thank God.

Soon as I sit down, I close my eyes and try to calm down. After this bus, another one to take me to the other end of the island. To my swimming lesson. This is crazy. I won't go! If I go it'll mess everything up... I shouldn't go... Why shouldn't I? He sees me. He really sees me... My hands are shaking. I hold one of them with the other. Like Teach did. On purpose. Last night. For the first time. And I'm going to see him again. This time with U's words ringing in my ears. Did I hear them or did I dream them?

'The next time whiteboy lays hands on the black queen, ask him this. Is it love or is it jungle fever?' Did he say *the* black queen or *my* black queen?

Dear God. What would Rosie do? Holy shit. She's ninety-two years old.

I open my eyes. U's up ahead, stopped on the side of the road, talking to somebody else on a bike... their heads so close together. As the bus draws parallel to them, I see who he's with. My stomach flips over. Malachi. Already bad in Primary One. The bus passes them and I turn and see them getting smaller and smaller.

Maybe it wasn't Malachi.

Rosie

Rosie walked out towards the water as the sun was going down. This was her favourite time of day with the sky flushed pink and the sea all golden. It was the moment when she liked to be alone – and the moment when all the relatives, neighbours and friends felt the need to check on her. She had taken to answering the phone with, 'No. I'm not dead yet.' Nina had told her to behave herself. 'It's only because we care, Rosie.' 'Well *you* do,' Rosie had grumbled, 'but not so sure about some of them others. Just want to be able to tell their pastor that they're ministerin to the sick and the shut-ins.' But she didn't do it again. She didn't mind annoying Nina but didn't like to upset her. That's why she made up a story about always taking an evening stroll to see Sister Edith and Sister Mavis at the end of her road. They were the perfect alibi. A dozen years younger than Rosie, but they were so far gone they didn't know a visitor from a hole in the ground. They would never tell.

She felt bad using the old maid sisters this way, but she looked forward with ever more eagerness to the minutes she spent at the water's edge. She knew this evening would be special. Because the day had been so good. Nina's girl. The boy the spit of Johnny. The things she had been able to give them. To make them grow.

Yes. This evening they would come.

She looked down at her feet, bare, wrinkled, her toes clutching the rock made smooth when the tide was high. She closed her eyes and heard the water singing for them to come. She lifted her arms, first up then out, palms up, and she began a slow spin, to the left, to the right, twisting from her broad waist, head tilted back loosening her long hair. Her body was alert to every breeze, every whisper on the shore. She was an open invitation for them to come.

And soon they did. In splendid dress they came, in indigo, in animal hides, in tartan cloths, adorned with beads and feathers, with silver pins, playing the fife, pounding on drums, coming across the water in rowboats, in canoes, in sloops with full white sails. When they drew near this time, she saw their faces were calm, not enraged or fearful or murderous as they sometimes were. Two men set foot on land together, one young, one old. Father and son. She knew them well. They came to her framed in sunset, walked straight to her. She held out her hands in welcome. The others took their places and the dance began, and as she danced, the years rolled back and back into the haze of the setting sun.

Round and round they went, the circle spreading ever wider but never broken.

CHAPTER 12: THE WICKEDEST MONTH

Hugh

'Meet me at the Crown and Anchor tables at noon,' G had said. 'I'll get there somehow.'

Hugh looked down at his wrist. 12:36. The sound system next to him belted out: *Cup Match time in Bermuda... Baccanal! Baccanal! Go Go Go Arrow! Go Go Go Arrow!*

Someone bumped into him. A sudden shock of cold liquid. 'Sorry, sweetie,' a husky voice said. A woman stopped for a second and dabbed his arm with a paper napkin. Her head was full of braids threaded with red and blue ribbon to match the red and blue stripes of her dress. With her face only inches away from his, she breathed rum at him. 'Too cute to be here on your lonesome.' With a toss of her braids, she pushed through the crowd, her drink held high. Hugh licked his arm. Black Seal with a hint of ginger beer. From being a real-ale purist, he was starting to acquire a taste for their rum. Maybe he'd get a drink. Better than standing around being pitied. But suppose she came and didn't see him?

He leaned against a pole supporting the canopy of one of the dozens of Crown and Anchor tables loaded with markers and fifty-dollar bills. He tried not to see those fat wads of dollars! He'd brought some money, as she'd instructed him, but knew that his chapel upbringing was going to make it hard for him to enjoy throwing away his hard-earned money on a game of chance. And what about the other game – the one on the field, the one people were supposed to be here to watch? His game was rugby. Cricket was for upper-class English twits. And this... this wasn't even cricket. This was an excuse for drinking, smoking, eating, gambling, parading... and, how would she say it? Gettin down. Hookin up and gettin down... Plenty of that.

The commentator's voice was an incessant drone.

Here comes Basden... With a full toss...

A sharp crack of willow on leather cut through the noise of the crowd followed by something like silence. Then a gasp.

Six! It's a six! O. J. Pitcher has smacked Jabari Basden right out of...

A roar, horns blaring, drums beating and the sound of the bleachers groaning under the weight of celebration or grief.

He's got his century!

Punters with their backs to the game raised their arms and wound up their hips. Someone brandishing a huge dark and light blue flag ran onto the pitch and embraced the batsman. Others followed, stuffing dollars in his pockets, ignoring the gesticulations of the umpire. Everywhere the sound systems cranked up the volume in a monumental clash. *Jam Bermuda! Jam Bermuda...* went to war against *You got it goin on...* which took on *Walk like a champion! Talk like a champion.*

In the pandemonium, Hugh could only raise a weak smile. Over the babel of voices and rhythms came a song, a phrase that eliminated the competition and rocked the earth Somerset Cricket Club stood on. *Got it goin on... Baby come to me,* the singer crooned.

As though beamed down from space, she appeared. Genesis, moving through the crowd, wearing dark pink and gold. She walked straight to him, smiling, talking to the person at her side. Lizzie.

Each girl kissed him on his cheek, then together led him away. He couldn't get his head around Lizzie being there. When he'd last looked, he was sure she didn't like Genesis and she'd certainly made it clear that she didn't rate him. But come to think of it, Genesis had mentioned that Lizzie had been stopping by recently. Didn't matter. On Cup Match Day, all bets were off. That much he understood. Within moments, he had a drink in his hand and was parading through the crowd, flaunting one beauty on each arm. Soon after, they hit the Crown and Anchor tables. The first time he played, he won back his stake. The second, he doubled it. He lost the third and fourth times, but the fifth time, when he put his markers on a crown, an anchor and a club, the dice came good with all three. Hugh saw the look the banker gave him – fifty percent happy, because a big winner was good for business and fifty percent unhappy, because this particular winner had taken enough of his damn money. Hugh did a quick calculation of probabilities in his head, hugged his two companions and turned his back on the tables.

But it was too late, he admitted to them. He was corrupted.

'Emancipated,' Genesis said. 'Not corrupted. Cup Match is all about Emancipation. From this day on, we're all free!'

She and Lizzie were in high spirits, full of the story of how Lizzie had liberated G from Nina's camp. Best view, best shade, best food. But completely dry and irredeemably well behaved. Lizzie had stopped by because she'd heard Nina's people did a great camp and wanted to check it out. There she'd found Genesis looking like a doomed soul among the teetotal cousins, uncles and grandmas. She had sat herself down and talked and laughed and eaten with Nina and her people for a full half hour, then she'd said – like she was just having the thought – 'Why don't I take Gen with me for a while?'

'Nina gave her that look,' said Genesis, making a comic facsimile of Nina's truth-seeking stare.

'Then the sister...'

'Rita...'

'Just upped and said to us, "Go 'long." Said to Nina, "Let the girls have some fun. You remember that word, don't you?" She'd given Nina that look – must be a family thing – and that was it!'

They told Hugh the story a couple of times, each time more elaborately, and each time they cracked up until both of them were almost in tears.

'Right. Who's having what?' For the whole time they were in line for Dolly's Specials, they debated what Hugh needed to have, as part of his cultural education. He'd bet Cup Match, drunk Cup Match, walked Cup Match. Now he had to eat it. Although it was only the early afternoon of the first day, by the time they had reached the counter, Dolly and her crew had the glazed look of marathon runners. They walked away with mussel pie, beef pie, hash shark, peas n rice, conch stew, fried fish and more fries, hot sauce, ketchup and more seasoned salt than any human being should be allowed to look at, let alone eat.

'Look! Shade!'

They ran towards a straggly clutch of oleanders that offered the merest protection from the sun. While they ate, Lizzie and Genesis commented on the world passing by.

'Needed to get some liposuction before she put on those shorts. Definitely. Her pastor wouldn't like it.'

'Who's that following her? I think it's her pastor...'

Hysterics while Hugh rolled his eyes and pretended not to be with them.

'Look at what that one's wearing! Can't be more than twelve years old...'

'Disgustin! And those old guys over there... Can barely walk... Full hot already...'

'Oh God, Gen! There's that Ian from work. Look! Gone native! Already...'

'Not like that one over there. In his straw hat. Tie and blazer. In this heat! Crest and everything. What does MCC stand for? Hugh?'

'Marylebone Cricket Club,' he said grandly.

'Right.' Lizzie and Genesis looked at each other. 'We knew that!' they screamed in unison. Hugh shook his head and nearly choked as he tried to toss back a Dark n Stormy.

A shadow fell across them, interrupting the laughter. Lizzie looked up.

'Hey, you! Guys, this is my cousin, Tiago.'

A few minutes later, Lizzie was spirited away by Tiago to some other part of the field. As she left, she shouted over her shoulder, 'Be home at a decent hour, Gen. I gave Nina my word.'

Hugh leaned back against the tree and closed his eyes. Even in the short time they'd been there, the shade had vanished. Beads of sweat gathered at his temples 'Wouldn't it be great to be in the water...'

'Yes! Let's go!'

When he opened his eyes, because of the glare, he could barely see Genesis though she was right next to him. But he heard her say, 'I'd love to go swimming.'

There was that slightly ironic line of her mouth when she added, 'Cup Match isn't only about being at the game.'

When they reached Tess's car, Genesis raised an eyebrow.

'Tess said I could use it while she's away,' Hugh said. 'Gone to… where again?'

'Palm Springs.'

'Yes. There. Spending the weekend with Richard.' As he manoeuvred the car out of the tight parking space, he added, 'Imagine wanting to be anywhere else, when you could be here.'

'You mean that?'

'What?'

'About not wanting to be anywhere else?'

'Yes, I do.' He considered for a second then laughed out loud. 'I really do!'

She sank back into her seat. 'Where we going? All the beaches are going to be rammed…'

'I've got an idea… You'll see.'

They pulled up.

'Here?' She didn't look pleased at seeing Tess's house. 'I thought we were going to the beach.'

'We are! Just you wait!' Hugh was all energy as he hurried past Sweet Airs, down to his cottage at the water's edge.

'Don't move.' He sat Genesis on a chair in his living room while he rushed outside. When he came back, he was carrying a large canvas bag with a towel tumbling out. He looked at her again, picked up some oranges and stuffed them into the bag. At every moment, he felt her eyes following him as he darted about.

Finally, he stood in front of her with his hand extended.

They walked past the dock to the strip of rough sand where the punt and a few sunfish sailboats were normally beached. The punt was bobbing on the water with an outboard motor attached to it. Genesis stopped dead in her tracks.

Without a word, Hugh burrowed in the canvas bag, pulled out an orange life vest and offered it to her.

'Can't we swim here?'

'No. Where we're going is much nicer. An island in the Sound.' He pointed in the direction of a place on the other side of what now seemed, even to him, an immense body of water. 'See how calm it is?' It was. Smooth. Like a glinting mirror.

'But… but…' Hugh watched fear flooding her face and felt his fear of her refusal flooding his. But she turned to him, her face wide open.

'But Nina says that... whatever the weathermen say... the real hurricane season starts at the beginning of August... That the water starts to turn... Starts to go bad... And today is... the first of August!'

Hugh looked out at the shimmering Sound. He took her hand. 'I'm not going to let anything bad happen to you, G.' He touched her cheek. 'Have a little faith.'

She blinked, reached for the life jacket and entered the water.

They made swift work of crossing the Sound and were soon moving through a scatter of small islands until they were in a lagoon, circled by islets, a few with a solitary house, most covered only with bay grape and cedar. It was the smallest of these that Hugh had discovered a few weeks before.

He dropped anchor and jumped out. The water reached his waist. It was clear, warm, so much so that Genesis did not need any encouragement other than his outstretched hand. She whipped off the lifejacket and they waded ashore. The beach was just wide enough to accommodate their beach blanket, while overhead, the dark trees nodded and let only dappled sunlight in.

'Let's explore!' She didn't wait for him but headed for a break in the trees. He followed, their footsteps crunching the crisp leaves underfoot. Every now and then she would stop and exclaim. A large, jewelled lizard here; a scuttling crab there. Every time, he was there, his arm ever ready to touch, to hold, as though by accident. Always she slipped away through the light and shade, but always after his skin had imprinted itself on hers.

She called out to him. 'Look what I've found, Teach!'

'Why don't you call me by my name?'

'Oh. Look what I've found. Hugh.'

Crouching down, she pulled back some branches, revealing a bush, full of small red fruit. 'Cherries!' she said, her mouth full. 'Yummmm.' He looked doubtful. He'd seen these before, growing along the roadside. Somebody at work had said they were poisonous. She chose the largest one and waited for him to open his mouth.

'Come on,' she coaxed. 'Come on, Teach. Sorry. Hugh.' For

a moment, she reminded him of the school nurse trying to get him to take a medicated sugar cube. He opened his lips and let his mouth fill with the sweet flesh. He swallowed the seed by mistake. When he was about to ask her why she hadn't warned him about that, he saw that she was practically inhaling cherries.

He couldn't let it pass. 'Whose island is this anyway?'

'Mine.'

'Oh yeah?'

Soon they were wrestling on the ground, rolling over and over on the fragrant leaves, crushing the red berries, their juice bursting upon their skin.

At last she broke free and ran off, laughing. By the time he was on his feet, she had cleared the trees, had found another beach and was in the water, running from him, looking back at him saucily, hooting his name and scaring the birds.

'G! Wait!'

She kept going. 'Huuuuuuuugheeeeeeee! Huuuuuuuugheeee...'

A sudden panic came upon him. They were on the other side of the island where the water became suddenly deep. She was so busy teasing him. She didn't know that this beach was different from the one they'd landed on. With her long legs, a few more steps and she'd put her foot down and there'd be nothing but ocean beneath it.

What would that do to her?

'Genesis!'

He summoned all of his strength, made a clean dive and streaked through the water until he saw her legs, taking long confident strides towards the darker blue.

She disappeared.

But he was with her in a matter of moments, catching her first by the hand, then grabbing her under her arms and hauling her to the surface.

She clamped her arms around his neck, spitting out salt water, her face a mixture of disbelief and alarm. 'What the...'

Hugh said nothing. He was aiming at something floating near to them. An old-fashioned wooden mooring, a cross between a buoy and mattress. A place she could hold onto until she had processed the fact that she was in water where she could not stand.

He didn't have to tell her. By the time they reached the buoy and she was hanging onto the ropes looped around it, she understood. At first, she clung to the ropes with her head down, as though praying.

She raised her eyes to his. Treading water a few feet away, he wasn't sure what her look meant. Then her left hand let go of the rope it was clutching. 'I'm ready.'

'Come to me.'

She let go of the other rope and, her face contorted into a grimace, she splashed and grunted and kicked towards him, her head like a rod out of the water. She made it and he gathered her quaking body into his arms. He swam her back to the buoy and she did it again. And again, and again; each time, she relaxed a little bit more. Every now and then, he stretched out his arms and let her lie there on her back, her arms akimbo, her eyes veiled to the sun and he could see the fear draining away until, stealthily, he drew one arm away, then the other and watched her float free. He had not felt this joy before nor had he known attentiveness so deep that, at the merest flicker of her eyelid, his arms became her life raft again.

'I want to go in now,' she said. When she looked at him, Hugh looked away. Everything was gone from her eyes. Stripped away, washed away… leaving only a blackness that was not so much a colour but a language. Her lips were moving but her eyes were speaking.

'Put your… uh… arms around my neck. Try not to strangle me.' She didn't smile but did as he asked. Her arms were now speaking, burning him through the water, as they began their journey to the shore. She rode on his back, her breasts searing him, her belly pressing against his buttocks, burning, as they moved to the shore. When Hugh thought that they were no longer in deep water, he turned to face her. They flew together in a tangle of limbs. Above the water, their mouths feasted on each other. Hugh had miscalculated and when he went to touch bottom, there was nothing there. Down they went and the water engulfed them. They came up spluttering.

But Genesis was not afraid.

When the sea finally gave way to the land, they took a few steps and their knees gave way. They fell onto the sand with the gentle surf breaking over them. On the island, the trees whispered and the gulls screamed. For Hugh and Genesis there was no noise. Their bodies spoke and all other thoughts were silenced.

Genesis

Don't know what to say, how to put it in words.

Yesterday.

August the first. When the ocean changes.

I swam in the ocean.

I let it carry me.

There was this little island. Not like the island I know. Like no-one had ever set foot on it. That new. That pure.

Then there was the water. Light blue. Like the shell of the bluebird egg Uncle Jack once showed me. And so warm.

It covered my head twice.

The first time happened in a flash. I was running in, laughing, calling out, wading in till the water almost reached my shoulders. I heard a sound but didn't turn around, just kept moving forward, with the voice behind me. *Genesis!* was the last thing I heard as I took a step. Dropping. Dropping down. Till the water was on top of me...

No time to be scared. Because of the arms. Before I could breathe in the ocean, they were there. Strong. Gentle. Pulling me out of the deep water. Pulling me up into the air.

Those arms guided me to a life raft. I don't know where my mind went, don't know what I said. Until that voice said *Come to me.*

Then I saw him. Teach. Who made me feel that I could lie on the water with my head tilted back, could look the sun in the eye, my arms outstretched, my legs floating free. And that his arms and the ocean would hold me.

I went under one more time. But this time, with him. Down. With water beneath our feet and water above our heads. Our arms and legs were in a tangle by the time we landed on the sand. And there was no way to untangle them. No way to separate his from mine. To separate him from me.

★

Today… The last day of August.

I can hardly believe this is my life. One long year ago, I was on Planet Lockdown. Now when I look in the mirror, who do I see? A girl. Nearly a woman. On her way up. Taking a plane. Going to study, like all those others. Me. I'll be doing this. Thinking about things. Talking about things. Figuring out things. In serious, dark libraries. With shabby-looking rich chicks sitting under trees reading books.

Me. From the Robinson Home. I can do it!

Been four weeks since I started believing I can.

Been seeing Teach almost every day since the month began.

August is the month of people trying to squeeze things in before Labour Day. Locals rushing to take off on holiday. Tourists cramming cruise ships to come here. Horseshoe Bay crowded to bursting. Parents sweating to find fees for private schools or colleges away. Teenagers saving their summer wages then blowing them on one night out. Everybody trying to outrun summer.

In all of that, Teach and I have been together, and everybody's been too busy to see. All three of Tess's sons have come to visit. Even Richard shows up. Barbecues, fishing, parties. Always something. Lizzie is a regular now. Always gives me notice and never asks questions. Something's on her mind but who knows what. And as for Nina, she's trying to get used to me going away. Every day it's a new list of Do's and Don'ts for me to *mark, learn and inwardly digest*. Giving me stomachache, that's what her list is doing. But I think she's happy for me. I think she is…

One thing I know. The time I spend with Teach is the reason I can weave through the cracks opened up by August. Teach and I. It's like we've become a 'we'. Invisible to the busy people because we know the hidden places. The places that hear us when we're talking. See us when we're not. When we're in the sea or on the sand. They know us.

But when it's over and I'm on my way back home, I have this feeling. Let down? Worried? Some little crawling thing in my belly. After we're done, it's always there, bringing me down…

On the bus now, going from Sweet Airs to Salt Cay. A long ride in anybody's book.

Somebody comes and sits next to me. I'm looking out the window; I don't have to turn to know it's a man. An old man. I shoot a glimpse at him and the little crawling thing starts to grow.

Old Man Tucker. The first one to mess with me. I'd been with them for over a year and they'd been nice to me. I was so excited because they'd taken me for dinner at the Seahorse. All dressed up, I ate up the food and left space for my favourite dessert. Lemon meringue pie. I was special, the only one to have dessert. Neither of the Tuckers could because they both had sugar. When we got home, she went straight to bed. I don't want to get out of my good clothes so I'm kinda skipping around the front room. Old Man Tucker's in his armchair. As I skip past, he stops me with his arm. It's like rock. His face is all I can see. Greasy. *You got something around your mouth.* I raise my hand to wipe it off. His sweaty hand grabs mine. *No.* He leans close and touches my cheek. Then he slowly licks the corner of my mouth and my bottom lip. *Meringue.*

He stands up, a sly smile on his face. He's breathing heavy. My head only comes up to his waist and I see that something strange has happened at the front of his trousers. Something bad.

I scream and stumble backwards into Ma Tucker's table with the figurines on it. They break into a million pieces. She comes runnin out of her bedroom, cussin and carryin on about the figurines.

The next morning, I'm dumped at the Robinson Home.

I was eight years old.

The bell rings. It's Old Man Tucker's stop. I watch as he lumbers towards the door. His diabetes must be bad now. I know he didn't recognise me.

I reach Nina's house just in time. Never vomited like that before. Violent. Like the memory. And all the effort it's taken me to forget it.

I call Teach. Tell him I need to see him. Now.

Teach is there waiting when the taxi pulls up. He pays the driver and we walk down to the cottage.

He puts his hand on my shoulder. I jump. Electric shock. He takes a step away.

'What happened?'

I can't answer. All the way in the taxi, I been swept away by a flood of Old Man Tuckers shoving their tongues and fingers inside me. Did any of them ever do the Big Nasty to you, Amber had asked. Amber. The runaway. We'd shared a room and for a few months we were almost friends, until she ran away and never came back. No, I told her. How come? I always broke something they loved, dodged them like U taught me or woke the neighbourhood up with my screaming. I was trouble and all they wanted was to see the back of me. The social workers asked the same question Amber did. I always regretted telling them No. Because I knew they'd be relieved and would tell me that this was something I could get over. That what happened to me wasn't much.

Wasn't terrible.

Wasn't theft.

So when I was fourteen, I decided where and when the Big Nasty was going to happen to me. And how much it was worth. Sometimes it was just a sense of satisfaction. But most times, it was a thing. Never from the poor-ass foster parents. And never money. Things. Like CDs and makeup, hair extensions and, best of all, sneakers. One thing equals another thing. It's simple math.

But always, afterwards, there was that small crawling thing in my belly.

And now Teach is talking to me. He's been talking to me all this time, his voice so quiet I almost didn't hear it. I can't look at his face. But I see his arms. Those arms that kept me afloat.

'I saw the man who first... molested me.'

'Oh God! What did you do?'

'Nothing. He sat down. He said nothing. I said nothing. Then he got off the bus.'

'Do you want me to call somebody? Nina? Tess?'

'NO!'

He sits down and puts his head in his hands. I feel sorry for him. He's out of his depth.

He walks to the kitchen and I hear him moving about. He comes out and puts a cup of tea in front of me.

I stare at it without a smile, even though just a few hours ago, I'd teased the shit out of him about the British and their tea.

'Genesis, what did he do to you?' He sits across from me.

'I told you. Nothing.'

'I mean... when you were... how old?'

'Eight.'

'When you were eight. What did he do?'

I raise my eyes to his. I search for the real question. Amber's question.

I get up and start pacing around, throwing looks at him. Still searching.

'Why do you want to know? Isn't it enough that I know?'

He scrapes his hair back and shakes his head.

'I'm no therapist, G, but don't you think... don't you think that it would help if you... you told me. Got it out in the open?'

In three quick steps, I'm in front of him, pulling him out of his chair.

'No. NO! It won't help! When I was in the bus with that stinkin man next to me, I didn't just remember what happened. I was there! I was eight!' The words ricochet off the walls. 'Lived every moment of it! His sour breath, the breaking of glass... the shattering of everything. The taste of ashes...'

He staggers a little. Despite my trembling, I grab his arms so that he doesn't fall. Those arms should be rocking me and keeping back the flood. Instead, I'm holding them.

Our eyes crash together. And there it is.

Amber's question.

I drop his arms.

He's praying it wasn't the Big Nasty. I know it!

Because he can't love somebody like that.

I take my cell phone from my pocket.

'What are you doing?'

'Calling a taxi. Gotta get home before Nina.'

'You can't go now! Not until you feel... better.'

I give a short laugh as he holds onto his desk, as if he's trying to stay upright.

When I get to the door, he shouts, 'You need to stay and talk to me!'

'No, I don't. I know everything that happened to me. And that's all that counts. I'm still alive and I went to school, took exams and will soon get out of this island. While you... you've heard a tiny piece of my story and it's like somebody dropped a bomb on you.'

I give him a look. He shrinks before my eyes.

'No, Hugh. I'm not going to talk to you. You want me to remember. And I don't. You want me to talk. And I won't. Because if I do, some part of you will judge me...'

'An eight year-old?'

'I'm damaged goods. That's what you think.' As I say these words, I feel strong. The way truth makes you feel. 'There's no room for that in your nice clean life. Go find that girl you told me about. What was her name? A real whitegirl name. Oh yeah. Kate.'

'Kate's married.'

'Get another Kate then.'

I hear a car horn blowing. The taxi.

'Give me twenty-five dollars.'

'What?'

'For the taxi fare.'

He pulls out three ten-dollar bills from his wallet. He holds out the money and does not move. I have to go and get it. Six steps are all I need to reach him. I don't feel strong anymore but I cover the distance. I don't see the thirty dollars. I only see the arm covered in fine hair and reddish-brown freckles. One of the arms that saved me. A long time ago.

I run up towards the taxi, hardening my mind, clutching the money. Crushed in my hand, there's one thing. Behind the screen door, inside the cottage, there's another. One thing equals another thing. Nothing more to be won or lost.

Simple math.

CHAPTER 13: HURRICANE SEASON

Genesis

'We've got a problem,' Tess says, raking through her hair. 'Maybe two.'

Don't like the way Tess is mauling her $500-a-pop hairdo. Don't like being ordered to her office when I got better things to do. Don't like much of anything recently. But in three days' time, I'll be off this rock for good. There must be a God!

'I've just got off the phone with my friend Bob Berkowitz at the American Consulate,' she says. 'There's been some mistake with your passport...' More shoving around of her hair. 'Instead of issuing your I-20 here in Bermuda – like they were supposed to – they sent your passport to DC.'

'My passport's... in Washington?' My chest can't get enough air. 'How I'm supposed to travel on Saturday?'

Tess leans over and takes my hand. 'Look. It'll be tight but there's just enough time. Bob's located it and it should be here, maybe tonight. Tomorrow morning at the latest.'

'So it'll be all right... for me to leave in three days. On Saturday.' I pause. 'September the sixth.' Something in her face tells me not to exhale. Not yet.

She gets up, looks down at me, then sits down again. 'Haven't you been listening to the news, G? There's a hurricane heading our way. A big one.'

'They never hit us, Tess. They always turn off at the last minute.'

Tess hands me the newspaper. *Get Ready For A Direct Hit.* I look at the front page like I'm reading an exam paper. There's the information. The storm's due on Friday. In forty-eight hours' time. A strong Category Three. Time for the island to batten down. The airport will shut tomorrow afternoon.

Just words.

'They never hit.' I lock eyes with Tess until she blinks.

'In denial...' She starts acting all pissed, mumbling something. She rummages around her desk drawer. 'You have to face this, G!' She whips her hair on top of her head with a scrunchie. 'There may be a way out. Bob says that the diplomatic bag arrives after Consulate hours. If it's in the bag this evening, then he'll issue the I-20 himself. That way, we can get you out tomorrow morning. Before they shut the airport.'

'Does Nina know?'

'Yes. I talked to her when you were on your way here.' There's a dull pain in my temples. Tess sits next to me again. 'As soon as we get the passport, we can get you out. The airport is already a bloody mess. Those expats will trample over their grandmothers to get away. Paradise is great – until a hurricane comes... If there's no room on the flights, I can get Richard to send down the PJ. Tomorrow morning. One of us will go with you. Me or Nina. Or both...'

'The PJ?' I stare at Tess, then start to laugh. A crazy sound. I can't say anything for a long time. Eventually, 'And if I can't get out on tomorrow?'

Tess shrugs. 'Depends on what the storm does. How badly it treats the airport. It's pretty exposed out there...' She makes me stand up and her hands push back my shoulders back. 'The worst thing that can happen is that you'll be late starting classes.'

'I can't be late... Can't!' Can't control my voice either. What comes out of my mouth sounds like crying.

Tess stares at me. 'Okay. Okay. Wait a minute. I'll see what I can do.'

While she's getting busy on the phone, I try to find something to do with my hands other than wring the life out of my t-shirt. Because if I can't go tomorrow, I won't go. I can't be late. Can't arrive at that rich-ass school late. I'm not dumb but I am late. Don't know half of what they know already – things they breathed in when they were babies in their pretty houses with their maids and nannies and gardeners. Late for all that. If I set foot in that school on time, I would still have to play catch-up with all the things that they know without even knowing how they know them. But to show up a week late! They would scan me like a laser and know in a second that I could never catch up. And I would know that too.

Finally, Tess turns to face me.

'That was Pamela Freni.'

'Who?'

'The Admissions Officer at Sarah Morrison! She says it's OK. Can't argue with an act of God, she said. Even if you're a few days late, it's going to be OK. All we need to do now is to get the visa and get you out before they close the airport.'

I can't be late! I don't actually say the words but Tess catches the look on my face and gives me that phoney smile I know so well.

'Come on, now. You go home and make sure that you're completely packed. Be ready for a quick getaway.'

When I'm at the door, she says, 'You and Nina come up to the house tonight. We'll look at all the possibilities. Don't worry. Everything's going to work out.'

Everything's going to work out. When last did anything work out for me? Tess's scary old people are looking down at us from the wall. Is that them laughing?

I watch Nina and Tess in a huddle. It's starting to get dark outside but they don't notice. Too busy with the Plans. What if the visa doesn't come through? And what if it does? Then there's how to get sold-out tickets for planes crazy enough to land on an island with a hurricane breathing down its neck.

It's like I'm not even here. They're making lists. They're on the phone. Trying not to argue. It's all about them. If only they could blame each other! No such luck. Even they don't have control over the weather and American Immigration... So they have to try to see which one of them has the most pull. Tess has her aceboy at the Consulate. No news from him yet. Then there's the tickets when half of Bermuda is scrambling to get out. Nina comes out sluggin with the niece high up in American Airlines who just might be able to pull nonexistent seats out of a hat. Tess lands the final blow. The Private Jet.

This is not a spectator sport. Better if they did some mud

wrestling. Get all their shit out in the open. But I don't know. Maybe not even then... What's between them is really old. Maybe their generation has to die out for things to change. I'm not following anything they're saying. All I know is I've gotta get out tomorrow!

Look at them! They're ready to work with their worst enemy so they can both have bragging rights. But they still hold the key to my life. Because of them, I might still get on a plane tomorrow and get out. All I need is to get away from them. Get away from this place and the crap it's given me all my life.

But if I get on a plane tomorrow, it'll be because of them! Tess is paying for everything. Every last thing! And Nina... well... she's been working hard on my soul... I should be grateful...

Oh God! If you exist, please take me away from them.

And from him! I wish I couldn't see the cottage from here!

But I shouldn't blame him. It's not his fault. It's mine.

I let him in. Those arms... those same freckly arms made me believe that he would teach me, protect me, maybe even...

He liked to see me starting to think. He liked that a lot. He liked my body. Yes. He did. But as soon as he got a taste of my real life – what it was, the things that happened. When I looked into his eyes, I saw it.

Pure terror.

I can't believe how far I went with him. The things I said to him. The little stories that just slipped out. I broke my own rule about never telling... I almost told him. About Joy. Just as I was about to, my mind went blank. Nothing there.

My mama drowned in the sea. That's all I could say.

Why did I let him in? And the three bitches too. When did I forget that I'm from the Robinson Home? That I'm nobody's child who can't remember anything.

I have to get out of this room. Out of this house with its little cottage by the water.

Then Lizzie shows up and saves me.

'Can you drop me home, Lizzie?'

'I just got here.'

'Yes but I need to go home and finish packing. So I can leave tomorrow.'

My eyes meet Lizzie's and we both look at Nina and Tess so deep in their planning that we don't exist. Lizzie nods and in a loud voice says, 'I'm taking Gen home. She needs an early night.'

They look up. 'But we don't know yet...'

'It's O.K. I know you two. You've got this.'

And just like that, I'm in Lizzie's car. As soon as I get in, I see the light go on in his cottage. From then on, I can't say a word. When we reach Salt Cay, I try to say thanks but the word doesn't come. It never comes when I really want it to.

I get out of the car, turn to her and nod. I hope she sees how grateful I am to her for saving me from those women. And by not talking to me in the car.

Uriel

'Why don't you wait here? Or come back in twenty minutes?' Uriel's voice was urgent as the two bikes slowed down. 'Still don't see why you had to come.' He jumped off his bike and glanced over at Malachi. 'I can handle it.'

Malachi said nothing. He put the bike on its stand, removed his helmet, stowed it away, adjusted his shades and slowly covered his head with the dark hood of his jacket.

'Known each other since back in de day, U. Skipped class. Played football. Chased tail.' He leaned against a low wall almost obscured with vines. 'Even if we wasn't that tight... I always thought you was a pretty cool guy. Somebody you could chill with.' Malachi straightened up. 'But this is different.'

Uriel felt a cold ripple pass through his body when Malachi levelled those blank, fish eyes on him.

'You owe me money. I gave you stuff to sell and I'm still waitin for my cut.' Malachi sank back onto the wall, his head swivelling around as he took in the tangle of green with the odd bit of dumped trash. He picked up a rusty frying pan and threw it into the undergrowth. With a look of disdain on his face, he wiped his fingers.

'This better be the right place, U.'

'Sure it is... Right round the corner. Don't look like much from the outside. But every cent of the two grand is there. And more. I swear!' Uriel drew a sharp breath. 'But... why ya here, Ki?' Malachi stood up. He came to Uriel's shoulder. 'Why?' U's voice was stronger. 'Like you don't trust me... Like ya dissin me.'

U straightened, willing his body to its full height.

Malachi rose on the balls of his feet then let his heels come down, finding a place of balance for his short, stocky body. He smiled. A flash of gold winked between his lips. 'No, my man. No disrespect. Just protectin my investment.' He dusted off the back of his jeans. 'You tell me that money got stolen from the place you was stayin? I believe you. Yes. I do. That's why when we go down the road, we both know that ya callin the shots. I'm not gon say nothing. But...' Those fish eyes again... 'I got ya back, if you need it.'

'No way I'm gonna need it.'

'Whatever you say.'

They found Rosie in her yard struggling to close one of her shutters. They were almost upon her before she saw them.

'What you doin creepin up on me like that?' When her eyes lit on Uriel, she smiled. 'Oh, it's Mister. I s'pose Nina sent you. Good. Means she's given up the idea of takin me up her house to ride out the storm.' Uriel opened his mouth to speak and closed it again. 'Nossuh. I'm stayin put.' Then she saw Malachi.

'Who's this?'

'Malachi, Rosie. My friend Malachi.'

She walked up and stood in front of him. 'Take that thing off ya head, boy. And them glasses too. Can't hardly see you.'

Malachi tried to tough it out – but managed only a few seconds. He slid the hood onto his neck and put his shades in his pocket. His eyes shifted about while Rosie gave him a good going over.

'Malachi, eh? Last book of the Old Testament.' Malachi stood rigid as the old green eyes raked his face. 'God's Messenger... Yah. I know my Bible.' She turned back to Uriel. 'That storm's comin. I can smell it! Better enjoy tomorrow, Mister. Cause Friday, we're gon get some licks! Yassuh.' She gazed about her for a moment. 'Well, what you waitin for? Help me with them blinds.'

Rosie put their young man muscle to work, closing the heavy wooden shutters, overturning the rowboat and placing it in the lee, putting plywood on the south-facing windows. Her orders were clear and she didn't tolerate any shirking. It was dark by the time the job was done to her satisfaction.

'Better come in. Made some drink this afternoon... Gettin late though... I need to go to my bed...'

With the shutters pulled in and the windows boarded up, it was dark and stifling inside. When Rosie disappeared down the stone steps to her kitchen, Uriel and Malachi in their baggy jeans and outsized tops were left looking like ungainly giants in the small living room. They didn't make eye contact but when Uriel glanced in Malachi's direction, all he could see was his mouth set in an ugly line.

Malachi switched on the light.

'Uriel...'

Rosie came up the steps puffing and blowing. Uriel took the tray – big glasses full of ice and an oversized pitcher full of drink. Red this time.

'Sorrel,' Rosie said.

She filled the glasses and headed towards her special chair. Uriel took a sip. 'Nice,' he said. Malachi put his on the table without tasting it and cleared his throat. Rosie did not sit down.

'Rosie,' Uriel began. His head dropped to his chest. Malachi cleared his throat again. 'Rosie... remember when I was here last time?'

'With Nina's girl.'

'Yes! That time!'

'What other time was there?' Rosie swirled the ice in her glass, the only sound in the room.

'Rosie. You said something that time... and my mate here and I...' U raced along. 'We want to kinda help you with it... to make sure it's all right... to...'

Rosie put down her glass and looked from one boy to the other. 'Spit it out, Mister.'

Uriel turned to Malachi, who was standing behind him with his hands deep inside the pockets of his jacket. He felt a bitter panic rising in his chest.

'You said you were rich,' he blurted out. 'And that it was here. In this house... In that yard!' He pointed to the darkness outside.

Rosie's eyes widened.

Uriel tried to control his breathing, tried not to think about the figure behind him. 'We want to help you, Rosie. Want to make sure that money's safe. Suppose your house gets flooded? This hurricane's gonna be a bitch... Everybody says so.' He looked around him wildly for confirmation. 'So... we just wanna take it and put it... someplace. Someplace safe.' His voice was barely audible.

Rosie stepped forward. 'Mister. Look at me.' He couldn't. She took hold of his chin and turned his face towards hers. 'I ain't got no money. Look at this place!'

Uriel could hear Malachi shuffling around behind him.

'But you said, Rosie! You said!'

'What I said, boy? What you think I said?'

'You said... you said... you were rich. Said you had a fortune. In your house. In your yard...'

Rosie shook her head, slowly, painfully. 'I don't have no money, boy. All I have is what you see.' Her hand made an arc taking in the old TV, the well-used chairs, a fishing rod and tackle, a few books, a bag of knitting, the jug of drink made from sorrel flowers. And the photographs of Johnny, Nina, Dee and Tall Oak's boy. 'It's a fortune to me.'

Uriel felt steely fingers close around his arm. He faced Malachi. The dead fish-eyes had come alive.

'What the fuck is this? Huh? Huh? Hey, U!' He pushed Uriel backward, jabbing him, until he had him against the wall. Malachi's hand was at his throat, not squeezing hard, but flexing its muscle. Showing it would go the distance.

'It's not...' Uriel coughed. 'Not what you think, Ki.' Malachi's arm pinned Uriel to the wall.

'I want my money.'

From the corner of his eye, Uriel saw that Rosie had not moved but was trembling from head to toe.

'Let me talk to her. I know she's got it. Let me...' Malachi's hand slipped to his side as he turned his attention to Rosie.

'No. wait, Ki. Let ME talk to her. Just wait. Wait! Rosie,' he said. 'Oh God, Rosie, please just give me the money. Please... I don't want nothing bad to happen... But you got to give it to me.'

Rosie's trembling continued unabated. Malachi shoved Uriel onto the floor and faced Rosie.

'Now look, old lady...' She raised her eyes to his. 'What you gotta be so old for?' He looked back at Uriel. 'This is bullshit!'

Uriel was on his feet, pulling at Malachi's arm. 'Let's go, man. We ain't done nothing yet. Let's get outta here. It ain't worth it.'

'Not worth it?' The angry fish-eyes burned Uriel again. 'I'll give you not worth it!' One well-placed blow to the solar plexus put Uriel on the floor groaning while Malachi turned his attention to Rosie.

'Give me the money.'

Nothing.

Malachi's breathing began to accelerate.

'I know what this is. I heard about you old people hiding money... Like that... like that...' He looked for a response from Uriel, hunched over and coughing. 'Like that Hughes guy,' he said, snapping his fingers. 'Herbert Hughes! Lived like a tramp but was loaded. Richer than...' Malachi struggled to finish the sentence.

From the floor, Uriel could see that Rosie wasn't shaking any more. She was composed but looked very tired. He tried to get to his feet but before he did, he heard Malachi say, 'Oh yeah? Not talking?' He swept the frosty glasses from the table. The red liquid splattered everywhere, the walls, the linoleum, the front of Rosie's dress.

'Boy, you need to get out of my house.' Rosie's voice was no longer shaky.

'Talking now? Huh?' Malachi's chin jutted forward. 'I want my money!'

'Out of my house!'

He pulled the gun from his jacket and smashed the photographs with the butt.

'Son, you need to go home. Before you bring more shame on your family.' Her voice was quiet and firm.

Malachi waved the gun around and was seized by a bout of chilling laughter. 'Family? What family? My family are my boys! My BOYS! Always got my back. Not like this piece of shit here...' He gave Uriel a vicious kick and turned back to Rosie.

'Old lady, I'm giving you one last chance... Hey...' He choked on the word. 'What you doin? What the fuck you doin...'

Uriel, still doubled over on the floor, twisted his body in time to see Rosie tilt her head back, stretch her arms out, palms upwards and lift her heels from the floor.

'Stop that!' Malachi squealed as she began a slow spin from her broad waist, to the left, to the right, her head back, her eyes closed and her hair hanging down. On her lips, there was a slight smile. 'Stop fuckin doin that!' Inches away from the gun she was, her arms outstretched, the contours of her body growing and growing as she reached upward.

When the bullet flew, it carved a channel straight through her.

She made a startled noise, her eyes bulged from her head, her hands clawed her chest, she looked down and slumped to the ground, her descent muffled by the many layers of her clothing.

Later, all Uriel remembered was Rosie on the floor, looking so much smaller than moments before, with the sorrel staining her dress red and the blood pumping a darker red from the middle of her chest. One of her hands hovered above her heart, twitching; what was left of her life concentrated there. Then it fell silently across the great wound. He had knelt and cradled her. She was warm in his arms but her eyes were dead. He closed her eyelids and laid her on the floor where her blood was already pooling.

On his feet again, grief, shame and rage made him a different being.

Malachi didn't see him coming. He was just outside, his back to the door as Uriel flew at him.

'Why you did that?' Uriel screamed as he turned Malachi to face him, seeing in those fish-eyes shock, fear, then finally resistance. When he felt Malachi's muscles tense into stone, rage swept away all other feelings.

They fought to kill, snarling and biting, choking, pummelling, each trying to get the other flat on the ground. Uriel saw the gun skitter across the bricked path. He heard the clang of metal against stone. They fell on the ground, rolling over and over. Straining towards that dark shape on the path, Malachi's arm was at full stretch, almost touching the gun. They rolled over again. Malachi was underneath him now, still stretching, still groping. Uriel had his hands around his throat and could taste the pleasure of the kill.

He squeezed, then felt the pulse beneath his fingers. He couldn't help himself. His fingers loosened.

Malachi's hand closed around the gun.

Surprise was all that Uriel felt when, flat on his back, he was looking down the steady barrel of a gun. He could see the whites of Malachi's eyes, two pale slits in the darkness. Uriel closed his eyes and waited.

'Fuck this,' said the voice, followed by the sound of running and the screech of a bike engine.

Uriel lay with his eyes shut until the sound stopped whining in his ear. He opened his eyes and started to shiver. He passed his hand down the front of his shirt. There was blood everywhere.

He leapt up and stared at the house. The lights were still on. He pressed his hands to the sides of his head and started running. To the bushes. To the bike. Anywhere... but away... away from that house, that yard.

Where could he go? Who could he go to? With blood on his hands. Who...

In a daze, he ran to his bike and raced down the road with his head about to explode.

Only one thought.

Only one person.

Uriel sprang off the bike, flung it on the grass and pounded on the door. He had never been in this yard before but for months he would ride past the turning. He'd daydreamed of how one day he would walk through this door.

When she opened the door and saw him, he knew that this was no dream.

Silence that was louder than any words. Her scream was silent, his sobbing story was wordless, the silence that followed was deafening. When his knees went from beneath him, her arms held him and shook him into stopping his hysterical tears. She said nothing as she left the room and came back with a clean shirt. Then the squelch of the wet rag on his face as she wiped it clean. The voice on the other end of the phone line as she gave the address was loud. More silence until the taxi came to take them away.

At the police station, it was the same. The silence of turning himself in, of leaving G and going to be interrogated and the silence of the questions that he couldn't hear, but the noise of the policeman's pen as he wrote down his every word, the noise of the bloody T shirt coming out of the plastic bag and being taken away, the noise in his ears, of that dark tide rising in his head and Rosie saying son you need to go home and the noise of those fish-eyes shining in the dark.

When they were leading him away, he saw G there, through the glass partition. Silently waiting.

Nina

Nina drove home from Tess's house humming. She reached over and patted her bag. G's passport was in it. Bob Berkowitz had come through. The I-20 was signed and stamped and the visa issued. She looked at her watch. 21:42. He really had gone beyond the call of duty. When Tess had handed the passport over, she had given Tess a hug and said, 'Looks like our girl can go after all.' They indulged in a little celebratory drink – Chardonnay for Tess, apple juice for Nina. Tess had said, 'Let's call her!' Nina had said no. She wanted to tell her the news in person.

They decided that Tess would travel with Genesis the next day – thanks to the American Airlines niece – and that, all going well, Nina would join them after the weekend.

By Nina's car, they had lingered, rehashing their plans.

'See you tomorrow at the airport at 11:30.'

'Bring your tissues! I know you!'

Nina put the key in the ignition. 'Better get home. Check on G and give her the news. When I left home this morning, her suitcases were locked and right by the door.' Nina smiled. 'Should have seen the packing confusion last night! What goes in, what stays out… Finally, everything's set. As she said, she's been packing suitcases all her life!'

'This works out well for me,' Nina said. 'Once you leave tomorrow, I can go and get Rosie. Tie her up and bundle her into the car if I have to! And tell the people at the Home that I'm bringing Jack to the house until the storm blows over. Imagine Jack and Rosie under the same roof… the Gombey Captain and the Wild Indian! That's always a blast! With all this other stuff to do, I still have to get my house ready. You?'

'Oh, Simmons has been here today. By the time we leave tomorrow, it'll all be secure... You can tell it's coming though. After nine at night and still as hot as hell.'

'Can you hear it?'

They stopped talking to listen to the booming of the ocean.

It was much louder as Nina drove along the South Shore Road but it was just a background to her thoughts. It was so long since she'd felt truly happy.

She fiddled with the knob on her radio and found the Public Information station.

All interests in and around Bermuda should closely monitor Hurricane Fabian, the powerful storm that is heading straight for the island. From tomorrow, there will be large swells and dangerous surf conditions on the South Shore beaches. Once the storm makes landfall on Friday, there will be significant coastal storm surge and flooding in low-lying areas. Currently, Fabian is a Category Four hurricane packing maximum sustained winds of 140 mph. Preparations to protect life and property should be rushed to completion.

'It's a Four now,' she murmured as she drove into her yard.

A bike was lying on the ground.

The front door swung open as soon as she touched it.

'G?'

She stood in the entrance hall. The suitcases were there and lights were burning all over the house.

'Genesis?'

Her eyes moved rapidly around the living room and the kitchen. Nothing was out of place. Then she spotted something. A rag on the kitchen counter. With dark red stains on it.

The phone rang.

'Nina!' Her sister's voice was loud and panicked. 'Why don't you use your bleddy cell phone? I'm comin to get you!'

'What...'

'We're goin to King Edward. It's Rosie.'

It would take Rita one minute, maybe two, to get in her car and come down the hill. In the meantime, Nina went to turn off the lights. In her bedroom she was puzzled to see a closet door open.

Rita found her there.

Nina looked at her. 'Rosie? Where's G?'

In the car, Rita gave her the story. Rosie was dead. Shot. They had arrested someone. A kid. He was 'helping them with their inquiries'. G was at the police station with him. Nina heard the story without comment. At the hospital, she identified Rosie's body and smoothed back the white wings that framed Rosie's face, the only part of her hair that hinted at her age. She heard Rita say that she looked peaceful.

Back home, Rita didn't want to leave her. In the end, Nina persuaded her to. Said she needed to sleep. With Rita gone, she went into her room and to the closet that had been open. She saw an empty hanger where she was sure one of Dee's shirts had been. One shirt was missing. She sat in the dark, waiting for G to come home.

It was in the early hours of the morning when Genesis arrived back, driven by a police officer nephew of Nina's. He had already called and given Nina a full update on what had happened and the role that Genesis had played.

'We've got her statement,' the nephew said from the door. 'She's been very helpful.'

Genesis stood with her head down in front of Nina who still sat unmoving in her chair. Genesis didn't move until the police car could no longer be heard. Nina held out the bloodied rag and Genesis collapsed sobbing with her head on Nina's lap.

'Rosie, Rosie... Help me, Nina, help me...'

Nina lifted the girl's head and made her look at the rag.

'What's that, G? Why does it have blood on it?'

'I cleaned U's face. I didn't want him going to the station with his face bleeding.'

'You? You's face?' Nina's voice sounded strangled, like air being forced through a very narrow space.

'U. Uriel... Uriel, my... my...'

'Your friend. The one who killed Rosie?'

Genesis was on her feet. 'It wasn't him, Nina! I swear! It wasn't. It was Malachi!'

'It was Uriel's friend who killed Rosie? Is that it?'

'Malachi's nobody's friend. Not U's. Nobody's!' The words

came out fast, tumbling over each other. 'Uriel was there because... Malachi threatened to... Malachi and his boys... They're bad, Nina... Real bad... U didn't mean to... he just wanted to... to see if he could... to go get some money...'

Nina's raised her hand to stop Genesis speaking. 'Your friend. U. He went to rob Rosie. Did you know he was going to rob Rosie?'

'No! I loved her...' She grabbed Nina's knees and buried her head in her dress.

Nina stood and brushed Genesis away.

'Get up!'

The girl obeyed.

'This is the boy you promised not to see.'

Genesis nodded, her eyes and nose still streaming.

'This is the boy I told you would drag you down.'

Another nod.

'Listen very carefully. You did not kill Rosie. But that boy would not have known about Rosie if he hadn't known you. If he hadn't seen you long after you'd promised it was over.' Genesis was looking at her feet, her hand swiping at the tears and the snot.

Nina waited until she raised her eyes.

'I don't blame you. You didn't pull the trigger. But as long as I live, when I think of Rosie's death, I'll think of the day you walked into my life.'

Genesis's bottom lip twitched. She closed her fingers around the rag, rubbed it over her face, threw it on the floor and ran into her room and started banging things around.

Nina stepped in front of Genesis as she came out of the room, a small bag on her back. 'One more thing.' She held out the empty clothes hanger. 'Why did you give that boy my husband's shirt?'

'What...?'

'Dee's shirt! On your *friend's* back! On that creature's back! Not enough that I've lost Rosie. I've lost Dee all over again...'

Genesis stood, motionless and silent. 'I take the blame. I do. But you should too!'

'Me?' The word was faint.

'You coulda helped Uriel and you didn't! I begged you to. Begged you!' Genesis stabbed the air with her finger. 'But you wouldn't. Call yourself a Christian? You coulda saved us both. He's just like me. Got nobody! I got nobody now.' She slung her bag on her back. 'Sorry! You won't be able to brag about how you saved me.'

Nina sat in her chair with a whole ocean roaring in her head. In a weak voice she said, 'Genesis, you're not the person I thought you were.'

'Ha! The person you thought I was… It was all an act!' Her eyes fell on the two suitcases at the door. 'You like the truth? Oh, you love the truth… Here's another one.' She kicked one of the suitcases and sent it clattering to the ground. 'I'm fucking the white man! Right under Tess's nose! And yours!'

She slammed the door so hard that a few roosters in the neighbourhood began to crow prematurely.

Nina did not move until the sun had risen in an oppressive and strangely beautiful dawn. In less than twelve hours, the airport would shut.

HURRICANE

The shark's oil never lies.

Traditional

CHAPTER 14: FABIAN

Genesis

Gotta find someplace to shelter. Can't stay here, on this bench. Not today. Not here, just a few feet from the harbour, all revved up and angry, with waves crashing into the dock.

They say you can smell the storm coming, can smell the hurricane. I didn believe them. The usual bullshit. They're right. The air is heavy. Like a stone in my lungs. Behind me, every tree's moaning. No cars on the roads. No bikes. No people. No seagulls. All gone. I been up at dawn before and the sky's never been like this. Clouds streaming across, beautiful, red. When they part, there's the moon, misty, looking down.

Who am I? Who's this friggin person thinking about the moon and the air and the trees? Gotta keep it together, G! Breathe and stop your heart from racing! Gotta tough this one out, like I've done my whole life. I hold my bag tight and something pulls me forward until my toes are right at the edge of the wharf. There it is, the ocean in agony. A year ago, no-one would have *ever* been able to get me to come this close. Not even Uriel. Not even my poor U. I squeeze my eyes shut and his face and Rosie's rise up before me. My eyes fly open. Better to look at the water.

The cruise ship berths are empty. When they knew the storm was coming, they hustled out of here. The pleasure boats are pulling against their moorings. White hulls rocking. Hull, mooring, berth... all useless words Teach taught me this year. Teach. The word tastes sour on my tongue.

Like I need more punishment, I take *that* picture out of my pocket and look at myself with those three women. My three bitches. Just before the waiter snapped the picture, someone had cracked a joke and everybody broke up. Tried laughing like them, laughing like I meant it. Like Teach, they thought they could save me.

Oh God! A big wave has snuck up on me, exploded against the dock, drenching me and stinging my eyes. I jump back and strike my leg hard on the corner of the bench. I look at the picture again. Don't know which pain is worse. No. I do know.

I limp back to the very edge and rip the picture up and fling the pieces towards the water. Head towards the streets of the city.

Nina

Nina looks at her watch. 10:30.

'Don't worry,' she says, leaning out of the car window. 'I think I know where he is.'

The matron of the Home looks relieved.

'Better get inside!' Nina calls out as she reverses. 'Wind's already kicking up.'

Her words give no hint of blame. Inside she's seething. The matron has mislaid Uncle Jack; this woman, whom Nina had mentored as a community nurse years ago, has managed to lose him. But it gives her one clear thing to do, leaving no room for the grief, rage and chaos of the past twenty-four hours. And for that, she's thankful.

Uncle Jack is not the only one to think of Devonshire Bay this morning. The car park is full and Nina elbows her way through a crowd of locals and tourists. The sea's green and belligerent as it threatens the houses huddling on the shore. Nina shudders. Even in sunlit times, she and the sea were not friends. And now here it is, indifferent, powerful. Still, she has a job to do.

She looks around. 'Has anybody seen an old man around here… looking lost?'

Her question meets no interest from the crowd. They are too busy taking pictures of their adventure for the folks back home; the locals, mainly young and male, shout to each other in gleeful voices, glad to be relieved of the tedium of school or work. Then there are the media people, setting up their cameras for live feeds to networks on the East Coast.

Nina takes this in with a single withering glance and shoves aside a teenage boy blocking her path. The hoots from his friends last only an instant as another wave crashes against the rocks near them. She runs, slipping on the mossy rocks and trying to keep her balance, towards the most exposed part of the shore.

There he is, his feet only inches from where the rocky ledge falls into the sea. She recalls the compact, muscular force he was when she was a child, half Samson, half shaman. The person she sees is shrunken, his back bent.

'Uncle Jack!'

He turns, his body blurred by the turbulent ocean surrounding him. She glimpses the shadow of a smile.

'Come! Come away from the edge!' she calls, beckoning him.

He turns back to face the water, straightens his back and raises his arms, his cane held high, his sodden oversized jacket billowing out around him.

'No! Turn around! Walk towards me!' Nina darts forward and reaches him just in time to see the sea rising into a mountain. She throws her arms around his waist and with the wave tilting like a falling tower, pulls him flat onto the rock.

The ocean crashes down on them. Blinded, her limbs pinned to the rock, her lungs filled by a chaos of churning water, she can be sure of only one thing – her arm clamped around the old man's body.

The sea retreats and they lie spread-eagled. Nina rolls onto her side and, curled up like a foetus, can only gag and heave and try to expel the water she's swallowed. She sees another huge wave on its way to the shore. Scrambling to her feet, she grabs Uncle Jack under the arms and drags him to dry ground beneath a clutch of bay grape trees. She collapses next to him.

By the time the next wave strikes, Uncle Jack is walking unassisted, bewildered and incoherent, but more disturbed by the loss of his cane than by the near loss of his life. When they reach the car park, the group of teenage boys are still skylarking, revving up their bikes and putting their helmets on and off. Nina feels the muscles of her stomach clench.

'How you doin, lady?' one of the boys asks. 'How's he doin?'

'You okay?' another asks.

'We're... we're fine... Fine.' She looks into their faces. No malice there. Just kids, young and dumb. But she's still wary of their nearness. *Keep away. Keep away from me.*

She turns to find that Uncle Jack has wandered off. One of the boys has him by the elbow and is leading him back.

Nina rushes over, takes arm and hurries him to the car.

'Thanks', she manages to say. 'Got to get him home!' She pushes Uncle Jack into the front seat.

He's silent all the way home, his body shivering beneath his waterlogged clothing, his face vacant and greyish black. A hot bath, dry clothes and get something warm inside him. Cream of Wheat with raisins and lots of condensed milk. If that doesn't settle him down, nothing will. She need not have worried. As soon as the name 'Salt Cay' becomes visible on the gatepost, Uncle Jack sits up and smiles.

The next hours pass smoothly – bath, clothes, porridge, all accepted without demur. They go outside to make their final check that all the boards over the windows are secure, when suddenly the sky darkens and they make it inside as the first squall sweeps across the island.

Ocean, wind and rain roar. Inside Salt Cay, all is calm. After the bath, the tub has been scrubbed and filled with drinking water and Nina makes a large pot of soup that, with any luck, might last a couple of days in the heat of September. Now she and Jack have to sit it out.

Although it is still early afternoon, it's already dark, inside and out. Jack finds his violin and fingers the strings. Nina turns to the photographs that cover every ledge of the room. She picks up one, a tender smile on her face.

'Remember Arlene? Sixty-three, wasn't it, Uncle Jack?'

He starts to play his one tune.

'That was some storm... Remember? Had to push all the furniture up against the door and a chicken blew down the chimney! That was something, eh? Dee and I were just courtin... And what about when the...' With lids half-closed, she talks while he plays.

Without warning, Uncle Jack stops playing. Nina hears him moving about, his mumbling becoming louder. Reluctantly, she opens her eyes. She finds him right in front of her, holding out one of the photographs from the shelf.

In the early hours of yesterday morning, she had almost crushed that picture under her heel but decided instead to put it at the back, face down, behind the others. How did he find it? He stands there, waiting.

It is one of the few that is not of the Brangman, Fox and Dickinson clans. A memento of a day out, the photo of the three of them and the girl. There is Tess, with her thick blonde ponytail; Lizzie with shades perched atop short black curls; Nina herself, her reddish-brown skin glowing, her head thrown back. Lizzie, who had flirted so outrageously with the waiter, had given him her camera and they were all laughing when he took the picture. Including the girl, her smile flawless and wide. But guarded. Always holding back, even then, at the happiest of times. Lizzie had given them all a copy of that picture and until last night it had pride of place among the other members of her tribe.

She can't bear to look at it now.

'Girl! Girl! Where she to?' Uncle Jack spoke so rarely these days.

'Gone, Uncle Jack. She's gone.'

He looks accusingly at her.

'Back to her own people,' she mumbles.

The black skin of the old man's face puckers into deep folds as he considers this information. Without another word, he returns to his violin. Nina closes her eyes again and tries to resume old time story, as her grandfather used to call it. But as the winds wail and the rain beats down, it's the faces of the girl and the two other women who demand her.

For one sickening moment, Rosie's unmoving face flashes before her.

'How you could like her, Uncle Jack?' Her voice is loud, bitter. 'How… with all she stole from us… from me…'

She paces up and down on the creaky wooden floor. One of the strangest things about the past year was the empathy that had sprung up between the girl and Jack. While she and the other two had tried to keep her on the straight and narrow, the girl had dismissed them as do-gooders but would do anything Uncle Jack asked of her.

Nina takes a deep breath. She's trapped in her house with the hurricane beating at her door. No escape. She lies flat on the floor and tries to will herself into a state of calm. There's a candle next to her. She gazes into its flickering flame. Such a beautiful thing, the light of a candle. So many colours… She closes her eyes, the colours fade and she's back at Devonshire Bay, running towards the old man. She sees his arms open like dark wings with the ocean seeming to rise up at his command.

'Dear God!' she cries, jumping up and running over to the window. On the other side of the glass there's nothing but darkness. 'She's out there!' The old man keeps playing. She snatches his bow and holds it behind her.

'She's out in that storm! The girl! The girl. I… She …' Her fist strikes the sill. 'I told her not to… But she… she never…' The look on Jack's crumpled face opens the floodgate that she has been battling to keep tightly shut.

At last, she dries her tears.

'Genesis,' she says, saying the name aloud for the first time since the girl left.

His finger shakes as he points.

'Yes.' Nina whispers, 'Out there.' She gives the bow back to him and returns to her place on the floor.

The old man remains fixed in front of the blank window and starts to play his tune. In the half slumber that comes and goes for Nina during the storm, she hears this melody, over and over again, inseparable from the violence of the winds.

Lizzie

Somewhere in the house, Lizzie hears the grandfather clock strike three. Outside the wind. But mostly, she hears her mother.

'Making your father go out… in this… *sair na tempestade*!' Ines's head of steam continues to rise and Lizzie struggles to stay disengaged. It's the usual combination of aggression and blame from Ines, sulky defence from Lizzie until the mother weeps, pushed to extremes by a selfish, ungrateful daughter.

The phrase ending in *tempestade* signals an escalation.

'Making your father risk his life... To rescue you from your absurd... *absurdo*... apartment on the hill! A stupid, show-off con-do-min-ium. With a name. You name a house! Not an apartment! Called *Baleia*! Whale! Who ever heard of such... And you... Yesterday afternoon you were here in this house where you belong, safe and sound. Then you go creeping out in the middle of the night! Then refuse to answer your phone...'

'I did not creep out! I left you a note...'

She'd woken to the morning's crimson dawn and decided to cut and run. What a thrill it had been! The drive along empty roads and the satisfaction of entering her pristine, Ines-free zone, her own space... But then came the mounting fear as the storm gained momentum. With each shaft of forked lightning, with each growl of thunder, she'd resorted to her old strategy of slowly counting backwards. It had kept fear at bay for a little while.

Her mother's rant continues unabated, now fully in Portuguese. '...When everybody had to be inside by noon, your father had to...'

In her apartment at noon the power had gone, the building was shaking and the ocean view was blotted out by swirling sea spray. Her laptop was only working on battery power. Its screen-saver was the photo taken by that cute waiter. They all looked so relaxed though it showed that Tess's skin was fighting a losing battle against the sun, and Nina was still the archetype of the solid, respectable black woman, even in mid-laugh. And she herself really did have a killer body... She'd studied Gen's face last. The bones were good and the skin had lost most of those nasty teen bumps. But the smile. Was it real? It was then there'd been a knock at the door. Her father, come to take her home.

Her mother's voice is weakening. 'What would have happened if...' A convulsive shuddering of the shoulders. Another Oscar-winning performance. It was all so familiar. The knot in her stomach and the scene itself. Anything could trigger it – skirt too short, housework not gold standard, friends not Portuguese enough, or too Portuguese. Didn't matter.

Underneath it all, her mother was still punishing her for

bringing shame on the family and endangering their immortal souls. In the fourteen years since, every confrontation between them reeked of it.

João crosses the room and comforts his wife with tissues and soothing little noises. Finally he says to Lizzie, 'Go keep Avó company.'

'*Boa tarde, Avó.*'

'*Boa tarde, minha filha.*'

Avó's room, soft with candlelight, has none of the claustrophobia of the rest of the house. Lizzie holds her grandmother close, breathing in the scent of violets.

'They told me you were sleeping. I would have come earlier if I'd known you were awake.'

'The storm woke me up. She hasn't finished yet,' Avó says. 'She still has a lot of weeping to do before her suffering ends.'

Lizzie picks up the plastic cathedral from among the figurines, happy that after many years of treating her grandmother like a shadow, as the others did, she had got to know Avó, the storyteller, the teacher, the survivor.

She prowls around the room. In that companionable 'silence', Lizzie glances up at a painting she'd given to Avó.

'You've had it framed!' says Lizzie, beaming.

Lizzie holds her candle up to the small watercolour of men in a rowing boat. The flame lights up the sombre colours of the sea, the sky and the thrashing bulk of the whale. In the rolling boat, the men battle the waves, the wind and the beast. Two stand, balanced unsteadily, ready to fling their harpoons; two pull hard on their oars, fighting the massive swells; the faces of the last two are lifted heavenwards.

'Imagine! They used to go out in those tiny boats...'

'That's right,' says Avó, her voice brightening. 'And would come back with enough whale meat for the whole parish!'

Lizzie says gently, 'Go on.'

Avó shakes her head.

'Come on now,' says Lizzie, taking one of the arthritic hands in hers. 'Don't forget. It's because of your story that I named my place *Baleia*.'

The old woman settles back in her chair.

'Although my Vovo, Pedro, came to this island to work the land,' Avó begins, 'he never missed a chance to chase the whales, as he had done back home. In Açores. It wasn't easy for Vovo Pedro to do,' the old woman goes on. 'That work was for the black men. After a while, they saw his skill would be good when the water was big beyond the reef and the whale was making them run. Then one day...'

Avó's story continues. For Lizzie, both the familiar tale and the keening wind are silenced. All she can hear is the pounding of blood in her ears as she looks at the painting. One of the boatmen has overbalanced and is tumbling headlong into the mountainous seas. His companions reach out for him making their boat lurch drunkenly.

'Elisabete?' Avó stares at her. 'Why so pale?'

'I'm fine, Avó,' Lizzie says, trying to find her normal voice. 'Please finish it. Properly.'

'The day that the sea called Vovo Pedro, he did not come. And he never went to hunt the whale again.' Avó pauses. *'Deo gratias.'*

Lizzie tries to get up but her limbs seem locked. Even worse, tears – those despised tools of her mother – threaten. Through the veil of her cataracts, Avó sees this.

'What's the matter?'

'There's...' she said at last. 'There's somebody out there... Lost.' Lizzie's heart swoops in her chest. 'Alone and lost...'

Avó gets up and lays a hand on Lizzie's shoulder. 'Get up, my child. We will light a candle to Santo Cristo and pray that if the sea calls, your friend will find a way back home.'

Tess

Tess shouts, 'Come in here!'

'Oh, yes,' Hugh calls from the other room. 'It's just after four. I'd love a cup.'

'Tea!' Tess snorts. 'Is that all you English people think about?'

Hugh joins her in the kitchen. 'Welsh. Welsh!'

'Whatever. Come see this.' She points to a narrow glass vial mounted on the wall.

'The shark's oil never lies.' She points at the grey, viscous substance in the vial. 'Liquid and crystal-clear yesterday. Now looks like a cloud. A solid grey storm cloud.'

'More island voodoo?'

'Make fun all you like, but some things you scientists can't explain.' Tess hands a plate to Hugh, invited into the Sweet Airs house itself to ride out the storm. She thinks that Hugh's initial excitement over his first Atlantic hurricane is starting to dissipate as the unpredictability of it all starts to dig in.

They take their food into the gallery. Suddenly there's a deafening clatter from the aluminium blinds covering the room's six huge French doors. Tess is sure that Hugh flinched.

'Take it easy,' she shouts. 'It'll pass. It's just rain, hard rain. Maybe hail.' On cue, the squall sweeps past. Tess makes two drinks and hands him one. 'Time for some Dark n Stormies.' She clinks his glass. 'To Hurricane Fabian! May he rant and rave... May he put on a show... and then screw himself in the North Atlantic!'

'To Fabian!' Hugh says, enjoying the sweet consolation of black rum and ginger.

'And to September 5, 2003! Maybe today's going to be a day for the record books!' Tess says, clinking his glass again.

When it is time to down a second, she raises her glass in the direction of the portrait wall.

'Why do you always do that?'

'Oh, I don't know. Maybe because every last one of them liked a drink, no matter how good and worthy they were supposed to be.' In the half-light, the old men with superb moustaches look down at their daughter. She decides it's time for music – while they still have electricity.

The nasal voice and acoustic guitar cuts through the clamour of the storm.

Where have you been my blue-eyed son?

Hugh doesn't like the song. Too long before his time, though the title, 'A Hard Rain's Gonna Fall', was appropriate enough. Tess sings along, slightly off key but word perfect. She leans towards him.

'You want to know who I am? How a woman like me, living in a place like this...' Her arm encompasses the gallery. '...how I got to be – what do the papers call me – a social crusader – in brackets (White)? I'm a child of the Sixties. This is a song of my youth. Told me that change was possible. I sang it. I lived it.' She paused. 'I changed.' She glances up at the family portraits and purses her lips. 'They might not like it.' She drains her glass. 'But I did.'

They drink, she sings, time lengthens and the storm grows fiercer.

A gust of wind, stronger and louder than the rest, strikes the back of the house. The whole building shudders while the shark's oil on the wall darkens into a thundercloud. The lights flicker and die. Outside, the sound of something shattering cuts through the howling winds.

Hugh freezes.

'The dock,' Tess announces. 'Always the first thing to go...' She stands up and sniffs. 'Still... Time to go to the library. That room's like Fort Knox.' She gives Hugh a motherly pat. 'Parts of this house are almost three hundred years old. We'll be perfectly safe.'

They set up camp in the library, Tess's favourite room. The hurricane lamps cast an amber light on the cedar shelves and the leather-bound volumes. After the singing and the Dark n Stormies, the combination of heat, darkness and noise create an oppressive atmosphere that plunges them into silence.

Tess's mind wanders. Her sons, her granddaughter – all in distant cities. Her husband, ever absent, soon impossible even to reach by phone... Then there's the events now over a day old – Rosie, Genesis – the violent events she is still trying to process.

She hears a slight rustling sound.

'Where is she, Tess?' Hugh holds out a photograph he has taken out of his backpack. The picture of the four of them.

Tess takes it from him. Instead of looking at it, she peers at her watch. 5:35. The storm is far from over and the diversion of hunkering down with Hugh is wearing thin.

'Did she leave yesterday? Did she get out before the airport shut?' In a faint voice he says, 'I've been trying to reach her for almost two days... nothing but voicemail. Even Nina's not answering.'

'Who gave you this picture?' Tess asks.

'She did.'

Tess breathes out and pushes away some damp strands of hair from her forehead. She glances at her hands. Time for a manicure. 'And you had to see her so urgently... to give her... final mathematical instruction... before she flew out to go to college?' She hopes her voice masks the surprise she feels. Usually, she doesn't miss a trick. She's known for it! A young man, a young woman. Why hadn't she seen it?

He raises his eyes. 'I need to know where she is.'

She looks down at the photo of Genesis.

Tell him everything? The rumours? Or only part of what she is sure of? 'I don't know... No-one does. She left Nina's house early yesterday morning and hasn't been seen since.'

When he did not reply, she adds, 'Leave that girl alone.'

Hugh takes back the photograph and thrusts it in Tess's face. 'If anything happens to her... I'm holding you responsible! All three of you...'

Something explodes in the next room and the house flails about like a helpless creature. The library door flies open, slamming against the wall, the force behind it snapping one of the brass hinges. Hugh stares, open-mouthed. Winds are battering the ceiling-to-floor blinds, making the interlocking aluminium louvres shiver and warp. The blinds are about to give. Already, thick, sea-saturated air is seeping in.

'The old cellar!' Tess cries. 'Got to get there! Through the gallery...'

They stand rooted to the spot as the metal shutters bend and the ceiling undulates from the pressure of the turbulent air. Hugh makes a break for it, grabbing Tess by the hand, dragging her along. They push aside, jump over furniture, keeping clear of the bulging glass doors. Once through the gallery, Tess takes the lead. As they tear through the kitchen, she thinks, *The only thing that would make me go back to that cellar is this. Running for my life.* But a snarling monster is at their heels, turning the hanging copper pans into deafening cymbals. One of the blinds gives way behind them, buckling and shattering and the rain bursts in, horizontal and laced with salt. Tess glimpses Hugh looking over his shoulder at the hole in the metal and glass where the hurricane has entered the house, at the bulging ceiling, at the curtains, shredded and reaching out like yearning arms, parallel to the floor. She sees him stop.

'Keep going!'

Then a roar comes from the water's edge.

'What's... that?'

Tess knows. The ocean itself has risen from its bed and is walking the earth. They are in its path. Behind them, everything is being smashed to the ground. A high-pitched whining, and part of the roof is sheared off. There is a sudden brightness then all light is consumed. They reach the old disused kitchen, a small windowless space. Tess spins around, wild-eyed.

'This one! Help me!'

Hugh gives the door a vicious kick, which breaks up some of the ancient paint encrusting the hinges. With one frenzied pull, he opens it, shoves Tess in and scrambles through. They push across the four heavy bolts, fall down the steep staircase, made slick and deadly by the torrent, and land painfully on the dirt floor.

Hugh

The ceiling of the cellar is so low that he hits his head against the rough trunks of old cedars. Head down, he inches across the floor, feeling Tess's breath on his neck, trying to distance himself from the water pooling at the foot of the steps. He finds the wall furthest away and they sit down next to each other, leaning against it with their legs braced, praying that the groaning door will hold.

Images flicker across his eyes: curtains reaching out to him; chairs flying like paper planes; roof slates being ripped away.

Tess is saying nothing. She's slumped forward, her body gathered in a tight, shuddering knot. Once, her arms lash out in sharp, defensive movements and then are still.

Hugh can't keep silent over what he has seen.

'I saw it, Tess. The eye. The edge of it. When the roof collapsed, I saw it. I looked up to where the roof had been and saw a patch of blue sky with the sun shining from it. It lasted for just an instant and then... darkness.'

He wishes he could lose himself in sleep, as Tess seems to have done. As the beast rages on overhead, images and sounds grip his mind, taking him into a terrifying and trackless hinterland. He tries to think about the ocean and, as usual, it calms him.

What would it be like beyond the reef? Mountainous seas with no land to cramp them, waves towering and cresting, illuminated by lightning. An ocean in tumult with no horizons. And under the waves? Currents of warm sea water tumbling and boiling beneath the surface, shifting continents of sand, grinding down and sweeping clean the mountain ranges of the deep.

Blue surrounds him, the blue of the calmest of seas. He's diving through water pierced by sunlight. It's darkening but still clear. With every stroke of his arms and every kick of his feet, the sea reveals to him some new marvel. He sees a figure darting through the light-flecked indigo. He races towards it and sees a girl, a young woman, beckoning him with dark slender arms. They play together, endlessly delighting in the weightlessness, the freedom and the grace of this kingdom. She touches his face then swims away towards the black ocean floor.

He hears someone calling out. It's Tess. 'Keep away!' she's shouting, flailing her arms. 'All of you! Keep away!' She still seems asleep, her arms dropping to her sides. In a whisper, she repeats a phrase over and over, 'They called it... they called it... the...'

Hugh leans forward to listen more closely but can't find any meaning in her refrain. He slumps back again and shuts his eyes.

'Breaking room... Where they kept the slaves.'

He hears that and is gripped by a sudden dread of the dark that surrounds him. It seems a living thing, thick and heavy. It enters his body, clogging his nostrils. As he sits with his back propped against the earthen wall, his legs drawn into a triangle, he feels a wetness gathering beneath his bare feet, beneath his buttocks. He feels so tired of all the noise that he cannot make out the sound that might explain this water. They are nowhere near the cellar steps and the rain had stopped cascading down on them once they had bolted the door.

The water keeps coming. Hugh thinks he hears a scuffling, feels one, two, three bristly bodies scuttle over his foot. He tries to call out to Tess; his voice is strangled in his throat. He reaches out for her but clutches air. He cannot see her, cannot see his hand. He must run for it, to save his life, but can't move from the spot where the black water continues to climb up his body. It is slow, the rise, unbearably so, but steady. There is no stopping the rising tide, no escape from the flood that will surely drown him.

He screams.

'Hugh!'

Tess grabs him by the shoulders.

'What... What...' He leaps up, striking his head and looking wildly about him. 'The water! The water...' A single shaft of light comes through a crude circle of thick glass and illuminates the dry cellar floor.

'I saw it! Felt it! The water!'

'It's over,' she says. 'It's after midnight. You've been sleeping. We've been down here for more than six hours. Come.'

At the bottom of the steps, Hugh stops. Hot tears pour down his face and his body shakes, as in a fever. Tess lifts his chin with her hand and he notices how ravaged she looks and feels ashamed.

'I'm all right now,' he says.

They emerge from the cellar, pick their way through the house and stumble outside where a crescent moon sheds weak beams over a scene both wretched and spectacular. Two small sailboats lie splintered on the lawn; the trunk of the great old rubber tree has sheered off, as though cut with a chain saw and many of its boughs lie strewn about. Where the waterspout had spun out of the water and cut across the land, it has left among the ruins a clear black line from the rocks on the shoreline, neatly sidestepping Hugh's cottage, through the flattened fruit and shade trees right up to the wreckage of the library, the gallery and the kitchen.

'I didn't think I would miss them!' Tess says, pointing a shaky finger at what is left of the place where portraits of generations of her family had so proudly hung.

Hugh puts his arm around her and feels her silently weeping against him. 'Look, Tess! The rest of the house is okay... is still there.' A warm wind blows potbellied clouds racing across the moon and in that moment there is enough light to see that, though bloodied, Sweet Airs is still solidly anchored to the land.

'I guess, after three hundred years, it was our turn,' she says, wiping her eyes.

'Do you think everyone, I mean, other people, have been spared? Like us?' Hugh's voice is husky.

'Yes, Hugh. I'm sure she's all right.'

Genesis

I want to surface from the nightmare of the sea rolling over me, roaring and blind. There's two voices in the wind. One high, the scream of some crazy woman, and the other deep and old, the sound of the sea crushing the land. All night long the wind and the sea clutch me and don't want to let me go. But I know it's not only me. There are others caught in this terror, crying *Oh Lord Oh Lord. Let me live till the morning.*

I struggle to awake but sleep still claims me. Then I hear it. Music. It is sweet and moves backwards and forwards like the tide with one tune that is played over and over again.

Only then do my eyes open. At first I don't know where I am. Then I remember. In the evacuation centre with rows of people just like me. Their sleeping bodies are covered in sheets and old blankets. They have no homes, no hiding places. Last night we were told to stay inside here until we are given the all-clear. I step over the sleepers and go outside. The storm has passed. Apart from a few clouds huddled on the horizon, the sky is washed clean. The lovely tune is fading and if I close my eyes I can still see the stars. I'm happy that I've made it through the night.

I lick my lips. They taste of the sea. And right in front of me, there it is... The year. The whole friggin year that has led me to this place. I can't stay here.

AFTERMATH

the wrecks of our past become coral, become stone,
become islands up-rising through the light, become home.

Jane Downing

CHAPTER 15: ADIEUS

Lizzie

Late in the morning of the day after the hurricane, Lizzie watched from the window as her mother surveyed the intact roof of their house, put her hand on her heart and made the sign of the cross. Then she beckoned her family to come outside and restore order to the chaos in the yard. Lizzie's younger brother, Carlos, was about to fire up the chainsaw when Genesis appeared at the gate. Hearing the click, everybody stopped dead: João with a machete in his hand, Lizzie holding a rake and Avó supported by a large broom.

Lizzie's mind started racing. She knew that Rosie was dead. Killed. And Gen was missing. In a brief phone call, Tess had given her the barest outline of what had happened. Since then there'd been too much going on to find out more. But Tess had said, 'Seems like Genesis knows the guy who's been arrested.'

What the hell...

There stood Genesis at the entrance to their yard, furiously brushing off the twigs clinging to her clothes and hair. Then came a torrent of words.

'Had to jump over wires sparking on the road. Coulda killed me! Big trees leaning over or clean outta the ground. A huge branch fell and almost took me out! Couldn't hardly see the roads. Hardly see the way...'

Lizzie's eyes darted between Genesis and her mother, who looked outraged. Lizzie ran between them, just managing to block her mother advancing on Genesis.

Holding the rake like weapon, Lizzie shouted, 'Leave her be!' She pulled Genesis through the tangled mess of the yard to the house and its only sanctuary, Avó's room. Avó welcomed them in and closed the door behind them. It was three days before the main roads were pronounced safe.

The first day was the worst, at least the loudest, with Ines in a towering rage at the presence *in her house* of this stranger, this good-for-nothing, delinquent, protestant, vandal, this Jezebel, snake, devil spawn, gang member, terrorist, criminal. All day the invective was spewed out on the other side of Avó's door, sometimes ebbing, only to flow again with renewed vigour. Ines was in such a state that she spoke only Portuguese, but her meaning would have been clear to anyone.

Whilst the battery-powered lanterns were switched on in the main part of the house, in Avó's room, they still moved about in candlelight, covering the floor with the quilt and sheets that João had smuggled in. They talked in fits and starts, mainly about the storm. Fabian had been a new kind of hurricane, more violent and deadlier than anything that even Avó could remember. When the time came for sleep, Lizzie and Genesis blew out the candles and opened the window to the hot September night.

When she heard Avó's gentle snoring, Lizzie said softly, 'Tell me what happened, Gen.'

'No.'

'What do you mean, no?'

'No, I can't... can't talk... I'll leave if you like.'

'Where to? To Nina's?'

'No! That's the last place...' Genesis sat bolt upright. 'I'm the last person she wants to see...'

The snoring stopped. Avó was awake.

'Don't worry. You can stay with me as long as you need to.' Lizzie turned on her side and threw back the sheet. 'Try to get some sleep, Gen.' She felt Genesis hunkering down beside her and before long, heard Avó's snore start up again. Lizzie's thoughts bubbled. Who'd killed Rosie? What was going on with Nina? Then there was what Ines had called Gen. In all the years she'd been Gen's Big Sister, her mother had exhausted her prodigious store of insults, ancient and modern. But never 'criminal'. Questions whirled around Lizzie's head until she fell into a fitful sleep.

When she awoke the next morning, Genesis was sitting up, her back pressed up against the wall, her legs drawn up in a triangle, her chin resting on her knees. Avó had somehow dragged a chair next to the girl and was sitting with one hand on her shoulder. Lizzie sat cross-legged in front of them.

'What happened, Gen?'

There were long pauses as Genesis struggled for words or when she lost her way and had to say, 'I gotta go back further… so you can get what I'm sayin…'

But Lizzie did get what she was saying, even when Genesis seemed to be loving and hating the same person at the same moment. Especially then. When Genesis had finished, she lay down and almost immediately fell asleep.

'I'm going to get us something to eat, Avó,' Lizzie said and, feeling unexpectedly calm, she walked towards the kitchen where the rest of the family was waiting.

She lit a burner on the stove, carefully poured some stored water into a saucepan and set it to boil. When she turned to get a loaf of bread, Ines stepped forward and switched off the stove.

'That water, that bread is for us. Not for the person you have hiding in your grandmother's room. In the room of your father's mother.'

'Dad!' Lizzie sought out João, but all she could see was thick iron-grey hair on the top of his head. Her brother's head was also down. She'd embarrassed them by bringing this drama in their midst. All they wanted was to sweep up debris, to have a quiet life.

'Get her out of my house!' Ines bawled.

'When the roads are clear, we'll both leave.' Lizzie tried to sound calm though her heart was pounding.

'Get her out. Now!'

Shutting out her mother's command, Lizzie heard instead what Genesis had just said in Avó's room before she fell asleep. She described her losses – Rosie, Uriel, Nina – all gone. 'I had nowhere else to go, Lizzie.'

'Mother…' Lizzie said. Her father and brother still kept their heads down. She walked around Ines and relit the burner. 'She will stay here as long as I do. Not a moment more. Or less.'

'You've gone too far this time, Elisabete.' Ines said. 'Bringing a street person, a criminal into our home. Someone who could kill us in our beds!'

'Stop it, Mother,' Lizzie snapped. 'Stop talking trash!'

'Trash. Truth.' Ines balanced two invisible substances in her hands. 'Truth! That's what I've got! I know she helped kill that old St David's woman! You forget that your cousin Marco is a policeman! Who happened to be on duty on Wednesday night! And who happened to be here on Thursday helping us to batten down for the storm! He told me that he had seen that girl – that girl you've been throwing in our faces for years – he'd seen her at the Station being interviewed! That girl is in your grandmother's...'

Somebody coughed.

Avó.

She nodded at her granddaughter.

'I don't know what you think you know, what you think Marco told you,' Lizzie said. Trying to keep her hands from shaking, she took a slice of white bread from the loaf. 'But that girl...' She waved the bread in the direction of Avó's room. 'That girl has done nothing wrong.' She reached over for the carton of eggs. 'Her only crime is having nowhere else to go.'

Lizzie found a bowl, selected an egg and cracked it into the bowl. For a moment, Ines was as still as a statue as she watched her daughter.

'I know what that feels like,' Lizzie added.

Ines resumed her attack. 'You've always had somewhere to go. You've always had your family, your home to go to! Your parents!' She spun round to João and back to Lizzie. 'But you... you! With all we've given you, all you've ever done is to bring one thing into this house. One thing!'

Lizzie felt a scream powering upward through her body. To prevent it, she snatched up a fork and started to beat the egg, then cracked and beat five more until they were pale and frothy. Only when she was breathing normally did she look at her mother.

'Let me guess.'

'Yes. Shame! *Vergonha*!'

'So I brought it here when I was seventeen. It's a gift that keeps on giving.' She melted some butter in the large frying pan, added salt and pepper to the bowl and poured the eggs in. The only sounds in the kitchen were of the pan scraping on the burner and the fork swirling the eggs around.

'Well,' Lizzie said, 'I'm not having that gift anymore, Mother. I'm giving it back to you. I don't care what you do with it. You can wear it like a crown. You can bury it and bring it out on special occasions. Or you can throw it away. Whatever you do, the shame isn't mine anymore.' She returned to scrambling the eggs. 'It's yours.'

It seemed to take a long time for Lizzie's breakfast to be over. The eggs had to cook, Genesis and Avó had to be seated and given their food at the kitchen table and the dishes had to be washed, dried and put away. All this was witnessed by Ines; the men had retreated to the safety of the yard.

On the third day, the main roads leading to town and beyond were pronounced clear and Lizzie and Genesis left that morning. They said goodbye to Avó who was crocheting in her room. Her legs were paining her but her face was full of light and she sent Lizzie and Genesis off with her blessings.

João said he would drive them.

At the kitchen door, her father suddenly took her in his arms. She could hardly bear to look in his eyes. 'Things will change,' he whispered. 'Maybe now your mother... she'll let go of things that happened to her when she was young.'

Lizzie's eyes scoured his face. She felt his arms tighten around her, sensing that he was drawing strength from her. Over his shoulder she saw the unmoving figure of Ines.

Lizzie looked directly at her mother. Something ancient and something newly-born filled the space between them.

'*Adeus, mãe.*'

'*Adeus... minha filha.*'

No one spoke on the drive to Lizzie's apartment. Back there, Lizzie looked out over the broad sweep of ocean, patted the sign *Baleia* and ushered Genesis inside.

They'd been there for almost a week, when Lizzie's landline came suddenly back on with a call from Tess.

'Do you want a ride to say goodbye to Rosie?'

'How? The bridge is still broken.'

'*Miranda.*'

Nina

Nine days after the storm, we buried Rosie.

The whole population of the eastern tip of the island – cut off from the mainland by the shattered causeway bridge – came out to sing her home. For Rosie, they would walk through the stricken landscape to the Chapel of Ease that sat pale and intact, on the brow of a hill overlooking a now peaceful bay.

Nina and Uncle Jack led the mourners as they entered the lane behind the horse pulling a makeshift hearse. A farmer's cart bore her cedar coffin lying on a bed of fresh green fronds. Forgotten skills were remembered, forgotten rituals revived – because it was Rosie and because of the storm that had plunged the island back into its past. As the horse plodded on, all that could be heard was the sound its hooves and the creak of the wheels. A bough from an overhanging poinciana suddenly crashed to the ground, spooking the horse. Hands sprang into action, soothing Hairpins Foggo's old mare, repositioning the coffin and heaving away the broken tree limb.

Nina, who had stepped forward to rearrange the greenery surrounding the coffin, brought her hand to her face to inhale the scent of palmetto and cedar. Their sap was strong and filled her head with their fragrance.

The cortege moved off again and Nina felt satisfaction in what she'd managed to do – to bury Rosie on the hillside between her husband and her son and among all her ancestors, despite the lack of electricity, despite the absence of a bridge between Nina's part of the island and Rosie's. For nine days, everyone had been afraid to talk to her. She seemed impervious to anything that was not her task. When she was told of Malachi's arrest, she didn't bat an eyelid. The day that Uncle Jack had appeared at her door with Icewater Lewis in tow, she'd thrown a few things in a bag for herself and Jack and had taken the risk of travelling the length of the island in Icewater's fragile craft on still turbulent seas. Rosie's house was a crime scene and could not be touched, but neighbours took Nina and Uncle Jack in, and with their help she'd been able to find the undertaker, find the carpenter, find the cedar, the cart, the horse, the preacher... She didn't have to inform St. David's Island that there would be a funeral.

As she walked along the lane, littered with shredded blossoms and leaves, she felt calm but empty as she surveyed the crowd of people waiting quietly, patiently for a glimpse of Rosie on her way to her rest. They would honour her today for what she was to them – a great link to the past. For Nina, the people who lined the road were an undifferentiated mass, merging into the colours of earth and sky. When someone leaned towards her and whispered something in her ear, the words passed through her into the open air.

The cart groaned to a halt. Pallbearers hefted Rosie onto their shoulders and began to climb the stone steps leading to the church. Beyond the ranks of sago palm, the mourners stood, crowding the churchyard, the lane. Every now and then, Nina recognised somebody, but only in the vaguest way – relative or friend, male or female, young or old... Halfway up the steps, her eyes rested on two faces, with names attached. Tess. Lizzie. How did they get here? It all meant nothing. Her only concern was to mount the stairs towards the wooden door, leading into the darkness of the church.

Inside, Nina could sense nothing but vibrations, lapping against her skin like water – the humming of the congregation, then the bright timbre of their song, the words of the preacher washing over her like waves, the gentle pulse of laughter as person after person stood and gave a Rosie story. Her only real sensation was the feel of the rough skin of the hand holding hers. Uncle Jack. The first time he'd been in church for many years. Coming out of the cocoon she was in, she turned and looked at him, knowing he must be suffering agonies in a borrowed white shirt. The next time he comes to church will be his last – and then there will be nobody.

Uncle Jack squeezed her hand and Nina knew that the service was over and that she would have to struggle to the surface and play her part and walk behind the shining coffin as the voices joyfully sang, *When we all get to heaven...* She put one foot in front of the other, feeling the strength of Uncle Jack's arm holding hers. *What a day of rejoicing it will be...* One foot in front of the other, concentrating on the action, blocking out the song. *When we all see Jesus...* She struggled not to be defeated by the swelling sound. *We'll sing and shout the victory!* Its purpose was to lift her up, that great chorus of voices, but in the darkness of the church, in the darkness of her mind, it was pushing her towards a yawning hole... She gritted her teeth. She would keep it together. She would not be the ostentatious wailer who had irritated her at funerals so many times before.

At last they were outside. She breathed in the fresh air and saw the sunlight bouncing off the white headstones and sparkling on the bay. It would soon be over. She felt she could manage – even if it was the worst part – to watch Rosie's slow descent into the dark earth, the nearness of Dee's and his father's graves, the lifetime of memories she fought hard to keep back. She must manage this because her whole life had prepared her for this moment. She was the eldest child. The rock.

Earth to earth...

She looked down at the handful of cool earth ready in her fingers and she thought of Rosie bringing the soil from Dark Bottom for her tin.

Ashes to ashes...

Unstoppably, the images came. Rosie in her yard, Rosie fishing, Rosie telling off Dee, telling her off, telling off a roomful of people, then feeding them, Rosie comforting her when she felt she'd die of grief... Rosie silent and unmoving on the hospital bed...

Dust to dust...

From nowhere it came. The thing that someone had whispered in her ear on her way to the church.

'The girl. She's here.'

Nina's head jolted up and she saw her. Genesis, standing alone. In a white dress with her eyes down, with the sun shining behind her.

Nina's knees gave way. Uncle Jack caught her and stopped her from falling into the grave.

CHAPTER 16: AFTERSHOCKS

Nina

Nina knew he would come, just didn't know when. One by one she would be done with all of them. That shattered circle, with the girl at its centre.

Lizzie called often. It was hard to shake her off. But she was at least a source of information. Genesis was staying with her. Nina still shuddered at hearing the name. As for Tess, it seemed as though the storm had demolished both her and her precious Sweet Airs.

That left only Hugh. He was sure to come. But she would be ready for him.

When he arrived, Nina was in her yard with her head tied and knee-deep in fallen banana trees. Two nephews were inside the house doing work that generated a huge amount of noise. When she saw him coming towards her, his face flushed and anxious, she could only sigh and pass him her machete.

'Chop this back.' Pointing to the base of the tree, she added, 'Don't touch the root. If you leave the old root, a new one will spring up through it.'

This was all she said until he'd finished dismembering the trees. She wiped her hands on her overall, looked at him and said impassively, 'I suppose you've come about...'

There she stalled.

'Genesis.' Hugh handed back the machete. 'Do you know where she is? Have you had any word of her? Tess is a basket case and Lizzie won't tell me anything... I haven't seen her since before the storm. I've been so worried.'

'Why?'

'Sorry?'

'Why are *you* worried?'

'What do you mean? Why...' He stepped back involuntarily.

'You got everything you wanted. So why are you bothered now?'

'I don't understand...'

'Let me help you.' She passed the machete from one hand to the other. 'You had your way with her because you could. Because she's poor.' Her voice rose a notch. 'Because she's dumb.' Another notch. 'I guess she felt flattered.'

'Now you just wait!' Blood rushed to his face and neck.

'No, I won't wait!' She stepped towards him, the sunlight glinting off the blade. He didn't move. 'I could put you in jail for what you did!'

'What are you talking about?' He eyed the blade. 'Jail? Are you saying I had something to do with what happened to Rosie?'

'Dear God protect me from fools!' She laid the machete on the ground. 'Not what happened to Rosie! What happened to G, you jackass! You abused that child – when she was still a minor!'

'That's not true. When we became... intimate... she had already reached the age of majority...'

'Age of majority my ass! But... I guess I can't prove anything.' She picked up the machete and swiped viciously at one of the few banana trees left standing. 'Anyway, I don't know where she is and, even if I did, I wouldn't tell you! You deserve each other.' Another slice and ribbons of green flew through the air. 'A decent man would have told me. A decent woman would, too. After all, I'm her... I was her...' She drove the blade in the earth and added, 'You're two of a kind.'

He walked towards his bike, then turned back to Nina. 'She's not a child. And she's not dumb.'

'She was dumb enough to get involved with you!' she shouted. 'And that other one. The one in jail!'

Hugh walked back in front of her. A few inches of air shivered between them.

'She has a fine mind,' he said.

'It's the fine mind that excites you? And is it the fine mind that is excited by you? And is it the fine mind in the underaged body that you had sex with?'

The blood rose in Hugh's face and the sinews in his arms visibly stiffened.

'Don't mock me, Nina. Don't mock us!'

His quiet voice was at odds with his rigid body. 'She had already turned eighteen when we made love for the first time.' Nina caught her breath at the word. 'But I'd been in love with her for months before that.'

Twice in two sentences he'd said that four letter word. Only a few minutes ago, she'd been the warrior goddess slicing through his manhood. But with that word – uttered twice – she felt it was she who'd been cut off at the knees.

'Leave her alone.'

'Why? Because I'm white, I suppose.' Anger lit up his eyes.

'Yes,' Nina said. 'After a year in this island, you finally realise that whatever the question is, the answer is race.' She gave a bitter snort. 'Actually, in this case, it's only part of it.'

He grimaced.

'Hugh. You've got a mother and father, right?'

'Yes.'

'I know you've got a grandfather. G told me he was a miner. Right?'

'Yes.'

'You have brothers? Sisters?'

'One of each.'

'Uncles and aunts?'

'Yes.'

'They all cared for you, encouraged you, made sure you studied before sending you out in the world. Yes?'

'Where's this going?'

'You remember sitting at the table with them, having... what do you call it?'

'Tea.'

'Do you remember going to the beach or seaside or whatever you call it? And do you remember Christmas or birthdays or whatever you did with all those people you say you've got? Waking up in the morning and hearing somebody talking or moving about, brushing their teeth. Flushing the toilet.' She paused. 'And do you remember knowing, without even thinking about it, that, good, bad or indifferent, they're yours. That they're your people. Do you remember that?'

Hugh said nothing.

'Of course you do,' she said softly. 'G didn't have that. None of it. Nothing. Just look...' Nina picked up a handful of chaff from the ground. She blew it and they watched as bits and pieces of leaf and twig spiralled down before landing on the earth.

'Her life has been like this. And because of that... She can't feel what you want her to feel.'

'That's not a logical conclusion! You're all mad! You. Tess. Lizzie. The only sane one is Genesis!'

'She thought she cared about Rosie but see how that ended! She thought she cared about me but... All I know, all I know is you're wasting your time. She can't...'

'What right do you have to stand there and say that?' Hugh's muscles were tensing again.

'I have the right because when you know the truth, you can say it.' Nina picked up a small hand of premature bananas and threw them to a far corner of the yard. 'I don't know how I know but I just do.' Words she realised Rosie used to say.

'She can't love you.' There it was. The word she feared hearing or uttering. 'That's the simple truth. Nobody ever taught her how.'

She turned her back on him and walked towards her kitchen.

Tess

Tess was going into town for the first time since the hurricane. She checked herself in the rear-view mirror. Hair swept into the blonde ponytail, make-up carefully applied, a double string of pearls at her throat. But those eyes... Who did they belong to?

Her first stop was the architectural firm charged with reinventing her house. She was in and out inside fifteen minutes – their newest plans just would not do, but she put them in her briefcase and promised to study them and work out what she wanted.

Out on the street again, Tess pulled her sweater around her. November was well under way and the earth had begun to exude damp vapours that made her bones ache. But her heart was still in September. It had not budged since the hurricane which had not only blown apart the only home she'd ever known but ripped up the logic of her life. Much of the house was still standing but the sight of it so exposed and beaten, in places just a skeleton – she felt as though she herself had been swept away that night.

At 9:30 precisely, she entered the offices of one of the island's oldest law firms. It was her twice-yearly appointment to discuss her investments. As she crossed the threshold of her cousin Mickey's chambers, she felt first light-headed, then resolute.

The meeting's agenda would have to be changed.

'Good to see you, Tessie. Heard the old place took a real hit. Good thing Grandpa Nate didn't live to see it.'

The sound of her childhood name threw Tess back to a time when she and this bald man with a paunch – with her brother and a troupe of cousins – had spent wild summers together, in and out of the water, learning how to sail, their hair bleached white, their skins burnt red or brown, under the eagle eye of the grandfather they shared.

'Started to renovate yet?'

'No, not yet. Simmons and his son are just finishing the clean-up.'

'Simmons. Still there? Like he's always been there – even when we were all children. Guess he was a child too. So many good times spent up there...'

'I want a divorce.'

The smile froze on Mickey's face.

'Sorry, Tess. I thought I heard you say...'

'Yes, I did. And yes, I do.'

Mickey crossed to where she was sitting and squatted on his haunches before her. 'In God's name, why? Why now? After...'

'Thirty-nine years.'

'Why now?'

'I don't know,' Tess said. 'It's time.'

'I can't believe it...' Mickey stammered, rising. 'You and Richard...' He returned to his chair, this time speaking as a lawyer. 'You and Richard have considerable assets, Tess. This could be messy, if you can't prove he was at fault. Is he at fault?'

‘Probably. Who knows? There’s been some “other woman” for as long as I can remember. It hardly matters.’ Tess gave a short, disconcerting laugh. ‘I don’t want anything. Except my house. My grandfather’s house. And his grandfather’s... And his grandfather’s...’

‘This is nonsense. Richard had nothing when you married him. All the money he’s made since then was based on what you brought with you.’ He paused. ‘Our family money. Without you, he would still be trying to make it big. New York-style.’

‘Just the house.’ She thought about it. ‘And the money I brought with me.’

‘And the millions since then?”

Tess shook her head.

Mickey tapped the desk with a pencil. ‘If you insist, I’ll draw up the papers. As your lawyer, I must advise you to think carefully about refusing to claim what is rightfully yours.’

‘What’s rightfully mine is that house and my place in it.’ She leaned towards him. ‘He never understood anything. After the hurricane, he called to say I should pack up and leave. Come to live in the Manhattan apartment. Permanently. Said the storm had done us a favour by wrecking Sweet Airs.’ She laughed. ‘It was like he’d never known me – not for a single instant of those thirty-nine years. Like he never got it at all. My life here. My roots. He didn’t know that I could never leave!’

‘I’ll draw up the papers.’

Outside, Tess loosened her hair and breathed in the morning. Then she started making calls as she walked down the street with a swing in her step. On impulse, she decided there was one other thing she would do, and called her hairdresser to ask if she could be fitted in.

It was late afternoon when she reached home. She headed down the hill to Hugh’s place. The storm had left it untouched and, during the day when Hugh was at work, she’d set up base camp there, using its working kitchen and bathroom, meeting workmen and staring into space. She was at his kitchen table toying with a half-empty plate of food when Hugh walked in.

‘What happened to you?’

‘I decided it was time to make a change.’ Tess scraped off her plate into the trash and went to the sink. 'Decided to make some calls. Haven't done that since the storm. I went to the bank and opened an account for Genesis. Was in touch with the President of Sarah Morrison College. They're deferring her place until next September. Lizzie tells me she's… functioning, and starting to talk again. Not about college yet, but she'll get there.' She turned on the water. 'I'm trying to persuade her to spend the next six months in London, doing some courses. That way, she'll be ready to go to Sarah Morrison next September. She needs to be out of here, Hugh, and soon! What with Rosie and Nina, whom I hear has dropped her holier-than-thou act and turned really obnoxious… And that poor bastard in jail. And you, of course! That kid needs to get off this rock!'

Her back was to Hugh so she didn't see his reaction. She did notice, though, that the cottage had become quiet.

She dried her hands and picked up her bag with the plans sticking out. At the door, she said, 'I also decided to get my house in order.' She tapped her forehead with one finger. 'And file for divorce.' And touching the platinum crew-cut shaven to within a centimetre of her scalp, she added, 'and lose the ponytail. You like my new look? It's all the rage…'

By nine the next morning, Tess was back in Hugh's kitchen poring over sketches for the renovation. When Simmons appeared at the door wanting to know what Ma'am had for him to do today, she delivered a monologue outlining all the possible architectural options. Simmons made no reply and stared out of the window.

'Well, what do you think?'

He slowly fished around in his pocket for his cigar. 'Do you want it just like it was before, or do you want it different?'

'That's the question, isn't it?' She gave him an appreciative look. 'The hell with these!' She swept the plans off the table. 'Let's see for ourselves.'

They climbed the low rise that separated the cottage from the house. From this angle, it looked like the beaten face of an aging prizefighter. The spectacular glass front was a lattice of plywood and pitch pine; the patio was stacked with concrete blocks; the pool drained and where the roof had been blown off, tarpaulin flapped. Through a recently erected wooden door, they entered a world where plastic sheeting covered everything – boxes of books, paintings hidden in brown paper, bubble-wrapped porcelain, veiled sculptures, sofas under drapes – all eerie in their plastic shrouds. They walked through what had been the library, the gallery and the kitchen.

'I'm thinking that... I don't want it as big as it was before. I won't need it now.' She looked at him over her shoulder. 'Mr. Alexander and I are splitting up. No need for all that entertaining...' With a wave of her hand, she dispatched the gallery, the patio and hundreds, maybe thousands, of dinner party guests. 'No need.'

Simmons shifted on his feet.

'You know, I'm so ready for this. Ninety per cent of me has been ready for years. But that ten per cent wouldn't let go. Now it has, I feel... okay.' Tess blushed. 'Sorry. I'm embarrassing you.'

Simmons lit the stub of his cigar and through the smoke said, 'Lot of changes. Can't stop change.'

'Most of us try!'

She pulled aside a plastic curtain into the original kitchen and before her was the ancient door. 'Simmons!' she called out as she fiddled with the rusty bolts. 'Help me get in.'

He placed his considerable bulk between her and the door and gave it a good pull. The smell of damp earth and rancid air rushed up and spilled over them.

'We need some light. Wait here,' he said, turning back.

Since the night with Hugh when this room had provided shelter from the storm, Tess had tried to block it from her mind.

'Let's go.' Simmons switched on the flashlight and carefully followed its beam down the moss-covered stone steps, with Tess inching her way behind him.

The room was bigger than she remembered. The floor was partially cemented but the greater part was earth and overhead ran the untouched trunks of cedars. The walls were a patchwork of plaster and untreated stone. On the far wall, there was a pool of weak light emanating from the single rough window, the one that Hugh said reminded him of a porthole. The room felt so empty, so at odds with her memory of that night when it had teemed with hostile presences. She took a step closer to Simmons and reached for the flashlight.

'Have you been here before?'

'No. But I heard about it.'

'Who from? This cellar isn't on any of the plans.'

'My people's lived round here for generations. A good few of us've worked here. So yah, I been known about this place.'

Tess tilted the flashlight upwards full onto his face, as he was saying 'this place'. It startled him into stillness for a moment. Then he moved his head back into darkness. Tess knew that image would be graven in her memory – the thick grey hair springing out from beneath his cap; the creased brown-amber skin with the twin tracks running across the forehead; the grey-ish-brownish eyes, sometimes hooded, always watchful. Tess could not remember a time when this face, or some version of it, had not been there, next to her, as present as the house itself. Yet, in this dark and murmuring cave, it was the face of a stranger.

She put the flashlight on the ground.

'Did any close relative of yours work at Sweet Airs? Your parents? Grandparents?'

'My mama, no. Never.'

'Never?'

'No. Didn't want to.'

'Really?'

'She worked in the hotels. My granma, who raised me, she wouldn't work here either. No way. But *her* mama did. Not for long. She left when she was still young, my granma said.'

'Your great-grandmother. That was a long time ago.'

She walked around the room in silence, trailing her fingers along the rough damp walls. The presences were alive again, like they had been on the night of the hurricane, mumbling as though from a far place. Their language was indistinct but the sound familiar. There were questions she wanted to ask; if she could only talk to them.

The murmurings went quiet. A great weight descended on her. There would be no relief from this burden. *Wouldn't work here… Didn't want to… Never.* She went to pick up the flashlight from the ground, but her mind was so clouded that she tripped on the torch. Simmons reached to steady her. In the momentary tangle of arms, the beam fell on the arm that had kept Tess from falling.

His sleeve was rolled up. There was a raised brown spot, splayed like a spider, an inkspot, just visible on the dark amber of his skin. She dropped the flashlight and covered her own burning forearm with her hand. Covered the birthmark stamped on the arms of her family since their ancestor scrambled ashore three hundred years ago – the family brand.

She felt Simmons's eyes on her, scorching her as she took a few faltering steps backwards and sat down with her back braced against the wall.

He stood on the bottom step, struck a match and relit his cigar. Tess stayed seated on the damp earth as images and words assailed her. She was nine years old again, holding her grandfather's hand, trying to understand the words bursting from his mouth.

This is how it's done.

Rough… Make 'em holler.

Her heart was sore for Nate, who had tried not to be like his father. How many of the bearded patriarchs had been like Nate? How many like his father? *My great-grandfather.*

She saw the light of the burning cigar, smelled its smoke. She thought of the girls. The women. How many had there been? How many? In the breaking room.

His great-grandmother. Young. Shiny. Black.

'Why do you work here, Simmons?' Tess's breath came in uneven bursts. 'And why do I call you Simmons? You've got more than one name. Your name is…'

'Gladstone. Gladstone Whitfield Simmons.'

She gave a feeble laugh and put her head in her hands. 'I knew that. I've always known that! I know where you live. I know your wife's name. And your children's… But…'

Tess wanted to get up and face Simmons. But she seemed chained to the spot. All she could do was to lean towards the tiny point of light of his cigar.

'What made you come to work here? When your family refused… after all that had happened?'

'I wanted to quit lots of times.' His words had the tones of a stern schoolmaster. 'I coulda gone and worked construction. Made more money. But I thought I would wait.'

'Wait for over forty years? What for?'

'I'm a patient man.' Simmons tapped ash from his cigar. 'Maybe I was waiting for today. For right now.'

Her hand flew to her mouth but failed to suppress the cry. She managed to heave herself up and stagger towards him.

'It'll be a lot easier to quit now.' Simmons walked up the steps, head erect, taking care not to slip. At the door, he turned and spoke as though addressing an assembly. 'But not just yet.' He blew a perfect circle of smoke into the air. 'Nobody knows how to care for *Miranda* like me. And…' This time, he spoke directly to Tess. 'And besides, I'll need help when it comes time for Akeem to go to college.'

The tendrils of smoke spun and twirled and made their way into the farthest recesses of the room. For one moment, they defeated the bitter, stagnant air.

Tess slumped back down onto one of the cold stone steps, her shorn head drooping between her hands like a penitent who fears repentance has come too late.

Genesis

When I hear Lizzie's car pull up on the gravel drive outside the apartment, my guts cramp up and I start looking for ways to keep my hands busy. The food is cooked and ready and the table all set. There's a big smile on Lizzie's face when she comes in and sees dinner waiting, but how long before that smile is wiped off her face?

'Hmmm. What's it tonight?' Lizzie puts down her bag and peeps under the covered dishes. 'Smells good.'

'Chicken and mashed sweet potatoes. New recipe.' I take a deep breath. 'I'm expecting an important phone call tomorrow.'

'Oh?' Lizzie sits down and picks up a serving spoon. 'Who from?'

'Uriel.'

Lizzie says nothing for a couple of minutes, with the spoon dangling from her hand. I'm standing behind her so I can't see if her lips are moving, if she's counting backwards like she does when she's trying not to scream. She told me that. One of those secrets she let me in on.

'When did all this happen? Those guys... prisoners... can't call you up just like that. You have to make arrangements.'

'Been working on it for three weeks now.' I hand her an envelope lying next to my plate. 'A scheduled call. Tomorrow... ten o'clock.'

'Why didn't you say anything?'

No time for bullshit. 'Because I couldn't stand you trying to persuade me not to.'

Lizzie slaps three big dollops of potato onto her plate then shoves it away.

'I can't tell you what to do, Gen.'

'No you can't.'

Lizzie says nothing for a while, then bursts out, 'Don't you think you need to put some space between you and that boy? Give yourself some more time to get back on your feet... Because you're not over it yet. Talking to whatshisname again could set you back!'

'His name is Uriel, for Chrissake!' Why doesn't she understand? Why doesn't anybody?

'Listen!' I keep hearing myself like it's somebody else. I move so I'm facing her. 'I won't be able to get back on my feet living here in your apartment pretending there's no Uriel. Until I speak to him, better yet see him, I'm stuck, I can't move, I'm lame.' I can't tell her that his is the one face always with me, the one with the golden glow.

'Lizzie, you've given me a place to sleep, food to eat... You've been a friend.' I go and sit next to her, just inches away, but not touching. 'Thank you.' I say it and mean it. 'But he's been writing to me and I've been writing back.' I try not to think of his letters. 'I have to do this.'

Lizzie shakes her head but says nothing.

'I know you don't think it's a good idea. And I'm sorry.' Saying sorry and meaning it. Still new to me. 'There's no-one else. I've got to help him. I'm all he's got!'

Lizzie gets up from the table. 'I'm not hungry.' As she passes, she says, 'The only thing I really understand is the bit about being stuck. I know about that. I just hope that talking to Uriel won't make things worse for you. Good night.'

I take my time clearing up the kitchen. I put off going to bed as long as I can. I dread it these days. There's either terrifying nightmares or I sleep the sleep of the dead. Either way I wake up exhausted. I climb into bed and sleep comes quickly.

I am eighteen years old and I'm walking on the beach. A group of boys – ten, twelve years old – are playing. It's a rough game and they've found someone to push around. Trying to get him on the ground. A boy, small and skinny. But fast. He makes a break for it and dives into the water. The others follow, led by a short stocky boy. But if the game is rough, so is the water. In front of him are ocean swells piling in one after the other; behind him is the pack of howling boys.

I start running towards him. He sees me. A wave breaks over him and takes him under. His head breaks the surface of the water. I hear his voice. Clear, above the noise of surf and shouting boys.

Help me Genesis! Help me!

I wake up feeling rested and calm. When I hear Lizzie moving around getting ready for work, I put the finishing touches to my plan.

He will hear my voice and know he doesn't have to be that person who wrote those letters to me. Somebody should have to pay for letting children go through school and not be able to read or write! But despite the terrible spelling and worse punctuation, I could still hear his voice. *Dunno how Im gon do this G. Dunno how.* I can see him in his orange outfit, fighting with pen and paper, trying to tell me what it's like, his head down, his back hunched.

He will hear my voice and know he's not alone. We've had each other since Primary 1. He will hear my voice when I tell him about my plan. How I will find a way to get someone to listen to his story. Because the only way he can survive is if he has hope. I will find somebody to see what happened to him – not just on the night Rosie died, but every day since he was born. I will find somebody who will believe that he will grieve for Rosie every day of his life…

I will use everything I've learned to stop him giving up. My whole life is about that now. Nothing else matters. Nothing.

The phone rings. I'm ready.

'Hello.'

'Good morning. Is this Genesis Smith?'

'Yes.'

'This is Prison Officer Dwayne Trott from the Westgate Correctional Facility. Please confirm your postal address.'

'Number 5 Ocean Vista Drive, Southampton SB04.'

'And your relationship with inmate Uriel Caines?'

'He is my close friend.'

There's a pause. Like when I asked the first prison officer for permission for this call a few weeks ago. The problem? I'm not a family member. But I'd argued – in a way that I'd heard Tess argue and Nina argue, without cussin or raising my voice – that for years, his mother had been in and out of jail and that no other relatives had taken an interest in him. That he and I had been friends since we were children and still were. After some discussion, that officer had said yes.

But I'm worried about the pause from Prison Officer Trott.

'All right, Miss Smith. I see that you have made payment for this call at Central Office.' Another pause. 'Here is Inmate Caines. You have fifteen minutes.'

'Hey, U!' Last night, in bed, I'd practised my cheerful voice.

Nothing. Finally, a voice says, 'Hey, G.' I don't recognise the stranger's voice. Old. Rough. All cried out.

How to start. Try to sound like you have some answers. That you're not worried. That everything's going to be fine.

'Everything's going to be fine, U.'

There's silence on the other end of the line.

'Not you too. I never expected this bullshit from you, G!'

'What are you taking about?'

'Talkin about? Talkin about spendin the rest of my life here! When I shouldn... I didn... kill... nobody! Nobody! Specially not Rosie! I was there. That's it. I was there when it happened. That's it! And I know Malachi's tellin a whole pack a lies about me. He's not goin down without me that's for sure... He's gon take me down!'

'Stop!' I want to put a gag over his mouth to stop that sound in my ear. Like a child stamping its foot and bawling. 'Uriel, stop runnin your mouth! Listen. Listen to me! For the past couple of weeks, I've been looking things up in the library and online and trying to find out as much as I can about... what's happened to you. Researching. They're charging you for being there. Malachi's saying you knew all about it. That you and him's been planning it. They don't know if that's true. It's your word against his. But they will have to prove that you intended to commit a crime. That you had *intent*. I think with a proper lawyer, a good lawyer, that charge could change.'

'So you're lawyer now!'

'No. But I promise you on a stack of bibles that I'm gonna get you a decent one. A good one. I know people now! They'll help.'

'How you gon do that? You're just outta high school.'

'Don't you know me at all? I'm gonna do it!'

Silence again.

'I got one question for you.' It's something that's been bugging me. 'Why did Malachi do it? A ninety-two-year-old woman? That's messed up even for him.'

'That's easy.' I think I hear something like a laugh. 'Because he's fucked up!' By the last word, his voice had broken down. 'And now he's telling all these lies about me. You know I wouldn't hurt Rosie, don't you, G?'

I don't even say anything. That he could even ask that question...

'I'm so screwed, G. Not one member of my screwed-up family would stand up for me. Not one! Nobody! They say I'm a waste a time.' It sounds like he's crying.

'But you got me! I'm gonna help you find the lawyer that you need. I'll write, call and visit when they let me. And I'll go to court and I'll be a witness. I'll tell them who you are!' My voice. So strange. Like somebody else talkin.

'But...' He takes a breath. It's like I can hear him thinking. 'They say it can take up to a year for the trial.'

'Whenever it is, I'll be here.'

'But... what about... goin away? To that school you told me about? When you goin to school?'

'Don't worry about that, U.' I'm smiling and wonder if that makes my voice sound different. 'I'm not going there anymore. I'm staying right here. Nobody's gonna be able to say that you got nobody. You got me! And when you get out, I'll be there at the prison gates waiting for you.'

It's the idea that's been forming since the night it all happened, since the long hours of the hurricane, since I saw Nina almost fall into Rosie's grave. My heart's been bursting to tell him. And now he knows.

'Ya not goin away? Ya stayin here… to be with me?'

'That's right!' I *can* hear the smile in my voice.

He doesn't say anything. For a long time. I check my watch. Fifteen minutes will be up soon.

He clears his throat. 'G.' He clears his throat again. 'Genesis. I…'

As I try to work out what he's trying to say, I feel a terrible pressure in my head.

'I gotta go.'

Click.

The call is over.

CHAPTER 17: NOBODY'S CHILDREN

Uriel

Hey, G!

I tried writin you but couldn hack it so my PO says why don't I tape it so he lends me his tape recorder and gives me this tape. He aint bad.

Now!

I've already told my PO if you ask for another scheduled phone call the answer is no. Don call me and don try come or write. I know ya gonna be pissed at me but I'm serious! Ya not stayin here watchin me sweat bricks in this place! I mahswell lock you up myself and throw away the key.

If you don want to go away to school, that's ya business. But it won be because a me. No! Bad enough havin Rosie on my conscience. No way I'm havin you too.

No friggin way!

You was always a real smart somebody. Shouldn just be me that knows it. You need to go. Get outta this place. Forget me. And the Robinson Home. And the mamas and deddies what threw us away. Forget all that! All you gotta do is get that plane outta here.

Thinkin about that is the only thing that can make me lift my head up.

Don't take that from me, G!

[Clearing his throat]

G, I wanna tell you something. Wanna answer ya question. Why did Malachi do it? Why didn he shoot me? I was the one who didn give him his money. He shoulda shot me.

But he shot Rosie. If she'd a been cryin and beggin, he wouldna done nothin to her. She was scared alright. I was on the ground thinkin my guts was split open but I could see her. She was shakin all over.

All of a sudden she stopped. Stood there lookin straight at him. That woulda pissed him off. Wasn expectin it. So he smashed up her pictures. Then what she do? She tells him somethin bout bringin shame on his family. Ki don't like that kinda talk. He acts so hard but he don like that kinda talk. Specially from somebody who all of a sudden don look scared a him. Then she starts actin all weird. Head all back. Swayin. Arms out. Eyes closed. Like she don care. I never seen anything like that before. But that's Rosie. Sayin and doin things you can't understand!

But for Malachi, all he sees is somebody standin in front a him with her chest stuck out. Like she's darin him to do somethin.

I could only see his back. Couldn see his face. Just Rosie doin that crazy thing. But I did see his hand holdin the gun. It was shakin big time. But I didn think he'd use it.

He was outta there before she hit the ground.

I never seen somebody run like that in my life. Never seen nobody that scared.

So to answer ya question. He shot her because he thought she was dissin him. Cos for him, the world is dissin or not dissin. Anything else, he can't handle.

I'm in that world now. Yah. That's my world now. The first night I was here, when I heard my cell door slam shut, it was bad. It was real bad. I felt like pullin the blanket over me and goin in the dark. But part of me, G, you know... for part of me, it didn sound strange at all. It was like my whole life had been leadin me to that sound. Like I was kinda... home.

But not you. Not you. No! Not you!

You... gotta... get goin!

Get away from here! From me!

Get!

And don look back.

Nina

'Nina! You've got to come!'

'What the...'

'You've got to come!'

'Who's this?' Her mind cloudy with sleep, Nina squinted at the clock. 'Calling me at... twenty past twelve?'

'Nina! Get up! I need help!'

In the time it took her to throw off her bedcovers, Nina went from deep sleep to wide awake. 'What's going on, Lizzie?'

'Gen!'

'What's she doing?'

'She's been acting crazy since I got home round seven. Couldn't keep still. Never stopped walking around. Then around nine, she locked herself in her room. I've been talking to her through the door but she doesn't say anything. But I can hear her walking around, bumping into things. I think I hear a voice – a man's voice. Then hers, kinda mumbling. No words. No words I can understand... You need to come!'

'I'll be there in fifteen minutes.'

Ten minutes later, Nina was at Lizzie's door. One look at Lizzie made Nina wonder who the patient was.

Putting down her weathered bag from her community nursing days, she walked to G's door and called, 'Genesis. Are you all right?'

There was a loud thud as something hit the other side of the door.

'A slipper,' Nina said. 'Lizzie, put the kettle on. You're going to make us both a cup of tea and then tell me what's been going on.'

'You're not going to force her to open the door and make sure she hasn't done anything to herself?'

'No.'

Lizzie glared at her but nevertheless put the kettle on. Soon she was sipping tea and talking while Nina listened.

'I've had her here since Rosie died and... She's been sad but she was getting better. Doing things in the apartment. Going to town. Trying to cook. Getting better. Then she had this call from Uriel. Three days ago.'

'What! She's been in this state for three days?'

'No. She was upset after the call but calmed down. No! Something happened today!' Lizzie handed Nina an opened envelope addressed to Genesis. 'This came.'

'He wrote to her. Whatever he said...' Nina turned the padded envelope over and over, studying the uneven handwriting. 'It was the last straw.'

Nina went to G's door and gave it three sharp knocks.

'Genesis. It's me.'

Another missile hit the other side of the door.

'Open the door!' Nina tried the handle and in a low voice said, 'Please open the door. I have a question to ask you.'

There were more noises from the other side – something being dragged across the floor, fumbling, mumbling and then a man's voice saying something like *not you*. Then a click followed by G's voice saying *Not you. Not you*.

Just as Nina was trying to work if it was *not you* or *not U*, the door flew open. She was shocked at what she saw. Genesis prowling around the room, seemingly unable to keep still. One arm clutched something to her chest. Her lips were clamped shut and her eyes looked unfocused.

As she watched Genesis kick some random object aside, Nina thought of all her training, all her years in hospital wards, in clinics, in people's homes, but none of it was any help at all. What was she going to ask Genesis? What was the one question that the girl's confused mind might hear.

'Genesis, what do you want me to do?'

The girl sat stiffly on the bed, pressing her treasure between her breasts.

What should she do? Call 911, have her assessed, hospitalized? Should she speak lovingly to her, should she be severe, should she comfort her with the psalms? She had a Gideon bible in her bag. No. Of course not! Should she call Tess, maybe Hugh? God no. Should she contact Uriel? What! He's in jail and it's the middle of the night! He's the one who had finally broken her.

Genesis had wept a river of tears that night when she'd promised never to see Uriel again. No tears this time as she climbed onto the bed, lay there and seemed to fall asleep. Nina approached the bed. Whatever state G was in, it was not sleep. Eyes tightly shut, Genesis was on her side, a perfect straight line from head to toe, and buffeted by tremors. Nina's hand inched towards G's rigid body and brushed her bare arm. The arm jerked Nina's hand away as if it was an annoying insect.

Nina sat back and watched as Genesis, moaning, curved herself into a foetal position. As she did so, Nina caught sight of the cassette tape clutched in her hand.

Whatever was on the tape was the reason for the monumental

distress that Genesis was feeling. It threw her back to the past, to the moment when she had felt the longed-for life slithering out of her body. After years of trying, she and Dee had rejoiced at the miraculous pregnancy and one month later grieved at its bloody end in a toilet bowl.

As Rosie had done for her all those years ago, she climbed onto the bed and curled her body around G's. She would stay there within an inch of her until the trembling stopped.

Genesis

After I heard Uriel's tape, I didn't stop falling until I was lying at the bottom of the ocean.

I slept for many hours and did not dream. When I opened my eyes, Nina said I called, 'Mama' and then fell asleep again.

Didn't call out to Uriel who'd told me to get away from him. Get away from our good times. Get away from the only childhood I can remember. Get away from the feeling that I only had to see him smile and I would be all right. That one sound. *Get!* It cut me like a dagger.

And I agreed to go back to stay with Nina, against my better judgement. Why? Maybe calling out 'Mama' was the clue.

Back at her house, Nina wanted to talk about Uriel and what he'd said and what I'd said. I didn't feel like talking so she talked instead.

She told me she'd listened to the tape lots of times and knew why it made me fall off the cliff. She realised he was the only person who'd known me all my life. Well, not all, but most of it. That he and I had both known nobody wanted us. That during all our growing up, he alone had helped me and I alone had helped him.

She asked me why I'd told Uriel that I wanted to stay with him and not go away to school. That question hurt my head but I told her anyway. Told her that I would sacrifice anything if I thought it would give him hope.

Nina sat nodding. There's only one way to give Uriel hope, G. And that's for you to make something of yourself. Don't you understand, G? While you were trying to give him hope, he was trying to give you freedom. Your freedom is his hope.

I stopped talking again for a day or so while I twisted and turned around that conversation.

'I want to find out about my mother,' I said to her.

'What do you know about her?'

'That she drowned in the sea. And she was twenty-one years old.'

'What do remember about her, G?'

'Not a thing. Except the name. Joy.'

'Nothing? You were four years old when she died.'

'Every now and then, I get tiny flashes of something. But basically nothing.'

'Why do you want to find out about her now?'

'When I heard that tape for the first time, I remembered when Uriel and I met. My first day in big school. I was five. That means that I had a life before him. I want to know what that was like, my life before Uriel. I want to know what she was like. Before I lost her.'

Nina said okay and I know she started looking for information about my mother from that same day. Every evening, I waited for her to come home and tell me what she'd found out. She put her whole family to work. All her nurse and teacher nieces, her police and computer-nerd nephews, her born-again sisters, her Dark n Stormy brothers. Their project wasn't me anymore. It was Joy.

Every day, she brought something home. The first day, she brought one of those big picture albums that have pages covered in plastic. The next day, she brought a copy of Joy's birth certificate. I carefully peeled back the plastic, pressed the certificate onto the sticky page then smoothed the clear cover into place. Only then did I look at the details. Name. Date of Birth. Place of birth. Names of mother and father. This was the start.

It went on like that for weeks as I placed bits and pieces of her life in the album. Nina's people dug up a ton of stuff I never knew before. The computer geeks found entries in public records; the nurses got access – illegal? – to medical files; the babylon nephews found the coroner's report on Joy's death. The teacher nieces got their hands on report cards from Joy's school days. But the real gold came from a born-again sister and a Dark n Stormy brother. Each of them provided a key name from the past. One, an upright woman of God; the other, a sweet-talking, hard-drinking man of the street.

Eventually the album was filled with reports, articles and certificates, all records of my mama's life. There were a few pictures of her in school uniform. The last to go in was something that Nina wrote, where she put everything together.

Before she read it out to me, she said, 'I'm sorry, G, there's still a lot we don't know and I've talked to so many people in the past months.

It went like this:

'Bradshaw Smith and Agnes Lee were married in Charlestown, Nevis in 1958. Soon after that, they came to join Agnes's sister, Dorcas, who had worked in Bermuda for several years. Joy Hyacinth Smith was born here on April 19, 1960. When she was barely a year old, her parents took her back home on a visit but were tragically killed in a boating accident. Dorcas Lee went to Nevis and got her, brought her back to Bermuda and became her adoptive mother.

'Joy's primary and secondary school reports say that she was a good student, conscientious, but with a dreamy streak. Dorcas was well regarded at her job but kept to herself. She was a devout member of the Calvary Baptist church; even there, she kept the congregation at arm's length. She found Joy's open nature a trial and discouraged friendships with other children.

'When Joy was sixteen, she caught the eye of Maxwell Binns. For Dorcas, his worldly ways were an offence against God and she ordered him to keep away from Joy. But they continued to see each other secretly and she became pregnant with his child.'

Nina stopped and smiled at me. 'You.

'Dorcas never forgave Joy. She packed her bag and left Bermuda to go back to Nevis for good, soon after you were born.

'The relationship with Maxwell must have turned sour and Joy evidently spent the next four years trying to get away from him, but he was a possessive and controlling man and wouldn't let her go.

'This is what I have found out about the day Joy died. Some of this comes from police reports, some from people I've spoken to who were mentioned as witnesses in the newspapers, and some I've had to guess.

'From early morning, neighbours heard loud shouting in the apartment where they lived. They saw Maxwell storm out and, later, Joy and the little

girl also left home. They caught a bus to the beach. A couple on the beach that day said that it was sunny but a yellow warning flag was flying. One woman remembered the little girl and her mother laughing and playing in the sand with a bucket and spade. Then Joy went into the water. A witness said she looked happy, holding out her long white skirt, waving at her daughter, dancing in the shallow water, her back to the waves. Dancing with such abandon that she didn't realise what was behind her. Suddenly she lost her balance and went under as a large wave broke. The lifeguard saw her in a full panic, being pulled out into deeper and deeper water. He ran in with a life preserver and towed her ashore. He administered CPR but she was already gone. The police went to her apartment later and, in a bag under the bed, found a passport and two airline tickets for the next day, in the names of Joy and Genesis Smith.

'In the absence of any blood relatives, the congregation of Calvary organised Joy's funeral but it is not clear where she is buried.'

I took the paper from Nina's hand, carefully placed it in the album and walked outside. I knew if I allowed myself to feel even the tiniest thing, it might drown me.

But, now I knew her full name. Joy Hyacinth Smith. Her parents' names. And where they were from. And why I'd never heard of them. The name of the woman who raised, then abandoned her. And the name of the man she was running from, the man she almost broke free of. The name of my father.

I'd never had names before. Names that belonged to me.

*

I'm standing on cool wet sand at the edge of the water. Uncle Jack is with us – Nina and I. She gives me a garland of white flowers. The last breath of a tiny wave runs up to my toes but doesn't touch them. I make sure of that. But still I have to make an excuse.

'Can't trust this February sun, Nina. The water's gonna be really cold.'

The three of us look around at the wide, horseshoe shape of the beach. No litter. No loud music. No tourists. No locals. Only us. Clean sand and flat blue water with the early morning sun making it shine. Bubbles of surf almost catch my feet again. This time I jump back and can't stop shaking. Nina reaches for my arm.

'You don't have to do this, you know. I'll take the flowers in for you. The fact that you've been able to come here is enough.'

I look down at the sand and hand the flowers to her without raising my head.

'Genesis...' Nina speaks softly. 'G, we have so much more to find out about your mother. There are so many things we don't know. But we do understand one thing. The reason why you've spent your whole life fearing the water.' I know this is not quite true, but I've never spoken to her about learning to swim with Hugh. She steps away from me. 'And you're brave enough to return to the place where you saw it happen fourteen years ago. You've come to honour Joy and to invite her to become part of your life again.'

Even so, it's what I've been dreading... the trembling, the buckling knees, the racing heart. Someone grabs my shoulders. The same someone smiles at me. A smile without teeth. A smile without end. Nina is looking in Uncle Jack's direction, but it's as if she is looking past him. Who is she seeing? Where has her mind wandered to? To what past? I don't know. All I know is that, at this moment, when everything seems a blurred illusion of sun and cold sea and sand, present and past, living and dead, a pair of rough old hands are keeping me from falling.

Jack and I are witnesses when Nina walks into the water. The quick grimace on her face shows that it really is cold but she keeps going, one slow step after the other. The ocean is up to her knees when she turns around and holds up the flowers, showing me that she's doing this in my name.

Then Uncle Jack takes the first step towards the water. 'Nina!' I call out as Uncle Jack's feet meet the ocean an instant before mine. 'We're coming in!'

We catch up with Nina and the three of us wade in until we are waist, then chest deep in the barely stirring water. I feel my clothes as they mould to my body like a heavy new skin that's nudging me in one direction then another. To take the garland from Nina, I have to let go of Uncle Jack's hand. I let go... I'm on my own! I feel the movement of the ocean around me, its ebb and flow powerful, deceptive.

I rest the flowers on the water and gently push them away. Nina starts to hum some old-time tune and I join in as the garland floats away. When we're back on the shore, I turn. I can still see the white flowers drifting on the blue water. The colours remind me of something.

'Little things are starting to come back to me,' I tell them. 'Like holding a bus ticket in my hand and knowing I'm going to the beach.' I can almost feel the sun shining on the ticket in the palm of my little-girl hand. 'And something white – swirling on the water.'

Nina nods.

We are on the sand shivering in our wet clothes. The flowers are getting smaller and smaller but are still visible.

'Maybe it'll happen.'

'What?'

'Maybe I'll see her face one day.'

'But you've seen the pictures, G. You know what she looks like.' Nina wraps me in a thick towel. 'She looks like you.'

'I don't want the pictures.'

Nina looks puzzled.

'I want the memory!'

CHAPTER 18: RECKONING

Genesis

'Excuse me a minute. A work call… from abroad,' Hugh says as he glues his phone to his ear and hurries to his car. He can't wait to put some space between us.

I sigh, sit back on the picnic bench and look around. Trees. Boats. Shoreline. Rosie's house.

This was a bad idea. A very bad idea.

So many things are freaking me out.

First, the fear that he wouldn't come.

Second – when he came – that he has a car! What happened to his beat-up Scoopy? I loved that bike! I loved being on the back of that bike!

Third, now that he's here, it's like talking to stone. And when he does talk, his eyes shift away from mine.

Finally, he gets a phone call and has to go to his car to take it!

I thought that bringing him here would mean something to him. It means something to me. I thought it would be a place where I could try to speak some kind of truth. That's what I thought. Before today. Before right now.

For a long time, I couldn't set foot in this place. I couldn't even think about it. Then came the day that Nina said, 'I need some help clearing out Rosie's house.' She finished loading up the car with tools and equipment. 'When I was there last weekend, I realised I couldn't do it on my own.' This was the first time she'd ever asked for help. It was impossible to say no. We spent that Saturday here and I cried the whole day – pulling up weeds and crying, piling up branches and crying. The next weekend was the same, until it began to be the work I focused on, and after that, I started to look forward to being here.

Why would I expect it to mean something to him? He only met Rosie that one time up at Sweet Airs. The day he met me... He never laid eyes on her again. She was just another person belonging to a world that he didn't know.

When I had shown him the tidy garden with all its garbage cleared away, he nodded and tried to appear interested. I didn't mention that somebody had taken Johnny's rowboat for repair because it would have meant telling the whole story. And without Rosie's punchline, what was the use? It was the same with the house. With the outside painted and the shutters replaced, it looked like a doll's house, not a place of magic. And, inside the house... even worse! With all of Rosie's treasures sorted and taken away, it looked even smaller than before. It was only when we went down the stone steps into the ancient kitchen that something seemed to stir in him, especially when he saw the bottles of dried herbs and potions that Nina and I had not yet taken away. But by this time, I'd given up and said nothing.

We came outside, took a few steps beyond Rosie's gate and sat on the wooden bench. Even when I told him I was going to London to study, not to Tess's rich-girl college in the States – even then, he had almost nothing to say.

That's when his phone rang. He's been on it a good ten minutes already! Back in de day, I would've done something spectacular to make him pay attention. Not that I don't think he deserves it but I don't have the energy for all a dat anymore.

I stop craning my neck in the direction of his car. I'm so fed up with him and want this goodbye to be over. I'd wanted to say all the things I'd never been able to say but he's not having it. He's put up a high brick wall around himself. With nothing else to do, I look at what's in front for me. I really look. I don't think about Rosie and I don't think about him. Everything drops out of my mind except what I see.

And I am dazzled by it.

Everything is here in this small green space at the edge of the water. My eyes make a slow sweep and take in what Rosie called her fortune. Frame by frame, I take it in. The lacy tree with flashes of oleander and ocean peeping through. Twisted old branches leaning over rocks and white sand. Brown rocks slipping into water the colour of lemongrass tea then mixing with blue. Aquamarine? And over there, the rocky coastline enters the water and becomes smooth stepping-stones that lead straight to a tiny island. It has cedars bending over and a beach just big enough for two.

I wonder if I can walk on those stones, walk right out to the island. I don't want to let go of it.

A hand is shaking my shoulder. 'Genesis?'

There he is, with a worried look on his face. The brick wall has gone.

'Oh.' I'm being pulled back to reality. 'It's you.'

'Of course, it is.' He sits down close to me. 'What's wrong? Has something happened?'

'I was looking over there.' I point. 'Does that island remind you of something?' My voice has dropped to a whisper.

'I don't think we should go back there, G.'

'Yes, we have to. I need to tell you what it meant to me.' We don't touch. But he's so near to me I can see a vein on his temple throbbing. I can feel the heat of the red flag flying in his face but I'm not afraid to speak.

'I want to thank you, Hugh.'

'For what?'

'Without that other island, our Cup Match island, I would never have been able to see how beautiful this one is, and everything else around it. Thank you for giving me that.'

This isn't what he wants to hear. He starts rubbing his hands along his thighs. Again he looks away.

'Before I knew you, I was so busy trying to… get by, I didn't have time to look around me… To see things like this!'

He doesn't respond, but I can talk freely now. 'Before, I didn't think that the flowers and the sun and specially the water had anything to do with me. That they could be part of me. You gave me something wonderful.'

He finally turns to me. The flag is still flying.

'So why… did we have to stop?'

'Because…' My tongue is locked again. All the words that I'd rehearsed evaporate. All the reasons wiped out. Then they all come barrelling out.

'We should have been friends for five, ten, twenty years before...' The words burst from me. 'Before we did...' I almost said The Big Nasty. That's how fucked up I still am! 'Before we...' I hit a wall, take a breath and try again. 'You needed to know about everything that ever happened to me. Before we became... you know... close. I needed to be sure that you could know these things and think I was still an OK person. That I wasn't tainted down to the core.'

'I never thought that, G.' He shakes his head sadly.

'You see, that's the problem. You say you didn't think it. But I say you did. For a split second, I saw it in your eyes. I did... Oh, I don't know! Maybe it was what I thought about myself.'

He puts his head in his hands. But I'm on a roll. Can't stop now.

'And there's so much else you don't know about me. You don't know a thing about the people who are closest to me. The only one you know is Tess. You don't know Nina...'

'Oh yes I do!'

I laugh out loud. 'You just know attack-dog Nina. You don't know the other Nina, the real one. Or Rosie. Uncle Jack. You don't know Lizzie. You don't know Uriel!'

'But I know you!'

'That's what I'm saying! If you don't know these people, you can't know me. You can't separate me from them!' I grab his hand and won't let him pull away. Blood rushes to my head pushing words out before I can pull them back. 'I fell in love with you.' Oh God! I said it! 'With my teacher. You opened up a whole new world to me. Do you understand how that felt to me?' I feel the bubble burst and give him back his hand. 'But you didn't learn about my world, my people.'

From out of nowhere a single gull shoots by, calling out and skimming over the water. Without even glancing at him, I tell him, 'I was too messed-up inside to make sure that you did.'

He keeps shaking his head and saying nothing. Finally he says, 'So that's it.'

'I guess it is.' I try to smile. 'There was an "us" for a little while. But now, I've got to go. Got to leave this island and everybody in it. I need time to be... to become...'

I can't finish. I expect him to get up and leave. But he doesn't. It's like we're both in a daze watching as the sun slips slowly into the ocean.

At last he gets up. 'You're leaving tomorrow?'

'The day after.' I look at the light on the water. 'Will there be anything like this where I'm going?'

'No.' He grunts but I think there's a little smile in there somewhere. 'There are beautiful places where you're going… I hope you get to see some of them. But this…' He clicks an imaginary picture with his hands. 'This you will see nowhere else. Remember it.'

I walk with him to his car. Before he opens the door, he runs his fingertips slowly along my cheek. It feels exactly as it did the first time he touched me. 'The next time I see you, well, who knows?'

He turns to the car and fiddles with keys. 'By the way, I thought you might like to know…' With every word, his voice sounds more natural. 'Buddy and I are developing that Gurnet Rock project. You remember the one about…'

'The old cedar root thing? The one I had a tantrum about?' I wince at the thought. 'I remember.'

'We're doing it right this time. A proper programme. Working with all the schools.'

'Wasn't that my idea?'

He smiles, the first real one since he came.

'I feel kinda special!'

'Don't let it go to your head. But just so you know,' he says. 'We've decided to rename it.' He starts up the engine and begins to pull out. He seems to be saying something but the windows are up.

'I can't hear you, Teach!'

He stops and lowers a window. 'We're calling it the Genesis Project!'

Nina

'I remember this,' said Nina, sinking back into the leather sofa and trying to get used to the new configuration of Sweet Airs.

'And that.' She pointed outside to the swimming pool absorbing the colours of the retreating sun.

Despite having promised herself not to engage with Tess, she was here, their first encounter in months. 'But the rest of it is...' Nina made a gesture encompassing the gallery. It seemed to have doubled in size, its walls stripped bare, the nooks and crannies that had flaunted its works of art now naked and forsaken.

'Do you like it?' Tess asked, surveying the room with a satisfied smile.

Nina shrugged. 'What did you do with it all?'

'Lots of things. Several pieces were destroyed by Fabian. A couple needed to be restored. After that, I sent some of them to Richard as part of the divorce settlement. Gave some to the National Gallery and Masterworks. Sold a few to collectors. A handful of them I kept for myself.'

'Why don't you put them up? I don't know anything about art, Tess. But this room – if you don't mind me saying so – looks sad. An empty shell.'

'A clean slate!'

'Hmmm.'

Whether Tess's radical surgery to her home signalled the end or the beginning of something, Nina couldn't tell. She wasn't really interested. There was only one thing she wanted to know.

'We're all meeting to say goodbye to G tomorrow. Yet you wanted to see me today! Why? What's this about?'

'To talk about Genesis, of course. Although I haven't seen much of her since the hurricane, she and I have been in regular touch.'

Nina sat looking at her hands.

'I know she's back living with you. That you've arranged counselling for her – both academic and otherwise. That she's decided she wants to study in the UK not the US. That you've helped her a lot. Especially finding out about her mother.'

Nina exhaled loudly. 'And?'

'And... And I wanted you to know that I'll be funding Genesis.'

'I've known that for ages, Tess.'

'It's just for the first year of her studies.'

'Just the first year?'

'After that, we'll see.'

'Okay,' said Nina, rising to her feet. 'If that's all, I'll be going.'

'That's it? What now, Nina? What?' She tugged at the heavy bangle on her wrist. 'Genesis and I have been talking about this for months. She was the one who said it should only be for a year.'

'And why didn't you overrule her? Do you think the poor kid needs to worry about fees at the end of every school year?'

'She's the one who insisted that it should be only one year. After that, she'd be on her own. She doesn't want to depend on me! If you talked to her, you'd know that!'

'Who are you to tell me how to talk to Genesis?'

'I bet every conversation you have with Genesis ends in a fight! The way it does with me! Why can't you ever be civil?'

'I get it. You want me to be your friend! Look what happens when I try! Do you know the last time you and I had a civil moment?'

Tess pressed her lips shut.

'I do! It was the night we celebrated G going away to college. Just before the storm. In this very room. Remember that? While we were busy saying cheers, Rosie was being shot.'

The blood drained from Tess's face. 'And you really blame me for that?'

'No, I don't.' Nina shook her head slowly. 'G had too many holes in her life and Uriel was the only one who could come close to filling them. I've had to accept that. Even if you hadn't let her run wild that night, she would have found a way back to him.'

Tess looked relieved.

'Don't think you're off the hook!' Nina raised an accusing finger. 'Whatever it is you want from me – congratulations, friendship, whatever – forget it! It won't happen. Tess, I don't trust you! I don't trust any part of you. Your motives. Your values. Because… they all come from a position of privilege from the time that human beings first scrambled onto this godforsaken rock. And when somebody like me has the nerve to call out somebody like you about it, you complain that it's unfair! We are your blind spot. Your black blind spot!'

'Somebody like me! What about me? Me. The person!'

'I bet you think that getting rid of all the pictures and those expensive... knickknacks... You think that's going to change anything about this house and what it represents? About what *you* represent?'

She stood up and headed to the door.

'Stop!' Tess crossed the room and gripped Nina's arm and started pulling her back into the room.

'Let go!' Nina grabbed Tess's hand. 'Let. Me. Go!' Nina's bag clattered to the floor as she tried to push Tess away and block the blows from those flailing, slapping hands. 'Have you lost your mind?'

Tess dropped Nina's arm but still she barred Nina's path.

'You can't go! I need you to see something.' And she pointed through the new kitchen to what looked like an ancient door.

Tess opened it and disappeared into the darkness. Nina followed but remained pinned to the threshold and could only see the white-silver of Tess's cropped hair slowly descending. With one foot hovering over the first step, Nina stopped when a voice in her head cried *Don't!*

As she was about to leave, there was a click and light poured from a bulb hanging from the cellar's ceiling. Tess was at the bottom of the steps looking up.

'Simmons put the bulb up. Before, the place was pitch dark.'

With a cold sweat on her brow, still Nina did not move.

'Come.' Tess pointed to two plastic chairs positioned directly under the light. 'Sit with me.'

Nina took a deep breath and came down the steps – one foot then the other, on each step. At the bottom, she sat down, wondering how, in a matter of minutes, she'd passed from cracking the whip of authority to meek obedience.

Tess walked towards the second chair but didn't sit down. It was not ordinary conversation. It was a speech to a waiting multitude.

'I was nine years old when I first came down here. It was forbidden – like the Tree of Knowledge in the Garden of Eden – but my brother and I came down here anyway. We were punished for it. My grandfather who loved me, suddenly hated me and told me things that sounded like gibberish. All I understood was that this was a bad place. The only thing I learned was that I had to forget it. I had to purge the cellar from my memory.'

Nina absorbed every detail of the story she heard, the saga of a golden childhood before the coming of the shadow world, the drip drip drip of the shadow world. The world of the breaking room. The story bristled with formidable characters – the kindly, tormented grandfather, the unrepentant great-grandfather who'd sown his seed in fertile soil and the young black girls whose innocence he'd broken for sport. There were the other ancestors, the ones in the portraits, the ones who had actually been slave-owners. Had any of them been like Grandpa Nate or had they all been like his father? Did they break men too? Then there was Simmons, who, without knowing any detail, had known everything from the beginning. He was the scarcely visible presence whose shoulders had borne the yard, the boats, the house and all who lived in it – a trusted, beneficent figure. Until now. Simmons. From the way Tess told the story, Nina knew how much she struggled to comprehend the landscape of his heart. He had become an impossible enigma, though bound tightly to her by history and by blood.

As Nina listened to the story, she tracked Tess as she roamed around like a restless spirit, crisscrossing the room and sometimes pressing her hands flat against one of the uneven walls. Then Tess switched into a different mode. In the present, talking without a filter. What came from her lips were questions, messy questions.

What to do about Akeem? What did Simmons mean when he said he might need 'some help'? What would happen when the word got out? What should she do if she found a line of long-lost cousins at her door? Would she have to change the terms of her divorce so that she would have enough – to do the right thing? And what was that? Would there ever be enough? For a scholarship fund? A foundation? Could there ever be enough? Nina knew the familiar brainstorming, problem-solving language that Tess used in her professional life, but this was different. When she'd talked about her family's slave-owning past, there had been genuine horror, yes, but there'd also been a kind of melancholy that made it almost sound like a fairy tale. What she was talking about now seemed full of raw life-changing edges.

There was one question that Tess didn't ask but Nina sensed was behind it all: Can I atone?

That unasked question ricocheted around Nina's head, not because she didn't know the answer, but because she had a question of her own. Can I forgive? Instead of an answer, what bubbled up were images of the life she knew. The faces came without reference to time or importance. They were all important and belonged to all time. Her niece, Sharon, being baptized; photographs of the grandparents she'd never known; Dee and his smile like sunlight; Dee in the midst of the riot. An endless string of girls knocked up and locked up. Genesis, dancing. Joy. Uncle Jack, his Captain's cape whirling out around him. Rosie. Genesis curled up like a foetus. This was her world. She was sure it wasn't a world Tess knew, at best a shadow world.

She heard her name and felt herself being dragged up from the depths.

'How do I make this right, Nina?' Tess stood before her, her face open, imploring. 'This all happened so long ago. And yet I... know I still live with it, that I'm condemned for it in the eyes of people like you.'

Nina shook her head. She had troubles of her own. She was being overwhelmed by this place. Here on this island, there had been no 'great houses' that overlooked the slave dwellings. It was too poor for that. Here, the handful of slaves had lived in cellars like this, along with the sacks of provisions. A cheek-by-jowl slavery. Nina ran her hand along her arm. Not black but the colour of brown paper bag. There was a cellar somewhere in her past. A cellar or a cane field or a salt pond.

'Look at this!'

Tess was at the far end of the cellar. Although the light was dimmer there, Nina could see Tess running one hand along the wall, which, like the others, had been plastered unevenly, leaving patches of raw limestone. Tess was feeling a strip of untreated stone a few feet off the ground, her fingers gingerly working the space between two blocks.

'Is there something there?'

Tess didn't answer, just kept working. Suddenly she stopped and pulled out a dark coiled mass from between the stones. She pulled out some more then held it out to Nina.

'What is it?' Nina did not want to touch it.

'Let's take it up to the light.'

Directly beneath the harsh light from the bulb, they stared at what lay in the palm of Tess's hand.

'Could it be seaweed? It might be seaweed.' Tess looked behind her at the wall that it had come from. 'To block up holes. It's the north-facing wall! To block out the wind from the north!'

'For insulation!'

She emptied the contents of her hand into Nina's.

Nina thought of Uncle Jack and the tons of seaweed he'd collected during his lifetime. To fertilise the soil. To make things grow. And now – to keep out the north wind. It made sense, even if it looked different, even though there was no trace of the tiny balloons that kept the weed afloat. Time had wreaked its damage but enough of the weed had survived. It made sense.

With the gentlest touch, Nina ran her fingers along its intricate curves, its brittle coils. She was a child again, on a wintry beach, helping Uncle Jack to fill the crocus bag with the sea's abundant harvest and then to scatter it underneath the citrus trees. She felt her childish hands plunging into the weed's dense texture.

Something felt wrong.

'It's not seaweed!' Her eyes filled with tears.

'What is it, then?'

'It's hair. It's human hair.'

Nina drove her car out onto the main road, finally leaving Sweet Airs behind her. She wasn't sure how long she'd been there since they came up from the cellar. One hour, maybe two.

When she knew what they'd found, Nina had carefully replaced the hair in the crack between the stones. She'd glanced at Tess and shut down the possibility of any other action. They'd climbed the stairs and returned to the gallery. There they'd sat lost in their own thoughts.

In the cellar, there'd only been feelings. And they'd threatened to obliterate her. She'd read about the experiences of Black people from the Americas visiting African slave sites like Elmina Castle and Gorée Island, and what these places of degradation and death had made them feel. When she'd sat in the cellar, she'd felt that rage, that grief.

Then came the moment when she'd held in her hands the remains of people from centuries past.

'They wanted to live,' she'd said to Tess, who'd looked up but didn't seem to see her.

'Despite everything – in that cruel room – they wanted to live. They wanted to keep warm when the north wind blew. They were not just flogged people, raped people, broken people. They were people! Who loved, hated, listened, plotted, planted, prayed, danced, dreamed, dared, surrendered. Tried again. They didn't just survive. They lived!'

Nina saw Tess's eyes riveted on hers.

'And more than that, they knew there was a future. How do I know that? Because that hair in the wall was not just for insulation.' She was engulfed by a wave of excitement. 'It was a message! A remnant of their living bodies. Left for somebody in a future that they could not know. To say that they'd been here! That they had lived!'

Silence descended once more. In the end, she'd walked over to Tess, said a few things but was not sure that Tess heard her. She told her she should use her wealth and influence strategically, where it could do the most good. But that would be the easy part. The tougher part would be to continue the conversation that Simmons had started. To continue the hard digging until the spirits of the cellar could rest in peace.

By the time Nina reached home, all of the images that had overrun her mind had been distilled into one face.

Genesis. The future. The message in the cellar had been for her. Then came another face, veiled, whose features she did not know. But there was a name attached to it. It came to her on the back of the night wind.

Uriel.

CHAPTER 19: BEGINNING

Genesis
19:30

My three bitches are here to say goodbye.

I told them before not to bring anything. No more presents! Tess is funding the whole of my Foundation Year but expects me to get a scholarship for everything after that. She says that her work has always been for worthy causes and I'm one of them – most of the time. Lizzie has hooked me up with some friend of hers who has an apartment – a *flat* – near to my school and I can stay there as long as I don't screw things up. She says she's warned her friend about me. And as for Nina... it's all about things she's sure I'll need. Thermal underwear, colour-coordinated clothes for wet and miserable weather, six packets of salt codfish, black hair products, Jergen's body lotion, her Gideon bible, Limacol...

It's been going on for weeks, these visitations, these counselling sessions, these gifts. Tonight, with Hugh's last words to me still ringing in my ears, I take a mental picture of these three women who found a way to bring their own Genesis project to a conclusion.

As it's Nina's house, there's food; as it includes Tess, there's wine; and as Lizzie's here, there's talk of new things – job, car, house – but also talk of her Avó's stories. I'm glad they're here, my three bitches, with all their laughing and quarrelling. It even seems that, with Nina and Tess, the laughing is real and the quarrelling isn't. Can I believe this?

Nina starts looking at her watch.

'Tomorrow G goes. And I'm here to tell you two that you need to hit the road soon because this girl's got to have a good night's rest.'

Tess and Lizzie salute Commandante Nina but do not move.

'But before they go,' Nina says to me, 'we all have a special present for you.'

'Guys! You promised! No more presents!' I'm wailing because I really don't have an empty square inch in my bags.

'All right ladies, step forward.' At Nina's order, the others stand next to her. All of a sudden, I start to worry. That weird expression on their faces. What is it? We've been having fun. I don't want the messing around to stop.

As soon as Nina starts talking with her voice in that other gear, I know that the laughing is over.

'G, we have something for you. And it's not just from us. It's also from somebody who couldn't be here tonight.'

Nina turns around and takes something from a brown paper bag.

Oh!

'It's Rosie's tin can! I thought it was lost.'

'No. I put it in a safe place the first time I went to clear her house.'

I take it in my hands, this out-of-shape tin that used to sit on Rosie's window ledge with the pictures of her husband, of Nina and Dee on their wedding day and of the long-lost relative wearing feathers and beads.

'And she used to put dirt in it. Every time she passed that place in St. David's... What's it called, Nina?'

'Dark Bottom.'

'Dark Bottom. When she passed Dark Bottom, she would always go in there, in among the trees, and bring back a handful of dirt.' I look around at the others. 'I thought it was really strange. And special.'

'More than special, G. That place is sacred. It's where her ancestors and Dee's ancestors used to meet so long ago, and with their drumming and dances would remember who they were.'

'And didn't she...' The memory comes racing back. 'Didn't she once say that she wanted me to have it? Didn't she, Nina?'

'She sure did.'

I have to sit down. I can almost hear Rosie's throwaway line, like she was talking to herself. 'One day I'll probably give this to you.'

'When I told Tess and Lizzie that I was going to give this to you...' Nina's still in her sermon voice. 'I told them that I'd be adding some soil that had a special meaning for me. And they both said they wanted to do that too.' Nina smiles. 'You know them. Always have to keep up with me.'

Nina opens the battered lid and takes something from her pocket. 'This earth comes from Salt Cay, from beneath the cedar tree that guards the gate. My grandparents came to Bermuda from Turks Islands and before they died, they had bought the land and put a shack on it. The house itself was built by my parents and their friends and they added on to it as the family grew. When they died, they left it to be divided among their eight children. But we were raised right and when our parents passed, we didn't fight over it. Over the years, Dee and I were able to give each of my siblings their fair and equal share.'

She pours a handful of earth into the tin.

Next comes Lizzie.

'When you first knew me, Gen, my head was in a bad place. Now it's better. Not perfect, but better. I don't know if it's because of knowing you or because of something else altogether or a bit of both... but all I know is that now I can look back and not be ashamed. This morning, my cousin Tiago drove me right across the grounds of the Mid Atlantic Club – like riding on green velvet – to one of the few places that hint at what it must have looked like in the 1920s when my Vovo and the others started work on it. There's an old cedar there, bent double by the wind but still strong. It's on the edge of the cliff which falls down into the ocean. The soil around the roots is full of bits of limestone rock. This means something to me now. It never did before.'

The pieces of chipped rock clang against the side of the can before they come to rest.

It takes a few moments for Tess to come forward. Her face is ashen and her right hand is clenched.

'This comes from the cellar of my house.' I've never seen Tess look like this, never heard her sound like this. 'My ancestors did things... terrible things, that I can't undo.' She swings around and looks each of us in the eye. 'What can I do? They've cast such a... shadow over my life!'

She puts a hand over her mouth. Her nails are perfectly manicured and the bracelet on her wrist is heavy and elegant. But they aren't important. All I see is a person, like me, like all of us in this room, trying to find the next step of the path they're on.

Her hand drops to her side and her eyes are on us again. 'All I can do is to face them... and try to be better.'

And she empties the Sweet Airs earth into the tin. Something passes between the Nina and Tess. Something electric. The clang of weapons being laid down? I don't know. Only time will tell.

When the solemnity has gone on long enough, I say, 'Hey, you guys! How am I going to take this with me? What am I going to say to Customs? There's no space on the form for sacred soil!'

'We thought of that,' Nina says. 'The tin has to stay here. It belongs to you and it belongs here. You'll have to come back to claim it.'

I laugh. That Nina! Always with her hidden clauses.

Later on, long after the goodbye hugs from Tess and Lizzie and long after Nina herself has gone to bed, I leave my bedroom and creep out to the living room.

The tin can is where we left it in the centre of the table, in the centre of the room. All the lights are off but the room is filled with brightness. I look through the window and the moon is there, not quite full but almost, lighting up the sky. Its beams fall directly on my gift, calling to me like a siren song. I walk along its path until the tin is in my hand. I open the lid and I swear a rush of air rises up from it and into my face. I dip one hand into the cool earth. The soil and sand and pebbles flow over and between my fingers. My fingers dig deeper until they reach the bottom of the tin. I turn the soil over once, over twice, over three times and then it's done. When I run water over my hands, there is soil caught beneath my fingernails. I don't disturb it.

18:28

Two minutes before the official check-in opening time. I glance over at Nina as the glass doors open to receive us and the trolley carrying my two suitcases.

Nina and I have spent a quiet day together. The only thing that was different was that we went and brought Uncle Jack home for lunch. He was a bit confused because Nina came for him in the middle of the day and it wasn't the weekend. But he was happy. He brought his violin with him and after lunch he played his one tune. Nina had to go out for a while so Uncle Jack and I went down to the beach and gathered some seaweed. When we'd finished filling our bag, I sat on the sand and he went into the surf. I saw him in profile, dark against the bright water and far enough away that I didn't see an old man but a strong protector whose arm would always be there, whose smile would light my way, whose music would come to me in times of trouble. He scooped up a handful of water, passed it over his face and began to walk towards me. He stayed in the surf as long as he could before leaving it behind. Although he lived between sea and land, for him, the ocean was supreme.

When we dropped him off at the Home, I thought I would feel sad. But I didn't. How could I, with that smile safe inside me?

18:30
I check in.

We're early of course so we sit ourselves down in the airport café. We hardly have anything to say and concentrate on eating and drinking whatever it is we ordered. It seems to me that there's a lot of noise, of people laughing and talking, announcements being made, glasses clinking, forks and knives being pushed around plates. But it's not that. It's the noise of the last days, weeks and months of my life, of the last two years of it and of all the years before that. They are making a deafening noise as I sit next to Nina.

Then comes my announcement.

'Passengers on British Airways flight 2233 to London Gatwick are asked to proceed to Security.'

I get very busy picking up my jacket, my bag and my carry-on. Nina suddenly puts her hand on mine. I stop and, just as suddenly, all the noise goes away. Only then does she stand and take my chin in her hand.

'Everything's going to be all right,' she says, smiling. 'You're going to be fine.'

'And you, Nina? Are you going to be fine?'

She's surprised by my question.

'Yes, I will.' She pauses. 'I think I will! By the way, Uriel sends his best. He says you have to show those people over there how to dance like a Gombey.'

'Uriel? You spoke to Uriel?'

'Passengers on British Airways flight 2233 to London Gatwick are asked to proceed to Security.'

'Come on, G. That's you.'

'You saw Uriel?'

'Yes,' she said, trying to get me to move. 'Yes. I did. I went to see him this afternoon while you were with Uncle Jack.'

'You went to see Uriel?'

'And I'll be going to see him regularly from now on.'

'My God! My God…' My head is spinning. 'You… you…'

'Yes, I did.'

'Second call for BA 2233 which will be boarding shortly. All passengers are asked to proceed to Security.'

'He's dyslexic, Nina! Make sure he gets help.' I grab both of her hands and hold them tight. 'And get him a good lawyer! Promise!'

'I'll do my best.'

'Get Tess to help you!'

'You're going to miss your flight.'

'Promise!' She tries to take her hands away but I won't let her.

'I don't know, G.' She looks straight into my eyes. 'I don't know if Tess and I are there yet. Where we can work together…'

'Listen, Nina.' I'm squeezing her hands really hard. 'This is not about you. And it's not about Tess. It's about Uriel!'

She nods. 'All right. I will.' Then in a whisper she says, 'Yes… The future.' She takes my elbow and guides me to Security.

'Well, this is it.'

'I'm going.' I take my jacket from her. 'But this isn't it!' I lean forward until her face is only inches away from mine. 'You'll never get rid of me. Never!'

We're both smiling through our tears and we hug so tight I can hardly breathe. She lets me go, turns on her heel and walks away. Just before she reaches the doors, her back straightens, her head lifts and she walks out into the evening air.

I make a note to myself. *That's the way it's done.*

Before too long, I'm sitting in the Departure Lounge. I try to look nonchalant as I check out the other passengers – the ones buying duty-free with their credit cards, the man studying something on his laptop – a short business trip? – and the woman with her two girls. These kids have probably been travelling since they were born. Like a long car ride for them.

'British Airways invites passengers in First Class and Business Class to board from Gate A.'

My stomach tenses at the thought of these people who have everything, can do anything. All the grey thoughts I've ever had rise through my body. All the sad and cruel and hopeless things that hemmed me in and told me I can't!

I rush to the bathroom, splash some water on my face and look at myself in the mirror. I stare long and hard and everything goes strange. Looking back at me is a young woman dressed in white, her long skirt sweeping the sand, the blue ocean behind her, her hair covered in a white cloth, her smile like the sun, her skin like the night. She looks familiar. Like me, but with a beautiful softness in her eyes that I do not have. She places both hands over her heart and fades away. But in my mind, she remains. Not as a vision. Not as a photograph. But as a memory that has come back to me.

I return to the departure lounge feeling perfectly calm for the first time in my life.

More boarding calls are made and groups of people line up. The person sitting next to me slouches towards the end of the straggly line. I watch him carefully. The way he moves. Without poetry, without strength.

The announcer in my head says, 'You have to show those people over there how to dance like a Gombey!'

I laugh out loud. Like a Gombey! Like a warrior! Yes, U! Yes!

My row is called.

I jump up, sling my jacket over my shoulder and join the other passengers. I am one of them now. I approach the last security check before I go out onto the tarmac. I show the security man my passport and catch sight of that huge white bird waiting silently for me.

Outside in the dark, I climb the metal stairs into the plane. I fasten my seat belt like I've been doing it all my life. I stretch out my fingers and see that traces of Rosie's earth are making the journey with me. I feel the power of the engines as we roar down the runway and take to the night sky. I feel myself rising, rising, with a deep ocean dropping beneath me.

I look out of the window and there below is the island, the peak of a great sea mountain. It's lit up like diamonds, a fish-hook, which no matter how high I soar, will always be caught in my flesh. Will always bring me home.

WRITER

(for Angela)

A woman, the grey in her hair just beginning,
sits at her desk in a modest pink house
made of traditional Bermuda white coral.
She writes with a black marker on a whiteboard
'Bermuda's history: the story of Beginning'.
The tetrameters roll on like the waves of the sea.
Words become breakers over submarine rocks
Where once there were forests of towering cedars
and conch shells with barnacles older than the sea
older than legends older than history.
Longtails are circling their nests in the rocks.
A great storm is coming. The darkening sky
is heavy with cloud. Tank rain sings loud
in the veins of the house. The waves grow higher.
Liquid mountains are rising in the air.
The salt from their spume flies in the wind
and the smell of the sea is everywhere.
Hurricane winds are devils howling
at the end of the world and chaos beginning...
The writer erases the words on the board and writes
'Genesis.'

Michael Gilkes

ABOUT THE AUTHOR

Bermudian by birth, Angela Barry lived abroad for more than 20 years – in England, France, The Gambia, Senegal and the Seychelles – before returning to Bermuda, where she worked as a lecturer until retiring in 2016. She holds a PhD in Creative Writing from Lancaster University, for which she worked on cross-cultural projects, reflecting her connections with the African diaspora. Her work has been published in journals including *The Massachusetts Review*, *The Bermudian magazine*, *The Caribbean Writer* and *BIM: Arts for the 21st Century*. She is the author of *Endangered Species and Other Stories* (2002) and the novel, *Gorée: Point of Departure* (2010). She is a contributor to the Commonwealth Writers anthology, *So Many Islands: Stories from the Caribbean, Mediterranean, Indian Ocean and Pacific* (2018) and also to *New Daughters of Africa* (2019).

She is currently working on a new novel, provisionally entitled Island Arts.

ALSO BY ANGELA BARRY

Endangered Species

ISBN 9781900715713; pp. 232; pub. 2002; £8.99

Eve has to watch her husband bring his paler mistress to the party she has so carefully prepared; Esther to deal with her rebellious daughter, and the guilt which attaches to her own youthful revolt against racial oppression; Joelle and Maryse must find ways of dealing with the lack of comprehension between village Africa and chic Frenchness in their Ivoirean lives; Gambian Doudou wants a traditional wife to end his loneliness in London; and Julia, in the title story, must fight to find herself again when her oldest friend dies of cancer.

Whether living in Bermuda, America, London, the Gambia or the Cote d'Ivoire, the characters in these stories not only confront their individual traumas, but the ways in which, as people of the African diaspora, differences of colour, class and colonial heritage divide them both from each other and themselves.

We are given revealing insights into Bermudian society, its tensions of race and culture and the geography that pulls some of its people closer to the USA, while others look to links with the Caribbean or the even more submerged links with Africa. But if we see the pain and alienation of uprooted people, what also moves through the stories is a sense of identity not as something fixed, but as an Atlantic flow, a circuit of peoples and cultures which has Africa as one of its starting points. And in that lies a unity that is real, if submarine.

When Doudou listens to the Gambian music of his homeland in London, it is a music of multiple Atlantic crossings, powerfully influenced by Cuban rumba, itself born from African and European roots. And as Mame Koumba, pointing to his Black British grandchildren, tells Doudou, grieving for the loss of ancestral wholeness, 'They're not what you would have had in the Gambia. But they're what you have. And there's Africa in them all.' Angela Barry's stories demand an alertness to that kind of connection.

Gorée: Point of Departure
ISBN: 9781845231255; pp. 210; pub. 2010; £9.99

A chance encounter at Kennedy Airport with her ex-husband, Saliou Wade, takes Magdalene and their now adult daughter, Khadi, on a visit to him and his new family in Senegal.

Magdalene is understandably nervous about the return, remembering the pain of the mutual cultural incomprehension – she is a St Lucian – that ended the marriage almost twenty years before; but Khadi refuses to go without her. In Senegal, whilst the now cosmopolitan Saliou appears to exist comfortably in multiple worlds, there are more complex relationships to manage with members of his large extended family. But the sensitivities are not merely social and cultural. A visit Khadi and her half-sister Maimouna make to the slave port of Gorée has consequences that lay bare unfinished business between West Indians and Africans, between Magdalene and Saliou, and Khadi and her parents. And when Khadi and Hassim, Saliou's brother-in-law, are drawn together, those looking on must wonder whether history will repeat itself.